Five Weeks in a Balloon

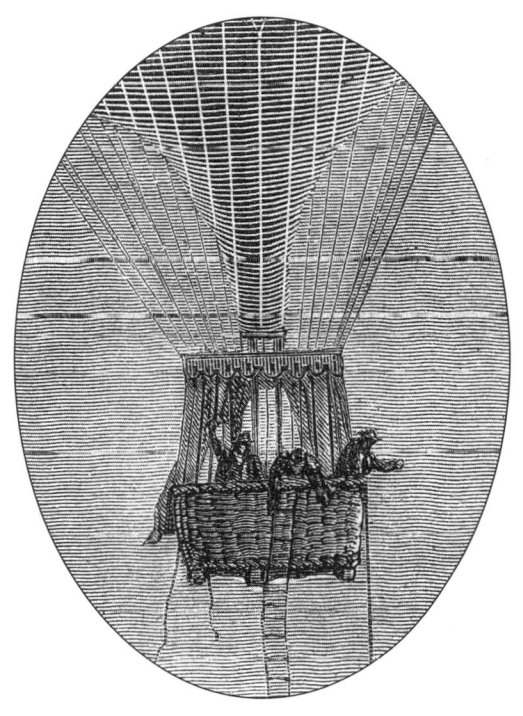

publication of this book is funded by the

BEATRICE FOX AUERBACH FOUNDATION FUND

at the Hartford Foundation for Public Giving

JULES VERNE

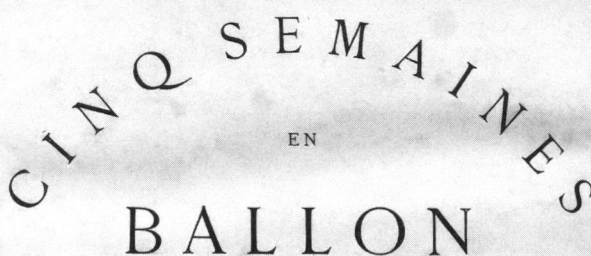

CINQ SEMAINES

EN

BALLON

VOYAGE DE DÉCOUVERTES EN AFRIQUE

PAR TROIS ANGLAIS

ILLUSTRATIONS PAR MM. RIOU ET DE MONTAUT

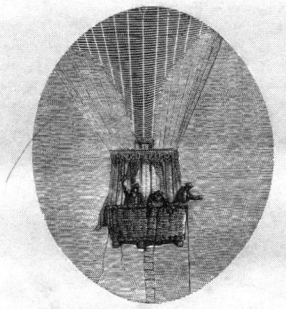

BIBLIOTHÈQUE
D'ÉDUCATION ET DE RÉCRÉATION
J. HETZEL ET Cie, 18, RUE JACOB

PARIS

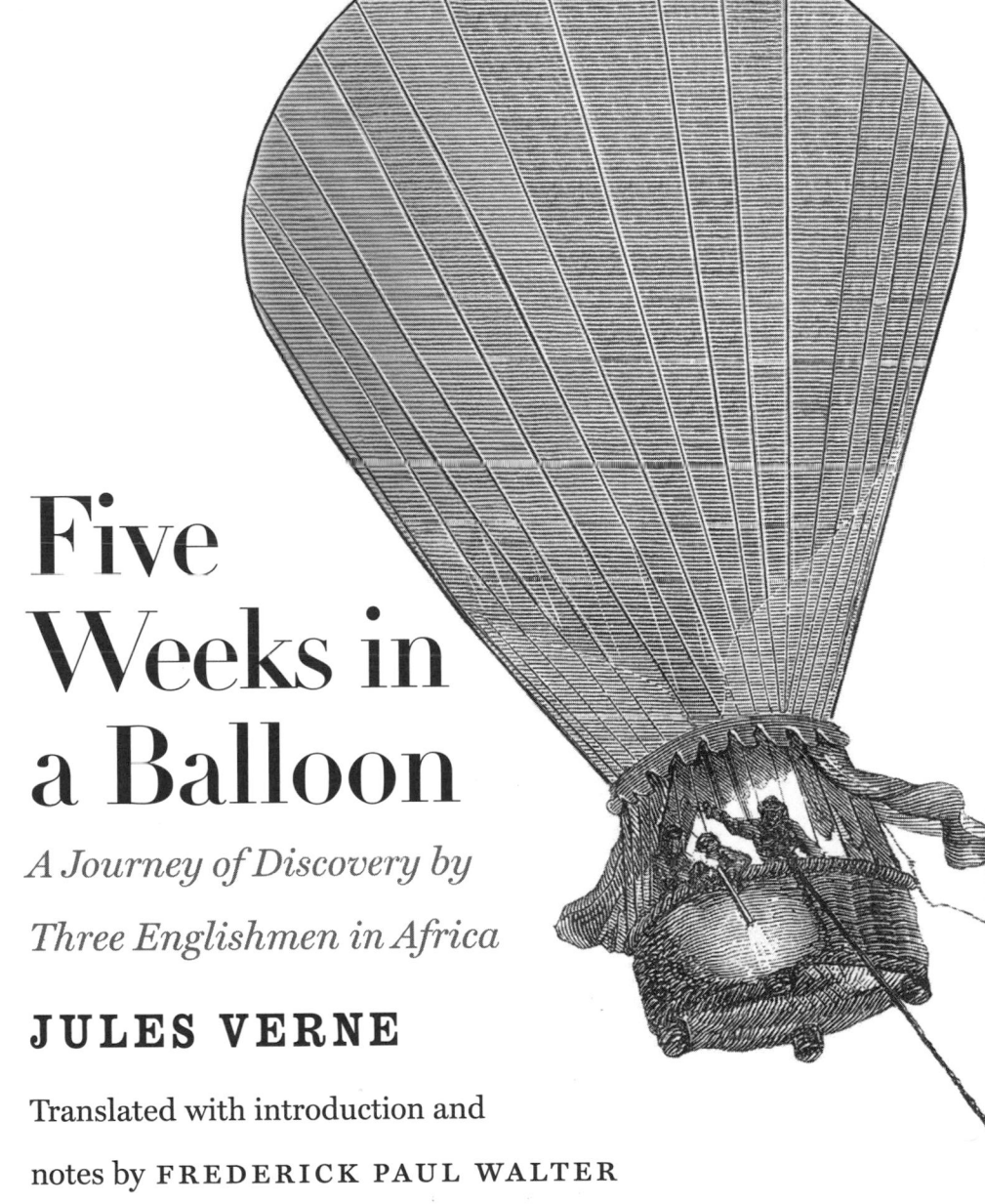

Five Weeks in a Balloon

A Journey of Discovery by

Three Englishmen in Africa

JULES VERNE

Translated with introduction and

notes by FREDERICK PAUL WALTER

Edited by ARTHUR B. EVANS

WESLEYAN UNIVERSITY PRESS *Middletown, Connecticut*

Wesleyan University Press
Middletown, CT 06459
www.wesleyan.edu/wespress
Translation and annotations © 2015 Frederick Paul Walter
Bibliography and biography © 2015 Arthur B. Evans
All rights reserved
Manufactured in the United States of America
Designed by Richard Hendel
Typeset in Miller, Didot, and Clarendon by
Tseng Information Systems, Inc.

publication of this book is funded by the
Beatrice Fox Auerbach Foundation Fund
at the Hartford Foundation for Public Giving

Wesleyan University Press is a member of the
Green Press Initiative. The paper used in this book
meets their minimum requirement for recycled paper.

Library of Congress Cataloging-in-Publication Data
Verne, Jules, 1828–1905.
[Cinq semaines en ballon. English]
Five weeks in a balloon: a journey of discovery by three
Englishmen in Africa / Jules Verne; translated with introduction
and notes by Frederick Paul Walter; edited by Arthur B. Evans.
    pages   cm — (Early classics of science fiction)
Includes bibliographical references.
ISBN 978-0-8195-7547-0 (cloth : alk. paper) —
ISBN 978-0-8195-7548-7 (ebook)
I. Walter, Frederick Paul, translator. II. Title.
PQ2469.C5E55 2015
843'.8—dc23   2014045129

5 4 3 2 1

Gratefully dedicated to the staff, volunteers, and aeronauts at the ANDERSON-ABRUZZO INTERNATIONAL BALLOON MUSEUM *in Albuquerque, New Mexico.*

Contents

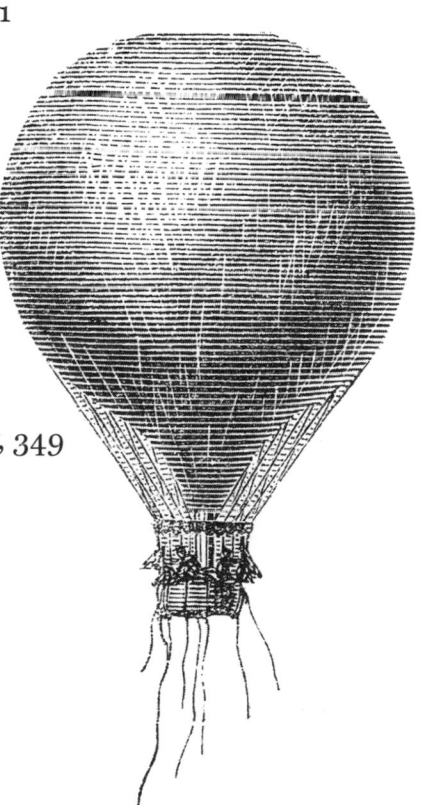

Introduction

Verne Takes Off

It's a balloonist's nightmare—a nutcase on board . . .

> "The higher we go, the more glorious our death will be!"
>
> All of her ballast tossed out, the balloon carried us to unreachable heights! The vehicle trembled in the air; the tiniest noises became explosions under the arching skies; our planet was the only object that caught my eye in that vastness, and it seemed ready for annihilation, while high above us the sky vanished into deep shadows!
>
> I watched the fellow stand up in front of me.
>
> "The time has come!" he told me. "We must die! All men reject us! They hold us in contempt! Let's crush them!"
>
> "No more!" I said.
>
> "Let's cut the ropes! This gondola will run loose in space! The force of gravity will change direction, and we'll head for the sun!"
>
> My despair galvanized me! I pounced on the maniac, and we grappled hand to hand, struggling fearfully! But he knocked me down, pinned me with his knee, and cut the ropes holding the gondola. . . .[1]

Verne was in his early twenties when he published the French originals of these lines. They come from a short story entitled "A Journey by Balloon" and they initially appeared in the August 1851 issue of the magazine *Musée des familles* (Family Gallery). It was only his second story to reach print; the first saw daylight the month before, same periodical, different genre—a Mexican adventure yarn.

Even so, "A Journey by Balloon" is an unsettling performance, among the darkest, fiercest things Verne ever penned. For one thing, it showcases two primordial fears—fear of heights and fear of falling. For another, it marks the debut of a crucial Vernian character—the renegade scientist. The plot is simple but riveting. The narrator, a French balloonist, stages a solo flight in a hydrogen balloon, only to have another Frenchman vault on board right at liftoff. The narrative instantly turns nasty. As the balloon rises into the air, the intruder assaults the balloonist, keeps throwing ballast overboard, and sends the vehicle over three miles up. The nameless skyjacker is dark, menacing, suicidal, apparently psychotic, thoroughly scary. The mix of high-impact fiction and news-making nonfiction seems immediately typical of this author.[2]

Balloon Beginnings

Human flight was still a new development—it had sprung up nearly full blown less than seventy years earlier and had barely changed in the decades since. The time was late in 1783. "Only rarely," historian Richard Hallion writes, "do revolutionary systems and technologies appear within the same year, but such is true of the balloon: the practical balloon constituted the dual invention of the papermaking brothers Joseph and Étienne Montgolfier and scientist Jacques Alexandre César Charles" (47).

The first launched the hot-air balloon, the second the gas balloon.

On October 15, 1783, the Montgolfiers sent their first man up in a hot-air balloon, a tethered flight—i.e., the balloon was literally on a leash. On December 1, 1783, Professor Charles went up himself in the first hydrogen balloon—an untethered journey that covered some twenty-five miles and ultimately climbed to 9,000 feet. Charles had recognized "that one could fly by creating a balloon filled with a lifting gas . . . namely the 17-year-old discovery hydrogen" (Hallion, 49). Isolated in 1766 by British chemist Henry Cavendish, hydrogen went by the nickname "flammable air," ranked as the lightest of gases, and offered the greatest lifting potential.

Furthermore, Charles's balloon was a surprisingly advanced vehicle: "a pattern of fishnet-like netting surrounded the upper hemisphere of the balloon . . . to form an attachment point for support ropes holding the ornate crew gondola" (Hallion, 56). As for the balloon's envelope, Henry Dale writes that Charles had "constructed a balloon of silk [which was] made impermeable to gas by varnishing it with dissolved rubber. They filled the envelope through lead pipes by adding sulphuric acid to iron filings which, in the process of oxidizing the iron, produced great quantities of hydrogen gas" (12).

Immediately these became the standard procedures, the same measures staying in force for many decades. As chapter 11 of this book reveals, not much had changed by Verne's day: the lifting gas in his fiction is invariably hydrogen. In fact, as George Denniston sums it up, "Hydrogen-filled balloons . . . became the balloons of choice throughout the world for almost two centuries" (16).

But if the procedures remained the same, so did the shortcomings. "The two big problems of lighter-than-air flight were propulsion and steering," as Dale notes (22). "Until they were resolved, the balloon for the most part remained a hobby for the rich and a fairground attraction for the masses rather than a practical vehicle for carrying passengers or freight."

Fledgling Flier

That's where things stood when Verne took on the topic of flight as a would-be author. High adventure and exotic locales had intrigued him from his boyhood—he grew up in the French industrial town of Nantes on the Loire River, a quick hop upstream from a busy Atlantic seaport. By then the machine age was well under way, steam-powered locomotives and ocean liners were practical parts of the culture, and flights by gas balloon were a major curiosity.

Samples of Verne's boyhood writing survive from his teens, including an unfinished novel from his eighteenth year (Herbert Lottman, 17). By the time of "A Journey by Balloon," he was twenty-three and had just broken into public print. Over the 1850s the *Musée des familles* published three short stories and two novellas by him, pieces in multiple genres: two tales of dark science, two Latin American adventure sagas, and a manhunt in the polar regions.

He was busier as a scriptwriter, although still not earning much. Over that same general period Verne penned some twenty plays and librettos, notably slapstick farces plus books and lyrics for musical comedies. His first professionally staged work, *The Broken Straws*, had a Paris run of about a dozen performances in 1850.

More than a decade would go by before Verne earned both fame and decent sales, so he was still a fledgling when "A Journey by Balloon" appeared. As indicated, it's a disturbing performance. Threats to life and limb throb under every paragraph, giving the tale unusual tension and ferocity. Verne's grip is so firm, the reader stays with him even through long stretches of expository material—in fact these educational digressions are almost a respite from the multiplying dangers, from our visceral fears. So as the intruder grows more crazed and the vehicle keeps climbing, we learn about early ballooning . . . its value in wartime . . . and its bloodcurdling failures, falls, and death tolls.

A dozen years later, several elements in this early story would be recycled in *Five Weeks in a Balloon*:

- The vehicle is a hydrogen balloon.[3]
- The skyjacker claims he has a way to steer balloons.
- Sophie Blanchard's death is described in detail.
- Likewise the flight of Garnerin's balloon to Rome.
- At the climax the gondola is cut loose.
- The narrator clings to the netting and reaches safety.

As for the educational matter on the history of ballooning, this is echoed in similar expository passages in *Five Weeks in a Balloon*—and of course, in much of Verne's fiction throughout his career.

In other ways too this powerful little story foreshadows Verne's later writing. Rejected by the scientific community, the maniacal skyjacker is the first of Verne's "dangerous scientists . . . the scientist who presents a serious danger to Nature, to society, and to humanity" (Arthur B. Evans, 1988, 83). He's the precursor of Verne's darker protagonists, his villain-heroes—Captain Nemo, the aeronaut Robur, the warmongering Schultze. And the story veers toward science fiction when it daydreams of balloons that are sky palaces, prefiguring futuristic vehicles such as Nemo's *Nautilus* or Robur's schooner-shaped helicopter.

Fans will recognize another old standby when the narrator plays word games with one of Newton's laws: "Their courage was in inverse ratio to the square of their speed of retreat." Verne rang further changes on Newton down through the years, sometimes seriously, as in *From the Earth to the Moon* (1865) . . . sometimes ironically, as in *Captain Grant's Children* (1867) where John hopes a flood rain will have a "duration in inverse ratio to its violence" . . . and sometimes comically, as in *The Earth Turned Upside Down* (1889) where a lovelorn widow "feels drawn to scientists in proportion to their mass and in inverse ratio to the square of their distance. And J. T. Maston was so plump, she just couldn't keep her distance."

However, it should also be noted that the educational matter in "A Journey by Balloon" tallies with accounts by today's scientists and historians, which means that Verne did a fair amount of homework. This raises the question: how did he become interested in this topic? Some scholars suggest he was inspired by Edgar Allan Poe's ballooning tales. Others point to his friendship with aeronaut and promoter Gaspard-Félix Tournachon, professionally known as Nadar. And still others deny he had any interest at all, asserting that "Verne did not like balloons" (William Butcher, 149). Yet this tightly detailed, solidly researched story from 1851 casts doubt on all of these theories.

First of all, Poe couldn't have been a factor. Jean Jules-Verne (30) reports that his grandfather read the American storyteller "in the years following 1848," yet young Verne had no English, and Poe's two ballooning yarns, "The Unparalleled Adventure of One Hans Pfaall" (1835) and "A Balloon Hoax" (1844), weren't available in French until *after* he had published "A Journey by Balloon." Translated by Alphonse Borghers, the first Gallic version of "Hans Pfaall" came out in 1853 (Arthur Hobson Quinn, 519); as for "Balloon Hoax," it appeared in 1856 as part of Charles Baudelaire's first Poe collection, *Histoires extraordinaires* (Lottman, 84). Furthermore, Nadar's influence figures even farther down the road: Butcher (145–46) has him entering Verne's life in 1861.

A number of Verne's interests seem to date from quite early on, certainly earlier than some have suspected. Take his fascination with polar exploration: when Poe's *The Narrative of Arthur Gordon Pym* (1837) first appeared in French translation in 1858, the young author was captivated. But he had already published his *own* tale of polar exploration, "Wintering in the Ice" (1855), which means that the interest was already there. And so it went with ballooning: he wasn't drawn to this activity because of Poe's or Nadar's influence—he was drawn to *them* because of a preexisting interest.

But again, where did it come from? Marcel Voisin suggests (135) that another literary figure may have been the catalyst: Paris journalist and poet Théophile Gautier had enthusiasms Verne was to share

(Stendhal, Wagner, Poe) and dabbled repeatedly in fiction and drama, stirring in such ingredients as well-made plots, submarines, and the Sepoy Rebellion. Young Verne may have hoped to emulate his career, and it seems significant that Gautier "published in *Le Journal* of September 25, 1848, an article entitled 'Concerning Balloons,' and another in *La Presse* of December 3, 1850, under the title 'Balloons'" (Voisin, 136).

One more thing: Voisin adds that Gautier frequently contributed to the *Musée des familles* "over the years 1840 to 1850."

Trial Balloon

Beneath all these influences and enthusiasms simmered Verne's "love of geography and exploration" (Butcher, 148), and he tried his hand a little later at straight nonfiction, a book-length travelogue based on his own wanderings over the British Isles. He finished the narrative in 1860, but it too came to nothing and wouldn't reach print for another 130 years—it appeared in English as *Backwards to Britain* (1993). Yet for a writer in love with geography, that era offered his mill plenty of grist. The world was full of unknown realms: both polar regions, South America, Canada, Mongolia, Siberia, Australia, the ocean depths, to say nothing of the moon and outer space. Right then the giant continent of Africa was making news: Burton and Speke had returned from it quarreling about the Nile's source, and in 1860 Speke had gone back "to prove that he was right." (Hazel Mary Martell, 30)

It was at this time too that African exploration was shifting into shameless colonialism, all Europe getting into the act. The continent's own people "were no match for the modern weaponry of the Europeans," as William Habeeb notes (30). "The French focused on North and West Africa, the British on southern and eastern Africa and Egypt, and the Portuguese on the southwestern and southeastern coasts." Not to mention the Belgians in the Congo, the Dutch in South Africa, and the Germans in East Africa. Ultimately it all led to the infamous 1884 Berlin Conference, where these factions parceled out the whole landmass for themselves. Not a single African was invited, the conference "gave no consideration to [their] needs and desires," and European rule persisted through much of the twentieth century (Habeeb, 30–31).

But as for Verne's career, it was going nowhere. Whether penning play scripts, short fiction, or full-length nonfiction, nothing worked until at last the tumblers clicked into place and he found his own winning combination: science . . . exploration . . . showmanship.

In 1862 he wrote a novel about a high-tech balloon trip across Africa.

It was finally his moment. As Evans describes it, Barth, Burton, Speke, Grant, and others were "creating widespread public interest in their continuing exploits. There is no doubt that Verne, conscientious as he was about staying abreast of such developments, saw in these explorations not only the ideal ingredients for his first [scientific novel], but also the strong likelihood of its immediate commercial success" (1988, 20).

This time around he had read Poe beforehand. Peter Costello writes that Verne's edition of Poe is dated 1862 and that he was critical of the American's two ballooning stories (70). He elaborated on his concerns in an analysis published a few years later: in *Edgar Allan Poe and His Works* (1864), he faults these tales for "brazenly transgressing the most elementary laws of physics and mechanics." As we'll see, Verne was determined to offer something more believable.

In the summer of 1862 he pitched his new manuscript to Pierre-Jules Hetzel, called by the author's grandson "one of the greatest publishers France has ever known" (Jules-Verne, 54). Hetzel's author list included the big names of nineteenth-century French literature: Honoré de Balzac, Victor Hugo, Émile Zola, George Sand, Baudelaire, Alexandre Dumas father and son. But the circumstances of his first meeting with Verne are hazy: it isn't clear how the young writer got his foot in the door or what took place after he did. Both of Verne's modern biographers bewail the lack of hard evidence, Lottman complaining that "there's precious little documentation" (83), Butcher suspecting that the details in earlier biographies might be fabricated: "Since no document has ever emerged, it remains perfectly possible that the biographers invented the whole story" (147).

The exact shape of Verne's new novel is also uncertain. Butcher even wonders if it *was* a novel (146–47), speculating that Verne offered the publisher a medley of nonfiction pieces about Africa and ballooning, Fergusson's adventure being simply a fanciful change of pace. But Hetzel called for revisions, and the author turned them around within two weeks (Jules-Verne, 56), so they hardly could have entailed a sweeping structural overhaul. Besides, there weren't any such medleys in Verne's earlier output, just short fiction, a couple dozen play scripts, and a book-length travelogue based on his *own* traveling. He had never been to Africa, and only later did he undertake a multipart geographical overview—and that was in an emergency and at Hetzel's behest.

More likely his text closely resembled what we know today as *Five Weeks in a Balloon*.[4] The revisions were in the details, edits, and refinements that could be decently managed in a fortnight. But this too remains uncertain: aside from some scraps of chapters 30 and 36, the manuscript is lost (Volker Dehs, 20–27).

Storytelling Strategies

Even so, the novel *is* distinctive in its structure. *Five Weeks* uses two separate strategies that Verne would resort to in many later narratives, although not necessarily together as he does here.

He takes exactly the first quarter of the book (chapters 1–11) to set up his journey. Initially he catches our attention simply by acting mysterious: the opening situation is fuzzy and unclear—we're curious to find out what in blazes is going on. In fact the yarn has an oddly disjointed, piecemeal exposition: chapter 1 hints at a daring expedition by the scientist Fergusson but gives few details—we know little more than what we can glean from the book's title page, namely that ballooning and Africa are involved. Then chapter 2 adds that Fergusson will fly east to west across the continent's midriff . . . after this, chapter 3 raises the notorious problem of how to steer a balloon . . . chapter 4 reveals that the trip aims to bridge two recent expeditions . . . and that's the rhythm. Later chapters keep adding dribs and drabs, culminating in chapter 10's by-the-numbers description of its innovative answer to the steering question. Verne has, in short, taken ten chapters to fit all the pieces into the puzzle, and we're finally ready for liftoff in chapter 11. To repeat: the engine that has pulled us along is our itch to find out "What's Going On?"

The remaining three-quarters of the novel have a different drive mechanism—they set measurable goals for the balloonists, goals that tease us with a new question: "Will They Make It?" Fergusson's first hope is to travel all the way to Senegal on Africa's west coast . . . his second is to link up the two earlier expeditions—Heinrich Barth's to the west in the vicinity of Timbuktu, Burton and Speke's to the east in the vicinity of the Nile's undiscovered source.

In those days England held a near monopoly on African exploration, and modern readers may not realize that the German Barth was in the pay of the British: "Barth was a Prussian, but he traveled under the British flag, wrote English for preference, and called himself Henry rather than Heinrich" (Felipe Fernández-Armesto, 344). This isn't as outlandish as it sounds, since Queen Victoria's mother and husband were both German-born; Anglo-Teuton relations could hardly have been closer. But the point is: Verne's hero Fergusson is working to connect the discoveries of *two English teams*.

A tangent to this objective is a third one that Fergusson tackles fairly early on: solving the age-old riddle of the Nile's source. As chapters 5 and 11 imply, the fictional Fergusson is in a race with an *actual* explorer, John Henning Speke. In 1860 the latter had gone back to Africa to settle this issue, which automatically means there are *other* true-life individuals in the race: Verne and Hetzel are hustling to write and publish the novel before it turns into old news. As Verne scholar Andrew Martin insists, "The main reason for speed in the preparation and execution of the expedition is that it is in danger of being overtaken by events" (36).

The danger didn't materialize, but in any case both of these storytelling strategies turn up in Verne's later fiction. If we're more familiar with the second (Will They Make It?), it's because his top sellers tend to advertise their objectives right in the title: *Around the World in Eighty Days* (1872), *Journey to the Center of the Earth* (1864), *From the Earth to the Moon*. In others the goals soon become clear in the text: *The Adventures of Captain Hatteras* (1866) is a quest for the North Pole . . . *The Mighty Orinoco* (1898) is a missing-person search . . . *The Wonderful Adventures of Mr. Antifer* (1894) is a treasure hunt.

As for the first strategy (What's Going On?), it rarely has to carry the whole narrative. *The Underground City* (1877) and *Robur the Conqueror* (1886) start with mysterious phenomena that the novels soon set about explaining. *The Castle in Transylvania* (1892) takes longer, holding off explanations until the end like your standard-issue whodunit. Even less orthodox is *Twenty Thousand Leagues under the Seas* (1870), which nails down the reader's interest by keeping Nemo, his crew, and their motives shadowy all the way through, prompting me to suggest elsewhere that "these mysteries are the book's undertow" (Walter, 320).

Five Weeks in a Balloon leaves no loose ends and closes firmly enough, but the novel is also notable for the variety of action and description in its final three-quarters, in the many episodes of the balloon's actual journey. Verne's book *is* episodic, built from individual stories, offering many chances for us to wonder if they'll make it. Some of these minidramas are one-chapter adventures—the outpost of Kazeh, the towing elephant, the battling cannibals, the ravaging locusts. Lengthier conflicts unfold later on—rescuing a missionary (three chapters), getting trapped in the desert (four chapters), Joe's disappearance (six chapters), the final sprint to the Senegal River (three chapters). But above them all is that overarching objective of reaching the African west coast.

Other key elements are Verne's plotting skills and gift of invention, especially his knack for conjuring up tight spots, cliff-hangers, and ingenious escapes—e.g., Joe's certain doom at the close of chapter 35 . . . the surprise rescue described in chapter 37 . . . the "setup" in chapter 34 that makes it all possible. This type of adroitness is often classed as "well-made plotting," and the term is apt here in the same sense that it applies to the play structures of Victorien Sardou and Henrik Ibsen or the detective novels of Agatha Christie and John Dickson Carr: developments and outcomes are cunningly prepared in advance and, even where surprising or shocking, come off as the logical effects of known causes.

Not unexpectedly, *Five Weeks* ends with a choice display of exactly this kind of virtuosity. Over chapters 38–43 the balloon *Victoria* keeps losing altitude and seems certain to crash to the earth. Yet each time we think the end is near, Verne finds another way out, reveals another card up his sleeve: they start by dropping all ballast . . . emptying water tanks . . . trying this, trying that . . . on and on through surprise after surprise. It's one of Verne's most entertaining traits, here and in the twists, turns, and trick endings of *Circling the Moon* (1869), *Eighty Days, Michael Strogoff* (1876), or *The Meteor Hunt* (1908).

Obviously *Five Weeks* was ideal for serializing. Its single-chapter adventures would give readers instant gratification, its cliff-hangers would keep them on pins and needles until the next installment. In fact, according to Daniel Compère, "Hetzel had first thought to issue *Five Weeks in a Balloon* in a periodical specializing in serializations that he'd published since 1860" (37). Ultimately Hetzel released it in an unillustrated softcover edition, but the following year he launched a *new* periodical in which Verne serializations would be the centerpiece for decades to come. One of history's first family magazines, it was a twice-monthly publication named the *Magasin d'éducation et de récréation*. As the title makes clear, it offered a mix of instruction and entertainment, and it grew into one of "the century's publishing phenomena" (Lottman, 95–6). Verne deserves much of the credit: he furnished Hetzel with a long series of adventure novels that were spiced with humor, hard science, dramatic derring-do, and visionary speculation. Following their serialization, they were republished in illustrated clothbound editions, and over the decades some sixty books appeared in this deluxe format, Hetzel marketing the franchise under the title *Voyages extraordinaires . . . Extraordinary Voyages* in literal translation . . . *Amazing Journeys* in snappier English.

Standard Ingredients

It may have been due to the saucy scriptwriting that intervened, but Verne's first novel is thoroughly different in tone from the dark terrors of his early short story "A Journey by Balloon."

For one thing, his characters are comedy material. Here, as in much of his fiction, they fall into three broad categories: the brain, the antagonist, and the stand-up comic. And these three—juggled, reworked, recombined, often divvied up—will soon became standard ingredients in Verne's storytelling.

The resident brain is usually a scientist or pedagogue: Dr. Fergusson is a generalist who knows his medicine, history, biological and physical sciences—a walking encyclopedia with countless facts, names, and dates at his fingertips, as he reveals at staggering length in chapters 30 and 38.

The role of antagonist is played by an old pal of Fergusson's, the rabid big-game hunter Dick Kennedy. In his case it isn't a full-time job—he opposes Fergusson's plans only in the first quarter of the book, is outmaneuvered, and after that turns into a well-meaning comrade.

Finally the stand-up comic provides chuckles, chapter taglines, and man-on-the-street perspectives. As is the case here, he's often a servant: Fergusson's valet is a pint-sized acrobat named Joe, who talks sense about giant redwoods ("If you live 4,000 years, isn't it perfectly natural to be on the tall side?"), adds a little social commentary ("If savages had the same tastes as aristocrats, how could we tell 'em apart?"), and even waxes philosophical ("A hunter doesn't know what hunting really is till he's the one being hunted!")

Shrewdly shuffled around, these roles were revived in other novels soon to follow. For instance *Journey to the Center of the Earth* has its own threesome, except in this case the scientist is the comic figure, his nephew is the skeptical opposition, and the servant is essentially a mute role. Among further variants, two very different scientists supply the brainpower in *Twenty Thousand Leagues*, while *The Mysterious Island* (1874) spreads the three roles over a sizable cast complete with understudies (e.g., Pencroff hands off to Joop). In short, there are endless combinations and permutations, and Verne's stories seem alert to them all. As for the oddity of Kennedy's short-lived antagonism in *Five Weeks*, it too reappears: Captain Nicholl badmouths the scheme to go *From the Earth to the Moon*, then happily signs on in time for blastoff.

Yet, despite its normally lighthearted tone, Verne's first novel *does* darken on occasion, although rarely in the vein of "A Journey by Balloon." Significantly, the most intense of these moments frame the book's halfway point: Chapter 20 unfolds a stomach-turning combat between two cannibal tribes; then come the events in chapters 21–23, less bloodcurdling but exceptionally somber for Verne as his heroes try to rescue a young missionary. In fact Verne repeatedly grieves the loss of European lives in Africa: Fergusson's blunt description (chapter 13) of a typical "surface journey" is troubling to read, and even Joe (chapter 35) finds the exploring efforts of Europeans "senseless and even sad." Still later, when his employer details the blood-spattered history of African exploration (chapter 38), the doctor's tagline takes the form of a despairing elegy: "This country . . . has witnessed the noblest kinds of dedication, for which, all too often, death has been the reward."

At times Fergusson seems to function as Verne's spokesperson, certainly he's our handy source for the information and insights that punctuate the action. Such educational nuggets are also standard ingredients in Verne, including full-scale lectures as in the just-mentioned chapter 38. Fergusson is no less diligent with the hard sciences, devoting all of chapters 7 and 10 to his balloon's inventive design. Finally, as a change of pace, Verne even has Joe deliver a mock lecture—in chapter 9 the servant delivers a bogus description of the cosmos, discoursing "about Neptune where seamen get a hearty welcome, and Mars where soldiers hog the sidewalks."

And finally *Five Weeks* contains pinches of the Vernian ingredient known to most: futuristic speculation. In chapter 16 Fergusson envisions a pattern of mass migrations with Africa emerging as "the center of the civilized world." We're not there yet, but another piece of speculation came to pass pretty quickly: in chapter 18 Fergusson and Co. pinpoint the Nile's source, and it's much as Henry Stanley confirmed it during the next decade. Prophetic also are the novel's new ballooning technologies: as Verne's grandson wrote a century later, "No satisfactory solution had yet been found for steering a balloon" (Jules-Verne, 57). His grandfather's scheme entails a hydrogen balloon, a double envelope, and a pioneering version of today's burner. Fergusson's vehicle rises and descends in order to find air currents heading in the desired direction. In the past this was accomplished only by dropping ballast or expelling gas—but after a while the balloon would run out of both and the journey inevitably grind to a halt. Fergusson's contribution is a heating system whereby the balloon "would rise to the appropriate altitude when the pilot heated water" (Lottman, xi). Warming up, the hydrogen expands and the balloon will climb; cooling off, the hydrogen contracts and the balloon will descend.

Critics Corner

It sounds simple and it is. Furthermore, Verne has been applauded by some commentators for coming up with an authentic innovation. The mechanism just described seems "to have been an invention of Verne himself," Costello writes (75), and Walter James Miller agrees that the Frenchman had "invented a new and plausible kind of balloon control" (xv). Even three decades later, Verne scholar Jean-Marc Deschamps concurs: "No balloon in Jules Verne's time had been equipped with such an ingenious arrangement" (15).

Yet Verne's contraption makes Deschamps jittery: he labels it "a flying bomb," marveling that it "never exploded despite the dangers lurking on every page" (15). Butcher likewise calls it a "frightening combination" (147), and naturally enough Verne's device sounds dubious today: hydrogen has long had a shady reputation, ever since taking the fall for the 1937 Hindenburg tragedy. But Verne's explanations were probably convincing in his own era when hydrogen was king—certainly Nadar was persuaded (Jules-Verne, 56). These days helium and propane often replace it, although it may be coming back in vogue: some space scientists now blame the Hindenburg fire on other causes, "as hydrogen produces none of the spectacular flames that consumed the airship" (David Owen, 63). In any case Verne's concept still operates in the burners used by today's hot-air balloonists: the purpose is still to climb and descend in search of favorable currents.

Other criticisms haven't always been well founded. Costello worries that Verne "does not seem to have considered how dangerous it would be if any oxygen leaked into the system" (75). And yet Verne repeatedly emphasizes (chapters 10, 12, 19, and 42) that the balloon's throat is hermetically sealed; further, when Fergusson finally resorts to oxygen for lift (chapter 43), the text explicitly tells us that "he took care beforehand to expel any remaining hydrogen through the valve."

Jacques Noiray has different doubts: he wonders if Verne's device is truly original, finding it "oddly similar" (45–46) to a so-called secret method used in an 1857 balloon flight to Algiers by the artist Paul Gavarni. I can find no official confirmation that the trip genuinely took place, but in any case it couldn't have had much in common with Verne's novel: Gavarni's vehicle boasted a propeller, two side-by-side balloons, and the usual release of gas in order to descend. The undisclosed method is alleged to have replaced the lost hydrogen—which makes it an entirely different animal from Verne's heating system.

As indicated, Verne's candidate for the Nile's source has sometimes been called prophetic: he opted for a stream flowing north from Lake Victoria (rather than Lake Tanganyika, as Burton argued). It was a prophecy "fulfilled in a matter of months when John Henning Speke returned from Africa to announce he had discovered the source of the Nile. But Verne's hero . . . had already made exactly the same discovery" (Miller, xv). The hard facts leave no wiggle room: *Five Weeks in a Balloon* rolled off the presses on January 31, 1863; Speke's famous telegram ("The Nile is settled.") reached London on May 6, 1863, appearing in the *Times* on the following day (Benjamin Disraeli, 275).

Given this chronology, it seems bizarre of Martin to disparage *Five Weeks* by claiming that Speke had found the Nile's source in 1858, long before the novel and that it was "something which has already been discovered" (35–36). Few agreed back then and few would agree now: as Fernández-Armesto reminds us, Speke "had seen only the southern shore of the lake and had not established how big it was or even whether it was a single body of water" (352). In fact Speke's later claim in 1863 (after he *actually* reached the northern end) also met with widespread resistance; it was only in the mid-1870s that an expedition under Henry Stanley "settled the question" and at last confirmed that Speke's hypothesis was correct (Fernández-Armesto, 355).

Generally, then, Vernians have high regard for *Five Weeks in a Balloon*. Butcher speaks for many when he notes its "innovative theme," calls it "a highly readable story," praises its "variety and pace," and labels it "quintessential Verne" (147–48). Not surprisingly, the book enjoyed strong sales, effectively launching Verne on a lifetime career. His grandson judged it "an immediate bestseller" (Jules-Verne, 57), while Lottman and Butcher both agree it was Verne's most successful title after *Around the World in Eighty Days*: the former (xiii) estimates that it was his second biggest seller in its original edition, while the latter (150) goes even farther: "Over Verne's lifetime . . . *Five Weeks* . . . [sold] second best among all his books, with an estimated one third of a million copies in French alone."

Aftermath and Influence

Verne stayed interested in aeronautics. Later in 1863 he joined Nadar in founding "a Society for Aerial Locomotion" (Jules-Verne, 57–58), then helped promote his friend's manufacture of a colossal balloon nearly as tall as Notre Dame cathedral. Christened the *Giant*, the vehicle was, in Miller's words, "one of the greatest publicity stunts of all time" (xiv), since it raised money for Nadar's aviation schemes while simultaneously boosting sales for Verne's new novel.

The author waited another decade before he went flying himself: "his first and only balloon flight . . . lasted only twenty-four minutes" (Lottman, 91). His pilot was the famous aeronaut Eugène Godard, and

Verne wrote up the experience in a newspaper article, "24 Minutes in a Balloon" (1873), for the *Journal d'Amiens*. His verdict on ballooning was positive: "It's even more than a journey, it's something like a dream, but a dream that's all too short!"

This brief account was one of several further pieces by him on the topic. Earlier, Verne had penned two articles for the *Musée des familles*, one on Nadar's colossal project entitled "Concerning the *Giant*" (1863), the other the aforementioned *Edgar Allan Poe and His Works*, in which he critiques Poe's ballooning stories. Following his twenty-four minutes with Godard, balloons would again play key roles in his novels (*The Mysterious Island, Hector Servadac* [1877], *Robur the Conqueror*), not to mention related gadgetry such as giant helicopters (*Robur* again), long-range missiles (*The Begum's Millions* [1879]), seaplanes on wheels (*Master of the World* [1904]), even manned kites (*A Two-Year Vacation* [1888]).

Beyond the aeronautics in *Five Weeks*, its events, settings, technology, and ethical content were additional influences on Verne's later fiction. Its side issue of determining the Nile's headwaters becomes a major objective in another novel about a big river, *The Mighty Orinoco*. Similarly, the lighthearted bets placed in chapter 2 are warm-ups for many a later wager, sometimes incidental *(The Meteor Hunt)*, sometimes pivotal *(Around the World in Eighty Days)*. In fact the latter dusts off several plotlines from *Five Weeks*: the rescue of the missionary from homicidal natives is echoed in the rescue of Lady Aouda from Brahman fanatics . . . the servant Joe gets separated from his master and two story lines advance concurrently, ditto with Passepartout in *Eighty Days* . . . and the last-minute dismantling of the balloon *Victoria* prefigures the climactic burning of the merchant steamer *Henrietta*.

As for settings, one geographic feature in *Five Weeks* became a leitmotif in these novels. The *Victoria* flies over a raging volcano in chapter 22, and this Vernian vision is amplified in most of his books over the next decade—*Journey to the Center of the Earth, Captain Hatteras, Captain Grant's Children, Circling the Moon, Twenty Thousand Leagues, The Mysterious Island* . . . and onward to the volcanoes in late-career titles such as *Propeller Island* (1895) and *Master of the World*.

Moving on to technology, the *Victoria*'s slow death in the desert (chapters 24–27) is the first instance of Verne devising an impressive vehicle, then evenhandedly exposing its Achilles heel (the balloon isn't self-propelled). A few years later he stages a similar exposé in *Twenty Thousand Leagues* when the submarine's single weakness (she can't manufacture oxygen) creates a life-threatening problem under the polar ice. And comparable things go wrong in *Circling the Moon*, *The Earth Turned Upside Down*, and *Propeller Island*. Verne may have faith in science, but it isn't blind faith.

Of course the close descriptions of Fergusson's mechanism are the forerunners of other famous hardware passages in these novels: the development-by-committee of the space capsule in *From the Earth to the Moon* . . . the specs on Nemo's diving gear in *Twenty Thousand Leagues* . . . the disquisitions on aerodynamics in *Robur the Conqueror*. But *Five Weeks* also offers another shrewd insight: men bond with machinery. As Alain Froidefond observes, Verne "eliminates or renders inaccessible female heroes as often as possible, instead giving a primal role to the machine" (24). Sure enough, the balloon *Victoria* is literally the love interest: "I've gotten attached to her," Joe admits in chapter 41. "It'll be hard to part with her!" Then at the close when she sinks into the Senegal River, he moans "Poor *Victoria*!" while even the doctor "couldn't keep back a tear." And this moist moment won't be the last in these novels. In *The Sphinx of the Ice Realm* (1897), when the stoic first officer sees his ship go down, Verne writes: "He was a man of the sternest fiber, and yes, he wept." Or in *The Steam House* (1880), when the robot elephant meets its explosive doom: "Poor creature!" the inventor says, and then follows up with "a huge sigh."

Five Weeks also introduces a number of ethical issues that are often debated in later books. One, Verne's pacifism, is only hinted at in chapter 20, where, as usual, Fergusson seems to be the author's mouthpiece: "If our supreme commanders could look down on their fields of operation as we're doing now, maybe they'd ultimately lose their stomach for blood and conquest." But two other issues get more extended coverage in Verne's first novel.

Greed and gold are the first. Kennedy leads off: early on he kills an elephant, damages one of its tusks, and bemoans the loss of thirty-five guineas. But the most biting passages are in chapter 23 and involve the valet Joe squabbling over gold deposits with Dr. Fergusson, who reveals an unsuspected gift for deadpan comedy. In essence Joe has great difficulty deciding between keeping his gold and dying of thirst, and this form of insanity is a thread Verne will follow repeatedly — mid-career in *Hector Servadac* and *The Earth Turned Upside Down*, near the end in *The Meteor Hunt* and *The Golden Volcano* (1906).

But ecological concerns seem to arouse Verne's deepest anxieties, and there are several caustic passages in *Five Weeks*. Dick Kennedy figures in most of them, a hunter so obsessed with his firearms (chapter 42) that he would rather finish the trip on foot than give them up. Elsewhere (chapters 28 and 31) he can't remember his kills and lives only for the next one — as an old adage on addiction puts it, "A thousand aren't enough." Finally in chapter 31 Fergusson reprimands him: "what's the point of shooting animals you can't make use of?" he asks the Scot. "To slay an antelope or gazelle for no good reason other than to satisfy your everyday hunting urges — that really isn't justified."

Verne takes up this environmental cudgel again in *Twenty Thousand Leagues*, accurately predicting the near extinction of many marine mammals. Here Kennedy's stand-in is Ned Land, a Canadian harpooner; when Land wants to attack a pod of inoffensive baleen whales, Captain Nemo's refusal expands on Fergusson's reprimand: "It would be killing just for the sake of killing. . . . When your colleagues, Mr. Land, destroy decent, harmless creatures like the southern right whale or the bowhead whale, they're guilty of criminal behavior . . . and they'll ultimately wipe out a whole class of beneficial animals."

Translating for Today

Even in the twenty-first century, then, *Five Weeks in a Balloon* is a novel with a good deal going for it:

- It's Verne's first novel, his breakthrough book.
- It was his second biggest seller, after *Around the World in Eighty Days*.
- It launched his famed series of *Voyages extraordinaires*.
- It's the classic ballooning novel.
- It's the first steampunk story.
- It's a triple-threat mix of adventure, comedy, and hard science fiction.

- It wrestles with ecological and economic issues that are still unresolved.

The present Wesleyan edition is the first complete English translation of this seminal work. It's not, however, the earliest translation in our language: the immediate popularity of *Five Weeks* led to the rapid publication of several English versions—nearly all in Verne's lifetime, during the high noon of his fame. As Evans reports in "The English Editions of *Five Weeks in a Balloon*" at the website *Verniana*, there have been six prior translations of this novel: three identify their translators (William Lackland, Frederick Amadeus Malleson, and Arthur Chambers), the other three keep them anonymous (the publishers are Chapman and Hall, Routledge, and Goubaud).

A seventh, much later version appeared in the 1960s under I. O. Evans's byline, but it proved to be an abridged spin-off of the Malleson rendering. Nor, alas, are any of the other editions responsibly complete. The Chapman and Hall text eliminates a good quarter of the book and goes to the rear of the class; Malleson, Routledge, and Goubaud condense almost every chapter, while Chambers's 1920s rendering often slurs details, seemingly out of carelessness. Lackland's is the fullest text, yet it has its problems too: the author's many footnotes are omitted, and there are a variety of small mishaps—dropped lines, missing details, technical errors, fleeting mistranslations, unnecessary glosses, etc.

Beyond these questions of omitting and condensing, there are language and style issues—severe ones. True, these are texts from another time and place, so reading them will naturally grow more difficult as the years go by. But they also present an uglier language barrier: in dealing with Africa and its peoples, these old British editions—Lackland's included—resort to racial epithets and pejorative slang, allowed in their day, despised in ours. Yet Verne's French is neutral and restrained, so as Evans concludes elsewhere (2005), the fault lies with the translators themselves: had they "chosen to be more faithful to what Verne had originally written, such terms would never have found their way into the English versions of [this novel] in the first place" (96).

So a complete, accurate, reader-friendly translation of Verne's early masterpiece is long overdue. This book has a twofold audience: first, the countless general readers who think Verne is fun to read, a population ranging from school kids to scientists to oldsters with fond memories. This new translation is particularly meant for them and works to balance the two methodologies Kieran O'Driscoll describes in his recent study of Verne in English: in brief, my text began life as a "highly accurate, source-oriented, imitative" rendering, which I then polished using "informal, idiomatic language" (251–52). As for other audience members, they include the growing battalions of scholars and specialists who, although they know their Verne from the original French, are still appreciative of textual detective work and stimulating critical materials. I encourage them to consult the endnotes, which address the policies, priorities, textual puzzles, and interpretive decisions affecting the translation. In short, to borrow another of O'Driscoll's phrases, this new, complete rendering of *Five Weeks in a Balloon* is "aimed at both a general and a scholarly readership" (190).

Frederick Paul Walter
Albuquerque, New Mexico

REFERENCES

Butcher, William. *Jules Verne: The Definitive Biography*. New York: Thunder's Mouth, 2006.

Compère, Daniel. *Jules Verne: Écrivain*. Geneva: Librairie Droz, 1991.

Costello, Peter. *Jules Verne: Inventor of Science Fiction*. New York: Scribner's, 1978.

Dale, Henry. *Early Flying Machines*. New York: Oxford University Press, 1992.

Dehs, Volker. "Les Manuscrits de *Cinq semaines en ballon.*" *Bulletin de la Société Jules Verne*, no. 183 (August 2013): 20–27.

Denniston, George. *The Joy of Ballooning*. Philadephia: Courage Books, 1999.

Deschamps, Jean-Marc. *Jules Verne: 140 ans d'inventions extraordinaires*. Paris: Du May, 2005.

Disraeli, Benjamin. *Letters: 1860–1864*. Edited by M. G. Wiebe, Mary S. Millar, Ann P. Robson, and Ellen L. Hawman. Toronto: University of Toronto, 2009.

Evans, Arthur B. "The English Editions of *Five Weeks in a Balloon.*" *Verniana* 6 (2013–14): 141–70.

———. *Jules Verne Rediscovered: Didacticism and the Scientific Novel*. New York: Greenwood, 1988.

———. "Jules Verne's English Translations." *Science Fiction Studies* 32, no. 1 (March 2005): 80–104.

Fernández-Armesto, Felipe. *Pathfinders: A Global History of Exploration*. New York: Norton, 2006.

Froidefond, Alain. "Jules Verne fabuleux." In *Jules Verne*, no. 8: *Humour, ironie, fantasie*. Edited by Christian Chelebourg. Paris: Lettres Modernes Minard, 2003.

Habeeb, William Mark. *Africa: Facts and Figures*. Philadelphia: Mason Crest, 2005.

Hallion, Richard P. *Taking Flight: Inventing the Aerial Age from Antiquity through the First World War*. New York: Oxford University Press, 2003.

Jules-Verne, Jean. *Jules Verne: A Biography*. Translated and adapted by Roger Greaves. New York: Taplinger, 1976.

Lottman, Herbert R. *Jules Verne: An Exploratory Biography*. New York: St. Martins Press, 1996.

Martell, Hazel Mary. *Exploring Africa*. New York: Peter Bedrick, 1997.

Martin, Andrew. *The Mask of the Prophet: The Extraordinary Fictions of Jules Verne*. Oxford: Clarendon Press, 1990.

Miller, Walter James. *The Annotated Jules Verne: From the Earth to the Moon*. 1978. 2nd ed. New York: Gramercy Books, 1995.

Noiray, Jacques. *Le Romancier et la machine: L'image de la machine dans le roman français, 1850–1900*, vol. 2. Paris: Corti, 1992.

O'Driscoll, Kieran. *Retranslation through the Centuries: Jules Verne in English*. Oxford: Peter Lang, 2011.

Owen, David. *Lighter than Air: An Illustrated History of the Development of Hot-air Balloons and Airships*. Edison, NJ: Chartwell, 1999.

Quinn, Arthur Hobson. *Edgar Allan Poe: A Critical Biography*. Baltimore: Johns Hopkins University Press, 1941. Pbk. ed., 1998.

Voisin, Marcel. "Théophile Gautier: Précurseur de Jules Verne?" In *Colloque d'Amiens* (1977), vol. 2: *Jules Verne: Filiations.Rencontres.Influences*. Paris: Lettres Moderne Minard, 1980.

Walter, Frederick Paul. *Amazing Journeys: Five Visionary Classics by Jules Verne*. Albany: State University of New York Press, 2010.

chapter I

The end of a wildly applauded speech—introducing Dr. Samuel Fergusson—"Excelsior"—full-length portrait of the doctor—a confirmed fatalist—dinner at the Travelers Club—many toasts to the occasion.

They had a packed house for the Royal Geographical Society's meeting on January 14, 1862, at 3 Waterloo Place, London. Their president, Sir Francis M——, made a major announcement to his distinguished colleagues during a speech that was frequently interrupted by cheering.

This choice bit of eloquence finally came to a close with several grandiose sentences brimming over with patriotic fervor:

"England has always marched in front of other nations" (because, mind you, nations are always marching on each other's fronts), "thanks to the valor of her explorers in the realm of geographical discovery. *(Much agreement.)* Dr. Samuel Fergusson, one of her glorious sons, won't disgrace his ancestry. *(No's from all directions.)* If this endeavor succeeds *(It will!)* we'll ultimately fill in the blank spaces on Africa's map *(hearty approval)*, and if it fails *(No, never!)* at the very least it will go down as one of the most courageous expressions of the human spirit!" *(Frenzied stamping of feet.)*

"Hooray! Hooray!" the gathering shouted, galvanized by these rousing words.

"Hooray for Fergusson the fearless!" exclaimed one of the audience's noisier members.

Enthusiastic yells rang out. Fergusson's name burst from every mouth, and we have reason to believe that it got an extra oomph from passing through English throats. The meeting room shook.

Yet many in the audience were seasoned travelers, dauntless, weather-beaten oldsters whose restless personalities had led them into

the five corners of the globe! Mentally or physically, one way or another, they all had survived shipwrecks, wildfires, Indian tomahawks, the war clubs of savages, burning at the stake, and the bellies of Polynesians! But nothing could quiet their pounding hearts during that speech by Sir Francis M——, which was definitely the grandest oratorical success at London's Royal Geographical Society within living memory.

But in England enthusiasm is more than a matter of words. It generates money quicker than molds at the Royal Mint.* They voted Dr. Fergusson a performance incentive on the spot, the lofty figure of £2500.[1] The significance of the sum was in keeping with the significance of the undertaking.

One of the Society's members queried the president on the issue of whether or not Dr. Fergusson would be formally introduced.

"The doctor is at the gathering's disposal," Sir Francis M—— answered.

"Bring him in! Bring him in!" they exclaimed. "A fellow as daring as all that is a sight worth seeing!"

* Monetary authority in London.

"Maybe," said a palsied old commodore, "this unbelievable proposal of his is just a prank he's playing on us."

"What if there's no such person as Dr. Fergusson?" a roguish voice exclaimed.

"Then we'd have to invent him!" replied a humorous member of this solemn Society.

"Have Dr. Fergusson come in," Sir Francis M—— merely said.

And the doctor came in to thunderous applause, but not the least bit impressed by any of it.

He was some forty years old, a man of average height and build; his dark-hued complexion hinted at an assertive personality; he had a poker face with regular features and a strong nose, a nose like a ship's prow for a man predestined to be a discoverer; his eyes were quite gentle, shrewd rather than bold, and lent real charm to his facial expressions; his arms were long, and he planted his feet on the ground with the confidence of somebody who takes everything in stride.

The doctor's entire person gave off a calm dignity, and you couldn't imagine him playing even the most innocent prank.

Accordingly, the hoorays and applause didn't let up until Dr. Fergusson called for silence with a genial wave of the hand. He headed over to the chair set out for his presentation; then, still on his feet, not moving, his eyes resolute, he pointed his right index finger at the sky, opened his mouth, and uttered this single word:

"Excelsior!"[2]

No surprise motion from Messrs. Bright and Cobden, no plea by Lord Palmerston for more money to fortify England's coasts, had ever created such a sensation! Sir Francis M——'s speech was left in the dust. At one go the doctor came off as enlightened, masterful, clear-headed, and temperate; he had said the word for the day:

"Excelsior!"

Completely won over by this unusual man, the old commodore moved that Fergusson's communication be inserted "in its entirety" into the *Proceedings of the Royal Geographical Society of London*.[3]

So who *was* this doctor, and what undertaking was he about to embark on?

During Fergusson's youth his father had been a gallant captain in the Royal Navy, and from his son's earliest years, he had acquainted the boy with the dangers and risks of his profession. The worthy lad seemed untouched by fear, quickly gave evidence of sharp wits, a questing intelligence, and a remarkable bent for scientific research; what's more, he revealed uncommon coping skills; nothing was ever awkward for him, not even using a fork for the first time, a test that youngsters generally fail.

Soon he was reading about bold undertakings, exploratory voyages, and they fired his imagination; he got all caught up in the discoveries that marked the first part of the nineteenth century; he daydreamed of the glory earned by Mungo Park, Bruce, Caillié, Levaillant—and even, I suspect, by Selkirk, who equaled them in his eyes. How many well-used hours he spent with that real-life Robinson Crusoe on his Juan Fernández Islands! Often he saw eye to eye with that marooned sailor; sometimes he disagreed with his plans and objectives; he would have acted differently and maybe done better—or, no doubt, at least as well! But one thing he was sure of—he never would have left that blissful island, where Selkirk had been as happy as a king without subjects . . . no, not even if he were to become First Lord of the Admiralty!

I'll let you decide if these tendencies blossomed during an adventurous youth that took him to the four corners of the world. His father was an educated man who never missed a chance to sharpen his son's keen intelligence with in-depth studies in hydrography, physics, and mechanics, plus a smattering of botany, medicine, and astronomy.

When the worthy captain passed away, Samuel Fergusson was twenty-two years old and had already traveled around the globe; he enlisted in the Bengal Corps of Engineers and gave a good account of himself in several skirmishes; but this life of soldiering didn't agree with him; he had little interest in commanding, so he wasn't keen on obeying. He submitted his resignation and set out for the northern regions of India's peninsula, crossing it from Calcutta to Surat, surviving as both hunter and gatherer. A mere pleasure trip.

From Surat we see him traveling to Australia and in 1845 taking part in Captain Charles Sturt's expedition, whose mission was to push inland and find that second Caspian Sea thought to exist deep in that continent then known as New Holland.

Samuel Fergusson went back to England around 1850; the demon of discovery possessed him more than ever, and until 1853 he accompanied Captain McClure on an expedition that skirted the American continent from Bering Strait to Cape Farewell in Greenland.

Despite exertions of every kind and in every climate, Fergusson's sturdy constitution held up marvelously; he was at home with the most hopeless hardships; he was the very model of your ideal traveler whose belly contracts or expands at will, whose legs grow longer or shorter depending on the bed improvised for the occasion, who can fall asleep at any hour of the day and wake up at any hour of the night.

After that, from 1855 to 1857, nothing could be less surprising than to find our tireless traveler visiting all of western Tibet along with the Schlagintweit brothers, then bringing back some intriguing cultural data from their investigations.

During these various journeys, Samuel Fergusson was the liveliest and most interesting correspondent on the *Daily Telegraph*, that one-penny newspaper whose daily circulation runs as high as 140,000 copies, barely enough for its several million readers. Accordingly, he was well known, this doctor, although he wasn't a member of any scholarly organization, neither the royal geographical societies of London, Paris, Berlin, Vienna, or St. Petersburg, nor the Travelers Club, nor even the Royal Polytechnic Institute, lorded over by his friend Cockburn the statistician.[4]

This sage actually proposed one day, as a friendly gesture, to solve the following problem for him: given the number of miles the doctor had covered in his journeys around the world, how many *more* miles had his head traveled than his feet, due to its greater radius? Or rather, supplied with the different mileages for the doctor's head and feet, what was his *exact height* to the nearest twelfth of an inch?

But Fergusson gave scholarly bodies a wide berth, being a member of the church of doers rather than talkers; his time was better spent in discovering than discussing, seeking than squabbling.

The story goes that an Englishman once visited Geneva intending to see the lake; they put him aboard one of those old-time carriages where the seats are mounted sideways and face out, as they do on the roof of an omnibus: now then, by chance our Englishman ended up in a seat that looked away from the lake; the carriage serenely circled it without the fellow thinking to turn around one single time, and he went back to London speechless over Lake Geneva.[5]

Dr. Fergusson, however, *had* turned around, and more than once during his travels, with the result that he had seen plenty. In this, moreover, he was just doing what came naturally, and we have grounds for thinking that he was a bit of a fatalist, but it was a very conservative sort of fatalism where he relied on himself and even on Providence; in his journeys he saw himself as pushed rather than pulled, as traveling the world like a railroad engine, which isn't steered but goes where the tracks do.

"I don't look for my path," he often said. "My path looks for me."

So nobody will be surprised by his composure as he received the Royal Society's applause; he was above such petty concerns, had no pride and even less vanity; he saw the proposal he had presented to Sir Francis M—— as perfectly simple and didn't even notice the immense effect it produced.

After the meeting, they took the doctor to the Travelers Club on Pall Mall; there he found a superb feast laid out for him; the dimensions of the dishes served were commensurate with the honoree's importance, and the sturgeon that figured in this splendid meal wasn't three inches shorter than Samuel Fergusson himself.

The diners lifted their glasses of French wine and proposed many toasts to the famous travelers who had earned renown in the land of Africa.[6] They drank to their health or memory in alphabetical order, being veddy British: to Abbadie, Adams, Adanson, Anderson, Arnaud, Avanchers, Baikie, Baldwin, Barth, Battuta, Beke, Beltrame, Belzoni, Bimbachi, Bonnemain, Bou Derba, Bowdich, Brisson, Browne, Bruce, Brun-Rollet, Burchell, Burckhardt, Burton, Cailliaud, Caillié, Campbell, Castel-Bolognesi, Chaillu, Chapman, Clapperton, Clot Bey, Colonieu, Courval, Cuny, Debono, Decken, Denham, Dickinson, Dickson, Dochard, Duncan, Durand, Duroulé, Duveyrier, El-Tounsy, Erhardt, Escayrac de Lauture, Ferret, Fresnel, Galinier, Galton, Geoffroy Saint-Hilaire, Golbéry, Gordon-Cumming, Hahn, Halm, Harnier, Hecquard, Heuglin, Hornemann, Houghton, Imbert, Kaufmann, Knoblecher, Krapf, Kummer, Lafargue, Laing, La Jaille, Lambert, Lamiral, John Lander, Richard Lander, Lefebvre, Lejean, Lemprière, Levaillant, Livingstone, MacCarthy, Magyar, Maizan, Malzac, Moffat, Mollien, Monteiro, Morrisson, Neimans, Overweg, Panet, Park, Partarrieu, Pascal,

Pall Mall feast

Pearce, Peddie, Peney, Petherick, Poncet, Prax, Raffenel, Rath, Rebmann, Richardson, Riley, Ritchie, Rochet d'Héricourt, Roscher, Roungawi, Rüppell, Saugnier, Speke, Steudner, Thibaut, Thompson, Thornton, Toole, Trotter, Tuckey, Tyrwhitt, Vaudey, Vayssière, Vincent, Vinco, Vogel, Wahlberg, Warrington, Washington, Werne, Wild,[7] and finally Dr. Samuel Fergusson, whose incredible endeavor aimed to link up the achievements of all these travelers and complete this series of African discoveries.

chapter 2

An article in the Daily Telegraph—*scholarly journals at war—Herr Petermann stands by his friend Dr. Fergusson—response from the learned Koner—sporting wagers—various propositions made to the doctor.*

The next day, in its January 15 issue, the *Daily Telegraph* published an article that read as follows:

At last Africa is going to turn over the secrets of her vast, lonely wastes: a modern-day Oedipus will be giving us the key to a riddle that the scholars of sixty centuries haven't managed to decipher. Formerly, to search for the source of the Nile—or, in the old Latin wording, *fontes Nili quærere*—was viewed as an insane endeavor, a fantasy that could never become reality.

Dr. Barth followed the route plotted by Denham and Clapperton as far as Sudan; Dr. Livingstone conducted many courageous investigations from the Cape of Good Hope to the Zambezi basin; Captains Burton and Speke discovered the great inland lakes. They blazed three trails for modern civilization; the spot where they intersect—which travelers still haven't managed to reach—lies in Africa's very heart. It's in this region that every effort needs to be made.

Now the deeds of those bold scientific pioneers will be tied together in this daring endeavor by Dr. Samuel Fergusson, whose splendid feats of exploration our readers have often relished.

This courageous discoverer[1] proposes to cross all Africa from east to west by balloon. If our sources are correct, the starting point of this astounding journey will be the island of Zanzibar off Africa's east coast. As for its endpoint, God only knows.

Yesterday the Royal Geographical Society heard a formal

proposal for this piece of scientific exploration; they approved the sum of £2500 to cover the undertaking's costs.

We will keep our readers up to date on this endeavor, which is unprecedented in the annals of geography.

As you might expect, this article had an enormous impact: at first it stirred up storms of skepticism; folks regarded Dr. Fergusson as an outright fantasy, an invention of Mr. P. T. Barnum—who, after working the states of the Union, was all set to "take in" the British Isles.

In Geneva a witty rebuttal appeared in the February issue of *Dispatches from the Geographical Society*; it poked fun at London's Royal Society, the Travelers Club, and the phenomenal sturgeon.

But Herr Petermann's *Mitteilungen*,[2] published in Gotha, reduced the Geneva journal to the most abject silence. Herr Petermann was personally familiar with Dr. Fergusson and vouched for the bravery of his daring friend.

Soon, however, there was no longer any room for doubt; preparations for the journey were under way in London; the factories of Lyon had received a major order for the taffeta needed to manufacture the lighter-than-air vehicle; lastly the British government put the cargo boat *Resolute*, skippered by Captain Pennet, at the doctor's disposal.

Instantly thousands offered him encouragement, thousands bombarded him with congratulations. Meanwhile details of the undertaking were published in the bulletins of the Paris Geographical Society; a notable article appeared in Monsieur V. A. Malte-Brun's *New Annals of Travel, Geography, History, and Archaeology*; a probing piece by Dr. W. Koner saw print in the *Zeitschrift für Allgemeine Erdkunde*,[3] triumphantly revealing the journey's potential, its chances of success, the nature of the obstacles ahead, the immense advantages of an airborne mode of travel; it criticized only the journey's starting point; instead it preferred Massawa, a little Ethiopian port from which James Bruce had set out in 1768 to search for the Nile's headwaters. But it unreservedly admired Dr. Fergusson's strength of mind and the bold-as-brass courage that could conceive and attempt such a journey.

The *North American Review* watched with little pleasure as England basked in all this glory; it laughed off the doctor's proposal and invited him to push on to America while the going was good.

In short, without listing every periodical on the planet, there wasn't a scientific forum from the *Journal of Evangelical Missions* to the *Algerian and Colonial Review,* from the *Annals of the Propagation of the Faith* to the *Church Missionary Reporter,* that didn't go into every aspect of this affair.

In London and across England, folks wagered sizable sums: 1) on whether Dr. Fergusson was a real or imaginary being; 2) on the journey itself, which some said wouldn't even be attempted and others said would be carried out in full; 3) on the issue of determining if it succeeded or not; 4) on the likelihood or unlikelihood of Dr. Fergusson ever coming back. The bookmakers logged enormous amounts on these wagers, as if they were taking bets at Epsom Downs.

As a consequence, believers, skeptics, dunces, and scholars all kept their eyes on the doctor; he became the lion of the day, without ever suspecting that he sported a mane. He was happy to provide detailed information on his expedition. He was easy to approach and the most straightforward fellow on earth. More than one bold adventurer turned up, eager to share in the glory and dangers of his endeavor; but the doctor refused without giving any reasons for his refusal.

Many inventors of gadgets devised for steering balloons came and proposed their methods to him. He wasn't in the market. To anybody who asked if he himself had discovered something of the sort, he consistently refused to elaborate and became more energetically involved than ever in the preparations for his journey.

chapter 3

The doctor's friend—where their friendship dated from—Dick Kennedy in London—an unexpected and unsettling proposition—a discouraging proverb—a few names from Africa's death register—advantages of a lighter-than-air vehicle—Dr. Fergusson's secret.

Dr. Fergusson had a friend. Not an *alter ego*, not a second self; a friendship couldn't exist between two perfectly identical beings.

But even though they boasted different traits, abilities, and personalities, Dick Kennedy and Samuel Fergusson marched to the exact same drummer, which didn't seriously bother them. On the contrary.

This Dick Kennedy fellow was a Scot in the fullest sense of the word—outgoing, decisive, bullheaded. He lived in the little town of Leith near Edinburgh, actually a suburb of "Auld Reekie."* He was sometimes a fisherman but at all times and places an avid hunter, not a bit surprising for a native of Caledonia who had done a little mountain climbing in the Highlands. He was renowned as a marvelous shot with a rifle; not only did he split bullets on a knife blade, he cut them into two equal halves—and if you weighed them afterward, you wouldn't find any noticeable difference.

Kennedy's looks strongly reminded you of the fiery Halbert Glen-

---

* Nickname for Edinburgh meaning "Old Smoky."

dinning as described by Sir Walter Scott in *The Monastery*; he stood over six English feet in height;[1] limber and alert, he seemed to be blessed with Herculean strength; a face deeply tanned by the sun, dark keen eyes, a bold and resolute nature; in sum, there was something solid and decent in the entire person of this Scot, and it boded well.

The two friends got to know each other in India, back when they both belonged to the same regiment; while Dick was hunting tigers and elephants, Samuel was hunting plants and insects; each could boast of being adept at his line of work, and more than one rare plant fell prey to the doctor, who valued this kind of conquest as much as any pair of ivory tusks.

These two young men never had a chance to rescue each other or to end up in each other's debt. Which means they had a lasting friendship. Fate sometimes kept them apart, but their mutual liking always brought them back together.

After their return to England, they were often separated by the doctor's expeditions abroad; but when he came back, he never failed to visit his Scottish friend and give a few weeks of himself unasked.

Dick chatted about the past, Samuel planned for the future: one looked forward, the other back. Hence Fergusson had a restless mind, while Kennedy was content with his lot.

After his trip to Tibet, the doctor went nearly two years without any talk of further exploring; Dick assumed that his urge to travel, his craving for adventure, had simmered down. To the hunter's relief. He figured that sooner or later the doctor was bound to come to a bad end; you can be an old hand with the human race and still not journey with impunity among cannibals and wild animals; so Kennedy urged Samuel to rest on his laurels, since he had done enough for science and more than enough to earn the gratitude of his fellow man.

To which the doctor was content to say nothing. He continued to look thoughtful, then indulged in mysterious calculations, spent his nights slaving over figures, even experimented with odd gadgets nobody could make sense of. You could tell that some grand idea was fermenting in his brain.

"What can he be working on?" Kennedy wondered, when his friend left him and spent the month of January back in London.

He found out one morning from that article in the *Daily Telegraph*.

"Merciful God!" he exclaimed. "That madman! That maniac! Go across Africa by balloon! That's all we need! So this is what he's been brooding about these past two years!"

Replace all these exclamation points with a fist smacking his skull, and you'll have an idea of the calisthenics our gallant Dick indulged in while he carried on this way.

When old Elspeth, his trusted housekeeper, ventured to hint that it might actually be a hoax:

"Get along with you!" he replied. "Don't I know him? Isn't this the doctor all over? Travel through the skies! Now he has eagle envy! No, this positively mustn't happen! It's up to me to put a stop to it! Lord, he'd be off to the moon one fine day if they let him!"

Half anxious, half furious, Kennedy caught a train that same evening at the main railway station and reached London the next day.

Forty-five minutes later a cab dropped him off at the doctor's humble abode on Greek St. in Soho Square; he went up the front steps and announced his coming by giving the door five firmly delivered thumps.

Fergusson opened it personally.

"Dick!" he said without much surprise.

"His own self," Kennedy shot back.

"What's this, my dear Dick—you're in London during the winter hunting season?"

"I'm in London."

"And why are you here?"

"To prevent an act of indescribable lunacy!"

"Lunacy?" the doctor said.

"Is it true what this paper says?" Kennedy responded, holding out the issue of the *Daily Telegraph*.

"Ah, that's what you're referring to! These newspapers are so irresponsible! But have a seat, my dear Dick."

"I won't have a seat. You're definitely intending to go on this trip?"

"Definitely; my preparations are coming along nicely, and I—"

"Where are they, these preparations of yours? Where are they? I'll rip 'em to pieces! I'll tear 'em to shreds!"

The worthy Scot was growing seriously angry.

"Easy, my dear Dick," the doctor went on. "I understand your annoyance. You're after me because I haven't told you yet about my new plan."

"He calls that a plan!"

"I've been so busy," Samuel continued, not acknowledging the interruption. "I've had so much to do! But never fear, I wouldn't have left without writing you—"

"Don't make me laugh!"

"Because I intend to take you with me."

The Scot gave a leap that would have done credit to a mountain goat.

"Hang it all," he said, "do you want 'em to lock us both up in Bedlam hospital?"*

"I'm absolutely counting on you, my dear Dick, and you're my first choice over many, many others."

Kennedy froze, totally astonished.

"Hear me out for the next ten minutes," the doctor replied serenely, "then you'll thank me!"

"You're serious about this?"

"Very serious."

"And what if I refuse to come along?"

"You won't refuse."

"But what if I do in the end?"

"I'll go alone."

"Let's sit down," the hunter said, "and let's talk without flying off the handle. If you aren't trying to be funny, maybe it's worth discussing."

* Insane asylum in London.

"We'll discuss it over breakfast, my dear Dick, if that meets with your approval."

The two friends took their seats at a little table, facing each other between a stack of sandwiches and an enormous teapot.

"My dear Samuel," the hunter said, "your plan's crazy! It's impossible! There isn't a thing realistic or workable about it!"

"We'll see after we've given it a try."

"But that's the point—you mustn't give it a try."

"Why not, if you please?"

"What about the dangers, all the different obstacles!"

"Obstacles," Fergusson replied solemnly, "are made to be overcome; as for the dangers, who can delude himself that he'll avoid them? Danger is a part of life; it can be dangerous to sit down at table or clap a hat on your head; in any case we must regard what's bound to happen as having happened already—and see only the present in the future, because the future is merely the present a little farther along."

"There you go!" Kennedy said, shrugging his shoulders. "You're always a fatalist!"

"Always, but in the positive sense of the word. So let's not agonize over what destiny has in store for us, and let's not forget our old English proverb: 'The man who was born to die on the scaffold will never die of drowning!'"

To this there was no comeback, which didn't keep Kennedy from dusting off a series of arguments easy to imagine but too long-winded to go into here.

"Anyhow," he said after a sixty-minute debate, "if you're dead set on going across Africa, if nothing else will make you happy, why not travel the usual way?"

"Why not?" the doctor replied heatedly. "Because all such efforts until now have come to grief! Think of Mungo Park who was murdered on the Niger, Vogel who vanished in Wadaï, Oudney who died in Murmur, Clapperton who died in Sokoto, the Frenchman Maizan who was sliced to pieces, Major Laing who was killed by the Tuaregs, Roscher from Hamburg who was slaughtered early in 1860—there are so many victims recorded in Africa's death register! Because it's an impossible struggle against the elements, against hunger, thirst, and fever, against wild animals and even wilder tribesmen! Because what can't be done

one way needs to be tackled in another! Because, in short, what you can't go through you have to sidestep or go over!"

"This isn't about going over," Kennedy fired back, "but *flying* over!"

"All right," the doctor went on with all the composure in the world. "What have I to fear? You'll readily agree that I've taken such thorough precautions, I won't need to worry if my balloon falls out of the sky; if she isn't equal to the task, I'll end up on the ground under the usual conditions other explorers face; but my balloon won't fail me, and we won't need to make any allowances."

"On the contrary, you *will* need to."

"Not so, my dear Dick. I don't intend to part company with her until I arrive on Africa's west coast. With her, everything is possible; without her, I topple back into the dangers and obstacles natural to such an expedition; with her, neither heat, torrents, storms, whirlwinds, unsanitary climates, wild animals, nor human beings are a concern! If I'm too hot, I go higher; if I'm cold, I descend; if there's a mountain, I pass it by; a precipice, I clear it; a river, I cross it; a downpour, I rise above it; a torrent, I skim over it like a bird! I press on without growing tired, I halt without needing to rest! I glide past new cities! I fly as fast as a tornado, sometimes high in the skies, sometimes just a hundred feet from the ground, and below is the great atlas of the world, with the map of Africa unfolding beneath my eyes!"

Our gallant Kennedy was starting to feel excited, but the mental picture in front of *his* eyes gave him vertigo. He looked at Samuel in wonderment, also in fear; already he felt he was swaying in the stratosphere.

"Hold on," he said, "hold on a second, my dear Samuel—does this mean you've found a way of steering a balloon?"

"Far from it. That's a pipe dream."

"But then you'll go—"

"Where Providence wills; but in any event from east to west."

"Why is that?"

"Because I'm counting on using the trade winds, which always blow in the same direction."

"Oh . . . right!" Kennedy said, thinking it over. "The trade winds . . . certainly . . . in a pinch . . . there's something to be said for 'em . . ."

"Something? No, my gallant friend, *everything.* The English government has put a cargo boat at my disposal; they've likewise arranged for three or four ships to cruise off Africa's west coast around the projected time of my arrival. In three months at the most, I'll be in Zanzibar where I'll set about inflating my balloon, and from there we'll launch her—"

"We?" Dick interrupted.

"Really now, have you a single objection left? Out with it, Kennedy old friend."

"A single objection? I have a thousand; but tell me, among other things: if you're counting on seeing the country, if you're counting on rising and descending at will, how can you do it without losing gas? So far there's no other way of proceeding, and that's why nobody goes on long outings in the clouds."

"My dear Dick, I'll tell you just one thing: I won't lose an atom of gas, not a single molecule."

"And you'll descend at will?"

"I'll descend at will."

"And how will you manage it?"

"That's my secret, Dick old friend. Trust me and make my motto yours: Excelsior!"

"Excelsior it is," replied the hunter, who didn't know a word of Latin.

But he was bound and determined to thwart his friend's departure in any way he could. So he pretended to agree but kept a careful lookout. As for Samuel, he went off to oversee his preparations.

chapter

African exploring parties—Barth, Richardson, Overweg, Werne, Brun-Rollet, Peney, Andrea Debono, Miani, Guillaume Lejean, Bruce, Krapf and Rebmann, Maizan, Roscher, Burton and Speke.

The course through the clouds that Dr. Fergusson intended to follow hadn't been chosen by accident; he had put serious thought into his

starting point, and it was with good reason that he decided to launch his balloon from the island of Zanzibar. Located off Africa's east coast, this island lies at latitude 6° south, in other words, 430 statute miles[1] below the equator.

The latest expedition in search of the Nile's headwaters had just set out from this island and was proceeding by way of the great inland lakes.

But it's important to point out which exploring parties Dr. Fergusson hoped to connect with each other. There were two main ones: Dr. Barth's in 1849 and the party led by Lieutenants Burton and Speke in 1858.

A native of Hamburg, Dr. Barth obtained permission for his countryman Overweg and himself to join an expedition under the Englishman Richardson; the latter had been entrusted with a mission in Sudan.

This huge country is located between latitudes 10° and 15° north—in other words, you have to push more than 1,500 miles[2] into Africa's interior to reach it.

At the time all that was known of this region came from the travels of Denham, Clapperton, and Oudney over the years 1822–1824. Keen on pressing their investigations farther, Richardson, Barth, and Overweg arrive like their predecessors in Tunis and Tripoli, then forge ahead to Murzuk, capital of Libya's Fezzan region.

At this juncture they take a sharp right turn to the west in the direction of Ghāt, accompanied by Tuareg tribesmen and plenty of complications. After a thousand episodes of thievery, humiliation, and armed assault, their caravan reaches the huge oasis of the Aïr by October. Dr. Barth separates from his companions, makes an excursion to the town of Agadez, and rejoins the expedition, which sets out again on December 12. It arrives in the province of Damergou; there the three travelers part company, and Barth takes the route to Kano, which he reaches by persevering and by paying sizable bribes.

Despite a high fever, he vacates this town on March 7, bringing only a single servant. His journey's main objective is to scout out Lake Chad, which still lies 350 miles away. So he presses on to the east and gets to the town of Zuricolo in Bornu, the heart of this large central African empire. There he learns that Richardson is dead, the victim of exhaustion and hardship. He arrives in Kouka, Bornu's lakeside capital. Three weeks later on April 14, he finally makes it to the town of Ngornu, 12½ months after leaving Tripoli.

We find him setting out again with Overweg on March 29, 1851, bound for the kingdom of Adamawa south of the lake; from there he gets as far as the town of Yola, a little below latitude 9° north. Which is the southernmost point reached by this bold explorer.

During the month of August, he goes back to Kouka, from there consecutively travels through Mandara, Bagirmi, and Kanem, then reaches his easternmost position, the town of Másena, located at longitude 17° 20′ west.*

On November 25, 1852, after the death of his last-remaining companion Overweg, Barth pushes into the west, visits Sokoto, crosses the Niger, and finally arrives in Timbuktu, where he's forced to sit out eight long months of misery, mistreatment, and humiliation by the sheik. But the presence of a Christian in town can no longer be tolerated;

* Calculated from the meridian occupied by England's Greenwich Observatory.

Fula tribesmen threaten to lay siege to the place. So the doctor clears out on March 17, 1854, takes refuge at the border where he stays for thirty-three days in a state of utter destitution, gets back to Kano in November, reenters Kouka, and from there goes home by Denham's route after a four-month layover; the doctor sights Tripoli again near the end of August 1855, and reenters London on September 6 without a single companion left.

And that's the story of Barth's bold journey.[3]

Dr. Fergusson was careful to note that he had halted in latitude 4° north and longitude 17° west.

Now let's see what Lieutenants Burton and Speke accomplished in east Africa.

The different expeditions that ascended the Nile were never able to reach that river's mystifying source. According to a report by the German doctor Ferdinand Werne, an expedition undertaken in 1840, under the auspices of Mehemet Ali, called a halt in Gondokoro between the 4th and 5th northern parallels.

In 1855 Brun-Rollet, a Frenchman from Savoy, was named consul of Sardinia in east Sudan, replacing Vaudey, who died by violence; disguised as a merchant named Yacoub, who dealt in gum and ivory, he set out from Khartoum, got to Belenia beyond the 4th degree, and returned in poor health to Khartoum, where he died in 1857.

Nor could anybody else approach the river's unattainable upper reaches—not Dr. Peney, head of the Egyptian medical service, who rode a small steamer one degree beyond Gondokoro and returned to die of exhaustion in Khartoum . . . not the Venetian Miani, who worked his way around the waterfalls located below Gondokoro and got to the 2nd parallel . . . not the Maltese trader Andrea Debono, who took his expedition even farther up the Nile.

In 1859 Monsieur Guillaume Lejean, entrusted with a mission by the French government, made his way to Khartoum via the Red Sea and boated up the Nile with twenty-one crewmen and twenty soldiers; but he couldn't get past Gondokoro and ran tremendous risks among Negroes who were in open revolt.[4] An expedition headed by Monsieur Escayrac de Lauture likewise tried to reach the notorious headwaters.

But this baleful objective has always stymied travelers; in the past Nero's emissaries got to latitude 9°; so in the eighteen centuries since, explorers have progressed only five or six degrees farther, a gain of just 300 to 360 statute miles.

Several travelers tried to reach the Nile's headwaters by using Africa's east coast as their starting point.

Over the years 1768–1772, the Scot James Bruce set out from the Ethiopian port of Massawa, crossed Tigray, visited the ruins of Aksum, viewed the Nile's source where it wasn't, and accomplished nothing of consequence.

In 1844 the Anglican missionary Dr. Krapf set up a colony in Mombasa on the coast of Zanj, discovering, along with Rev. Rebmann, two mountains 300 miles from that coast; they were Mt. Kilimanjaro and Mt. Kenya, which Messrs. Heuglin and Thornton have just scaled in part.

In 1845 the Frenchman Maizan went ashore by himself in Bagamoyo opposite Zanzibar, then traveled to Deje-la-Mhora, where a chieftain had him brutally tortured and put to death.

In the month of August 1859, a young traveler from Hamburg, Roscher, set out with a caravan of Arab merchants, got to Lake Malawi, and there was murdered in his sleep.

Finally in 1857 Lieutenants Burton and Speke, both officers in the Bengal army, were sent by London's Royal Geographical Society to explore Africa's great lakes; on June 17 they exited Zanzibar and pushed due west.

After four months of unheard-of suffering, their baggage being looted and their carriers beaten senseless, they arrived in Kazeh,[5] a central meeting place for traders and caravans; they were right in the Land of the Moon; there they gathered valuable documentation of the country's customs, government, religion, fauna, and flora; then they headed for the first of the great lakes, Tanganyika, located between latitudes 3° and 8° south; they reached it on February 14, 1858, and visited the various tribes along its shores, most of them cannibals.

They retraced their steps on May 26 and reentered Kazeh on June 20. There, an exhausted Burton lay ill for several months; during this time Speke went more than 300 miles north to Lake Victoria,[6] which he sighted on August 3; but he saw only its lower reaches in latitude 2° 30′.

He got back to Kazeh on August 25 and with Burton resumed the route to Zanzibar, where they arrived the following year during the month of March. Then these two bold explorers returned to England, after which the Paris Geographical Society awarded them its annual prize.

Dr. Fergusson was careful to observe that they hadn't cleared either latitude 2° south or longitude 29° east.

So the challenge was to tie Dr. Barth's exploring to Burton and Speke's; this meant crossing an expanse of country covering more than twelve degrees.

chapter 5

Kennedy's dreams—articles and pronouns in the plural—innuendos from Dick—jaunt over the map of Africa—what lies between two legs of a pair of compasses—current expeditions—Speke and Grant— Krapf, Decken, Heuglin.

Dr. Fergusson pressed energetically ahead with the preparations for his departure; he personally supervised the manufacture of his lighter-than-air vehicle, in line with certain modifications he was keeping strictly to himself.

For a good while he had been intently studying the Arabic language and various Mandingo dialects;[1] thanks to his polyglot inclinations, he was progressing rapidly.

Meanwhile his friend the hunter dogged his footsteps; probably he was afraid the doctor might take off without saying anything; he kept after him on this topic with his most persuasive arguments— which didn't persuade Samuel Fergusson—and poured his heart out in touching appeals—which left the doctor thoroughly unmoved. Dick felt him slipping through his fingers.

The poor Scot was honestly to be pitied; he no longer looked at a blue sky without dark forebodings; while he slept he had a queasy sensation of swaying to and fro, and every night he felt he was tumbling down from some boundless height.

We should add that during these dreadful nightmares, he fell out of bed once or twice. His first order of business was to show Fergusson the severe contusions his cranium had acquired.

"And," he added in a neighborly spirit, "I was only three feet up! No more than that! And look at this bump! Think what this means!"

This doleful innuendo failed to pluck the doctor's heartstrings.

"We won't fall out of the sky," he said.

"But what if we finally do?"

"We won't."

That was that, and there wasn't a thing Kennedy could say back.

What left Dick particularly exasperated was that the doctor seemed to utterly deny Kennedy's own free will; he saw the Scot as irreversibly fated to become his companion in the clouds. There was no longer any shadow of a doubt. Samuel was unbearable in his overuse of the first-person plural pronoun:

"*We* shall make steady progress . . . *we* shall be ready on the . . . *we* shall be leaving on—"

And likewise with the possessive adjective for singular nouns:

"*Our* balloon . . . *our* gondola . . . *our* excursion . . ."

And ditto for plural nouns:

"*Our* preparations . . . *our* discoveries . . . *our* ascensions."

Dick shuddered, although he was bound and determined to not go; but he didn't want to clash openly with his friend. Let's acknowledge, moreover, that without explaining himself to anybody, he quietly had his wardrobe put together and sent him from Edinburgh along with the finest shotguns in his armory.

One day, while recognizing that even unbelievable luck would give him only a one-in-a-thousand chance of success, he pretended to give in to the doctor's wishes; but in order to delay the journey, he brought up a wide variety of possible snags. He raised concerns about the expedition's value and timeliness. . . . Was there any real need to go looking for the Nile's headwaters . . . ? Would they truly be working for the benefit of humanity . . . ? If every tribe in Africa ultimately became civilized, would they be any happier . . . ? Besides, were they certain that civilization would fare any better in those parts than in Europe? (Maybe.) And in the first place, couldn't they just wait and see . . . ? One day somebody would certainly cross Africa and run fewer risks in the process. . . . In a month, in six months, before the year was out, some explorer would undoubtedly make it . . .

These innuendos had an effect exactly opposite to the one they aimed at, and the doctor trembled with impatience:

"O poor Dick! My faithless friend! So you want somebody else to get the glory? I have to disown my past? Shrink from obstacles that are trivial? Repay the English government and the Royal Society of London by turning into a wavering coward?"

"But . . ." continued Kennedy, who got a lot of mileage out of this conjunction.

"But," the doctor kept on, "can't you see that my journey has to compete with the achievements of undertakings already in progress? Don't you realize that new expeditions are now forging deep into central Africa?"

"And yet—"

"Listen closely, Dick, and take a look at this map."

Dick sighed and took a look.

"Follow the Nile upstream," Fergusson said.

"I'm following it," the Scot replied meekly.

"Go to Gondokoro."

"I'm there."

And Kennedy thought how easy such a journey was . . . on a map.

"Take this pair of compasses," the doctor went on, "and place one leg on this town that the boldest men have barely gotten past."

"It's placed."

"And now search along the coast for the island of Zanzibar at latitude 6° south."

"Got it."

"Now follow that parallel until you reach Kazeh."

"Done."

"Go up longitude 33° to the lower reaches of Lake Victoria, to the locale where Lieutenant Speke came to a halt."

"I'm there. Any closer and I'll fall in the lake."

"All right, do you know what we're justified in assuming, based on information supplied by the lakeside tribes?"

"No idea."

"It's that this lake, whose southern end lies in latitude 2° 30′, is sure to reach an equivalent 2½ degrees above the equator."

"Really!"

"Now then, from this northern end a stream flows that inevitably has to join up with the Nile, if it isn't the Nile itself."

"Interesting."

"Now then, take your pair of compasses and place the other leg at that end of Lake Victoria."

"Done, Fergusson old friend."

"How many degrees do you count between the two legs?"

"Barely two."

"And do you know what that amounts to, Dick?"

"Haven't the foggiest."

"That amounts to barely 120 miles — essentially nothing."[2]

"Well, almost nothing, Samuel."

"Now then, do you know what's taking place even as we speak?"

"I honestly don't."

"This. The Royal Geographical Society sees it as very important to explore this lake that Speke glimpsed. Under their auspices Lieutenant (now Captain) Speke has teamed up with Captain Grant of the Indian army; they're heading a sizable and well-funded expedition; their mission is to go all the way up the lake, then continue on as far as Gondokoro; they've received a grant of more than £5000, and the governor at the Cape has put his Hottentot soldiers at their disposal; they left Zanzibar at the end of October 1860. In the meantime the Englishman John Petherick, Her Majesty's consul in Khartoum, has received upwards of £700 from the foreign office; he's to equip a steamboat in Khartoum, stock it with adequate provisions, and make his way to Gondokoro; there he'll wait for Captain Speke's caravan and will be in a position to replenish the captain's supplies."

"Good thinking," Kennedy said.

"You can easily see how urgent this is, if we're to take part in these exploring activities. And that's not all; while some are well on their way to finding the source of the Nile, other travelers are charging boldly into Africa's heartlands."

"On foot?" Kennedy said.

"On foot," the doctor answered, ignoring this new innuendo. "Dr. Krapf proposes to press on to the west via the Djob, a river located below the equator. Baron von der Decken has left Mombasa, has scouted out Mt. Kenya and Mt. Kilimanjaro, and is now pushing toward the center."

"Still on foot?"

"On foot still, or on muleback."

"Same exact thing in my opinion," Kennedy remarked.

"Finally," the doctor went on, "Herr von Heuglin, Austria's viceconsul in Khartoum, has just organized a highly important expedition whose primary objective is to search for Vogel, the traveler sent to Sudan in 1853 to assist with Dr. Barth's work. In 1856 he left Bornu and decided to explore the unknown country that stretches from Lake Chad to Darfur. Well, he hasn't been seen since then.* Letters reaching Alexandria in June 1860 report that he was murdered by order of the King of Wadaï; but other letters, addressed to the traveler's father by Dr. Hartmann, quote a *felata*³ from Bornu who indicated that Vogel would merely be held prisoner in Wara; therefore they shouldn't abandon all hope. A committee has been formed, and it's presided over by the Duke Regent of Saxe-Coburg-Gotha; my friend Petermann is secretary; a national funding drive has taken care of the expedition's costs, and many experts have signed on; Herr von Heuglin set out from Massawa during the month of June, and while looking for traces of Vogel, he's supposed to scour the country lying between the Nile and Lake Chad, in other words, to link Captain Speke's operations with Dr. Barth's. And then explorers will have crossed Africa from east to west."

"Well," the Scot went on, "since everything's off to a flying start, what's left for *us* to do down there?"

Dr. Fergusson didn't answer and settled for shrugging his shoulders.

chapter 6

An unbelievable valet — he can see Jupiter's moons — Dick and Joe lock horns — doubt and belief — the weigh-in — Joe honors Wellington — he gets a half-crown.

Dr. Fergusson had a valet; he answered to the name Joe and with dazzling speed; was exceptionally good-natured; swore absolute fidelity and boundless devotion to his master; anticipated his every wish and shrewdly translated it into reality; was a Caleb who never grumbled or

---

* Following Dr. Fergusson's departure, it came out that after some debate, Herr von Heuglin took a route different from the one assigned to his expedition, whose command has reverted to Herr Munzinger.

got in a bad mood; and couldn't have been better at his job if he had been born for it. Fergusson turned the details of his daily life completely over to him, and quite rightly. Trusty Joe, one in a thousand! A valet who knows your favorite foods, who shares your tastes, who packs your bags and doesn't leave out a single sock or shirt, who's the keeper of both your keys and your secrets yet doesn't take unfair advantage of the fact!

Because, to our worthy Joe, the doctor was a man among men! How confidently and respectfully Joe received his decisions. Once Fergusson had spoken, only a moron would try to talk back. Everything he thought was correct; everything he said, reasonable; everything he ordered, doable; everything he undertook, possible; everything he finished, admirable. You could slice Joe to pieces (although you probably would rather not) without changing his opinion of his master.

Accordingly, when the doctor came up with his plan to cross Africa by air, Joe saw it as a done deal; obstacles no longer existed; the instant Dr. Fergusson decided to leave, he was as good as there—along with his loyal servant, because the gallant lad knew without being told that he would be going too.

Besides, his cleverness and his marvelous agility were bound to be a big help. If the zoological gardens had needed somebody to teach gymnastic tricks to the monkeys (who are pretty adept already), Joe would have gotten the job in a heartbeat. Leaping, climbing, soaring, performing a thousand impossible stunts—for him, kids' stuff.

If Fergusson was the brains and Kennedy the muscles, Joe supplied the sleight of hand. He had already gone with his master on several journeys and had picked up a smidgen of science in his own way; but he was especially remarkable for his cheery outlook, his engaging optimism; he found everything easy, reasonable, and natural, consequently he never saw any need to moan or groan.

Among other gifts, he enjoyed eyesight of amazing strength and range; he shared with Maestlin, Kepler's teacher, the rare ability to see Jupiter's moons without a spyglass, and he could count fourteen stars in the Pleiades group, whose farthest members are of the ninth magnitude. But he didn't let this talent go to his head; on the contrary, he waved to you from afar and sometimes could put his eyes to very good use.

Portrait of Joe

Given the confidence that Joe placed in the doctor, it isn't surprising that continual arguments broke out, with all due deference, between Kennedy and the worthy servant.

One doubted, the other believed; one stood for farsighted caution, the other blind faith; the doctor was flanked by both doubt and belief! I must say that he didn't worry his head over either.

"Well, Mr. Kennedy?" Joe said.

"Well, my lad?"

"The time's coming. Looks like we're off to the moon."[1]

"You mean the Land of the Moon, which isn't quite as far; but don't worry, there are just as many dangers."

"Dangers! With a man like Dr. Fergusson!"

"I don't want to rob you of your illusions, my dear Joe, but this undertaking of his is sheer madness: it'll never happen."

"Never happen! So you haven't seen his balloon at the Mitchells' workshop[2] in the Borough?"*

"I'm not going near the bloody thing."

"You'll miss out on quite a sight, sir! What a rare piece of work! What a smart design! What a delightful gondola! How comfy we'll feel inside!"

"You're seriously expecting to go with your master?"

"I am," Joe fired back with conviction. "Why, I'll go with him any-placc he wants! That's all he needs! To head off by himself when we've traveled the world together! Who would buck him up when he's done in? Who would give him a strong helping hand over a precipice? Who would look after him if he comes down sick? No, Mr. Dick, Joe'll stay on duty by the doctor—where Dr. Fergusson is, I'll always be around."

"Good lad!"

"Anyhow you're coming with us," Joe went on.

"Of course!" Kennedy said. "In other words, I'll go along and at the last minute I'll keep Samuel from committing this piece of lunacy! I'll follow him right to Zanzibar—that way, a friendly hand will be there to stop him from carrying out this crazy scheme."

"With all due respect, Mr. Kennedy, you won't be stopping anything. My master isn't some crackpot; he gives a lot of thought to his undertakings, and when he makes up his mind, the devil himself couldn't change it."

"That remains to be seen!"

"Don't get your hopes up. But the main thing is, you're coming. For a hunter like you, Africa's a marvelous country. So in any case, you won't be sorry you took this trip."

"No, I definitely won't be—if that bullheaded doctor finally wakes up to reality."

* Suburb south of London.

"By the way," Joe said, "you know that today's the weigh-in."

"Huh, weigh-in?"

"That's right, my master, you, and me—all three of us will be getting weighed."

"Like jockeys?"

"Like jockeys. Only don't worry, you won't have to slim down if you're too heavy. They'll take you the way you are."

"I'm positively not getting weighed," the Scot said firmly.

"But his machinery seems to need it, sir."

"Well, his machinery will just have to manage without it."

"Blimey, if we don't have the right numbers, suppose we can't get off the ground!"

"By God, that's all I ask!"

"Look here, Mr. Kennedy, my master will come and fetch us any second."

"I won't go."

"Oh, you don't want to give him trouble now."

"Yes I do."

"Fine!" Joe said with a laugh. "You're talking like this because he isn't here; but when he says to your face: 'Dick!' (with all due respect), 'Dick, I need to know exactly what you weigh,' I guarantee you'll go."

"I won't go."

At that moment the doctor reentered his study, where this conversation was taking place; he turned to Kennedy, who wasn't feeling fully at ease just then.

"Dick," the doctor said, "come along with Joe; I need to know what the two of you weigh."

"But—"

"You can keep your hat on. Come along."

And Kennedy did.

The three of them made their way to the Mitchells' workshop, where one of those scales called a steelyard balance had been set up. The doctor absolutely had to know his companions' weight in order to determine the buoyancy of his lighter-than-air vehicle. So he made Dick climb onto the platform of the scale; the hunter didn't put up any resistance, saying under his breath:

"Fine! Fine! Doesn't mean I'm agreeing to it."

"A hundred and fifty-three pounds," the doctor said, scribbling this number in his notebook.

"Am I too heavy?"

"Naw, Mr. Kennedy," Joe shot back. "Anyhow I'm on the light side, so I'll make up for it."

With that Joe took the hunter's place, and so enthusiastically that his momentum nearly tipped the scale over; he mimicked the statue of Achilles that honors Wellington at the Hyde Park entrance—and he looked impressive even without a shield.

"A hundred and twenty pounds," scribbled the doctor.

"Hoho!" Joe threw in while grinning smugly. Why the grin? He wasn't saying.

"Now my turn," Fergusson said. And he scribbled 135 pounds for himself.

"The three of us," he said, "weigh no more than 400 pounds."

"But master," Joe continued, "if your experiment called for it, I could easily lose another twenty pounds by skipping meals."

"No need, my boy," the doctor replied. "Eat all the meals you like; here's a half-crown, take on as much ballast as you want."

chapter 7

Geometric details—calculating the balloon's capacity—the two-piece vehicle—the envelope—the gondola—the mysterious mechanism—provisions—the bottom line.

Dr. Fergusson was busy for a good while with the details of his expedition. You can appreciate that his balloon, that wondrous conveyance designed to carry him through the clouds, was the recipient of his constant attention.

First of all, to keep his lighter-than-air vehicle from taking on excessively grand dimensions, he decided to inflate her with hydrogen, a gas that's 14½ times lighter than oxygen. This gas is easy to produce and has provided the best results in experiments with lighter-than-air vehicles.

Working with ultracareful calculations, the doctor found that in order to bring the articles essential to his journey, plus his mechanism, he needed to carry aloft a weight of 4,000 pounds; so he had to find out what the lifting power would be that could heft this weight, and consequently, what its capacity would be.

A weight of 4,000 pounds is equivalent to 44,847 cubic feet[1] of displaced air, which is just another way of saying that 44,847 cubic feet of air weighs about 4,000 pounds.

When you give the balloon this capacity of 44,847 cubic feet and replace air with hydrogen (a gas that's 14½ times lighter and weighs only 276 pounds, a difference of 3,724 pounds), you affect the vehicle's buoyancy. It's this difference between the gas's weight inside the envelope and the air's weight outside that constitutes the balloon's lifting power.

Even so, if the balloon took in that 44,847 cubic feet of gas we're talking about, she would fill up completely; now then, that's a nonstarter, because as the balloon rises into thinner layers of air, the gas inside her tends to expand and will pretty quickly burst the envelope. So as a general rule, balloons are only two-thirds full.

But due to certain plans known only to him, the doctor decided to fill his lighter-than-air vehicle only halfway, and since he had to carry aloft 44,847 cubic feet of hydrogen, to give his balloon roughly twice the capacity.

He designed her with that stretched-out shape we know to be preferable; the horizontal diameter was 50 feet and the vertical diameter 75;* in this way he got a spheroid with a capacity that amounted to 90,000 cubic feet in round numbers.

If Dr. Fergusson had been able to use two balloons, it would have increased his chances of success; in essence, if one of them happened to rupture in the air, you could drop some ballast and stay aloft with just the other. But handling two lighter-than-air vehicles turns out to be quite tricky when it comes to giving them the same lifting power.

After mulling it over a good while, Fergusson devised a clever arrangement that combined the advantages of two balloons without the drawbacks; he built two different-sized envelopes and enclosed one inside the other. His outer balloon, which kept the dimensions we've given above, contained a smaller one the same shape with a horizontal diameter of only 45 feet and a vertical diameter of 68 feet. So the capacity of this inner envelope was only 67,000 cubic feet; it would float in the elastic fluid that surrounded it; a valve opened from one balloon to the other, allowing for contact between the two as needed.

The advantage of this setup was that if you had to let out gas in order to descend, you could release it from the outer balloon first; even if you needed to empty the bigger one completely, the smaller one would stay intact; so you could get rid of the outer envelope as an inconvenient burden, and the second envelope, left on its own, would give the wind less purchase than half-deflated balloons do.

Furthermore, in the event of a rip or other accident happening to the outer balloon, the inner one had the advantage of being protected.

---

* These dimensions are nothing extraordinary: in Lyon back in 1784, Monsieur Montgolfier built a lighter-than-air vehicle with a capacity of 340,000 cubic feet, and she could heft a weight of twenty-two tons.[2]

This two-part vehicle was manufactured with twill taffeta from Lyon that had been coated with gutta-percha. This is a resinous, rubbery substance that's completely watertight; it's also totally impervious to acids and gases. A double layer of taffeta covers the very top of the sphere, which takes almost all the strain.

This envelope could hold its elastic fluid for an unlimited period of time. It weighed half a pound for every 9 square feet. Now then, the outer balloon had about 11,600 square feet of surface, so its envelope weighed 650 pounds. The second balloon's envelope had 9,200 square feet of surface and weighed only 510 pounds: so the two came to 1,160 pounds.

The netting designed to hold up the gondola was made of extra-tough hempen rope; the two valves were looked after as meticulously as if they were a ship's rudder.

The wickerwork gondola was circular in shape, 15 feet across, reinforced with a light iron framework, and decked out underneath with elastic springs designed to deaden shocks. Gondola and netting together weighed no more than 280 pounds.

Beyond this, the doctor had ordered four tanks built from sheet metal a sixth of an inch thick; they were connected to each other by pipes equipped with spigots; attached to them was a coil made of two-inch-wide tubing that ended in two straight, different-sized extensions, the longer measuring 25 feet in height, the shorter just 15 feet.

The sheet-metal tanks were fitted into the gondola in such a way as to take up the least possible space; the coil didn't need to be eased in until later and was packed separately, as was a very powerful Bunsen battery. This mechanism had been so cleverly put together, it weighed no more than 700 pounds, even with its special 25-gallon water tank.

The instruments set aside for the journey consisted of two barometers, two thermometers, two compasses, a sextant, two chronometers, an artificial horizon, and an altazimuth, a telescope for surveying things far away and out of reach. The Greenwich Observatory had put itself at the doctor's disposal. But Samuel didn't propose to do any physics experiments; he simply wanted to work out his heading and fix the positions of the chief rivers, mountains, and towns.

He also took along three well-tested iron anchors, likewise a 50-foot ladder of light, tough silk.

He calculated as well the exact weight of his provisions; they consisted of tea, coffee, crackers, salted meat, and pemmican, a mixture that contains many nourishing ingredients in concentrated form. In addition to an adequate supply of brandy, he arranged for two water tanks that held 22 gallons apiece.[3]

Consuming these various foods would gradually lower the weight that their lighter-than-air vehicle had to carry—because it's essential to realize that a balloon's buoyancy in the air is tremendously sensitive. Even an almost unnoticeable weight loss is enough to cause a distinct change in her handling.

The doctor didn't forget to bring a tent for covering part of the gondola, nor the blankets that would make up their entire bedding for the journey, nor some hunting rifles, nor supplies of gunpowder and bullets.

Here's a summary of his different calculations:

Fergusson	135 pounds
Kennedy	153 "
Joe	120 "
Weight of the first balloon	650 "
Weight of the second balloon	510 "
Gondola and netting	280 "
Anchors, instruments, firearms, blankets, tent, various utensils	190 "
Meat, pemmican, crackers, tea, coffee, brandy	386 "
Water	400 "
Mechanism	700 "
Weight of the hydrogen	276 "
Ballast	200 "
Total:	4,000 pounds

This was the breakdown of the 4,000 pounds that Dr. Fergusson proposed to carry aloft; he brought just 200 pounds of ballast "for unexpected developments only," he said, because he definitely intended not to use any . . . thanks to the presence of his mechanism.

8

Joe's value—the Resolute's *commander—*
arrangements[1]—Kennedy's arsenal—the farewell
dinner—departure on February 21—science sessions
with the doctor—Duveyrier, Livingstone—specifics
of air travel—Kennedy reduced to silence.

By about February 10 preparations were nearing completion, and the envelopes, one inside the other, were totally finished; their walls had been subjected to intense air pressure and had passed the test; this spoke well for their strength and bore witness to their painstaking manufacture.

Joe was beyond happiness; he beat a steady path from Greek St. to the Mitchells' workshop, always bustling and beaming, eager to give the details of the business to anybody who didn't ask, prouder than ever of going with his master. I even think that in showing off the lighter-than-air vehicle, talking up the doctor's ideas or designs, and pointing him out through a partly open window or on his way down the street, the worthy lad earned a half-crown or two; but there's no need to wrinkle your nose; he had every right to turn a little profit on the wonderment and curiosity of his age.

On February 16 the *Resolute* arrived and dropped anchor off Greenwich. A local vessel of some 860 tons burden,[2] she was propeller driven, made good time, and had been entrusted with replenishing Sir James Clark Ross's supplies during his latest expedition to the polar regions. By reputation Commander Pennet was a genial chap, and he took a special interest in this journey, being a longtime fan of the doctor's. This Pennet fellow was more of a scholar than a soldier, which didn't keep his ship from carrying four short-bodied naval cannons, although they had never harmed a soul and went off only during peacetime ceremonies.

The *Resolute*'s hold had been arranged explicitly to house the lighter-than-air vehicle; she was loaded on board with the greatest care during the day of February 18; to avert any accidents, they stowed her deep in the ship; under Fergusson's eyes they also lashed down the gondola and its accessories—the anchors, lines, and provisions, plus the water tanks that were to be filled on arrival.

To produce the hydrogen gas, they took on board ten barrels of sulfuric acid and ten of ground scrap iron. These amounts were more than enough, but it was essential to guard against possible losses. The mechanism designed for expanding the gas included some thirty casks, and the whole works were stowed deep in the hold.

These various preparations were complete by the evening of February 18. Two comfortably furnished cabins were waiting for Dr. Fergusson and his friend Kennedy. Swearing that he wasn't going, the Scot made his way on board with an authentic hunter's arsenal—two fine breech-loading, double-barreled shotguns and a top-of-the-line rifle from the factory of Purdey, Moore and Dickson in Edinburgh; with a weapon like this, a hunter wouldn't be hard pressed to put a bullet in a mountain goat's eye at 2,000 paces; in addition he had two Colt six-shooters for sudden surprises; his powder supply, cartridge pouch, shot, and bullets were ample for his needs but didn't exceed the weight limits spelled out by the doctor.

The three travelers took up residence on board during the day of February 19; they were welcomed with pomp and circumstance by the captain and his officers, the doctor as cool as ever and concerned strictly with his expedition, Dick excited but trying not to show it, Joe bounding around and bursting with smart-aleck remarks; he quickly became the wit of the wardroom, where they saved him a place.

On February 20 the Royal Geographical Society threw a big farewell dinner for Dr. Fergusson and Kennedy. Commander Pennet and his officers were in attendance at this meal, which was very lively and heavily given over to toasting and well wishing; they drank to each other's health and longevity often enough to guarantee every guest centuries of existence. Sir Francis M—— presided with emotional restraint, dignified as ever.

Much to his befuddlement, Dick Kennedy received a good share of

these bacchic congratulations. After drinking to "Fergusson the fearless, the glory of all England," they just had to drink to "Kennedy the courageous, his no-less-daring companion."

Dick turned beet red, which they took for modesty: the clapping increased. Dick turned redder still.

A message from the Queen arrived during dessert; she presented her compliments to the two travelers and wished them every success in their undertaking.

Which called for a new round of toasts "to Her Most Gracious Majesty."

At midnight, after fervent farewells and hearty handshakes, the guests took their leave.

The *Resolute*'s longboats were waiting by Westminster Bridge; the commander got in along with his passengers and officers, then the swift current of the Thames ferried them to Greenwich.

They all were on board by one o'clock and fast asleep.

By three o'clock the following day, February 21, the furnaces were throbbing; at five o'clock the crew weighed anchor, and under her propeller's thrust, the *Resolute* headed for the mouth of the Thames.

No need to point out that conversations on board revolved entirely around Dr. Fergusson's expedition. His looks and his words inspired such confidence, soon nobody other than the Scot doubted that his undertaking would succeed.

During the voyage's long, idle hours, the doctor taught an honest-to-goodness course in geography down in the officers' quarters. The young fellows were enthralled by the discoveries made over the last forty years in Africa; he told them about the exploring parties of Barth, Burton, Speke, and Grant; he painted them a portrait of that mysterious region scientists were freely investigating from every direction. In the north young Duveyrier was exploring the Sahara and bringing Tuareg chieftains back to Paris. Under the urging of the French government, a couple of expeditions were in preparation, one southbound and one westbound, the two planning to intersect in Timbuktu. Farther south the tireless Livingstone was drawing still closer to the equator, and since March 1862 he'd been going up the Ruvuma River

The Resolute

together with Mackenzie. The nineteenth century would certainly not end without Africa revealing the secrets buried for 6,000 years in her bosom.

Dr. Fergusson aroused his audience's particular interest when he gave them the details of his journey's preparations; they insisted on double-checking his calculations; they argued about them, and the doctor was happy to participate in the debate.

On the whole they were amazed at the relatively limited number of provisions he was taking along. One of the officers questioned the doctor about this one day.

"That surprises you?" Fergusson responded.

"Definitely."

"But how long do you think my journey will take? Months? That's where you're quite wrong; if it dragged on, we'd be done for, we wouldn't make it. Please understand that it's no more than 3,500 miles—make that 4,000 miles—from Zanzibar to the Senegal coastline.[3] Now then, traveling day and night at the rate of 240 miles[4] every twelve hours (nowhere near the speed of our railway trains), it will take seven days to cross Africa."

"But then you wouldn't be able to see anything, or take topographical readings, or scout out the countryside."

"And yet," the doctor replied, "if I'm in control of my balloon, if I go up and down at will, I can call a halt whenever it suits me, especially when the air currents are so strong that they threaten to carry me off."

"And you'll run into some," Commander Pennet said. "There are hurricanes that go over 240 miles per hour."

"See?" the doctor shot back. "At that kind of speed, you'd cross Africa in twelve hours; you'd wake up in Zanzibar and go to bed in Saint-Louis."

"But," another officer resumed, "could a balloon be swept along at that speed?"

"One already has," Fergusson replied.

"And the balloon held up?"

"Perfectly. It happened in 1804 at the time of Napoleon's coronation. In Paris at eleven at night, the balloonist Garnerin launched a lighter-than-air vehicle that bore the following inscription printed in gold letters: *Paris, the 25th day in the Month of Frost during the 13th year of the French Revolutionary Calendar, coronation of the Emperor Napoleon by His Holiness Pope Pius VII*. At five o'clock the next morning, the citizens of Rome saw the same balloon soar over the Vatican, cross the Roman Campagna, and splash down in Lake Bracciano. Therefore, gentlemen, a balloon *can* withstand such speeds."

"A balloon, yes; but a man . . ." Kennedy ventured to say.

"A man as well! Because a balloon is always motionless in relation to the surrounding air; it isn't the balloon that moves, it's the mass of air itself; accordingly, if you light a candle inside your gondola, the flame won't flicker. A balloonist riding in Garnerin's vehicle wouldn't suffer in the slightest from her velocity. But I don't hold with such high-speed experiments, and if I can hitch up to some tree or crag during the night, I'll do so without fail. In any case we're taking enough provisions to last us two months, and there's nothing to prevent our crack hunter from furnishing us with plenty of game when we're on the ground."

"Ah, Mr. Kennedy! You'll squeeze off some prize-winning shots!" a young midshipman said, looking at the Scot with envious eyes.

"Not to mention," another went on, "that you'll have all the glory as well as all the fun!"

"Gentlemen . . . ," the hunter replied, "I truly appreciate . . . your compliments . . . but I don't deserve such . . ."

"Huh?" everybody interrupted. "Aren't you going too?"

"I'm not going."

"You won't be leaving with Dr. Fergusson?"

"I not only won't be leaving with him, I've come along to stop him at the eleventh hour."

All eyes turned to the doctor.

"Pay him no mind," he replied in his calm way. "There's no need to discuss this; deep down he's perfectly aware that he's going."

"I swear by St. Patrick—" Kennedy exclaimed.[5]

"Don't swear another word, Dick old friend; you've been measured, you've been weighed—you, your powder, firearms, and bullets; so there's nothing more to say."

And in fact, from that day until their arrival in Zanzibar, Dick didn't reopen his mouth; he had nothing more to say on this subject or any other. Not one word.

chapter 9

Rounding the Cape—the forecastle—a course on the cosmos taught by Professor Joe—on steering balloons—on searching for air currents—Εὑρηκα.[1]

The *Resolute* headed swiftly toward the Cape of Good Hope; the sky stayed clear, although the sea was beginning to run high.

On March 30, twenty-seven days after leaving London, they saw Table Mountain outlined on the horizon; located at the foot of a natural amphitheater formed by the hills, Cape Town was visible through the ship's spyglasses, and the *Resolute* soon dropped anchor in its harbor. But the commander made a layover only to take on coal; this was a day's work; the next morning his ship stood into the south to round Africa's lowermost point and enter the Mozambique Channel.

This wasn't Joe's first ocean voyage; he wasted no time in making himself at home on board. Everybody liked him for his spontaneity and high spirits. A good part of his master's fame had rubbed off on him. Folks listened to him as if he were an oracle, and his forecasts weren't much wider of the mark than anybody else's.

Consequently, while the doctor was busy providing clarification in the officers' quarters, Joe lorded it over the forecastle, where he laid out his own version of things—a procedure followed, incidentally, by leading historians from the dawn of time.

The balloon journey was naturally the topic that came up. Joe had trouble getting some of the diehards to buy into the undertaking; yet once the sailors did so, their imaginations, stimulated by Joe's anecdotes, were ready to believe anything was possible.

Our dazzling storyteller convinced his audience that after the present journey, folks would go on plenty of others. This was just the beginning of a long series of superhuman undertakings.

"You see, my friends, once you've sampled this type of gadding about, you just can't do without it; so for our next expedition, instead of heading sideways, we'll go straight up and keep on going."

"Wow! Right to the moon!" a listener said in amazement.

"Not the moon!" Joe fired back. "Criminy, that's old news. Everybody heads that way in these things. Anyhow there's no water on the moon, and you'd have to take along a gigantic supply—and even flasks of air if you plan on breathing."

"Fine, but can you get a flask of gin up there?" said a sailor deeply enamored of that beverage.

"Not a drop, me hearty. Thumbs down on the moon! But we'll take a stroll around those pretty stars and lovely planets my master's often talked to me about. Consequently we'll start by dropping in on Saturn—"

"The one with the ring?" the quartermaster asked.

"Right, a wedding ring. Except nobody knows what happened to his wife!"

"What! You'll get as high as that?" a wide-eyed cabin boy asked. "He's the very devil, your master."

"The devil? Naw, he does too many good deeds."

"And what happens after Saturn?" asked one of his more restless listeners.

"After Saturn? Well, we'll pay a visit to Jupiter; an odd locality, mind you, where the days are only 9 ½ hours long, which is just fine for slackers, and the years, by jingo, last twelve times longer than ours, which is beneficial for folks who have no more than six months to live. They get a little added bonus!"

"The years are twelve times longer?" the cabin boy went on.

"Yes, laddie; so in those parts your mama'd still be nursing you, and that geezer there, who's coming up on fifty, would be a little tyke 4½ years old."

"You're pulling our legs!" the whole forecastle hooted in unison.

"Gospel truth," Joe said confidently. "But what do you expect? When folks keep stagnating down here on earth, they don't learn anything and stay as dumb as dolphins. So head up to Jupiter for a little while and see for yourself! But for pity's sake be careful on the way, because those moons of his are a pain to bump into!"

And they laughed but half believed him; and he told them about Neptune where seamen get a hearty welcome, and Mars where soldiers hog the sidewalks to the point of tedium. As for Mercury, that's a nasty world of bandits and merchants who are so similar, it's hard to tell them apart.[2] And lastly he drew them a truly seductive picture of Venus.

"And when we come back from this expedition," said our genial storyteller, "they'll award us that Southern Cross gleaming up there in the good Lord's buttonhole."

"And you'll have earned it!" the sailors said.

So those long evenings in the forecastle went by, full of lighthearted chitchat. And meanwhile the doctor carried on with his educational talks.

One day the conversation got around to steering balloons, and they invited Fergusson to give his views on the matter.

"I don't believe," he said, "that we'll manage to steer a balloon. I'm acquainted with all the methods attempted or proposed; not one of them has worked, not one of them is feasible. You can appreciate that I've had to spend time on this problem, that it was bound to be of great interest to me; but I couldn't solve it with the means available from contemporary mechanics. We'd need to come up with a motor that's both amazingly strong and unbelievably light! And if we did, we wouldn't be able to withstand air currents of any significance! What's more, until now we've been more concerned with steering the gondola than the balloon. That's a mistake."

"But there are major similarities," somebody countered, "between a lighter-than-air vehicle and a ship you can steer at will."

"No, there are few to none," Dr. Fergusson replied. "The air has infinitely less density than the sea, in which a ship is only half submerged, while a lighter-than-air vehicle is fully immersed in the atmosphere and stays motionless in relation to the elastic fluid surrounding her."

"So you think the science of air travel has nothing more to offer us?"

"Not at all! It just needs to look for different answers, so if you can't steer your balloon, at least you can keep her in favorable air currents. The higher we go, the steadier they are in their speed and direction; they aren't troubled anymore by the valleys and mountains that crisscross the earth's surface, and these, as you know, are the main reason that the wind shifts and blows erratically. Now then, once these different zones have been identified, all the balloon will have to do is get situated in the currents that suit her needs."

"But in order to reach them," Captain Pennet went on, "you'd have to go up and down continually. That's the real difficulty, my dear doctor."

"And why, my dear commander?"

"Let's be clear on this: it would create difficulties and obstacles for journeys of long duration, if not for little day trips."

"And your reason, please?"

"Because you rise only if you drop ballast and you descend only if you let out gas, and in the process your supplies of ballast and gas would soon be used up."

"My dear Pennet, that's the heart of the matter. That's the single difficulty science needs to go forth and conquer. This isn't about steering a balloon; this is about moving her up and down without sacrificing the gas that's her strength, blood, and soul as it were."

"You're right, my dear doctor, but the problem still hasn't been solved, the way to do this still hasn't been found."

"Begging your pardon, it *has* been found."

"Who found it?"

"I did."

"You?"

"Otherwise, as you can appreciate, I wouldn't have risked this balloon trip across Africa. I'd be out of gas by the end of the first day!"

"But you didn't say anything about this in England!"

"No. I didn't want to become embroiled in public controversy. It wouldn't have served any useful purpose. I conducted my preparatory experiments in secret and to my satisfaction; so there was nothing more I needed to learn."

"Well, my dear Fergusson, can you let us in on your secret?"

"Here it is, gentlemen—the way I do this is quite simple."

Audience interest was at its highest pitch as the doctor serenely took the floor, then spoke as follows:

chapter 10

Prior efforts—the doctor's five tanks—the gas burner—the heating system—method of maneuvering—guaranteed success.

"People have often attempted, gentlemen, to rise or descend at will without wasting a balloon's gas or ballast. A French balloonist, Monsieur Meusnier, tried to achieve this objective by pumping air into a bag inside the envelope. A Belgian, Dr. Van Hecke, used wings and windmill blades to work up a vertical force that in most cases wouldn't have been sufficient. The practical results achieved by these different methods have been unimpressive.

"So I decided to tackle the problem more realistically. And at the outset I eliminated ballast from the equation, except in dealing with acts of God such as damage to my mechanism or the need to rise suddenly in order to dodge an unforeseen obstacle.

"My method of ascending and descending involves nothing more than changing the temperature to make the gas expand or contract inside my lighter-than-air vehicle. And here's how I achieve this result.

"You saw several tanks brought on board along with the gondola, tanks whose functions are a mystery to you. There are five of them.

"The first holds about 25 gallons of water, to which I add a few drops of sulfuric acid to increase its ability to conduct electricity, and I break it down using a powerful Bunsen battery. You know the gases that make up water: it's two parts hydrogen and one part oxygen.

"When the battery is in operation, the oxygen makes its way via the positive pole into a second tank. A third, positioned above the second and twice its capacity, receives the hydrogen reaching it via the negative pole.

"Spigots — one with an opening twice as big as the other's — put these two tanks in contact with a fourth known as the mixing tank. There the two gases we get by breaking down water are indeed mixed. The capacity of this mixing tank is about 41 cubic feet.[1]

"The upper part of this tank has a pipe made of platinum and equipped with a spigot.

"You can already see what we have, gentlemen: the mechanism I've described to you is nothing less than a kind of blowtorch — it's a burner fed by oxygen and hydrogen, and it's hotter than a furnace in a foundry.

"That settled, I'll move on to the second part of the mechanism.

"Two roughly adjacent pipes emerge from the lower part of my balloon, which is hermetically sealed. One comes from the upper reaches of the hydrogen gas, the other from the lower reaches.

"These two pipes are equipped at various points with strong rubber joints, which allow them to flex as the vehicle shakes and shivers.

"Both of them go down into the gondola and vanish into a cylindrical tank made of iron and known as the heating tank. Two strong disks of the same metal close it off at both ends.

"The pipe from the balloon's lower regions penetrates into this cylindrical container through its bottom disk; inside, it takes the form of a spiral-shaped coil whose rings rise one above the other, reaching almost to the top of the tank. Before emerging, the coil makes its way into a little cone whose convex base[2] is lowermost and looks like a bowl-shaped skullcap.

"The second pipe emerges from the peak of this cone and makes its way, as I've told you, into the balloon's upper reaches.

"The bowl-shaped skullcap on the little cone is made of platinum to keep it from melting while the burner is in operation. That's because the burner sits at the bottom of the iron tank in the middle of the spiral-shaped coil, and the tip of its flame will gently lick at this skullcap.

"You're familiar with those heating systems, gentlemen, that are designed to warm apartments. You're familiar with how they work. The air in an apartment is driven through its pipes and sent back out at a higher temperature. Now then, what I've just described to you is, in all honesty, simply one of those heating systems.

"What will actually take place? Once the burner is lit, the hydrogen in the coil and the convex cone heats up and swiftly rises through the pipe leading to the upper regions of my lighter-than-air vehicle. The vacuum created below draws the gas from the lower regions, warms it in turn, and is continually refilled; in the pipes and coil, then, there's a tremendously swift stream of gas that keeps emerging from the balloon, returning to her, and heating back up.

"Now then, the gases will increase by $\frac{1}{480}^3$ of their volume for every additional degree of heat. So if I make the temperature 18 degrees hotter,[4] the hydrogen in my lighter-than-air vehicle will expand by $\frac{18}{480}$, or 1,674 cubic feet,[5] so it will displace an extra 1,674 cubic feet of air, which will increase my lifting power by 160 pounds. It's the same, then, as dropping that amount of ballast. If I increase the temperature by 180 degrees,[6] the gas will expand by $\frac{180}{480}$: it will displace an extra 16,740 cubic feet, and my lifting power will be 1,600 pounds greater.

"As you can appreciate, gentlemen, it's easy for me to significantly impact my buoyancy. I've calculated the volume of my lighter-than-air vehicle so that when she's half inflated, she displaces a weight of air exactly equal to the envelope with its hydrogen plus the gondola with its travelers and all its accessories. Reaching this stage of her inflation, she's at a point of perfect buoyancy in the air and neither climbs nor descends.

"To get her to ascend, I use my burner to make the gas hotter than the surrounding air; this additional heat builds up more pressure and further inflates the balloon, which keeps climbing the more her hydrogen expands.

"Naturally I descend by reducing the heat from my burner and letting the temperature cool back down. Generally it takes much less time to ascend than to descend. But that's a lucky state of affairs; I've never put much stock in descending quickly, whereas, by contrast, a swift upward movement lets me dodge obstacles. The dangers are down below, not up above.

"Besides, as I've told you, I have a nominal amount of ballast that will let me rise even more swiftly if I need to. My valve, which is located at the very top of the balloon, is nothing more than a safety valve. The balloon always has the same amount of hydrogen; the changes in temperature that I produce inside this imprisoned gas are enough in themselves to move me upward and downward.

"Now, gentlemen, as a practical detail, I'll add this one thing.

"The combustion of hydrogen and oxygen at the tip of the burner produces nothing but water vapor. So I've equipped the lower part of the cylindrical iron tank with an exhaust pipe that has a valve operating at a pressure less than two atmospheres; consequently, as soon as the steam reaches this intensity, it escapes on its own.

"And now let's carefully run the numbers.

"Twenty-five gallons of water, broken down into its constituent elements, will give 200 pounds of oxygen and 25 pounds of hydrogen. This represents, with the atmospheric pressure, 1,890 cubic feet of the first and 3,780 cubic feet of the second, or 5,670 cubic feet for the whole mix.[7]

"Now then, when my burner's spigot is wide open, it uses up 27 cubic feet per hour,[8] and its flame is at least six times brighter than the biggest streetlights. So on an average, to keep myself at a middling altitude, I wouldn't burn more than 9 cubic feet per hour;[9] therefore my 25 gallons of water offer me 630 hours of airborne travel, or just over twenty-six days.

"And yet, since I can descend at will and replenish my water supply on the way, my journey can be of indefinite duration.

"That's my secret, gentlemen; it's simple, and as simple things do, it will succeed without fail. My method consists of making the gas expand and contract in my lighter-than-air vehicle, and there's no need for clumsy wings or driving devices. A heating system to produce my changes in temperature, a burner to supply the heat—nothing that's inconvenient or burdensome. So I believe that I've assembled all the prime ingredients for success."

That was the close of Dr. Fergusson's speech, and it was heartily applauded. There wasn't a single objection to be raised; everything had been anticipated and resolved.

"Even so," the commander said, "there could be some dangers."

"If it works," the doctor merely replied, "who cares?"

chapter **11**

*Arriving in Zanzibar—the English consul—hostile
reception by the natives—Koumbeni Island—the
rainmakers—inflating the balloon—departure on
April 18—final farewell—the* Victoria.

A continually favorable wind meant that the *Resolute* made excellent
time to her port of destination. The Mozambique Channel was especially smooth sailing. This trip through the waves was a good omen for
their trip through the clouds. Everybody was eager for the moment
when they would arrive and put the finishing touches on Dr. Fergusson's preparations.

Finally the vessel came in sight of Zanzibar, the town located on the
island of the same name, and at eleven o'clock in the morning on April
15, she dropped anchor in the harbor.

The island of Zanzibar belongs to the Imam of Muscat, an ally of
France and England, and it's clearly his prize colony. The harbor wel-
comes a large number of ships from neighboring regions.

The island is separated from Africa's coast by a channel, no more
than thirty miles across[1] at its widest point.

It does a booming business in gum, ivory, and especially "ebony," because Zanzibar is the leading slave market. This is the gathering place
for all the conquered booty from the battles continually indulged in
by chieftains inland. This trafficking in humanity also extends along
the entire east coast, even up to the latitudes of the Nile, and Monsieur G. Lejean has seen this trade openly carried on under the flag of
France.

As soon as the *Resolute* arrived, the English consul in Zanzibar
came on board to put himself at the doctor's disposal, since, over the
past month, European newspapers had kept him up to date on Fergusson's plans. But until then he had belonged to the sizable phalanx
of the skeptical.

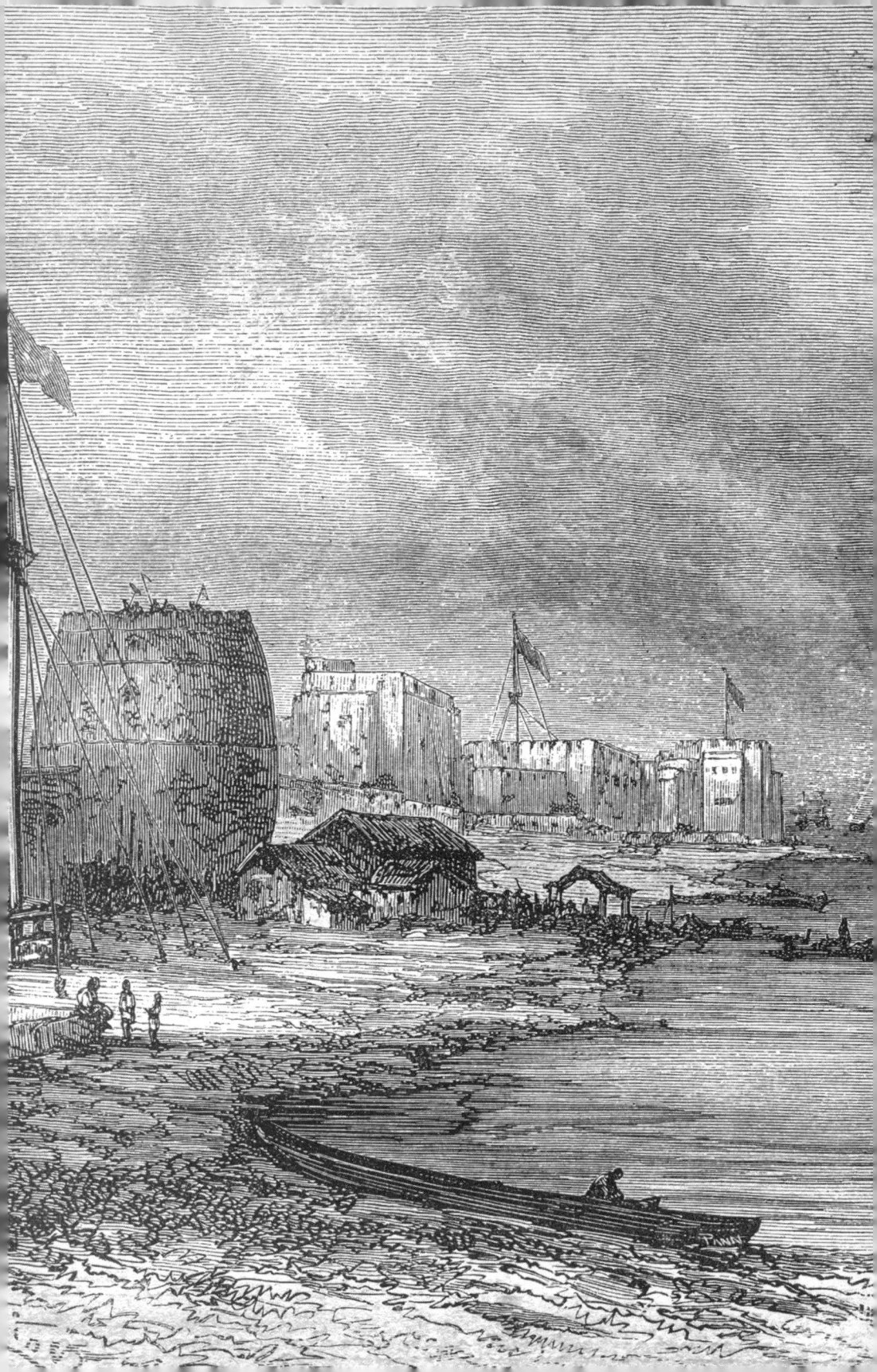

"I had my doubts," he said, holding out his hand to Samuel Fergusson, "but not anymore."

He offered his own home to the doctor, Dick Kennedy, and of course our gallant Joe.

As a further kindness, he acquainted the doctor with various letters he had received from Captain Speke. The captain and his companions had suffered dreadfully from hunger and foul weather before reaching the country of Ugogo; they found it tremendously difficult to make any headway and no longer thought they could send back news in a timely manner.

"Those are perils and hardships we'll be able to avoid," the doctor said.

The three travelers had their baggage transferred to the consul's home. The crew got ready to unload the balloon on the beach in Zanzibar; there was a promising location next to the signal mast and near an enormous edifice that would shelter it from easterly winds. It was a huge tower shaped like an upended barrel—the Heidelberg cask is a humble keg by comparison—and it functioned as a citadel with Balochi enforcers carrying lances and standing watch on its platform, a gang of noisy idlers.

But as they were about to unload the lighter-than-air vehicle, the consul learned that the local population would oppose this move by force. Nothing is blinder than fanatical fervor. The island chafed at the news that a Christian had arrived and meant to ascend into the skies; Negroes were more perturbed than Arabs and viewed the scheme as intentionally hostile to their religion; it looked to them as if somebody had designs on the sun and moon. Now then, those two heavenly bodies are subjects of veneration for African tribes. So they were determined to oppose this sacrilegious expedition.

Alerted to these developments, the consul, Dr. Fergusson, and Commander Pennet put their heads together. The seaman didn't want to retreat in the face of these threats; but his friend made him listen to reason on the matter.

"We'll definitely prevail in the end," he told him. "Even the imam's enforcers will lend us a hand if need be; yet, my dear commander, acci-

View of Zanzibar

dents can happen in a second; one piece of mischief could be enough to cause irreversible damage to the balloon, and our journey could be jeopardized beyond repair; so we must proceed with great caution."

"But what can we do? If we go ashore on the African mainland, we'll run into the same difficulties! What can we do?"

"Nothing could be simpler," the consul answered. "Look at those islands located beyond the harbor; unload your vehicle on one of them, put a cordon of sailors around her, and you'll be out of harm's way."

"Perfect," the doctor said, "and we'll complete our preparations at our leisure."

The commander went along with this advice. The *Resolute* drew up to Koumbeni Island. During the morning of April 16, they put the balloon in a place of safety inside a clearing among the big trees that dot this landscape.

They stood two masts on end, 80 feet high and positioned the same distance from each other; sets of pulleys were attached to the tips of these, able to raise the lighter-than-air vehicle with the help of a crosswise cable; at that juncture the balloon was completely deflated. Fastened to the top of the outer envelope, the inner one would be lifted up along with it.

They fitted the two intake pipes for the hydrogen into the lower appendix[2] of each balloon.

They spent the day of the 17th setting up the mechanism designed to produce the gas; it consisted of thirty barrels in which a large amount of water was broken down by mixing in scrap iron and sulfuric acid. Getting washed as it went, the hydrogen made its way into a huge central cask, from there entering each envelope by the intake pipes. In this fashion each of them got filled with an accurately measured amount of gas.

For this operation it was necessary to employ 1,866 gallons of sulfuric acid, 16,050 pounds of iron,[3] and 9,166 gallons of water.[4]

The operation got under way the following night around three o'clock in the morning; it went on for nearly eight hours. The next day, complete with her netting, the lighter-than-air vehicle swayed gracefully above her gondola, held down by a good many bags of dirt. They assembled the inflation mechanism with great care, taking the pipes

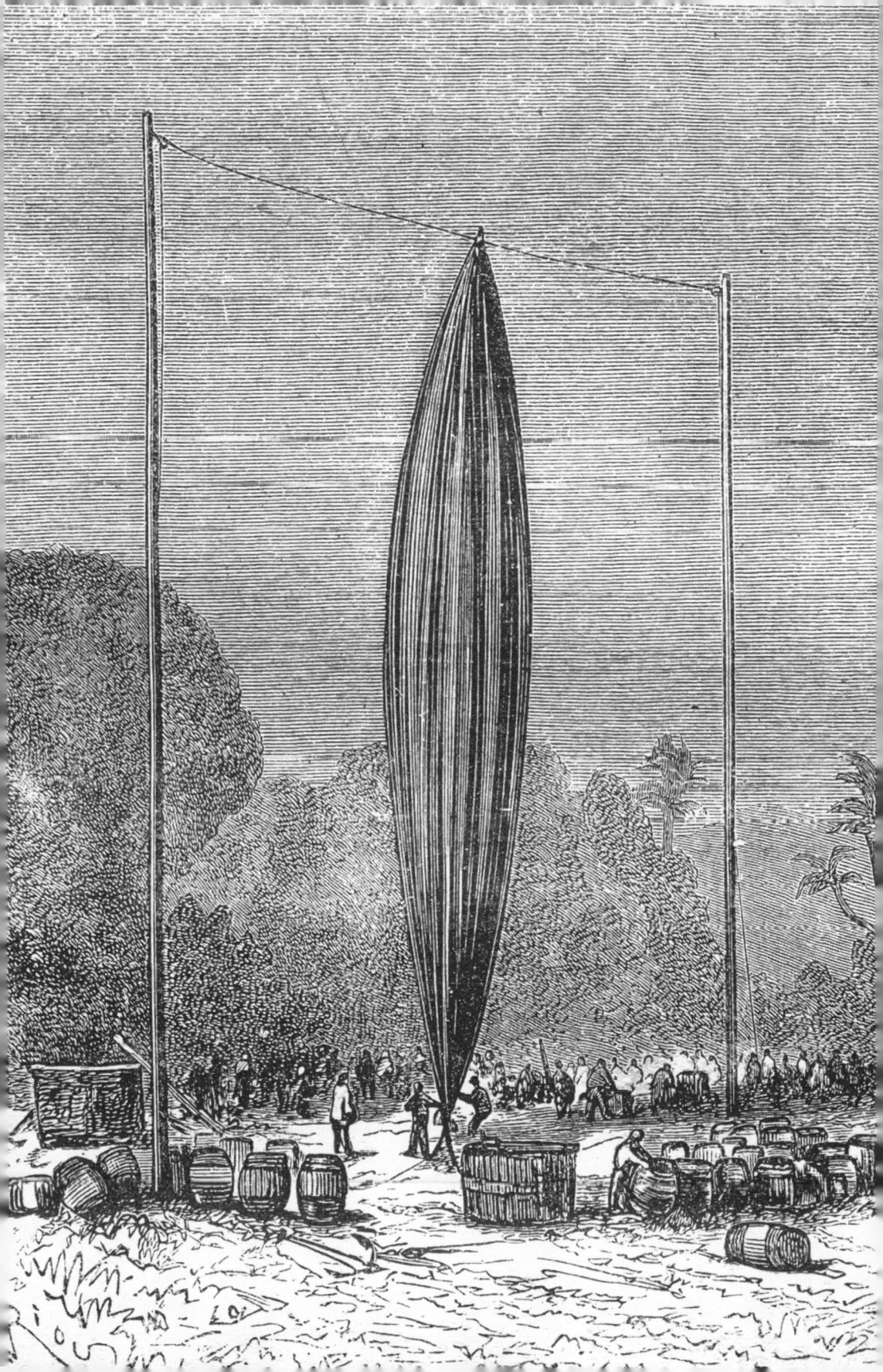

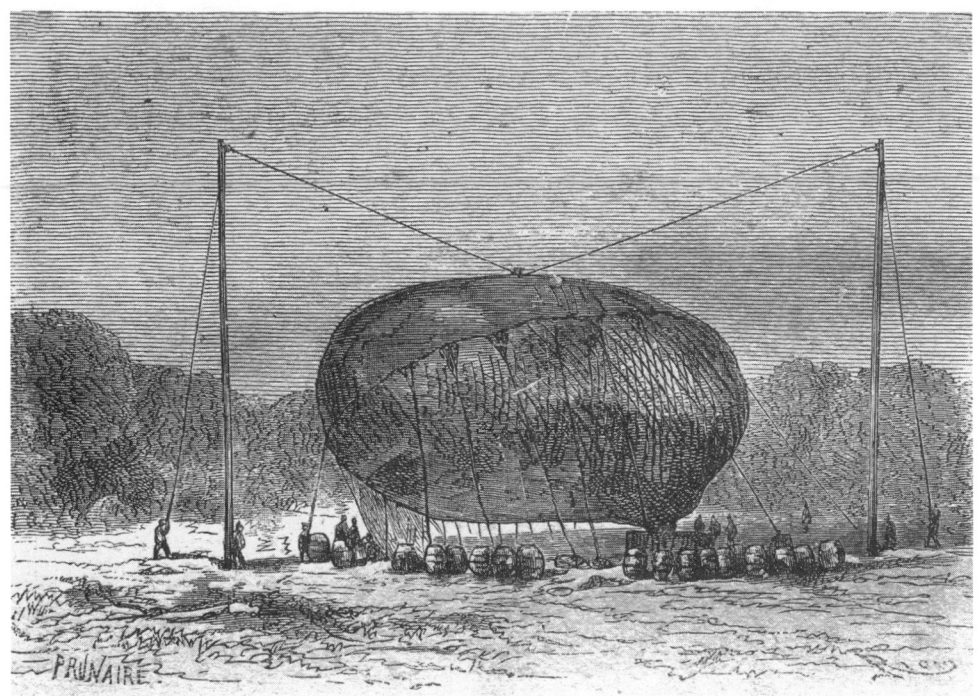

that emerged from the vehicle and fitting them into the cylindrical container.

They stocked up on water in Zanzibar; the anchors, lines, instruments, travel blankets, tent, provisions, and weapons went into their assigned places in the gondola. The 200 pounds of ballast were divvied up into fifty bags, then stowed within easy reach at the bottom of the gondola.

These preparations were complete by about five o'clock in the evening; sentries were on continual watch around the island, and the *Resolute*'s longboats crisscrossed the channel.

The Negroes continued to express their displeasure by yelling, scowling, and writhing about. Witch doctors roamed among the angry crowds, fanning the flames of their anger; some fanatics tried to swim out to the island, but they were easily driven back.

Then it was time for magic spells and mumbo jumbo; claiming to control the clouds, rainmakers prayed for hurricanes and "pebble

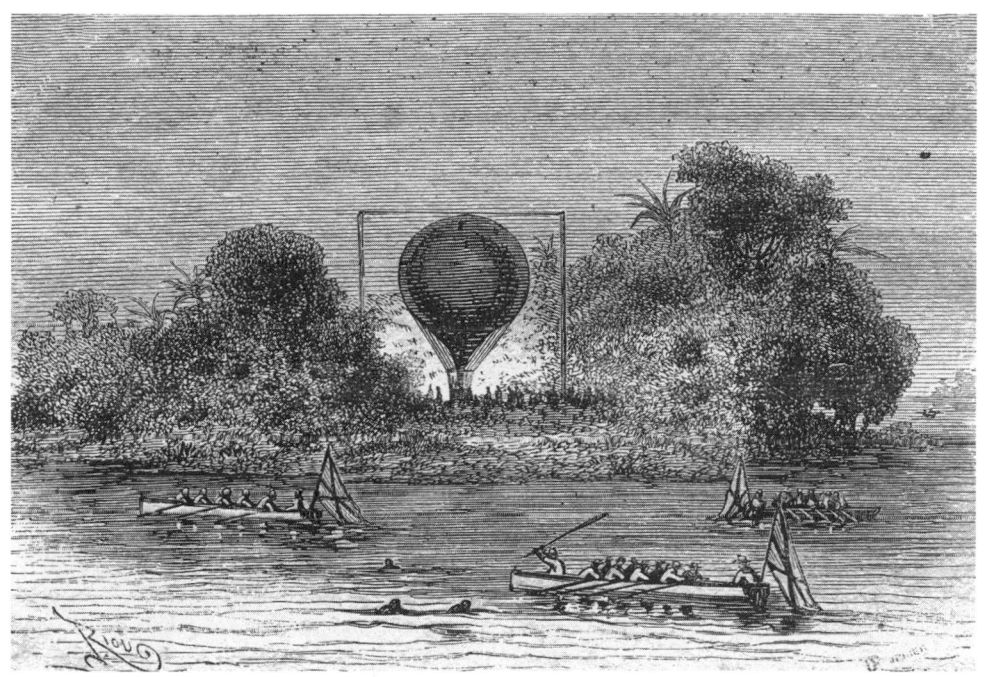

showers";* to this end they gathered leaves from every type of tree in the country; they boiled them over a low fire, meanwhile killing a sheep by plunging a long needle into its heart. But despite these solemnities, the sky stayed clear, and their sheep and scowls went for nothing.

The Negroes then indulged in furious orgies, getting tipsy on *tembo*, hard liquor extracted from the coconut palm, or a tremendously intoxicating beer called *togwa*. Their songs had no melodies to speak of, although the rhythms were pretty catchy, and they didn't let up until well into the night.

Around six o'clock in the evening, the travelers got together for one last dinner at the table of the commander and his officers. Kennedy, whom nobody paid attention to anymore, muttered unintelligible words in an undertone; he didn't take his eyes off Dr. Fergusson.

Anyhow it was a gloomy meal. The crowning moment was at hand, and it inspired troubling thoughts in everybody. What did fate have

* Name that Negroes give hailstorms.

in store for these bold travelers? Would they ever rejoin their circles of friends, return to enjoy the pleasures of hearth and home? If their means of transportation proved inadequate, what would happen to them in the midst of those fierce tribes, in those unexplored regions out in that immense wilderness?

Until then they had attached little significance to such scattered thoughts, but now their keyed-up imaginations were under siege. Still cool and composed, Dr. Fergusson chatted about this and that; but he tried without success to dispel this outbreak of gloom; it was beyond him.

Fearing acts of violence against their persons, the doctor and his two companions slept aboard the *Resolute*. At six o'clock in the morning, they left their cabin and made their way to Koumbeni Island.

An easterly wind was blowing, and the balloon swayed gently. Twenty sailors had taken over from the bags of dirt holding her down. Commander Pennet and his officers were in attendance at this departure ceremony.

Just then Kennedy went straight to the doctor, clutched his hand, and said:

"You're really determined to go, Samuel?"

"Bound and determined, my dear Dick."

"I've done everything in my power to put a stop to this trip?"

"Everything."

"Then my conscience is clear on that score, and I'm coming along."

"I was sure of it," the doctor responded, a hint of emotion visible for one second in his features.

It was the moment for final farewells. The commander and his officers gave hearty hugs to their courageous friends, including our worthy Joe, full of pride and joy. Every attendee wanted a chance to shake hands with Dr. Fergusson.

By nine o'clock the three traveling companions had taken their places in the gondola: the doctor lit his burner and turned up the flame to produce heat more quickly. Held to the ground in a state of perfect buoyancy, the balloon started to lift off after a few minutes. The sailors had to pay out the mooring lines a little. The gondola rose about twenty feet.

"My friends," the doctor called, standing between his two companions and doffing his hat, "let's give our airborne vessel a name that will bring her good luck! Let's christen her the *Victoria!*"

A fearsome hooray rang out:

"Long live the Queen! Long live England!"

Just then the lifting power of their lighter-than-air vehicle increased prodigiously. Fergusson, Kennedy, and Joe threw their friends one last farewell.

"Let her go!" the doctor called.

And the *Victoria* rose swiftly into the skies, while aboard the *Resolute*, four short-bodied naval cannons thundered away in her honor.

chapter 12

Crossing the strait — Mrima — Dick's remarks and Joe's recommendation — recipe for coffee — the district of Uzaramo — the unfortunate Maizan — Mt. Dutumi — night over a prickly pear[1] — the doctor's maps.

The sky was clear, the wind moderate; the *Victoria* rose nearly straight up to an altitude of 1,500 feet, which was indicated by a drop of 1 and ⅚ inches[2] in the mercury column of their barometer.

At that altitude a more emphatic current carried the balloon toward the southwest. What a magnificent sight unfolded beneath our travelers' eyes! The island of Zanzibar offered a view of its entire expanse, standing out in a darker color as if on a huge world map; its fields reminded you of different-colored swatches in a sample book; woods and thickets were big leafy clusters.

The island's residents looked like insects. The hoorays and shouts gradually died away in the air, and only booms from the ship's cannons ruffled the envelope's lower edges.

"What a gorgeous view!" Joe exclaimed, the first one to break the silence.

Nobody answered him back. The doctor was intently studying the changes in his barometer and recording the various details of his ascension.

Kennedy was looking too, and his eyes needed to be everywhere at once.

The sunlight came to the aid of their burner, and the gas's pressure increased. The *Victoria* reached an altitude of 2,500 feet.

The *Resolute* took on the humble appearance of a small craft, and Africa's coast was visible in the west as an immense border of foam.

"You're not talking?" Joe said.

"We're busy looking," the doctor replied, aiming his spyglass at the mainland.

"As for me, I just have to talk."

"Feel free, Joe! Talk all you like."

And Joe treated himself to an awesome feast of nonsense syllables. Oohs, ahs, and wows erupted from his lips.[3]

While crossing the sea, the doctor thought it best to stay at that altitude; he could study a greater expanse of coastline; his thermometer and barometer hung inside the partly open tent, always within view; placed outside, a second barometer was for their use when they stood watch at night.

Propelled at a speed slightly faster than eight miles per hour, the *Victoria* had almost made it to the coast after another two hours. The doctor decided to drop closer to the ground; he cut back the flame of his burner, and the balloon soon descended to an altitude of 300 feet.

She hovered above Mrima, the name given this part of Africa's east coast; heavy borders of mangroves protected its edges; the low tide exposed their thick roots, gnawed by the teeth of the Indian Ocean. The sand dunes that used to form the coastline were swelling along the horizon, and the summit of Mt. Nguru reared up in the northwest.

The *Victoria* passed close to a village that the doctor identified as Kaole on his map. All its citizens had gathered and were letting out shrieks of anger and fear; they fired their arrows in vain at this monster of the skies, which swayed majestically above all that impotent sound and fury.

The wind blew to the south, but the doctor had no worries about heading that way; on the contrary, it let him keep an eye on the trail blazed by Captains Burton and Speke.

After a while Kennedy grew as chatty as Joe; approving comments shot back and forth between the two.

"Who needs stagecoaches!" one of them said.

"Who needs steamboats!" said the other.

"Who needs railways," Kennedy fired back. "You ride 'em across a country and can't see where you're going!"

"Now take a balloon!" Joe went on. "You feel like you aren't even moving, while nature goes to the trouble of unrolling right under your eyes!"

"What a sight! What a marvel! What a thrill! Like dreaming in a hammock!"

Crossing the strait

"How about some lunch?" asked Joe, who had worked up an appetite in the open air.

"That's a thought, my lad."

"Well, cooking it won't take long! It'll just be crackers and canned meat."

"And all the coffee you like," the doctor added. "I'll let you borrow a little heat from my burner—it has plenty to spare. And this way we won't have to worry about fires."

"Which would be dreadful," Kennedy went on. "Like having a powder magazine overhead."

"Not quite," Fergusson replied. "But if the gas did ignite, it would ultimately burn itself out little by little, and we'd sink to the earth, which would be aggravating for us; but never fear—our lighter-than-air vehicle is hermetically sealed."

"Then let's eat," Kennedy said.

"Here you are, gentlemen," Joe announced, "and while I'm at it, I'm going to brew you some coffee to write home about."

"Among Joe's thousands of virtues," the doctor added, "is his truly

remarkable talent for brewing that tasty beverage; it's a blend he concocts from a variety of sources, which he has never revealed to me."

"Well, master, since we're up where nobody can overhear, I'll let you in on my recipe. The blend is simply equal parts mocha, arabica, and robusta."[4]

A few seconds later three steaming cups were in front of them, the close of a quality lunch topped off by the diners' high spirits; then each of them went back to his observation post.

The country was notable for its tremendous fertility. Narrow, winding trails plunged beneath canopies of greenery. Our explorers passed above tilled fields of fully ripened tobacco, corn, and barley—plus, here and there, huge rice paddies with their straight stems and reddish blossoms. They saw sheep and goats locked up in big cages, which were raised on pilings for protection from the fangs of leopards. Luxuriant vegetation tumbled over this extravagant soil. Again and again the many villages were filled with shouts and astonishment as the *Victoria* came in sight, and Dr. Fergusson wisely kept her out of range of the villagers' arrows; for a good while the natives gathered outside their clusters of huts, hurling empty curses after the travelers.

At noon the doctor checked his map and judged they were passing above the district of Uzaramo.* The landscape turned out to be dotted with coconut palms, papaya trees, and cotton plants, over which the *Victoria* seemed to dance on by. Joe found this vegetation perfectly natural, since, after all, this *was* Africa. Kennedy spotted some jackrabbit and quail that were just begging for a bullet; but it would have been a waste of gunpowder, seeing that he couldn't possibly retrieve the game he had shot.

Our balloonists were traveling at a speed of twelve miles per hour and soon were above the village of Tounda at longitude 38° 20′.

"That's the place," the doctor said, "where Burton and Speke came down with intense fevers and thought for a moment that their expedition was in jeopardy. And yet they weren't very far from the coast, although exhaustion and hardship had already taken a heavy toll on them."

In fact malaria reigns around the clock in this region; the doctor himself could escape its clutches only by lifting his balloon above the reek of that damp earth, whose fumes are drawn out by the hot sun.

Sometimes they could spy a caravan resting in a kraal, waiting for the cool of the evening before getting under way again. Surrounded by hedges and jungles, these are huge enclosures where traders take shelter not only from wild animals but also from the thieving tribes in these parts. You could see the natives running every which way at the sight of the *Victoria*. Kennedy wanted to take a closer look at them; but Samuel continually opposed this notion.

* "U" and "ou" mean *region* in the local language.

"The chieftains are armed with muskets," he said, "and our balloon would be such an easy target for their bullets to hit."

"Would a bullet hole make us fall out of the sky?" Joe asked.

"Not immediately; but that hole would soon turn into a huge rip, and all our gas would escape."

"Then let's keep a respectful distance from those rascals. What do you figure they're thinking as they see us soar through the air? I bet they're dying to worship us."

"They're welcome to do so," the doctor replied, "but from afar. That's always a good policy. Look—the country's already changing in appearance; there are fewer villages; the mango trees have died out; they don't grow at this latitude. The terrain is turning hilly, which suggests that mountains aren't far off."

"Actually," Kennedy said, "there *does* seem to be higher ground on this side."

"In the west . . . those are the first mountain chains of the Ourizara range . . . that's probably Mt. Dutumi, and I hope we can take shelter behind it during the night. I'll turn up the flame of my burner—we need to stay at an altitude of 500 or 600 feet."

"All the same, sir," Joe said, "that's a first-class gadget you've put together. It isn't tricky or tiring to work with—turn on a spigot and you're in business."

"We're better off up here," the hunter said when the balloon had climbed higher. "The sunlight reflecting on that red sand was getting hard to take."

"What colossal trees!" Joe exclaimed. "Maybe they're perfectly natural down here, but they're still something to see! It wouldn't take a dozen of 'em to make a whole forest."

"Those are baobab trees," Dr. Fergusson replied. "By Jove, the trunk on that one could be a hundred feet around. Maybe it was at the foot of that same tree that the Frenchman Maizan lost his life in 1845, because we're above the village of Deje-la-Mhora, which he ventured to alone; a chieftain in this region captured him and tied him to the foot of a baobab tree—then that brutal Negro slowly amputated his limbs while a war song echoed in the background; after that he began to slit his captive's throat, stopped to sharpen the dull blade of his knife, then tore away the poor man's head before it had been cut off! That unfortunate Frenchman was just twenty-six years old!"

"And France didn't demand vengeance for that crime?" Kennedy asked.

"France filed charges; the Sultan of Zanzibar did everything he could to apprehend the murderer, but he wasn't successful."

"I request we hang out somewhere else," Joe said. "Take her higher, master, if you want my opinion."

"More than happy to, Joe, since that's Mt. Dutumi up ahead of us. If my calculations are correct, we'll pass it by before seven o'clock this evening."

"We aren't traveling at night?" the hunter asked.

"Not if we can avoid it; if we're alert and careful, there wouldn't be any risk, but it isn't enough just to cross Africa, it's essential to see it."

"No reason to complain so far, master. Instead of a wilderness, we've got the best tilled and most fertile land in the world! So much for the geography books!"

"Hold on, Joe. Let's see what tomorrow brings."

Around six-thirty that evening, the *Victoria* hovered opposite Mt. Dutumi; in order to clear it, they had to climb more than 3,000 feet, and for that to happen, the doctor had to raise the temperature just eighteen degrees.[5] To maneuver his balloon, he truly took a hands-on approach, you might say. Kennedy pointed out the obstacles they needed to rise over, and the *Victoria* flew higher, still hugging the mountain's surface.

At eight o'clock she went down the far slope, which had a gentler incline; they tossed the anchors out of the gondola, and one of them caught on the paddles of an enormous prickly pear, then stayed stuck. Immediately Joe slid down the rope and secured it with great thoroughness. They lowered the silk ladder, and he climbed deftly back inside. Sheltered from easterly winds, their lighter-than-air vehicle remained virtually motionless.

They got their evening meal ready; exhilarated by that jaunt in the sky, the travelers put a big dent in their provisions.

The balloon caught on the paddles of a prickly pear

"How far did we go today?" Kennedy asked, downing a fearsome mouthful.

The doctor took some lunar sights and fixed his position, checking the superb map that functioned as his guidebook; it belonged to the atlas *Der Neuester Entedekungen in Afrika,*[6] published in Gotha by his learned friend Petermann, who had sent him a copy. The doctor would use this atlas over his entire journey, because it contained the itinerary of Burton and Speke to the great inland lakes, Sudan according to Dr. Barth, the lower Senegal River according to Guillaume Lejean, and the Niger Delta per Dr. Blaikie.

In addition Fergusson came equipped with a volume that combined under one cover all of the accumulated thinking on the Nile; it was entitled *The Sources of the Nile: Being a General Survey of the Basin of That River and of Its Head-Streams, with the History of the Nilotic Discovery*, by Charles T. Beke, Ph.D.

He also had those superb maps published in the *Bulletins of the Royal Geographical Society of London*, so details of all the explored regions were at his fingertips.

Plotting their course on his map, he found it had taken him two degrees of latitude (or 120 miles) to the west.[7]

Kennedy commented that their course was southerly. But the doctor had no problem with this heading, since, wherever possible, he wanted to follow in the footsteps of his predecessors.

They decided to divide the night into three watches, so each of them in turn could look after the safety of the other two. The doctor would stand guard at nine o'clock, Kennedy at midnight, and Joe at three in the morning.

Wrapped in their blankets, Kennedy and Joe stretched out under the tent and slept peacefully while Dr. Fergusson kept watch.

chapter 13

*Change in the weather—Kennedy's fever—the doctor's
medicine—surface journeys—the Imengé basin—
Mt. Rubeho—6,000 feet up—a daytime layover.*

The night was peaceful; yet when Kennedy woke up Saturday morning, he complained of cold sweats and feeling run-down. The weather was changing; up in the sky, the heavy cloud cover seemed to be laying in supplies for a second Noah's Flood. A depressing country, this Zungomero—it rains continually here, except for maybe a couple of weeks during the month of January.

It wasn't long before a violent downpour assaulted the travelers; below them were trails carved out by *nullahs*, a sort of temporary torrent, and they would become unusable, since, in addition, they were clogged with thornbushes and gigantic creepers. You caught a distinct whiff of those hydrogen sulfur fumes that Captain Burton mentions.

"As he rightly put it," the doctor said, "you'd think a corpse was hidden behind every hedge."

"Nasty country," Joe replied, "and it seems like Mr. Kennedy didn't spend a very restful night here."

"Actually I'm running a pretty high fever," the hunter said.

"That's nothing surprising, my dear Dick, since we're in one of Africa's unhealthiest regions. But we won't stay here any longer. Let's get going."

Joe unhooked the anchor in one deft motion, then went back up the ladder into the gondola. The doctor promptly got to work, the gas expanded, and the *Victoria* lifted off again, driven by a tolerably stiff breeze.

A few shanties were barely visible in the midst of that infected fog. The country took on a different appearance. In Africa it often happens that unsanitary regions aren't very sizable and border on districts that are perfectly healthy.

Kennedy was obviously ailing, the fever beating down his hardy constitution.

"This is the wrong time to get sick," he said, wrapping himself in his bedclothes and lying down under the tent.

"A little patience, my dear Dick," Dr. Fergusson replied, "and you'll be on the mend in no time."

"On the mend! Confound it, Samuel, if your portable medicine chest has a drug that'll straighten me out, give it to me this second. I'll close my eyes and gulp it down."

"I've got something better, Dick old friend—a natural way to cool you off where there's no price to pay."

"And how will you do that?"

"It's quite simple. In a nutshell, I'm going to climb above these clouds that are soaking us and get away from this infected air. Just give the hydrogen ten minutes to expand."

Before those ten minutes had gone by, the travelers were out of that moisture zone.

"Wait a bit, Dick, and you'll experience the effects of clean air and sunshine."

"Now there's a miracle cure!" Joe said. "It's downright magical!"

"No, it's perfectly natural."

"Well, I can't argue with that."

"I gave Dick a change of air, just as they do every day in Europe, and just as I'd send a patient in Martinique to the Carbet Mountains* to escape a yellow fever outbreak."

"Man, this balloon is heaven!" Kennedy said, already feeling better.

"At any rate it's heading that way," Joe replied with a straight face.

They were a rare sight, those masses of clouds piling up under the gondola just then; they tumbled over each other, reflecting the sunshine, blending into a magnificent burst of light. The *Victoria* reached an altitude of 4,000 feet. Her thermometer indicated that the temperature was definitely dropping. You couldn't see the ground anymore. Some fifty miles to the west, Mt. Rubeho reared its glittering crown; it walled off the country of Ugogo at longitude 36° 20′. The wind blew them along at twenty miles per hour, but our travelers weren't con-

* Among Martinique's highest.

scious of this speed; they didn't feel any vibrations, didn't have any sense of even being in motion.

Three hours later the doctor's forecasts came true. Kennedy's cold sweats were gone, and he ate a hearty breakfast.

"Sure beats quinine sulfate,"[1] he said with relief.

"Far and away," Joe agreed. "This'll be the rest cure for me when I'm an old duffer."

Around ten o'clock in the morning, the skies cleared.[2] There was a rift in the clouds; the ground reappeared; the *Victoria* inched closer to it. Dr. Fergusson was looking for an air current that took him more to the northeast, and he ran into one at an altitude of 600 feet. The country was getting hillier, mountainous even. The district of Zungomero faded into the east along with the last coconut palms in that latitude.

Soon the ridges of a mountain jutted out more abruptly. Peaks rose here and there. Every second they had to watch for sharp pinnacles that seemed to shoot up without warning.

"We're surrounded by reefs," Kennedy said.

"Don't worry, Dick, we won't run aground."

"Nice going anyhow!" Joe remarked.

In fact the doctor maneuvered his balloon with marvelous skill.

"If we had to trudge over that sopping terrain," he said, "we'd get bogged down in some unhealthy mudflat. Since our departure from Zanzibar, half of our pack animals would already be dead of exhaustion. We'd look like ghosts, and our hearts would be full of despair. We'd always be brawling with our guides and carriers, always at the mercy of their wanton brutality. By day, the heat is damp, intolerable, and overpowering! By night, the cold is often unbearable, and you'd be bitten by flies whose mandibles can pierce the heaviest canvas and drive you mad! Not to mention every other kind of calamity from ferocious beasts to barbaric tribes!"

"I'm all for not going there," Joe merely remarked.

"I haven't exaggerated a thing," Dr. Fergusson went on, "because if you read the accounts by travelers who dared venture into these parts, they'll bring tears to your eyes."

At about eleven o'clock they went past the Imengé basin; the tribes scattered over these hills threatened the *Victoria* in vain with their weapons; she finally reached the last rollings of the terrain leading up

to Mt. Rubeho; these form the third and highest chain in the Usagara system.

Our travelers could fully appreciate how the mountains were laid out in this country. Mt. Dutumi forms the first stage of three offshoots, which are separated by huge lengthwise plains; these high knolls are made up of rounded pinnacles, the ground in between sprinkled with pebbles and occasional rocks. The steepest incline in these mountains looks toward the Zanzibar coast; the western slopes are nothing but slanting mesas. Dips in the terrain are covered with dirt that's dark, fertile, and full of hardy vegetation. Various streams flow eastward to join up with the Kingani River, among gigantic clusters of such trees as sycamores, tamarinds, calabashes, and palmyra palms.

"Watch out!" Dr. Fergusson said. "We're coming up on Mt. Rubeho, which means 'passageway for winds' in the local language. When we go around its sharp ridges, we'd be wise to stay well above them. If my map's correct, we'll be operating at an altitude greater than 5,000 feet."

"Will we get many chances to reach those upper zones?"

"Very few; the elevations of Africa's mountains come off as minuscule next to peaks in Europe and Asia. But in any event our *Victoria* will have no trouble clearing them."

The gas quickly expanded as the heat increased, and the balloon began ascending in no uncertain terms. Even so, the hydrogen's expansion didn't present any dangers, and the vehicle's huge envelope was only three-quarters full; the barometer dropped nearly eight inches, indicating an altitude of 6,000 feet.

"How long can we go up like this?" Joe asked.

"The earth's atmosphere is 36,000 feet high," the doctor replied. "With quite a large balloon, you'll go a good way up. That's what Messrs. Brioschi and Gay-Lussac did; but then blood issued from their mouths and ears. The air didn't have enough oxygen. A few years ago two bold Frenchmen, Messrs. Barral and Bixio, also ventured into the upper regions; but their balloon ripped—"

"And they fell out of the sky?" Kennedy asked instantly.

"Of course! But they fell as quick-witted men should—without getting hurt."

"Well, gentlemen," Joe said, "feel free to have another go at it; but as for me, I'm a dimwit and would rather stick with a happy medium, not too high, not too low. Mustn't be greedy."

At 6,000 feet up, the air's density is noticeably thinner already; sounds carry with difficulty, and it's harder to make yourself heard. Objects grow blurry. Your eyes see only big, poorly defined masses; people and animals become totally invisible: roads are shoelaces, lakes are fishponds.

The doctor and his companions felt they had entered the realm of the abnormal; an air current of tremendous speed swept them past arid mountains, their summits covered with huge patches of snow that amazed the eye; the contorted appearance of these peaks pointed to undersea upheavals during the first days of the world.

The sun was shining at the zenith, and its rays fell straight down on these deserted summits. The doctor made an accurate sketch of these mountains, which consisted of four distinct knolls nearly in a straight line, the most extensive one being farthest to the north.

Soon the *Victoria* descended the slope opposite Mt. Rubeho, going along a wooded hillside sprinkled with trees colored a very dark green; then came some ridges and ravines in a sort of wilderness area that led to the country of Ugogo; yellow plains spread out farther down, scorched and cracked, littered here and there with saline plants and thornbushes.

Adorning the horizon were thickets that turned into forests farther off. The doctor dropped closer to the ground, they tossed out the anchors, and one of them soon hooked onto the branches of a huge sycamore.

Joe slid quickly into the tree and carefully secured the anchor; the doctor left his burner on, giving his vehicle enough lifting power to keep her aloft. There had been an abrupt lull in the wind.

"Now, Dick old friend," Fergusson said, "take two shotguns, one for you, the other for Joe, and the two of you try to bring back some choice cuts of antelope. They'll be our dinner."

"The hunt is on!" Kennedy exclaimed.

He disembarked by climbing down from the gondola. Joe had let himself drop from branch to branch and was waiting for him while doing limbering-up exercises. Minus the weight of his two companions, the doctor could turn his burner off.

"Don't fly away without us, master!" Joe called.

"Never fear, my boy, I'm securely in place. I'm going to organize my notes. Happy hunting, and be careful. Anyhow I'll keep an eye on the area from up here, and if anything seems even a bit suspicious, I'll fire a rifle shot. That will be your signal to report back."

"Can do," the hunter replied.

chapter 14

Arid and parched, its clayish earth cracking open from the heat, the country seemed deserted; here and there you saw a few traces of caravans, the bleached bones of men and animals, half gnawed, crumbling into the same dust.

After walking for half an hour, Dick and Joe plunged into a forest of gum trees, eyes on the lookout, fingers on the triggers of their shotguns. They weren't sure what they were up against. Although he wasn't a marksman, Joe was handy with a firearm.

"Walking does a body good, Mr. Dick, but the going isn't too great on this terrain," he said, blundering into the quartz fragments scattered around.

Kennedy motioned to his companion to keep quiet and not move. They had to manage without hunting dogs, and as nimble as Joe was, he didn't have the nose for it like a pointer or a greyhound.

In a riverbed that still had a few stagnant pools, a herd of some ten antelope were quenching their thirst. The graceful animals seemed uneasy, as if scenting danger; in between sips, their shapely heads darted upward, their supple nostrils sniffing the air to windward of the hunters.

Joe stood still while Kennedy circled some shrubbery; he got within shotgun range and fired. The antelope herd vanished in the blink of an eye; hit in the small of the shoulder, a lone male dropped in his tracks. Kennedy rushed up to his prey.

It was a *blaue bock*,[1] a magnificent animal, pale blue turning to gray, belly and insides of the legs as white as snow.

"A shot in a thousand!" the hunter exclaimed. "He's a very rare species of antelope, and I hope I can treat his hide so it'll keep."

"Whoa! You really mean that, Mr. Dick?"

"Positively! Look at this handsome coat."

"But Dr. Fergusson would never take on all this extra weight."

"You're right, Joe! Still, he's quite an animal, and it's a shame to leave the whole works behind!"

"The whole works? No way, Mr. Dick; we'll remove all his nutritional benefits, and with your permission, I'll carve him up as expertly as the staff of the Worshipful Company of Butchers."[2]

"Have at it, my friend; but when I wear my hunter's hat, I can skin a piece of game as smartly as I bag it."

"I'm sure you can, Mr. Dick; so it'll be a snap for you to set up a grill over three stones; you've got lots of deadwood, and I need just a couple of minutes to put your hot coals to use."

"I'll be finished in no time," Kennedy shot back.

He instantly went to work building his fireplace, which was ablaze in a matter of moments.

Extracting a dozen chops and the juiciest tenderloin cuts from the antelope's carcass, Joe soon transformed them into mouthwatering meat dishes.

"They'll be a treat for our friend Samuel," the hunter said.

"Know what I'm thinking about, Mr. Dick?"

"Why, fixing your steaks, what else."

"Not even close. I'm thinking about the faces we'll make if we don't find our balloon again."

"Good lord, what an idea! You're expecting the doctor to leave us behind?"

"No, but what if his anchor happened to pop loose!"

"Impossible. Anyhow Samuel wouldn't have a problem bringing his balloon back down; he maneuvers her pretty expertly."

"But what if the wind carried him away, what if he couldn't get back to us?"

"Stow it, Joe, enough of your what ifs; they're not funny."

"Look, sir, it's natural for all sorts of things to happen in this world; now then, anything can happen, which means we need to be ready for everything—"

The antelope
hunt

Just then a gunshot rang out overhead.

"Huh?" Joe said.

"My rifle! I'd know that sound anywhere."

"A signal!"

"We're in danger!"

"Maybe he is too," Joe countered.

"Come on!"

The hunters quickly gathered up the results of their hunting and returned in their tracks, following the branches Kennedy had broken to

guide them back. The heavy undergrowth kept them from seeing the *Victoria*, although she couldn't have been very far away.

They heard a second gunshot.

"It's urgent," Joe said.

"Good lord! He just fired again."

"Sounds like he's defending himself."

"Let's get moving."

And they ran at top speed. Reaching the edge of the woods, they immediately saw the *Victoria* in her berth and the doctor in the gondola.

"So what's going on?" Kennedy asked.

"Good God!" Joe exclaimed.

"What do you see?"

"Down there, a band of Negroes surrounding the balloon!"

Sure enough, two miles away some thirty individuals were crowding around the foot of the sycamore, waving, howling, and jumping about. A few of them were climbing the tree and heading for its highest branches. The danger seemed clear and present.

"My master's done for!" Joe exclaimed.

"Come on, Joe, calm down and look sharp. We've got the firepower to pick off four of those rascals. Let's go!"

They covered a mile with tremendous speed, then another gunshot came from the gondola; it took out one big devil who was hauling himself up the anchor rope. His lifeless body tumbled from branch to branch, then hung there twenty feet up, two arms and two legs swaying in the air.

"Huh?" Joe said, coming to a stop. "How the devil's that creature hanging on?"

"Who cares," Kennedy answered. "Keep running!"

"Aw, Mr. Kennedy," Joe exclaimed, breaking into laughter, "he's hanging by his tail! By his tail! He's an ape! They're all just apes!"

"Well, we're better off with their kind!" Kennedy shot back, rushing into the midst of that howling mob.

It was a fearsome pack of baboons, savage, vicious, and a horrific sight with their doglike muzzles. But a couple of gunshots quickly sorted things out, and the rest of that scowling horde took to their heels, leaving several of their brethren on the ground.

In a second Kennedy was clinging to the ladder; Joe hauled himself into the sycamore and detached the anchor; the gondola dropped down to his level, and he got back inside without difficulty. A few minutes later the *Victoria* rose into the air, heading east under the impetus of a moderate wind.

"That was some attack!" Joe said.

"We thought the natives had you surrounded."

"Fortunately they were only apes!" the doctor replied.

"We couldn't tell from far away, my dear Samuel."

"Or even closer," Joe remarked.

"Be that as it may," Fergusson went on, "this ape attack could've had the direst consequences. If the anchor had come loose after all the shaking they gave it, who knows where the wind might've taken me?"

"What'd I tell you, Mr. Kennedy?"

"You were right, Joe; but on top of being right, you also were fixing some antelope steaks back then, and I was starting to drool at the sight."

"I can well believe it," the doctor replied. "Antelope meat is superb."

"As you can judge for yourself, sir—dinner is served."

"Gad," the hunter said, "this hunk of venison has a woody aroma I can't resist."

"Yum!" Joe replied, talking with his mouth full. "I could live on antelope the rest of my days, especially with a glass of grog to aid the digestion."

Joe brewed the above-cited beverage, which they sipped reverently.

"Things are going pretty well so far," he said.

"Very well," Kennedy remarked.

"Say, Mr. Dick, are you sorry you came along?"

"Not a man alive could've held me back!" answered our hard-nosed hunter.

By then it was four o'clock in the afternoon; the *Victoria* found herself a faster air current; the terrain was inching upward, and soon the column of their barometer indicated an altitude of 1,500 feet above sea level. For the gas to expand enough to keep his vehicle aloft, the doctor needed to have his burner going continually.

Around seven o'clock the *Victoria* soared over the Kanyemé basin; the doctor instantly identified that huge clearing, ten miles in expanse, its villages lost in the midst of baobab and calabash trees. This is the residence of one of the sultans in the country of Ugogo, where maybe folks are more civilized because it's rarer for them to sell members of their own family; but all its citizens, whether man or animal, live together in round shanties that don't have any framework and look like haystacks.

After Kanyemé the terrain turned arid and stony; but an hour later, in a fertile hollow some distance from Mdaburu, the vegetation was back in force. As the light died out, so did the wind, and the very air seemed to fall asleep. The doctor searched the different altitudes for a current but without success; looking over this calm expanse, he decided to spend the night in the skies, and for greater safety he rose to an altitude of about a thousand feet. The *Victoria* stood still. The night was magnificently starry and dead silent.

Dick and Joe stretched out on their peaceful bed and slept like logs during the doctor's watch; the Scot relieved him at midnight.

"Wake me up if anything happens, no matter how trivial," he told Dick. "And above all, don't take your eyes off the barometer. It's like a compass for folks in our shoes!"

The night was cold, its temperature as much as twenty-seven degrees lower[3] than during the day. Once the darkness came on, it was shattered by a nocturnal chorus of creatures whom hunger and thirst had driven out of their lairs; frogs made a racket in the soprano register, jackals chimed in with their yelping, while lions warmed up their imposing bassos, filling out the harmonies of this high-spirited orchestra.

Resuming his post in the morning, Dr. Fergusson checked the compass and saw that the wind had changed direction during the night. Over the past two hours or so, the *Victoria* had drifted some thirty miles to the northeast; she passed above Mabunguru, stony country bulging with humpbacked crags and scattered with finely polished chunks of an igneous rock called syenite; similar to the boulders in Carnac, conical masses dotted the ground like so many dolmens from the days of the Druids; sundry buffalo and elephant bones added touches of white here and there; not many trees were around, except some extensive woods to the east, hiding a couple of villages in their depths.

At about seven o'clock, a circular rock appeared, nearly two miles in expanse, looking like an immense carapace.

"We're heading the right way," Dr. Fergusson said. "There's Jihoue-la-Mkoa, where we'll call a brief halt. I'm going to replenish the water supply I need for my burner—let's try to hitch up somewhere."

"There aren't many trees," the hunter replied.

"We'll try in any case; Joe, toss out the anchors."

The balloon gradually lost her lifting power and dropped closer to the ground; the anchors ran; a fluke on one of them lodged inside a crevice in a boulder, and the *Victoria* stood still.

You mustn't assume that the doctor could turn his burner off during these layovers. He had calculated the balloon's buoyancy while at sea level; however, the terrain was continually rising and anytime it got to an elevation of 600 or 700 feet, the balloon would have an automatic tendency to ride at a level lower than the ground itself; so to keep her aloft, the gas definitely needed to expand. A dead calm would be the only circumstance in which the doctor would let the gondola rest on the ground—but then his lighter-than-air vehicle would be relieved of considerable weight and would stay aloft without any help from his burner.

His maps indicated huge ponds on the western slope of Jihoue-la-Mkoa. On his own Joe made his way to them, carrying a cask that could hold some ten gallons; not far from a small deserted village, he easily found the designated locality, saw to his water supply, and was back in less than forty-five minutes; he hadn't spotted anything out of the ordinary except some immense elephant traps; he very nearly fell into one of them, which had a half-eaten carcass lying inside.

He brought back from his excursion a species of medlar, a plumlike fruit that apes eat with enthusiasm. The doctor identified it as coming from the *mbenbu* tree, quite plentiful over the western part of Jihoue-la-Mkoa. Fergusson waited for Joe with some impatience, because even a quick layover in this unfriendly land left him in constant dread.

They got the water on board without difficulty, the gondola having dropped nearly to the ground. Joe was able to jerk the anchor loose, then nimbly climbed back in next to his master. The latter immediately turned up his flame, and the *Victoria* resumed her course through the skies.

By then she was about a hundred miles from Kazeh, a major settlement in Africa's interior, where, thanks to a southeasterly current, our travelers could hope to arrive that same day; they were traveling at

a speed of fourteen miles per hour; it was getting fairly difficult to guide their vehicle; they couldn't go too high without the gas expanding a good deal, because the country already had an average elevation of 3,000 feet. Now then, the doctor preferred, as far as possible, to not overdo the expanding; so he deftly followed the windings of a fairly steep incline, hugging the villages of Thembo and Tura-Wels. The latter form part of Unyamwezi, a magnificent region where trees reach the most enormous dimensions and even cactuses grow to whopping sizes.

Around two o'clock, under magnificent skies and a fiery sun that gobbled up the tiniest current of air, the *Victoria* soared above the town of Kazeh, located 350 miles from the coast.

"We left Zanzibar at nine o'clock in the morning," Dr. Fergusson said, checking his notes. "And with all our detours, we've gone nearly 500 statute miles[4] after just two days of travel. Captains Burton and Speke took 4½ months to cover the same distance!"

chapter 15

Kazeh—the noisy marketplace—the Victoria *puts in an appearance—the* wagangas—*the sons of the moon—the doctor's stroll—townspeople—the royal* tembé—*the sultan's wives—royally drunk—Joe adored—how they dance on the moon—about-face— two moons in the sky—the fickle glories of godhood.*

A major locale in central Africa, Kazeh isn't a town; to tell the truth, the interior doesn't *have* any towns. Kazeh is just an assemblage of six huge clearings. Inside them are huts, slave shacks with small courtyards and small, carefully tended gardens; onions, spuds, eggplants, pumpkins, and superbly tasty mushrooms grow in them to perfection.

In the Land of the Moon, Unyamwezi is the community beyond

View of Jihoue-la-Mkoa

compare, Africa's garden spot, fertile and magnificent; the district of Unyanembé lies in its center, a delectable area where a few Omani families lead lazy lives, being authentic pureblood Arabs.

For years they have done business in Africa's interior and Arabia; they have dealt in gum, ivory, print fabrics, and slaves; their caravans have crisscrossed these equatorial regions; in addition their convoys visit the coast in search of luxuries and playthings for these wealthy merchants, and the latter lounge in the midst of their wives and servants, leading the least agitated and most horizontal of existences in this delightful district, always reclining, laughing, smoking, or dozing off.

Around these clearings are many native huts, huge enclosures for marketplaces, fields of *cannabis* and moonflower, lovely trees and cooling shade—there you have Kazeh.

This is the general meeting place for caravans: those from the south with their slaves and shipments of ivory; those from the west that export cotton and glass beads to tribes around the great inland lakes.

And perpetual pandemonium reigns in the marketplaces, an indescribable ruckus that mingles the yelling of half-breed carriers, the playing of drums and cornets, the neighing of mules, the braying of donkeys, the singing of women, the squealing of children, and the shaking of wooden rattles by *jemadars*,* who give the beat for this pastoral symphony.

Spread out there in no particular order—and even in delightful disorder—are gaudy fabrics, beadwork, ivory tusks, rhinoceros horns, shark teeth, honey, tobacco, and cotton; and there the oddest bargains are struck, where the asking price of each article is based on how badly the buyer wants it.

All at once this pandemonium, running around, and noisemaking abruptly died out. The *Victoria* had just appeared in the sky; she soared majestically overhead and dropped straight down little by little. Men, women, children, slaves, merchants, Arabs, and Negroes all slithered across the *tembés*[1] and vanished into their shanties.

"My dear Samuel," Kennedy said, "if we keep having this kind of effect, it'll be hard doing business with these people."

"But simple doing some funny business," Joe said. "We could quietly

* Caravan leaders.

disembark, then walk off with the most valuable merchandise without bothering about the merchants. We'd be rich."

"Steady there!" the doctor remarked. "These natives were frightened to begin with. But their curiosity or their superstitious beliefs will win out, and they'll soon be back."

"You think so, master?"

"We'll see; but it wouldn't be wise to get too close to them, since the *Victoria* isn't covered with armor plate or chain mail; so she's not immune to bullets or arrows."

"So, my dear Samuel, you're figuring to enter into negotiations with these Africans?"

"If it's possible, why not?" the doctor responded. "There must be Arab merchants in Kazeh who are less barbaric and better educated. I recall that Messrs. Burton and Speke had nothing but praise for the hospitality of the townspeople. Therefore it's a risk we can run."

As the *Victoria* inched closer to the ground, one of her anchors latched onto a treetop near the marketplace.

Just then the whole populace reemerged from where they were holed up; heads peeked out cautiously. Identifiable from their regalia of conical seashells, several *wagangas*[2] strode boldly forward; they were the local witch doctors. From their belts dangled little black gourds coated with grease, plus various magical props that were grimy from long professional use.

Little by little the crowd moved in the travelers' direction, women and children circling below them, drums competing in clamor, hands colliding and then reaching for the sky.

"They're pleading," Dr. Fergusson said. "That's how they go about it; and if I'm not mistaken, they'll call on us to play a major role."

"Fine, sir, play it!"

"You too, my gallant Joe—maybe they'll turn you into a god."

"Oh, that wouldn't bother me, sir. I don't mind incense."

Just then one of the witch doctors, a Myangan,[3] gestured for silence, and all the hubbub died down into utter stillness. He spoke a few words to the travelers, but in a language they didn't know.

Not understanding him, Dr. Fergusson took a chance, threw out a few words of Arabic, and got an immediate answer in that language.

The speaker delivered a long-winded, flowery address to his tolerant audience; the doctor soon realized they had quite simply mistaken the *Victoria* for the moon herself; they thought that good-hearted goddess had deigned to drop in on their town along with her three sons— a never-to-be-forgotten honor in that land so loved by Old Sol.

With great dignity the doctor replied that the moon toured the provinces every thousand years, feeling a need for closer contact with her devotees; so he urged them to breathe easy and take advantage of her divine presence by making their wants and needs known.

The witch doctor answered in his turn that the sultan, the *mwani*, had been sick for many years and had begged the heavens for help; he invited the son of the moon to come see him.

The doctor reported this invitation to his companions.

"And you're going to see this Negro king?" the hunter said.

"Certainly. These people seem well disposed toward us; the sky's calm; there isn't a puff of wind! No need to worry about the *Victoria*."

"But what are you going to do?"

"Don't be concerned, my dear Dick; with a little medicine I'll see it through."

Then, speaking to the crowd:

"The moon feels compassion for this sovereign so dear to the children of Unyamwezi, and she has entrusted us with healing him. Have him prepare to welcome us!"

The hubbub, singing, and outbursts grew louder, and that huge anthill of black noggins started off again.

"Now, my friends," Dr. Fergusson said, "we need to be ready for anything; we might have to leave in a hurry at any given moment. So Dick will stay in the gondola and maintain adequate lifting power with the burner. The anchor is firmly secured; there's nothing to fear. I'll climb down to the ground. Joe will disembark with me; except he'll remain at the foot of the ladder."

"What! You're going to that rascal's lair by yourself?" Kennedy said.

"What!" Joe exclaimed. "You don't want me sticking with you, Mr. Samuel?"

"No, I'll go alone; these good people imagine that their great moon goddess has come to visit them, hence their superstitious beliefs will protect me; so don't worry, and both of you stay at the posts I've assigned you."

"Fine, have it your way," the hunter replied.

"See that the gas keeps expanding."

"Right."

The natives were shouting with greater intensity; they were vehemently demanding that the heavens intervene.

"Tsk, tsk," Joe commented. "I think they're a little bossy with their kindly moon and her divine sons."

Equipped with his portable medicine chest, the doctor disembarked, Joe climbing down first. The lad was as solemn and dignified as you could want, sitting at the foot of the ladder, crossing his legs under him in good Arab fashion, while part of the crowd formed a respectful circle around him.

Meanwhile, guided by the sounds of instruments, escorted by ritual war dances, Dr. Fergusson headed slowly toward the royal *tembé*, located some distance outside the town; the time was about three o'clock, and the sun shone resplendently, which was the least it could do on such an occasion.

The doctor walked with dignity; the *wagangas* surrounded him and took care of crowd control. Soon Fergusson was joined by the sultan's bastard son, a rather good-looking lad who, in line with local custom, would inherit all of his father's goods, to the exclusion of the legitimate children; he fell prostrate before the son of the moon; the latter graciously motioned him back up.

Going down shady lanes, surrounded by every luxuriant form of tropical vegetation, that fired-up procession arrived forty-five minutes later at the sultan's palace, a squarish edifice called *Ititénya* and located on a hillside. Formed by a thatched roof, a sort of veranda dominated its exterior, supported by wooden posts that had some pretensions to being carved. Drawn with reddish clay, long streaks decorated the walls and tried to reproduce the figures of men and snakes—the latter with more success than the former, naturally. The roof over this dwelling didn't rest right on the walls, and air could circulate freely; otherwise no windows, and barely a door.

Dr. Fergusson was welcomed with great ceremony by the guards and the sultan's favorites, men of fine Nyamwezi stock, the most characteristic of central Africa's people, strong, sturdy, well put together, sound in mind and body. Divided into a large number of little tresses,

their hair fell over their shoulders; their cheeks were striped with blue or black incisions from temples to mouth. Their earlobes were fearfully stretched, hung with wooden disks and shards of gum copal;[4] they were dressed in brilliantly painted fabrics; the soldiers wielded hardwood lances, longbows, barbed arrows poisoned with spurge sap, cutlasses, long saw-edged sabers called *simes*, and small battle-axes.

The doctor went inside the palace. There, despite the sultan's illness, the uproar increased when he arrived, although it was already horrendous. He noted some rabbit tails and zebra manes dangling from the lintel of the door as if they were amulets. His majesty's entire harem welcomed him to the mellifluous harmonies of the *upatu*—a sort of cymbal made from the bottom of a copper pot—and to the banging of a *kilindo*, a drum five feet tall, carved from a tree trunk, and which two virtuosos were working over with smacks of the fist.

Most of the sultan's wives seemed quite pretty, laughing as they smoked tobacco and weed in big black pipes; they looked very shapely under their long, gracefully draped gowns, and they wore a kind of "kilt" made from calabash fibers and fastened around their waists.

Six among them weren't any less merry than the rest, although shunted off to one side and on reserve to be cruelly sacrificed. When the sultan died, they were to be buried alive next to him, to divert him in his eternal solitude.

Taking in the whole scene at a glance, Dr. Fergusson walked up to the sovereign's wooden bed. There Samuel saw a man of around forty—he was in a total stupor from every kind of carousing, and nothing could be done for him. The illness that had hung on for so many years was simply perpetual intoxication. This regal drunk was pretty much dead to the world, and all the ammonia water in existence wouldn't straighten him out.

His wives and favorites stayed on bended knee during this solemn visit. The doctor uncorked a bottle that contained a powerfully invigorating stimulant, and with a few drops he momentarily revived the stupefied hulk; the sultan stirred, and given a carcass that had shown no other signs of life for some hours, this development led to louder shouting in the physician's honor.

Samuel had seen enough, quickly sidestepped his gushing admirers, and left the palace. He headed for the *Victoria*. It was six o'clock in the evening.

During his absence Joe waited serenely at the foot of the ladder; the crowds paid him the highest homage. Like a true son of the moon, he let them. For a divinity he acted like a pretty regular bloke, not stuck up, even sociable with the young African girls who couldn't take their eyes off him. Of course he got into chummy conversations with them.

"Adore me, girls! Adore me!" he told them. "I may be the son of a goddess, but I'm still a little devil!"

They undertook to appease him by presenting him with gifts, which normally they would have dropped off at a *mzimu* (fetish hut). These consisted of barley ears and some *pombé*.[5] Joe felt obligated to sample this potent breed of beer; but although he had refined his palate on gin and whiskey, this brutal brew was too much for him. He reacted with a hideous scowl, which his audience mistook for a lighthearted grin.

And then, joining their voices in a droning chant, the girls performed a solemn dance around him.

"Aha! You're dancing," he said. Then, not to be outdone: "All right, I'll show you how we dance where *I* come from!"

And he cut loose with a jig to make your head spin, weaving, stretching, crouching, dancing on his feet, dancing on his knees, dancing on his hands, performing outlandish contortions, striking unbelievable poses, mugging outrageously, and in the process giving these townspeople the oddest notions of how deities dance on the moon.

Now then, all these Africans had the mimicking skills of monkeys, and they promptly set about imitating his faces, his leaps, his jiggles; they didn't miss a single move, they didn't forget a single expression; so it was a free-for-all, perpetual motion, chaos that words can't describe, even feebly. At the height of the festivities, Joe spotted the doctor.

Fergusson was coming back in a big hurry, in the midst of a howling, disorderly mob. The witch doctors and chieftains seemed positively manic. They surrounded the doctor; they crowded against him, they threatened him. A strange about-face! What had happened? Did the sultan bungle things and die under the care of his celestial physician?

At his post, Kennedy saw the danger but didn't understand the cause. Strongly urged by the expanding gas, the balloon strained against her mooring line, impatient to rise into the sky.

The doctor made it to the foot of the ladder. Their superstitious fears still held the crowd back and deterred any acts of violence against his person; he went swiftly up the rungs, and Joe nimbly followed.

"We haven't a second to lose," his master told him. "Don't try to unhook the anchor! We'll cut the rope! Follow me!"

"But what's wrong?" Joe asked, scrambling into the gondola.

"Did something happen?" Kennedy said, rifle in hand.

"Look," the doctor replied, pointing at the horizon.

"What?" the hunter asked.

"The moon, that's what!"

In essence the moon was rising, red and resplendent, a fiery globe in a field of pale blue! There she was! Right next to the *Victoria*!

Either the earth had two moons, or these visitors were nothing but imposters, schemers, false gods!

That's how the crowd very naturally reasoned it out. Ergo this about-face.

Joe couldn't keep back a huge roar of laughter. Realizing that their prey were giving them the slip, the people of Kazeh let out a long wailing howl; muskets and longbows took aim at the balloon.

But one of the witch doctors motioned to them. They lowered their weapons; he shinnied up the tree, intending to grab the anchor rope and pull the contraption to the ground.

Joe dashed over, hatchet in hand.

"Should I cut it?" he said.

"Wait," the doctor replied.

"But that Negro . . . ?"

"We may be able to save our anchor, and that's preferable. There will always be time to cut it."

High in the tree, the witch doctor was so efficient at breaking branches, he managed to unhook the mooring line; pulled violently upward by the ascending balloon, the anchor caught the witch doctor between the legs, and he took off into the stratosphere like a horseman straddling a hippogriff.

When the crowds below saw one of their *wagangas* shooting into space, they were filled with immense awe.

"Hooray!" Joe yelled, while the *Victoria* climbed with great speed, thanks to her lifting power.

"He's hanging on tight," Kennedy said. "A little sightseeing won't do him any harm."

"Should we let go of this Negro all at once?" Joe asked.

"Certainly not!" the doctor countered. "We'll let him down gently; and in the eyes of his fellows, I suspect, this adventure will significantly enhance his status as a magician."

"They might look on him as a god," Joe exclaimed.

The *Victoria* had made it to an altitude of about a thousand feet. The Negro clung to the rope with dreadful energy. He didn't say a word, he

just kept staring. He was a mix of terror and amazement. A mild westerly wind swept the balloon a good way out of town.

Half an hour later, finding the country deserted, the doctor cut back the flame of his burner and dropped closer to the earth. Twenty feet above the ground, the Negro made a quick decision; he jumped for it, landed on his feet, and ran off toward Kazeh; meanwhile, suddenly relieved of his weight, the *Victoria* climbed back into the sky.

chapter 16

Signs of a thunderstorm — the Land of the Moon — the future of the African continent — the doomsday machine — scenic views at sunset — flora and fauna — the thunderstorm — the zone of fire — the starry sky.

"That's what we get," Joe said, "for playing the moon's sons without her prior approval! Our satellite almost got even with us! By any chance, master, did you sully her reputation with your medicine?"

"By the way," the hunter said, "what was he like, this Sultan of Kazeh?"

"Like an old drunk with one foot in the grave," the doctor replied, "and he won't be badly missed once he's gone. But the moral of it all is that honor and glory are fleeting, so we mustn't get too attached to them."

"That's a shame," Joe remarked. "They worked for me! Being adored! Playing God at my leisure! But what do you want? When the moon arrived, she was all red, which goes to show that we'd riled her up!"

During these and other conversations in which Joe examined that glowing orb from an entirely new perspective, the sky filled with huge clouds to the north — grim, heavy clouds. A fairly brisk wind was blowing some 300 feet up, driving the *Victoria* north-northeast. Above her,

The witch doctor gets carried off.

the vault of the heavens was pale blue and unblemished, but the air had a sultry feel.

Around eight o'clock in the evening, our travelers lay in longitude 32° 40′ and latitude 4° 17′; influenced by an approaching thunderstorm, air currents drove them along at a speed of thirty-five miles per hour. Below their feet the fertile, rolling plains of Mfuto went swiftly by. It was a marvelous sight, and they marveled at it.

"We're deep in the Land of the Moon," Dr. Fergusson said, "a name it has kept from ancient times, no doubt because its people have worshipped the moon throughout history. It's truly a magnificent region, and it would be hard to find a place with lovelier plant life."

"If we had some in London, it wouldn't exactly be natural," Joe replied, "but it'd be mighty enjoyable! Why are these beautiful things limited to such backward countries?"

"And are we so sure," the doctor countered, "that this region won't become the center of the civilized world someday? Maybe future populations will move here, once all Europe is too depleted to feed her citizens."

"You think so?" Kennedy asked.

"Definitely, my dear Dick. Look at the course of human events; think about the consecutive mass migrations, and you'll reach the same conclusion I have. Asia was the first to suckle the world, true? She was in constant labor for maybe 4,000 years, she conceived, she bore fruit, and finally when stones sprang up instead of old Homer's golden crops, her children turned away from her withered and depleted bosom. Then you see them flocking to young, energetic Europe, and she nurtured them for 2,000 years. But already her fertility is on the wane; her reproductive powers are declining by the day; those new diseases that annually attack her produce, those failed harvests, those shrinking resources—they're a sure sign of deteriorating vitality, of impending depletion. Accordingly we already see hordes of people rushing to America's nourishing breasts, a source not inexhaustible but not exhausted as yet. This new continent will grow old in her turn; her virgin forests will fall under the axes of industry; her soil will weaken from meeting the excessive demands placed on it; where two crops used to flourish each year, barely one will emerge from those lands at the end of their strength. Then Africa will offer new races the treasures that have accumulated for centuries in her bosom. These climates so fatal to foreigners will be cleansed by crop rotation and soil drainage; these scattered watercourses will be combined into one common bed and will form a thoroughfare for shipping. And this country we're soaring over will become more fertile, wealthy, and vital than any other— a great kingdom that will make discoveries even more amazing than steam and electricity."

"Oh, sir," Joe said, "I'd really like to see that!"

"You entered the world too soon, my boy."

"Besides," Kennedy said, "it might be a pretty tiresome time if industry takes over the globe and runs everything for profit! After inventing machines, man will be devoured by 'em! I've always figured that doomsday will come when some huge boiler gets heated to three billion atmospheres, then blows up the planet!"

"And I'll add," Joe said, "that the first ones fooling with the contraption will have been Americans."

"Quite so, they're great boilermakers!" the doctor replied. "But without getting all caught up in these discussions, let's be content to marvel at this Land of the Moon, since it's right beneath our eyes."

Below the masses of piled-up clouds, the sun shed its last rays and draped the ground's tiniest irregularities in gold trim: gigantic timber, treelike weeds, and mosses flush with the soil all shared in this outpouring of light; the mildly rolling terrain swelled here and there into little conical hills; no mountains were on the horizon; immense brushwood barriers, impregnable hedges, and prickly jungles partitioned off the glades where the many villages were spread out; gigantic spurges erected natural fortifications around them, intermingling with the coral-shaped branches of the shrubbery.

Soon the Malagarasi River, Lake Tanganyika's chief tributary, began winding beneath the clumps of greenery; it offered sanctuary to the many watercourses arising from swollen torrents during the flood season, or from ponds gouged into the ground's clayish bedrock. For watchers on high, it was a network of waterfalls pouring over the entire western face of the country.

Livestock with big humps grazed on the lush meadows, vanishing into the tall weeds; magnificently aromatic forests pleased the eye like huge bouquets; but inside those bouquets lions, leopards, hyenas, and tigers[1] took refuge to escape the heat of the dying day. Sometimes the top of a thicket would ripple as an elephant passed underneath, and you could hear trees cracking as they gave way to its ivory tusks.

"What a country for a hunter!" Kennedy exclaimed gleefully. "If you fired a shot at random into any part of that forest, you'd hit something worthwhile! Couldn't we give it a quick try?"

"Not yet, my dear Dick; night's falling, a threatening night with a thunderstorm to keep it company. Now then, the soil in this region acts like an immense electric battery, so the thunderstorms are dreadful."

"You're right, sir," Joe said. "The heat's stifling, and there's no wind at all; you can tell something's in the works."

"The atmosphere is overloaded with electricity," the doctor replied. "Every living thing is attuned to the conditions in the air that precede a battle of the elements, and I confess I've never seen those conditions as pervasive as this."

"Well," the hunter asked, "wouldn't it be a good time to descend?"

"On the contrary, Dick, I'd rather go higher. I'm only worried about being carried off course by these crosscurrents in the air."

"You don't want to stick with the heading we've followed since we left the coast?"

"If at all possible," Fergusson replied, "I'll bear more to the north for seven or eight degrees; I'll try to go back up to the supposed latitudes of the Nile's headwaters; maybe we'll spy a few traces of Captain Speke's expedition, or even Herr von Heuglin's caravan. If my calculations are correct, we're at longitude 32° 40′, and I'd like to head straight up past the equator."

"Look at that!" Kennedy exclaimed, interrupting his companion. "Look at those blood-colored masses of flesh, those hippopotamuses wriggling out of the ponds—and those crocodiles inhaling the air so noisily!"

"They feel stifled!" Joe noted. "Ah, what a dandy way to travel, and we can truly look down on those nasty varmints! Mr. Samuel! Mr. Kennedy! Look at those packs of animals moving in tight ranks! There's a good 200 of 'em; they're wolves."

"No, Joe, they're wild dogs; a notorious breed that doesn't shrink from attacking lions. They're the most dreadful thing a traveler could encounter. They'd instantly tear him to pieces."

Hippopotamuses on the surface of a pond

"Whoops. Just don't put Joe in charge of muzzling the brutes," replied that blithe youth. "Anyhow, if that's the nature of the beast, we shouldn't hold it against 'em!"

Little by little the landscape fell silent under the thunderstorm's influence; apparently the heavier air became unfit for transmitting sound; the atmosphere seemed packed in cotton wool, swallowing up every noise like a room hung with tapestries. Falcons, gray-crowned cranes, red jays, blue jays, mockingbirds, and phoebes all vanished into the tall trees. Everything in nature pointed to an impending cataclysm.

By nine o'clock in the evening, the *Victoria* hung motionless above

Mséné, a huge gathering of villages barely standing out in the shadows; sometimes a stray beam of light reflected off a dreary patch of water, indicating regularly laid out ditches; and through a last rift in the clouds, your eyes could catch the dark, quiet shapes of palm trees, tamarinds, sycamores, and gigantic spurges.

"It's stifling!" the Scot said, inhaling the biggest lungful he could of that thin air. "We're stock-still! Should we take her down?"

"But what about the thunderstorm?" the doctor said with some uneasiness.

"If you're worried about being carried off by the wind, I don't think you have a choice."

"Maybe the storm won't burst tonight," Joe went on. "The clouds are awfully high."

"That's the very reason I'm reluctant to go above them; we'd have to climb to a great altitude, lose sight of the earth, and not know the entire night if we were moving forward or in what direction."

"Make a decision, my dear Samuel, the clock's ticking."

"It's aggravating that the wind died out," Joe continued. "It would take us far away from the thunderstorm."

"Which is regrettable, my friends, because the clouds are a danger to us; they contain countercurrents that could ensnare us in their eddies, also lightning flashes that could set us on fire. On the other hand, if we dropped anchor in some treetop, the squall could be forceful enough to slam us to the ground."

"Then what can we do?"

"We need to keep the *Victoria* in a neutral zone between the earth's perils and the sky's. We have ample water for the burner, and our 200 pounds of ballast are intact. In a pinch I can make use of them."

"We'll keep watch with you," the hunter said.

"No, my friends; put the provisions under cover and go to bed; I'll wake you if necessary."

"But we aren't in danger yet, master—wouldn't it be better if you got some rest yourself?"

"Thank you, my boy, but no—I'd rather stand watch. We aren't moving, and if our circumstances don't change, tomorrow we'll be in exactly the same place."

"Good night, sir!"

"Good night, if that's still a possibility."

Kennedy and Joe got comfortable under their blankets, and the doctor stayed by himself out in the vastness.

But the clouds were like a domed ceiling that kept inching downward, and the darkness deepened. The black vault of night closed in around the planet earth, as if bent on crushing it.

Violent, swift, incisive, a flash of lightning suddenly sliced through the gloom; the gash it made hadn't closed before a frightful thunderclap shook the heavens to their depths.

"Everybody up!" Fergusson shouted.

Aroused by the horrific racket, the two sleepers stood by for orders.

"Are we descending?" Kennedy asked.

"No, the balloon wouldn't hold up under it! Let's go higher before these clouds transform into water and the wind increases!"

And he got busy shooting the flame of his burner into the loops of the coil.

Thunderstorms in the tropics develop with as much speed as violence. A second flash of lightning ripped through the cloud bank, then twenty others instantly followed. Electric sparks streaked the sky, crackling under the heavy raindrops.

"We're too late," the doctor said. "Now we have to cross a zone of fire in a balloon filled with flammable gas!"

"So take her down! Take her down!" Kennedy kept repeating.

"We'd have about a fifty-fifty chance of being hit by lightning, and we'd quickly rip apart on some tree branch!"

"We're climbing, Mr. Samuel!"

"We need to go faster, still faster!"

During equatorial thunderstorms in this part of Africa, it isn't rare to count thirty to thirty-five flashes of lightning per minute. The sky is literally on fire, and the thunderclaps never let up.

The wind cut loose with frightful violence in that burning atmosphere; the white-hot clouds buckled under the assault; you would have sworn that the air from some immense blower was fanning those flames.

Dr. Fergusson kept his gas burner going full blast; the balloon expanded and ascended; Kennedy knelt in the center of the gondola and tied down the tent flaps. The balloon was whirling fast enough to

give you vertigo, and our travelers had to put up with nerve-wracking shakes and shivers. Big hollows took shape in the envelope of their lighter-than-air vehicle; the wind swooped down savagely, and the taffeta cracked like a gunshot under the pressure. Making a furious racket, a sort of hail crossed the skies and drummed on the *Victoria*. But she continued her upward trek; flashes of lightning scrawled fiery tangents to her circumference; she was in the heart of the blaze.

"God help us!" Dr. Fergusson said. "We're in His hands; He alone can save us. Let's be ready for any eventuality, even catching on fire; our fall may not be swift."

The doctor's voice barely carried to the ears of his companions; but they could see his calm features in the midst of crisscrossing flashes of lighting; he was watching the phosphorescent phenomena caused by St. Elmo's fire, which played along the netting of their lighter-than-air vehicle.

The *Victoria* kept whirling and twirling, but she continued to climb; after a quarter of an hour, she had gone beyond the zone of storm clouds; the extensive outpourings of electricity below her were like a huge halo of fireworks hanging from her gondola.

It was one of the most gorgeous sights nature can offer to man. Below, the thunderstorm. Above, the starry sky—serene, silent, self-contained, with the moon shedding her peaceful rays over those peevish clouds.

Dr. Fergusson checked the barometer; it gave an altitude of 12,000 feet. The time was eleven o'clock in the evening.

"The dangers are behind us, thank heaven," he said. "All we have to do is stay at this altitude."

"That was scary!" Kennedy replied.

"Oh now," Joe countered. "It added a spot of variety to our trip, and I don't mind watching a thunderstorm from a little higher up. It's a colorful sight!"

The Victoria *in the middle of a thunderstorm*

chapter 17

*The Mountains of the Moon — an ocean of greenery —
they drop anchor — elephant towing service — running
fire — death of a pachyderm — country kitchen — meal
on the grass — a night on the ground.*

On Monday the sun rose above the horizon around six o'clock in the morning; the clouds broke up, and a pleasant breeze cooled the early morning hours.

The sweet-scented earth grew visible again to the travelers' eyes. Twisting in place among the countercurrents, their balloon had barely drifted; letting his hydrogen contract, the doctor dropped down to catch a more northerly heading. He searched without success for a good while; the wind took him to the west until he sighted the famous Mountains of the Moon, which curve in a semicircle around Lake Tanganyika's lower tip; their slightly jagged offshoots stood out against the bluish horizon; they were like a natural fortification, too hard for central African explorers to climb; a few isolated pinnacles bore hints of year-round snow.

"Now we're in unexplored territory," the doctor said. "Captain Burton pushed quite far into the west, but he couldn't reach these famous mountains; he even denied they existed, although Speke vouched for them; Burton claimed they sprang from his companion's imagination; for us, my friends, no more doubts are possible."

"Will we fly over 'em?" Kennedy asked.

"No, God willing; I'm hoping to find a favorable wind that will bring me back to the equator; I'll even wait for one if need be — I'll have the *Victoria* drop anchor like ships do in contrary winds."

But it wasn't long before the doctor's expectations were fulfilled. After trying out a few different altitudes, the *Victoria* proceeded northeast at a moderate speed.

"We're moving in the right direction," he said, checking the compass, "and we're barely 200 feet in the air, highly promising conditions for scouting out these new districts; when Captain Speke left Kazeh and went on to discover Lake Victoria, he headed up a straight line that lay more to the east."

"Will we be at this a long time?" Kennedy asked.

"Maybe; our objective is to travel in the direction of the Nile's headwaters, and we have over 600 miles to cover before getting to the farthest point reached by explorers coming from the north."

"And we won't set foot on solid ground," Joe asked, "in order to stretch our legs?"

"Of course we will; besides, we'll need to go easy on our provisions, and you, my gallant Dick, will be supplying us with fresh meat on the way."

"Anytime you like, Samuel old friend."

"We'll also have to replenish our water supply. Who knows if we won't be carried off to more arid regions? So we can't be too cautious."

At noon the *Victoria* lay in longitude 29° 15′ and latitude 3° 15′. She passed over the village of Uyofu on the northernmost edge of Unyamwezi, which was abreast of Lake Victoria, invisible as yet.

The tribes closer to the equator seem a bit more civilized, although governed by absolute monarchs whose tyranny knows no bounds; the province of Karagwah constitutes their most tightly knit community.

Our three travelers made up their minds to dock at the first promising locale. They needed to call an extended halt and give their lighter-than-air vehicle a thorough going-over: the doctor cut back the burner's flame; the anchors, tossed out of the gondola, were soon skimming over the tall weeds of an immense meadow; from the air it seemed to be covered with a closely trimmed lawn, but in reality this lawn was seven or eight feet high.

Like a gigantic butterfly, the *Victoria* scarcely brushed these weeds, not even bending them back. There wasn't an obstacle in sight. It was like an ocean of greenery without a single reef.

"We could go on like this a good while," Kennedy said. "I don't see a single tree we can pull up to; I think our hunt's in trouble."

"Hold on, my dear Dick; you couldn't hunt in these weeds, they're higher than you are; we'll end up finding a more promising area."

In truth it was a delightful outing—an honest-to-goodness boat ride over this sea that was so green, so nearly transparent, and rolling so gently beneath the passing breezes. Their gondola truly lived up to its name and seemed to cleave the waves, sometimes causing flocks of splendidly colored birds to burst out of the tall weeds with a thousand merry squawks; the anchors dipped into this lake of blossoms, tracing a furrow that closed behind them like a ship's wake.

All at once the balloonists felt a sharp jolt; no doubt the anchor had bitten into some rocky crevice hidden under that gigantic lawn.

"It caught hold," Joe said.

"Good, drop the ladder!" the hunter shot back.

These words were barely out of his mouth when a shrill hooting sound echoed in the air, and the following sentences, punctuated with exclamations, burst from the lips of our three travelers:

"What was that?"

"A weird sort of hooting!"

"Good heavens! We're in motion!"

"The anchor came loose!"

"No, it's still holding," Joe said, tugging at the line.

"The rock itself is in motion!"

There was a huge amount of movement in the weeds, and soon a long sinuous shape rose above them.

"A snake!" Joe said.

"A snake!" yelled Kennedy, cocking his rifle.

"Nothing of the sort!" the doctor said. "It's the trunk of an elephant."

"An elephant, Samuel?"

And with that Kennedy sighted down the barrel of his weapon.

"Hold it, Dick, hold it!"

"No question! That animal's towing us."

"And in the right direction, Joe, the right direction."

The elephant was moving at a spanking pace; soon he got to a clearing, and there they could see all of him; he was magnificent, an animal of gigantic size, and the doctor identified him as the male of the species; he had two whitish, marvelously curving tusks that might have been eight feet in length; the anchor's flukes were stubbornly stuck between them.

Using his trunk, the beast was making vain attempts to break free of the line connecting him to the gondola.

"Giddyup, big fella!" Joe exclaimed in high delight, doing his best to spur on this unorthodox draft animal. "It's the last word in travel! Horses are out this year! We'll have an elephant if you please."

"But where's he taking us?" Kennedy asked, his rifle quivering and his fingers itching.

"He's taking us where we want to go, my dear Dick! Have a little patience!"

"Whig-a-more,[1] as Scottish farmers say!" Joe yelled cheerily. "Giddyup! Giddyup!"

The animal broke into a healthy gallop; he hurled his trunk right and left, and whenever he lunged, he gave the gondola a violent jolt. The doctor stood ready, axe in hand, to cut the line if he had to.

"But," he said, "we won't part with our anchor until the last possible moment."

This chariot race—with an elephant in the traces—lasted nearly an hour and a half; the beast didn't seem at all tired; these enormous pachyderms can manage remarkably long hauls, and they're known to cover immense distances from one day to the next—like whales, which are also big on bulk and speed.

"In fact," Joe said, "we practically *have* harpooned a whale, and whatever whalers do on their fishing expeditions, we need to get the hang of it."

But a change in the nature of the terrain forced the doctor to revise his method of propulsion.

A dense grove of camel thorn trees[2] came into view north of the meadow, roughly three miles off; the balloon now had a serious need to part company with her chauffeur.

So Kennedy was entrusted with stopping the elephant in his tracks; he sighted down the barrel of his rifle; but he wasn't in a favorable position to get at the beast, at least not in any effective way; hitting the animal's cranium, his first bullet flattened out as if it had struck sheet iron; the beast didn't seem at all bothered; but the crack of the rifle made him pick up the pace, and he had the speed of a horse at full gallop.

"Bloody hell!" Kennedy said.

"What a hardheaded brute!" Joe added.

"We'll try a couple of conical bullets in the small of the shoulder," Dick went on, carefully loading his rifle. Then he fired.

The animal let out a dreadful hooting sound and ran like nobody's business.

"Look here," said Joe, who was packing a shotgun, "I'd better give you a hand, Mr. Dick, or we'll never finish the job."

And two bullets lodged in the beast's flanks.

The elephant pulled up, raised his trunk, then resumed his high-speed course toward the grove; he shook his huge head, and blood began to cascade from his wounds.

"Let's keep up our fire, Mr. Dick."

"And keep up a running fire," the doctor added, "because we're less than forty yards from the grove!"

They squeezed off ten more rounds. The elephant gave a fearful leap; there was a cracking noise that was so loud, you would have sworn the gondola and balloon had gone completely to pieces; the jolt knocked the axe out of the doctor's hands onto the ground.

At this juncture they were in a dreadful fix; the anchor rope was securely caught, and our travelers couldn't work it free or cut it with their knives; the balloon was rapidly approaching the grove, then a bullet struck the animal in the eye just as he raised his head; he stopped, wavered; his knees buckled; his flank swung sideways to the hunter.

"Got him in the heart!" the Scot said, after firing his rifle one last time.

The elephant let out a bellow of distress and mortal agony; he straightened for an instant, trunk writhing, then he fell with all his weight onto one of his tusks, which snapped clean off. He was dead.

"He snapped off his tusk!" Kennedy wailed. "In England ivory fetches thirty-five guineas[3] for every hundred pounds!"

"That much?" Joe said, wriggling down the anchor line to the ground.

"Why are you crying over spilt milk, my dear Dick?" Dr. Fergusson replied. "Are we ivory traders? Did we come here to strike it rich?"

Joe inspected the anchor; it was solidly caught on the tusk that was still intact. Samuel and Dick leaped to the ground, while the half-deflated balloon swayed above the animal's corpse.

"What a magnificent beast!" Kennedy exclaimed. "Look at the size of him! I never saw any elephants this big in India!"

"Nothing surprising in that, my dear Dick; the world's finest elephants are in central Africa. Hunters such as Andersson and Gordon-Cumming have bagged so many down by the Cape, the creatures are migrating toward the equator, and there we'll often find them in sizable herds."

"Meanwhile," Joe replied, "I wish we could have a bite or two of this specimen! I hereby propose to serve you a sumptuous meal at the beast's expense. Mr. Kennedy can go hunting for a couple of hours, Mr. Samuel can knuckle down to inspecting the *Victoria*, and in the meantime I can do some serious cooking."

"Well thought out," the doctor replied. "Wish granted."

"As for me," the hunter said, "since Joe has deigned to offer me two free hours, I'll take 'em."

"Off you go, my friend; but no foolish heroics. Don't wander too far away."

"Relax."

And Dick plunged into the grove, carrying his shotgun.

Then Joe got busy with his kitchen duties. First he dug a hole in the earth that was two feet deep; he filled it with the dry branches covering the ground, which came from trees shouldered aside by passing elephants, whose tracks were still visible. After filling the hole, he built a two-foot pyre above it and set it aflame.

After that he went back to the elephant's carcass, lying barely sixty feet from the grove; he deftly removed the trunk, which was nearly two feet wide at the base; he selected the daintiest part of it, adding one of the animal's cushioned feet; in essence these are morsels beyond compare, like a bison's hump, a bear's paw, or a boar's head.

The flames consumed the pyre completely from the outside in, and after its coals and embers were cleared away, the hole was extremely hot; wrapped in aromatic leaves, the elephant morsels took their places inside this improvised oven under a covering of hot embers; then Joe built a second pyre over it all, and after the wood was consumed, the meat cooked to perfection.

Then Joe took the dinner out of the blaze; he arranged this mouth-watering meat over green leaves, positioning the meal in the middle of a magnificent patch of grass; he brought out crackers, brandy, and coffee, then drew some fresh, clear water from a nearby stream.

Laid out in this way, it was a feast that was pleasing to the eye—and Joe wasn't bragging when he told himself it would be even more pleasing to the taste buds.

"Travel without getting tired or running risks!" he said over and over. "Meals anytime you want! A hammock all day long! What more could you ask for? And our good Mr. Kennedy didn't want to come along!"

For his part Dr. Fergusson got on with a studious examination of his lighter-than-air vehicle. Apparently she hadn't suffered during the turmoil; the taffeta and gutta-percha had proved marvelously resilient; given the ground's current elevation, and taking the balloon's lifting

Dr. Fergusson's drawing

power into account, he was pleased to see that she held exactly the same amount of hydrogen as before; so far the envelope had remained completely watertight.

Our travelers had left Zanzibar just five days earlier; they still hadn't opened the pemmican; their stores of canned meat and crackers were ample for a long journey; so nothing needed replenishing except the water.

The pipes and coil seemed in perfect shape; thanks to their india-rubber joints, they were ready for the balloon's every shake and shiver.

His examination over, the doctor got busy organizing his notes. He made a rough but very successful sketch of the surrounding country-side, its long meadow vanishing into the forest of camel thorn trees, the balloon motionless above the elephant's monstrous body.

At the end of his two hours, Kennedy came back with a string of plump partridges and a thigh from an oryx, a type of gemsbok belonging to the most agile species of antelope. Joe took charge of preparing these additional provisions.

"Dinner is served!" he called soon after in his most dulcet tones.

And our three travelers merely had to sit down on the green grass; they gave the elephant's trunk and foot a grade of excellent; they drank to England as usual, and the savory aroma of Havana cigars wafted over this delightful district for the first time.

Kennedy did enough eating, drinking, and babbling for four people; he was feeling no pain; he solemnly proposed to his friend the doctor that they take up residence in this forest, build a hut out of foliage, and start a dynasty of Congo Crusoes.

His proposal died in committee, although Joe volunteered to play the role of Friday.

The countryside seemed so tranquil, so deserted, the doctor decided to spend the night on the ground. Joe built fires all around them, a barricade essential for keeping out wild animals; drawn by the smell of elephant meat, hyenas, cougars, and jackals were prowling the neighborhood. Kennedy had to fire his rifle several times at these overaggressive visitors; but the night ultimately ran its course without any disagreeable incidents.

chapter 18

At five o'clock the next morning, preparations for departure got under way. Using the axe he had luckily recovered, Joe cracked the elephant's tusks. Set free, the *Victoria* carried our travelers off to the northeast at a speed of eighteen miles per hour.

The doctor had carefully determined his position by taking star sights the evening before. He was at latitude 2° 40′ below the equator, i.e., 160 statute miles away; he crossed over many villages without worrying about the uproar his appearance provoked; he noted the physical layouts of these places with a cursory glance; he cleared the slopes of Mt. Rubemhé, almost as steep as summits in the Usagara system, and later in Tenga he came to the first spurs of the Karagwah chains, which, in his opinion, logically stem from the Mountains of the Moon. Even so, there's an old legend that calls these mountains the cradle of the Nile, and it isn't far from the truth, because they border Lake Victoria, supposedly the storage tank for the great river's contents.[1]

From Kafuro, the country's great mercantile district, he finally spotted that long-sought lake on the horizon, the lake Captain Speke glimpsed on August 3, 1858.

It was an emotional moment for Samuel Fergusson; he had almost completed a major stage of his exploring, and with his spyglass to his eye, he didn't miss one contour of this mysterious region, whose details looked like this:

Below him the land was generally eroded; barely a few ravines had been tilled; littered with moderately high pinnacles, the terrain flattened out closer to the lake; fields of barley took the place of rice paddies; plantain grew there for the country's wine production, also *mwani*, a wild plant that stands in for coffee. Karagwah's capital amounted to a community of some fifty circular shacks, covered with thatched roofs that were actually in bloom.

You could easily see that they were an attractive race of people, folks whose startled faces had a yellowish-brown coloring. Some incredibly overweight women lumbered around the plantations, and the doctor thoroughly amazed his companions by telling them that this highly prized obesity results from a compulsory diet of coagulated milk.

By noon the *Victoria* lay in latitude 1° 45′ south; by one o'clock the wind was driving her over the lake.

Captain Speke's name for this lake was Nyanza Victoria.* In this locality it might have been ninety miles wide; at its southern end the captain found an island group that he named the Bengal Archipelago. He scouted out the area as far as Muanza on the east coast, where he was warmly welcomed by the sultan. He conducted a topographic survey of this part of the lake, but he couldn't lay hold of a small craft to cross it or to visit Ukerewe Island; this huge, densely populated isle is governed by three sultans and at low tide changes into a mere peninsula.

The *Victoria* came at the lake farther to the north, much to the doctor's regret since he had wanted to verify its outlines lower down. Dotted with thornbushes and tangled shrubs, its shores literally vanished beneath myriads of light brown mosquitoes; surely nobody lived there or *could* live there; herds of hippopotamus were visible, wallowing in forests of reeds or scooting into the lake's whitish waters.

Viewed from the air, the *nyanza* boasted a western horizon so wide, you would have sworn this was a sea; the two shores are so far apart, they can't keep in contact; what's more, storms are both frequent and forceful, because winds run amuck in this high, uncovered basin.

The doctor had trouble staying on course; he was afraid of being swept east; but luckily a current carried him due north, and by six o'clock that evening the *Victoria* had taken up residence on a small deserted island in latitude 0° 30′ and longitude 32° 52′, twenty miles offshore.

* "Nyanza" means *lake*.

The travelers managed to hitch up to a tree, and after the wind died out toward evening, they rode quietly at anchor. Climbing down to the ground was unthinkable; here legions of mosquitoes covered it in dense clouds, as they did on the *nyanza*'s shores. Joe actually re-emerged from the tree covered with bites; but he wasn't fuming because he found this behavior perfectly natural on the mosquitoes' part.

Less sanguine, the doctor payed out all the line he could to escape those merciless insects, which rose into the air with a creepy buzzing.

The doctor put the lake's elevation at 3,750 feet above sea level, just as Captain Speke had calculated.

"So we're on an island, are we?" Joe said, scratching hard enough to dislocate his wrists.

"We could circle it in seconds," the hunter replied, "and except for those friendly insects, there isn't a living thing in sight."

"In all honesty," Dr. Fergusson replied, "the islands scattered over this lake are simply the summits of submerged hills; but we're lucky to have found shelter among them, because the lakefronts are populated by fierce tribesmen. So go to sleep, since the sky has a quiet night in store for us."

"You aren't going to do likewise, Samuel?"

"No, I wouldn't be able to shut my eyes. My thoughts would keep me wide awake. If the wind's favorable tomorrow, my friends, we'll travel due north and we might just discover the source of the Nile, a mystery that's still unsolved. We're so close to the great river's headwaters, I couldn't possibly sleep."

The doctor stood guard while Kennedy and Joe, significantly less invested in such scientific concerns, dozed off in short order.

At four o'clock on Wednesday morning, April 23, the *Victoria* weighed anchor under a grayish sky; nighttime had trouble leaving the lake's waters, which were wrapped in dense fog, but a sharp wind soon broke the mists up completely. For a few minutes the *Victoria* wavered between this and that heading, then finally proceeded due north.

Dr. Fergusson clapped his hands in delight.

"We're going the right way!" he exclaimed. "We'll have a chance to see the Nile, it's now or never! At this moment, my friends, we're crossing the equator! We're entering our own hemisphere!"

"Aha!" Joe said. "You figure the equator runs through here, master?"

"Exactly here, my gallant lad!"

"Well, with all due respect, I think we'd better drink to the occasion without wasting another second."

"A glass of grog would be appropriate!" the doctor replied with a chuckle. "You have a true grasp of what's important in this cosmos of ours."

And that's how they celebrated "crossing the line" aboard the *Victoria*.

Their balloon made excellent time. In the west you could see a low, slightly jagged coastline; to its rear, the loftier mesas of Uganda and Usoga. The wind speed increased enormously: nearly thirty miles per hour.

Violently whipped up, the *nyanza*'s waters were foaming like ocean waves. Thanks to certain ground swells that shimmied a good while after subsiding, the doctor deduced that the lake had to be extremely deep. A small craft or two were the only primitive vessels they glimpsed during this quick crossing.

"Due to its high elevation," the doctor said, "this lake is obviously nature's storage tank for rivers in the eastern part of Africa; water evaporates from its tributaries, then comes back to it as rain from the sky. This has to be the Nile's source, I'm positive of it."

"We'll see," Kennedy remarked.

The western shore drew near around nine o'clock; it looked wooded and empty. The wind picked up a little toward the east, and you could glimpse the lake's other side. It curved around to finish in an extensive obtuse angle, thereabouts of latitude 2° 40′ north. Tall mountains lifted their arid peaks at that end of the *nyanza*; but between them a deep, winding gorge provided the frothing river with a way out.

While maneuvering his lighter-than-air vehicle, Dr. Fergusson examined this country with eager eyes.

"Look!" he exclaimed. "Look, my friends! The Arabs' accounts were correct! They mentioned that Lake Victoria empties its waters into a river that flows north—this river exists, we're descending along with it, and it's moving at a speed comparable to our own! And this trickle of water running beneath our feet is surely going to merge with the waves of the Mediterranean! It's the Nile!"

"It's the Nile!" Kennedy echoed, catching Samuel Fergusson's enthusiasm.

"Long live the Nile!" Joe said, ready to wish anything a long life when he was in a good mood.

Here and there enormous rocks impeded the course of this mystifying river. The water foamed; it fashioned rapids and waterfalls, confirming the doctor's expectations. Many torrents poured out of the nearby mountains, foaming as they fell; your eye counted them by the hundreds. You saw thin, scattered threads of water well up from the ground, intersect, merge, run races, and flow together into this budding brook that becomes a river after it takes them in.

"That's clearly the Nile," the doctor repeated with assurance. "The origin of its name has fascinated scholars as much as the origin of its waters; they've tracked it back to documents in Greek, Coptic, and Sanskrit;* yet that scarcely matters, since it finally has been forced to give up the secret of its headwaters!"

"But," the hunter said, "how can we be sure this is the same river that's been explored by travelers out of the north?"

"If the wind stays favorable for another hour," Fergusson replied, "we'll have definite, conclusive, and unfailing proof."

The mountains parted, giving way to many villages, to tilled fields of sesame, Egyptian corn, and sugarcane. The tribes in these regions looked agitated, hostile; they seemed more angry than adoring; they treated travelers as foreigners, not deities. To them, tracing the Nile's headwaters was akin to grand larceny. The *Victoria* needed to keep out of range of their muskets.

"Landing here will be tricky," the Scot said.

"Ah well, that's the natives' loss," Joe remarked. "They'll miss out on the pleasure of our conversation."

"But I need to disembark," Dr. Fergusson replied, "if only for a quarter of an hour. Otherwise I can't authenticate the results of our exploring."

"So it's essential, Samuel?"

"It's essential, and we'll disembark even if we have to exchange gunfire!"

"Fine with me," Kennedy replied, patting his rifle.

"Whenever you're ready, master," Joe said, girding for battle.

"And science marches on, weapon in hand," the doctor replied. "It won't be the first time—the same thing happened in the mountains of Spain when a French scholar was measuring the earth's meridian."

"Relax, Samuel, and trust your two bodyguards."

* One Byzantine scholar thought that *Neilos*, the Greek word for Nile, had a mathematical significance. The letter N stood for 50, E for 5, I for 10, L for 30, O for 70, and S for 200—which adds up to the number of days in a year.

"Is it time, sir?"

"Not yet. We'll go higher still and get the exact lay of the land."

The hydrogen expanded, and in less than ten minutes the *Victoria* was soaring at an altitude of 2,500 feet.

From that height you could make out a hopelessly tangled network of brooks that the river took to its bed; additional ones came from the west, flowing between the many hills out in that fertile countryside.

"We're barely ninety miles from Gondokoro," the doctor said, tapping his map, "and less than five miles from the position reached by explorers out of the north. Let's drop down with caution."

The *Victoria* sank over 2,000 feet.

"Now, my friends, let's be ready for any eventuality."

"We're ready," Dick and Joe replied.

"Good!"

Soon the *Victoria* was moving along the riverbed, barely a hundred feet in the air. The Nile measured a hundred yards across at this locality, and natives were furiously milling around in the villages that lined the banks. At latitude 2° north the river turns into a ten-foot waterfall that drops straight down, consequently it isn't navigable.

"There's the very waterfall Debono mentioned!" the doctor exclaimed.

The river basin widened and was sprinkled with many islands on which Dr. Fergusson feasted his eyes; he seemed to be searching for a landmark that hadn't come in sight as yet.

Beneath the balloon, a few Negroes were drawing nearer in a small craft; Kennedy greeted them with a shotgun blast, which fell short but motivated them to head back to shore at high speed.

Joe wished them good riddance. "If I were them, I wouldn't come back for seconds! I'd be awfully leery of a monster that spits lightning bolts on demand."

But at this point Dr. Fergusson suddenly grabbed his spyglass, aiming it at an island that sat in the middle of the river.

"Four trees!" he exclaimed. "See, down there!"

Yes, four freestanding trees loomed at one end.

"It's Benga Island! It truly is!" he added.

"Well, and so?" Dick asked.

"That's where we'll disembark, God willing!"

"But there seem to be people there, Mr. Samuel!"

"Joe's right; if I'm not mistaken, about twenty natives are crowding around."

"We'll send them packing; it won't be difficult," Fergusson replied.

"Good as done," the hunter remarked.

The sun was at the zenith. The *Victoria* drew near the island.

The Negroes belonged to the Makado tribe and were letting out energetic yells. One of them wore a hat made of tree bark and he waved it in the air. Kennedy got him in his sights, fired, and the hat flew away in pieces.

There was a general rush for the exits. The natives jumped into the river and swam back across; hailstorms of bullets and cloudbursts of arrows came from both banks, although without endangering the lighter-than-air vehicle, whose anchor had bitten into a crevice in the rock. Joe slid down to the ground.

"Drop the ladder!" the doctor ordered. "Follow me, Kennedy."

"What's up?"

"We're both disembarking; I need a witness."

"Count me in."

"Joe, keep a good lookout."

"No problem, sir, I'll take care of things."

"Come along, Dick," the doctor said, stepping down onto the ground.

He led his companion to a group of rocks standing at the tip of the island; there he searched for a while, ransacking the thickets and bloodying his hands.

All at once he clutched the hunter tightly by the arm.

"Look," he said.

"Letters!" Kennedy exclaimed.

Yes, two letters were carved on the rock, standing out with perfect clarity. You could easily read:

A. D.

"A. D.!" Dr. Fergusson continued. "Andrea Debono! The traveler who got the farthest up the Nile's bed—this is practically his signature!"

"It's conclusive, Samuel old friend."

"Now you're convinced?"

"This is the Nile! We can't doubt it for a second."

The doctor took one last look at the precious initials, copying down their exact shape and size.

"And now," he said, "off to the balloon!"

"Better hurry, because some natives are fixing to come back over the river."

"It barely matters now! If the wind drives us north for a few hours, we'll make it to Gondokoro and shake hands with our countrymen!"

Ten minutes later the *Victoria* lifted off majestically, while Dr. Fergusson announced his triumph by unfurling a flag with England's coat of arms.

chapter 19

The Nile — the quivering mountain — homesickness —
the Arabs' accounts — the Nyam-Nyams — Joe talks
sense — the Victoria dodges a few bullets — Madame
Blanchard[1] — ascensions by lighter-than-air vehicles.

"What's our heading?" Kennedy asked, watching his friend check the compass.

"North-northwest."

"Bloody hell, that isn't exactly north!"

"No, Dick, and I think we'll be hard pressed to reach Gondokoro; that's disappointing, but we've finally linked the exploring parties from the east to those from the north; we have no cause for complaint."

The *Victoria* was wafting farther and farther from the Nile.

"Take one last look," the doctor said, "at this insurmountable latitude that the bravest travelers could never get beyond! Those were the same intransigent tribesmen reported by such travelers as Messrs. Petherick, Arnaud, Miani, and young Monsieur Lejean, who've left us the best work on the upper Nile."

"Does this mean," Kennedy asked, "that our discoveries match up with the scientific theories?"

"They match up perfectly. The headwaters of the White Nile, the *Bahr-el-Abiad*, are submerged in a lake the size of a sea; that's its birthplace; of course the imaginative arts will lose out as a result; people loved thinking of this king of rivers as heavenly in origin; the ancients referred to it as an ocean and they weren't far from believing it flowed directly from the sun! But sometimes we have to lower our expectations and abide by what science teaches us; there will always be dreamers, but there might not always be scholars."

"You can see some more waterfalls," Joe said.

"That's Makedo Falls at latitude 3° north. Nothing could correspond more closely! If only we could have followed the Nile's course for a few hours!"

"And down there ahead of us," the hunter said, "I see a mountaintop."

"That's Mt. Logwek, known to Arabs as 'the quivering mountain'; Debono visited this whole region, calling himself Latif Effendi while traveling through it. The tribes along the Nile are deadly enemies and wage genocidal war on each other. You can easily judge the perils he had to face."

By that point the wind was carrying the *Victoria* to the northwest. To dodge Mt. Logwek, they needed to find a steeper current.

"My friends," the doctor told his two companions, "this is where our African crossing truly begins. Until now we've mainly followed in the footsteps of our predecessors. From this point we'll plunge into the unknown. Courage won't be a problem for us, will it?"

"Never!" Dick and Joe exclaimed in unison.

"Then off we go, and heaven help us!"

By ten o'clock that evening, after passing over ravines, forests, and scattered villages, our travelers had reached the flanks of the quivering mountain and were skirting its gentle gradients.

On that memorable day of April 23, propelled by a brisk wind during a fifteen-hour run, they had covered a distance of more than 315 miles.[2]

But this latest part of the journey left them in a melancholy mood. Utter silence reigned in the gondola. Was Dr. Fergusson all caught up in his discoveries? Were his two companions brooding over their trip through these unknown territories? No doubt these matters were mixed in with aching memories of England and faraway friends. Only Joe seemed to have a carefree outlook, finding it perfectly natural that his homeland was somewhere else the moment he left it; as for the tight-lipped Samuel Fergusson and Dick Kennedy, he let them be.

At ten o'clock that evening, they "tethered" the *Victoria* alongside the quivering mountain,* packed in a substantial meal, then took turns sleeping and standing watch.

* Tradition has it that whenever a Muslim sets foot on the mountain, it quivers.

Next day, calmer thinking prevailed when they woke up; the weather was pleasant, and the wind was blowing the right way; breakfast, brightened by Joe in top form, ultimately restored their cheery high spirits.

They were crossing an immense region at that moment; it lies between the Mountains of the Moon and the Darfur range, an expanse as big as Europe.

"No doubt," the doctor said, "we're crossing over what's believed to be the kingdom of Usoga; geographers have maintained that a huge basin existed in the middle of Africa, an immense central lake. We'll see if this formulation bears any resemblance to reality."

"But where did that belief come from?" Kennedy asked.

"From accounts by Arabs. Those people are adroit storytellers, maybe too adroit. Reaching Kazeh or the great inland lakes, a few Arab travelers saw some slaves hailing from these central regions, questioned them about their country, slapped together the records of their various answers, and used that as the basis of their formulations. Deep down we still find a little truth there, and as you saw, they weren't mistaken about where the Nile originates."

"They were spot on," Kennedy replied.

"Those records led them to rough out some tentative maps. Accordingly I'm going to follow our course on one of them, correcting it where I need to."

"Do people live all over this region?" Joe asked.

"They do, troublesome people."

"I was afraid of that."

"These scattered tribes are lumped together under the general name of Nyam-Nyams, and this label is nothing but a nonsense word; it's supposed to sound like chewing."

"It does a perfect job," Joe said. "Nyam! Nyam!"

"My gallant Joe, if you were on the receiving end of this nonsense word, you wouldn't find things so perfect."

"What do you mean?"

"I mean these tribes are viewed as cannibals."

"That's a fact?"

"An established fact; people also claimed these natives came equipped with tails like common quadrupeds; but it soon emerged that these appendages belonged to the animal skins they were wear-ing."

"What a shame! A tail's mighty nice for chasing mosquitoes away."

"Maybe so, Joe; but these need to be relegated to the realm of tall stories, just like those dog heads that the traveler Brun-Rollet attrib-uted to certain tribes."

"Dog heads? Handy for barking and for biting people too!"

"Which, unfortunately, is what has proven true about these ferocious tribes—they're so greedy for human flesh, they hunt for it obsessively."

"All I ask," Joe said, "is that they don't obsess too much over mine."

"You do go on!" the hunter said.

"Here's how I see it, Mr. Dick. If there's ever a food shortage and I have to be eaten, I want it to benefit you and my master! But stuff those rascals' stomachs? No way, I'd die in dishonor!"

"Well, my gallant Joe," Kennedy said, "you've made it clear: we can count on you when the cupboard's bare."

"Yours to command, gentlemen."

"Joe's talking this way," the doctor remarked, "so we'll coddle him and fatten him up."

"Could be," Joe replied. "Humans are such self-centered creatures!"

In the afternoon a warm fog seeped from the soil and covered the sky; its fine spray barely let you make things out on the ground; fearful of banging into some unexpected mountaintop, the doctor accordingly called a halt around five o'clock.

The night was uneventful, but the murkiness was so intense, they had to be exceptionally vigilant.

Throughout the next morning a monsoon blew with tremendous force; the wind surged into the balloon's lower cavities; it gave a good shaking to the appendix that the inflation pipes fitted into; they had to be secured with lines, an operation in which Joe acquitted himself with great dexterity.

At the same time he verified that the balloon's throat was still her-metically sealed.

"That's doubly important to us," Dr. Fergusson said. "First, we avoid any loss of our precious gas; next, we don't leave a flammable trail around us, which might end up catching on fire."

"That wouldn't be one of our journey's highlights," Joe said.

"We'd be hurled to the ground?" Kennedy asked.

"Not hurled, no! The gas would burn quietly, and we'd descend little by little. This kind of accident happened to a French balloonist, Madame Blanchard; her balloon caught on fire while she was setting off fireworks, but she didn't fall out of the sky, and she probably wouldn't have been killed if her gondola hadn't banged into a chimney and thrown her to the ground."

"We'll hope nothing like that happens to us," the hunter said. "Till now this trip hasn't struck me as dangerous, and I don't see anything that'll keep us from reaching our destination."

"Nor do I, my dear Dick; but accidents have always been caused by the balloonist's carelessness or the faulty construction of his equipment. Even so, out of several thousand ascensions in lighter-than-air vehicles, there have been fewer than twenty fatal accidents. As a general rule it's the liftoffs and landings that present the greatest dangers. Consequently these are the moments in which we mustn't overlook any precautions."

"And now it's lunchtime," Joe said. "We'll have to settle for canned meat and coffee, till Mr. Kennedy finds some way to dish us up a decent hunk of venison."

chapter 20

The bottle from heaven — the fig-palm — the "mammoth trees" — the war tree — the team of winged steeds — two tribes battle it out — slaughter — divine intervention.

The wind turned violent and erratic. The *Victoria* truly dodged some bullets up in the sky. Sometimes tossed back to the north, sometimes to the south, she just couldn't find a steady breeze.

"We're going very fast without making much progress," Kennedy said, noting how often the magnetic needle on their compass shook and shivered.

"The *Victoria*'s moving at a speed of at least thirty miles per hour,"[1] Samuel Fergusson said. "Lean over and watch how quickly the countryside vanishes from view beneath our feet. There! That forest looks like it's rushing at us!"

"That forest has already changed into a clearing," the hunter replied.

"And the clearing into a village," Joe shot back a few seconds later. "See the faces on those Negroes—they look pretty startled!"

"Perfectly understandable," the doctor replied. "When balloons first arrived on the scene, French peasants fired at them overhead, thinking they were sky monsters; so it's acceptable for a Sudan Negro to look wide-eyed."

"Bless me!" Joe said, while the *Victoria* hugged a village, barely a hundred feet up. "By your leave, master, I'll throw 'em an empty bottle; if it arrives safe and sound, they'll worship it; if it breaks, they'll make amulets out of the pieces!"

And with that he tossed a bottle over the side; it promptly smashed to smithereens while the natives let out loud shrieks and dashed into their round huts.

A little farther along Kennedy exclaimed:

"Look at that odd tree! It's one species higher up and another down below."

"Wicked!" Joe said. "Here's a country where trees grow on top of each other."

"It's simply the trunk of a fig tree on which a little organic soil got spilled," the doctor replied. "One fine day the wind blew some palm seed over it, and this palm tree sprang up as if it were out in a field."

"A first-rate method," Joe said, "and I'll export it to England; it'll do famously in London's parks; not to mention it'll encourage orchards to be fruitful and multiply; we'll have gardens rising into the air, piggybacking on each other; folks living in garrets will love it."

Just then the *Victoria* had to climb higher and clear a forest of trees that were over 300 feet tall, a type of banyan tree as old as the hills.

"What magnificent trees!" Kennedy exclaimed. "These ancient forests are more impressive than anything I know. Feast your eyes, Samuel!"

"The height of these banyans is truly marvelous, my dear Dick; and yet they wouldn't be at all surprising in the forests of the New World."

"What! There are taller trees around?"

"Surely—among those referred to as 'mammoth trees.' Thus in California there was a cedar 450 feet tall, higher than the clock tower at the Houses of Parliament[2] and even the Great Pyramid of Egypt. It was 120 feet around at the base, and the annual rings in its wood gave its age as over 4,000 years old."

"Aw sir, there's nothing amazing in that! If you live 4,000 years, isn't it perfectly natural to be on the tall side?"

But while the doctor lectured and Joe responded, the forest had already given way to a large assemblage of shacks arranged in a circle around an open area. A solitary tree grew in the middle, and Joe exclaimed at the sight:

The cannibal tree

"Well, if those are the blossoms that one's been sprouting for 4,000 years, I'm not giving it any prizes."

And he pointed to a gigantic sycamore whose trunk vanished completely from view under heaps of human bones. The blossoms Joe spoke of were freshly decapitated human heads, which were hanging from daggers stuck in the bark.

"A cannibal tribe's war tree!" the doctor said. "Indians take scalps, Africans entire heads."

"Matter of style," Joe said.

But the village of bloody heads had already vanished below the horizon; another farther away offered a sight just as repulsive; there were half-eaten corpses, skeletons crumbling into dust, human limbs scattered here and there, all left as fodder for hyenas and jackals.

"No doubt those are the bodies of wrongdoers; as the practice is in Ethiopia, they're left in the open for wild animals, who kill them by going for the jugular, then feed on them later whenever it's convenient."

"Not much crueler than hanging 'em," the Scot said. "Just messier, that's all."

"In parts of southern Africa," the doctor went on, "they settle for locking the wrongdoer in his own shanty, along with his livestock and maybe his family; they set the shack on fire, and all of them burn together. I call that cruelty, but I agree with Kennedy that if hanging's less cruel, it's just as barbaric."

Joe, putting his superior eyesight to good use, spotted a few flocks of carnivorous birds soaring along the horizon.

"They're eagles," Kennedy exclaimed, looking them over through a spyglass. "Magnificent birds that fly as fast as we do."

"Heaven help us if they attack!" the doctor said. "From our standpoint they're more to be feared than wild animals or savage tribesmen."

"Rubbish!" the hunter replied. "We'll send 'em on their way with a shot or two."

"I'd rather not tap into your talents, my dear Dick; the taffeta composing our balloon wouldn't stand up to jabs from their beaks; luckily, I think those awesome birds are more afraid of our vehicle than attracted to it."

"Say, here's an idea," Joe said, "and they're coming to me by the dozen today; if we managed to harness a team of live eagles, we could hitch 'em to our gondola, and they'd pull us through the skies!"

"This method has been seriously proposed," the doctor replied, "but I doubt if it would be very feasible with creatures so skittish by nature."

"We'd break 'em in," Joe continued. "Instead of bits in their mouths, we'd direct 'em with blinders that can cut off their view; blind one of their eyes, they'd go right or left; blind both eyes, they'd come to a stop."

"Allow me, my gallant Joe, to prefer a favorable wind to your team of eagles; it's cheaper to feed and more dependable."

"You're allowed, master, but I'll stick with my idea."

It was noon; for some time the *Victoria* had adopted a more moderate pace; the country below her merely went by; it no longer flew.

All at once the sounds of shouting voices and whistling arrows reached our travelers' ears; they leaned over and on the open plain saw a sight that affected them strongly.

Two tribes were at war, battling relentlessly and filling the sky with clouds of arrows. Consumed with killing each other, the combatants didn't notice the *Victoria*'s arrival; some 300 of them had collided in a hopelessly tangled free-for-all; most were red with blood from their wounded foes, were wallowing in it, and presented a horrifying picture.

They paused when the balloon appeared; their howls intensified; a few arrows flew at the gondola, one coming near enough for Joe to snatch it from the air.

"Let's climb out of range!" Dr. Fergusson exclaimed. "No risk taking! That's the rule for us."

Waged with axes and hardwood lances, the slaughter continued on both sides; as soon as an enemy fighter fell to the earth, his opponent raced over to decapitate him; weaving through the crowds, women gathered the bleeding heads and piled them at both ends of the battlefield; they often squabbled over the possession of these horrid trophies.

"What a ghastly scene!" Kennedy exclaimed in deep disgust.

"Nasty fellows!" Joe said. "All they need are uniforms and they'd be like any other warriors on the planet!"

"I've a good mind to intervene in that scrap," the hunter went on, shaking his rifle.

"Absolutely not!" the doctor replied instantly. "We mustn't meddle, it isn't our affair! Do you know the rights and wrongs of it, you who'd play the role of Providence? Let's get away from this repulsive sight as quickly as possible! If our supreme commanders could look down on their fields of operation as we're doing now, maybe they'd ultimately lose their stomach for blood and conquest!"

The chieftain of one of those savage factions was remarkable for his athletic stature and Herculean strength. With one hand he plunged his spear into the tight ranks of his enemies, with the other he made huge gaps in them with a swing of his axe. At one point he threw down his blood-reddened lance, rushed at a wounded man, sliced off his arm with a single stroke, took this arm in his other hand, lifted it to his mouth, and bit into it ravenously.

"Oh, that horrible brute!" Kennedy said. "I can't take any more of this!"

And the warrior fell backward with a bullet through the forehead.

At his collapse, the deepest astonishment overcame his warriors; that supernatural assassination terrified them, meanwhile reviving the spirits of their opponents, and in a flash half the combatants had deserted the battlefield.

"Let's go higher and find a current that will sweep us away," the doctor said. "I'm nauseated by this sight."

But they didn't leave fast enough to avoid seeing the victorious tribe rush at the dead and wounded, quarrel over the still-warm flesh, and revel in it voraciously.

"Ugh!" Joe said. "Revolting!"

The *Victoria* went higher as her hydrogen expanded; the howls of that frenzied horde stayed in their ears for a few seconds; but finally, carried back to the south, they left that scene of bloodshed and cannibalism.

Then the terrain presented various irregularities, with many watercourses flowing east; no doubt they emptied into Lake Nu's tributaries or the Gazelle River, which Monsieur Guillaume Lejean has described so intriguingly.

Night fell, and the *Victoria* dropped anchor in longitude 27° and latitude 4° 20′ north, after a 150-mile trip.

chapter 21

Muffled noises from somewhere — a nocturnal attack — Kennedy and Joe up a tree — two gunshots — "Help! Help!" — daybreak — the missionary — reply in French[1] — the rescue plan.

The night was quite dark. The doctor couldn't identify the country they were in; he had hitched up to an extremely tall tree, whose blurred form he could barely make out in the gloom.

As was his custom, he took the nine o'clock watch, and Dick came to relieve him at midnight.

"Look sharp, Dick, keep a careful lookout."

"Something new afoot?"

"No, but I thought I detected some muffled noises below; I'm not too sure where the wind carried us; it can't hurt to be extra cautious."

"You might've heard some wild animals chattering."

"No, it seemed like something quite different; anyhow don't fail to wake us at the tiniest hint of trouble."

"Relax."

Listening intently a second time, the doctor didn't hear anything, threw himself down on his bedclothes, and soon fell asleep.

Heavy clouds covered the sky, but there wasn't a puff of wind stirring overhead. Held by a single anchor, the *Victoria* neither shook nor shivered.

Leaning back in the gondola to watch the burner at work, Kennedy eyed that calm darkness; he examined the horizon, and as happens with uneasy minds expecting the worst, his eyes sometimes thought they detected faint glimmers.

At one point even, he definitely thought he detected something 200 paces off; but it was just a flash, after which he didn't spot anything else.

No doubt it was one of those flickering illusions your eyes see when it's pitch black.

Kennedy shrugged it off and fell back into his aimless ruminating, then a sharp hissing sound pierced the air.

Was it some animal calling, some nocturnal bird? Did it come from human lips?

Kennedy fully understood the seriousness of the situation and he was on the verge of waking his companions; but he told himself that the men or animals were out of range in any case; so he inspected his weapons, took his night glass, and again peered out into the void.

Soon he thought he glimpsed some faint shapes creeping toward the tree below him; a moonbeam glinted like lightning between two clouds, and he clearly picked out a band of individuals stirring in the gloom.

The episode of the baboons popped back into his head; he put his hand on the doctor's shoulder.

Fergusson woke immediately.

"Hush!" Kennedy said. "Talk in a low voice."

"Something's up?"

"Yes, let's rouse Joe."

The instant Joe was awake, the hunter described what he'd seen.

"Those ruddy apes again?" Joe said.

"Possibly; but it's essential to take precautions."

"Joe and I," Kennedy said, "will climb down the ladder into the tree."

"And meanwhile," the doctor added, "I'll take steps to ensure we can lift off in a hurry."

"Good idea."

"Let's head down," Joe said.

"Use your weapons only if all else fails," the doctor said. "It does us no good to trumpet our presence in these parts."

Dick and Joe pantomimed their answers. They slid silently down into the tree, taking their places in a fork of the tough branches that gripped the anchor.

For a few minutes they listened in the foliage, silent, not moving. Then something scraped lightly against the tree bark, and Joe clutched the Scot's hand.

"Hear that?"

"Yes, it's coming closer."

"What if it's a snake? That hissing sound you picked up—"

"No! It had something human about it."

"I'll take savages any day," Joe mused. "Reptiles give me the willies."

"That noise is louder," Kennedy continued a few seconds later.

"Yes! Somebody's climbing up, getting higher."

"Watch this side, I'll take care of the other."

"Right."

The two men sat in seclusion at the top of a main branch, which grew smack in the middle of that one-member forest known as a baobab tree; the darkness was intense, deepened by the density of the foliage; but Joe leaned close to Kennedy's ear, pointed to the lower part of the tree, and said:

"Negroes!"

The natives were talking in low voices, a few words actually reaching our two travelers.

Joe sighted down his shotgun.

"Wait!" Kennedy said.

Sure enough, the savages were scaling the baobab; they were emerging on every side, slipping over the branches like reptiles, climbing slowly but surely; then their body odor gave them away, that septic grease they rubbed over themselves.

Soon two heads rose up in view of Kennedy and Joe, exactly level with the branch they occupied.

"Ready . . . fire!" Kennedy said.

The two shots echoed like thunder, dying away in the midst of agonized yells. In an instant the whole horde had vanished.

But in the midst of the shrieking, they heard a strange, unexpected, impossible shout! A human voice clearly called out these words in French:

"Help! Help!"

Astounded, Kennedy and Joe instantly climbed back into the gondola.

"Did you hear that?" the doctor said to them.

Two gunshots

"You bet! It's uncanny—somebody just yelled for help!"

"Some Frenchman in the hands of those barbaric people!"

"A traveler!"

"Maybe a missionary!"

"Poor devil!" the hunter exclaimed. "They're murdering him, they're martyring him!"

The doctor was unable to conceal his emotion.

"No doubt about it," he said, "some unfortunate Frenchman has fallen into the hands of those savages. But we won't leave without doing everything possible to rescue him. Your gunshots told him that unexpected help was near, a heaven-sent intervention. We won't disabuse that notion. Are you with me?"

"We're with you, Samuel, and we'll do anything you say."

"Then let's put our heads together, and at daybreak we'll try to save him."

"But how will we get around those wretched Negroes?" Kennedy asked.

"From the way they cleared out," the doctor said, "they obviously aren't familiar with firearms; so we need to make the most of their fears; but we must wait until daylight before taking action, and we'll form our rescue plan depending on the lay of the land."

"The poor fellow can't be far off," Joe said, "because—"

"Help! Help!" the voice called again, weaker this time.

"Those barbarians!" Joe exclaimed, all aquiver. "But what if they kill him tonight?"

"You hear, Samuel?" Kennedy continued, clutching the doctor's hand. "What if they kill him tonight?"

"It isn't likely, my friends; these savage tribes put their captives to death in broad daylight; they need sunshine!"

"What if I took advantage of the dark," the Scot said, "and snuck down to the poor fellow?"

"I'm going with you, Mr. Dick!"

"Hold on, my friends, hold on! This scheme does credit to your decency and courage; but you'd endanger us all, and you'd do even more harm to the man we're trying to rescue."

"What do you mean?" Kennedy resumed. "Those savages are scared and on the run! They won't be coming back."

"Dick, I beseech you, do as I say; I'm acting for the good of everyone; if by any chance they surprised you and captured you, it would be all over for us."

"But that poor fellow's waiting, hoping! And getting no answers! Nobody's coming to help him! He must think his senses played tricks on him, and he didn't really hear anything . . . !"

"We can reassure him," Dr. Fergusson said.

And standing up in the darkness, making a megaphone with his hands, he called out forcefully in the foreigner's language:

"Whoever you are, take heart! Three friends are looking after you!"

A dreadful howling answered him, probably to drown out the captive's reply.

"They're cutting his throat! Or they're going to!" Kennedy exclaimed. "Our intervening will just speed up his execution. We've got to do something!"

"How can we, Dick? What could we attempt in all this darkness?"

"Crikey, if it was just daylight!" Joe exclaimed.

"Oh? And what if it *were* daylight?" the doctor asked in an odd tone of voice.

"Nothing simpler, Samuel," the hunter replied. "I'd disembark and scatter the blighters with a couple of gunshots."

"How about you, Joe?" Fergusson asked.

"Me, master? I'd be cagier. I'd tip off the captive to light out in some prearranged direction."

"And how would you share that information with him?"

"I'd send him a note attached to this arrow I caught in the air—or I'd simply tell him in a loud voice, since these Negroes don't understand our languages."[2]

"Your plans aren't feasible, my friends; the hardest thing will be for that poor fellow to actually get away, assuming he manages to thwart the vigilance of his persecutors. As for you, my dear Dick, with all your daring and your playing on their fear of firearms, your scheme might just succeed; but if it came to grief, you'd be done for, and we'd have two men to rescue instead of one. No! We must get all the odds in our favor and proceed quite differently."

"But right away," the hunter countered.

"Maybe!" Samuel replied, lingering over the word.

"Does this mean, master, that you could bust up this darkness?"

"Who knows, Joe?"

"Wow! If you pull off something like that, I'll hail you as the world's brainiest man!"

The doctor kept still for a few seconds; he was mulling things over. His two companions watched him intently; they were on tenterhooks over this extraordinary situation. Soon Fergusson took the floor again:

"Here's my plan," he said. "We have 200 pounds of ballast left, since the bags we've brought are still intact. I'm assuming that this captive, a man obviously worn down by suffering, weighs as much as one of us; that will still leave us 60 pounds of ballast to drop if we need to climb in a hurry."

"So how do you intend to maneuver?" Kennedy asked.

"This way, Dick: you'll admit that if I get to the captive and drop an amount of ballast equal to his weight, I won't have changed my balloon's buoyancy in any way; but if I want to bring off a quick ascension to escape that tribe of Negroes, I'll have to use more dynamic methods than my burner; however, if I dump that leftover ballast at the needed moment, I'm sure to lift off with great speed."

"Obviously!"

"Yes, but there's one hitch; in order to descend later, I'd need to let out an amount of gas commensurate with the extra ballast I'll have dropped. Now then, our gas is a precious commodity; but we can't worry about losing it when a man's safety is at stake."

"You're right, Samuel, we must risk anything to rescue him."

"Then let's get to work and arrange these bags around the edge of the gondola, so we can dump them in one fell swoop."

"But what about this darkness?"

"It will conceal our preparations and won't be dispelled until they're complete. Take care to keep all our weapons within easy reach. It may be necessary to open fire; now then, the rifle gives us one round, the two shotguns four, the two revolvers twelve, making seventeen rounds in all, which we can squeeze off in fifteen seconds. But maybe we won't need to resort to all that noisemaking. Are you ready?"

"We're ready," Joe answered.

The bags were in place, the weapons at hand.

"Fine," the doctor continued. "Keep an eye out for anything. Joe will handle dropping the ballast, and Dick will save the captive; but don't make a move until I say so. Joe, you go first, free the anchor, and climb right back into the gondola."

Joe slid down the rope, then reappeared a few seconds later. Liberated, the *Victoria* drifted into the air, barely moving.

Meanwhile the doctor verified the presence of enough gas in the mixing tank to fuel the burner, delaying for a good while any need to fall back on the services of his Bunsen battery; he drew out—keeping them absolutely apart—the two conducting wires that functioned to break down water; then, rummaging in his travel bag, he took out two pieces of charcoal sharpened to a point, which he fastened to the tips of the two wires.

His two friends watched without comprehending but kept their mouths shut; when the doctor finished his work, he stood in the center of the gondola; he held the pieces of charcoal, one in each hand, then brought the two points close to each other.

Suddenly there was an intense, blinding glare, an unbearable glow generated between the two charcoal points; an immense shower of electric light literally shattered the darkness of the night.

"Yikes, master!" Joe yelped.

"Not a word!" the doctor said.

chapter **22**

The shower of light—the missionary—saved by a beam of light—the Lazarist priest—faint hope— medical attention—a life of self-denial—passing over a volcano.

Fergusson flashed his powerful light beam into various parts of the void and brought it to rest over a locality where shouts of fear were audible. His two companions looked eagerly in that direction.

Nearly motionless, the *Victoria* was moored over a baobab standing in the center of a clearing; among fields of sesame and sugarcane, you

could make out some fifty low, cone-shaped shanties with many tribesmen swarming around them.

A hundred feet below the balloon, a stake stood in the ground. A
human being lay at the foot of this stake, a young man no more than
thirty years old, with long black hair, half naked, emaciated, drenched
in blood, covered with wounds, head sunk onto his chest like the cru-
cified Christ. On top of his head, the hair was more closely cropped,
hinting at a tonsure now half grown out.

"A missionary! A priest!" Joe exclaimed.

"Poor devil!" the hunter replied.

"We'll rescue him, Dick!" the doctor said. "We'll rescue him!"

The crowd of Negroes saw the balloon, which looked like an enormous comet with a brilliantly glowing tail, and you can easily imagine the terror gripping them. Hearing their shouts, the captive lifted his head. His eyes lit up with sudden hope, and although he understood little of what was going on, he stretched his hands toward his unexpected rescuers.

"He's alive! He's alive!" Fergusson exclaimed. "God be praised! Those savages are in a first-class panic! We'll rescue him! Are you ready, my friends?"

"We're ready, Samuel."

"Joe, turn off the burner."

He carried out the doctor's order. Pushed quietly along by a barely noticeable breeze, the *Victoria* hovered over the captive, simultaneously inching downward as her hydrogen contracted. She continued to drift for about ten minutes, surrounded by waves of radiance. Fergusson doused the crowd with glowing rays, splashing quick, bright patches of light here and there. Under the sway of indescribable fears, the tribesmen vanished into their shanties one by one, leaving the area around the stake deserted. So the doctor had been right to rely on the phantasmagoric effect of the *Victoria* shooting sunbeams into that intense darkness.

The gondola drew near the ground. But a few bolder Negroes came back, shouting loudly, realizing their victim was about to escape. Kennedy grabbed his shotgun, but the doctor ordered him to hold his fire.

On his knees, the priest no longer had the strength to stand up, and he wasn't even tied to that stake, because his weakened condition made it unnecessary to bind him. Just as the gondola was inches from the ground, the hunter dropped his weapon, seized the priest around the body, and set him down inside the gondola, while at the same instant Joe abruptly dumped their 200 pounds of ballast.

The doctor had figured he would climb with tremendous speed; but contrary to his expectations, the balloon rose just three or four feet and stood still!

"What's holding us back?" he exclaimed, alarm in his voice.

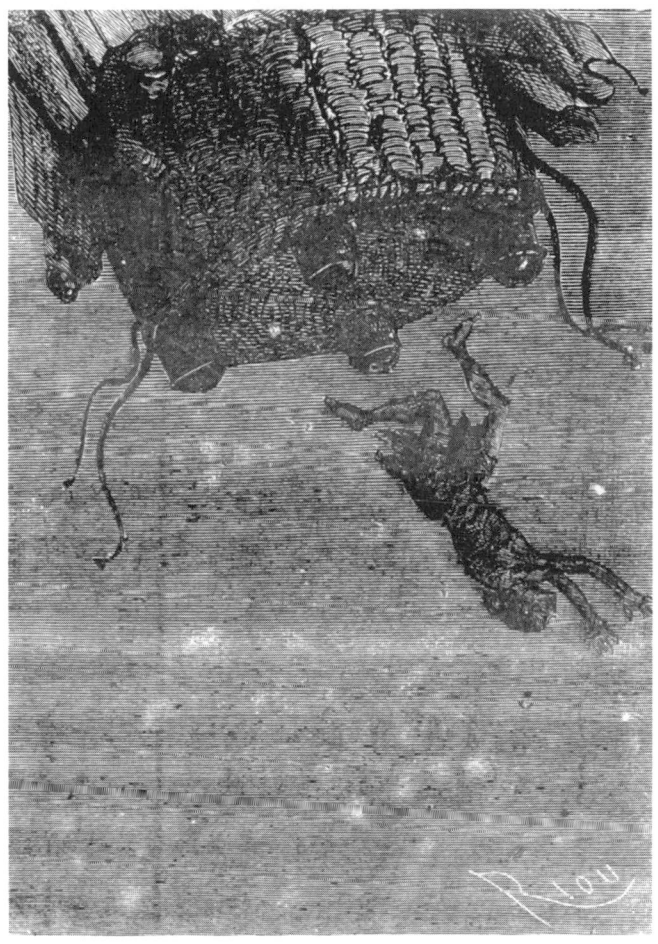

A few savages rushed up, letting out fierce yells.

"Blast!" Joe exclaimed, leaning over the side. "One of those ruddy Blacks is hanging on under the gondola!"

"Dick! Dick!" the doctor snapped. "The water tank!"

Dick read his friend's mind, lifted up a water tank that weighed more than a hundred pounds, and heaved it overboard.

Suddenly much lighter, the *Victoria* gave a 300-foot leap into the skies, the tribesmen howling as their captive escaped in a dazzling flash of light.

"Hooray!" yelled the doctor's two companions.

All at once the balloon gave another leap, which carried her over a thousand feet up.

"What happened?" Kennedy asked, almost losing his balance.

"Nothing! That ruffian just let go of us," Samuel Fergusson replied quietly.

Quickly leaning over the side, Joe could still see the savage, hands outspread, whirling in the air, soon crashing into the ground. Then the doctor drew his two electric wires apart, and the darkness was as intense as before. It was one o'clock in the morning.

The unconscious Frenchman finally opened his eyes.

"You're safe," the doctor told him.

"Safe!" he replied in English with a wistful smile. "Safe from dying a cruel death! Thank you, my brothers; yet my days are numbered, even my hours, and I haven't much longer to live!"

And the missionary, exhausted, relapsed into unconsciousness.

"He's dying!" Dick exclaimed.

"No, no," Fergusson replied, bending over him. "But he's quite weak; let's lay him under the tent."

And with gentle care they placed his poor, emaciated body on their bedclothes, a body covered with scars and still-bleeding wounds, iron and fire having left their harrowing fingerprints in twenty places. The doctor made a length of bandage out of a handkerchief, then stretched it over the wounds after bathing them; he ministered to the Frenchman adroitly, with a physician's skill; from his medicine chest he took a bottle that contained an invigorating stimulant, then poured a few drops over the priest's lips.

Feebly holding the doctor's compassionate hands,[1] the young man barely had the strength to say, "Thank you! Thank you!"

The doctor saw that he needed absolute rest; he lowered the tent flaps and went back to guiding his lighter-than-air vehicle.

Taking their new guest's weight into account, the balloon was now 180 pounds lighter; so she stayed aloft without the burner's help. At daybreak a gentle current drove her west-northwest. Fergusson spent a few seconds checking on the unconscious priest.

"He's a heaven-sent companion—we've got to save his life!" the hunter said. "Any grounds for hope?"

"Yes, Dick, with medical attention and this bracing air."

"That man has really suffered!" Joe said with feeling. "You know, he's done braver deeds down here than we have, going among those tribes all by himself!"

"No argument there," the hunter replied.

That whole day the doctor wouldn't let anybody disrupt the poor man's sleep; he was unconscious a good while but occasionally broke into anguished mutterings, which didn't fail to worry Fergusson.

Toward evening the *Victoria* came to a full stop in the midst of the gloom, and that night, while Joe and Kennedy took turns at the sick man's bedside, Fergusson watched over the safety of them all.

By next morning the *Victoria* had drifted only slightly to the west. It promised to be a magnificently clear day. The sick man was able to call his new friends in a firmer voice. They raised the tent flaps, and he happily breathed the crisp morning air.

"How do you feel?" Fergusson asked him.

"Maybe a little better," he answered. "But you, my friends, I've seen you only in a dream till now! I can scarcely grasp what has happened! Tell me who you are, so I don't forget your names in my last prayers!"

"We're English travelers," Samuel replied. "We've been attempting to cross Africa by balloon, and along the way we've had the good fortune to rescue you."

"Science has its heroes," the missionary said.

"But religion has its martyrs!" the Scot replied.

"You're a missionary?" the doctor asked.

"I'm a Lazarist priest, a member of the Congregation of the Mission. Heaven sent you to me, and heaven be praised! The life I've sacrificed is complete! But you come from Europe. Tell me about Europe, about France! Five years have gone by since I've had any news!"

"Five years by yourself, among these savages!" Kennedy exclaimed.

"They're souls needing redemption," the young priest said, "our primitive, unenlightened brothers whom only religion can educate and civilize."

Honoring the missionary's wishes, Samuel Fergusson talked at length about France.

The priest listened eagerly, and tears flowed from his eyes. The poor young man took Kennedy's and Joe's hands in turn—his own were burning with fever; the doctor fixed him a few cups of tea that he drank with pleasure; then he had the strength to sit up partway, and he smiled to see himself carried through such a clear sky!

"You're bold travelers," he said, "and you'll succeed in your courageous undertaking; you'll see your relatives again, your friends, your country, you'll—"

Then the young priest grew so much weaker, he sank back again. He lay in a state of collapse for some hours, as if near death, while Fergusson ministered to him. The doctor couldn't contain his emotion; he felt the priest's life slipping away. Would he lose the man so quickly after rescuing him from torment? He changed the bandaging on the martyr's horrible wounds, then had to sacrifice the better part of his water supply to cool the priest's burning limbs. He showered him with the gentlest, wisest care. Little by little the sick man was born anew in his arms, returning to awareness if not to activity.

Out of his broken words, the doctor pieced together his life story.

"Speak your native language," Samuel had said to him. "I understand French, and it won't be as tiring for you."

The missionary was a poor young man from the village of Arradon in central Morbihan, a department in Brittany; from early on he had a religious calling; in addition to a life of self-denial, moreover, he was willing to *risk* his life, so he joined the priestly order known as the Congregation of the Mission, whose illustrious founder was St. Vincent de Paul; at the age of twenty he left his country for the unfriendly shores of Africa. And there, overcoming obstacles, weathering hardships, traveling, and praying, he gradually made it to the heartland of the tribes who live along the tributaries of the upper Nile; for two years they rejected his religion, ignored his zeal, and looked askance at his charitable deeds; he was held captive by one of the cruelest Nyambara tribes, and they subjected him to a thousand forms of ill treatment. But he kept preaching, teaching, and praying. Run out of the region, this tribe left him for dead after one of their all-too-frequent battles with other tribes, but instead of returning in his tracks, the young man continued his evangelical pilgrimage. Sometimes people mistook him for a madman, and those were his periods of greatest peace; he was acquainted with the dialects in these regions; he tried to make converts. In sum, he roamed these barbaric lands for another two full years, driven by a superhuman, God-given strength; he lived for a year with that tribe called the Barafri, one of the most savage of the Nyam-Nyams. Their chieftain had died a few days ago, and they blamed the priest for his unexpected demise; they decided to put the Frenchman to death; his torture had already been under way for forty hours; he was to die beneath the noonday sun, as the doctor had assumed. When he heard the sound of firearms, his instincts took over: "Help! Help!" he shouted; and he thought he was dreaming when a voice from the sky offered him words of consolation.

"I don't regret," he added, "that my existence is waning—my life belongs to God!"

"Don't give up hope," the doctor answered him. "We're at your side; we'll save you from death, just as we rescued you from torment."

"I don't ask that much of heaven!" the priest replied with calm acceptance. "Blessed be the Lord for granting me the joy, before I die, of clasping friendly hands and hearing my native language."

The missionary grew weaker again. The day went by in this way, alternating between hope and fear, Kennedy deeply moved, Joe turning aside to wipe his eyes.

The *Victoria* made little headway, as if the wind tried to go easy on her precious burden.

Toward evening Joe sighted an immense glow in the west. At higher latitudes you would have sworn it was a huge aurora borealis; the sky seemed on fire. The doctor carefully examined this phenomenon.

"Maybe it's only an erupting volcano," he said.

"But the wind's carrying us over it," Kennedy insisted.

"Well, we'll clear it by a comfortable margin."

Three hours later the *Victoria* was in the midst of mountains; her exact position was longitude 24° 15′ and latitude 4° 42′; in front of her a blazing crater poured out torrents of molten lava, hurling slabs of rock to a great height; streams of liquid fire fell back in blinding cascades. It was a magnificent sight but a dangerous one, because the wind blew with unchanging constancy, carrying the balloon toward that scalding air.

It was an unavoidable obstacle, and they had to clear it; the burner was going full blast, and the *Victoria* made it to 6,000 feet, leaving more than 600 yards between herself and the volcano.

From his sickbed the dying priest could watch that fiery crater, while a thousand dazzling showers came roaring out of it.

"It's so beautiful," he said, "and God's power is infinite, even in its most terrifying manifestations!"

That outpouring of red-hot lava covered the mountainside in a genuine carpet of flame; the balloon's lower half glittered in the night; a scorching heat rose up to the gondola, and Dr. Fergusson was quick to flee from this perilous situation.

Around ten o'clock that evening, the mountain was nothing more than a red speck on the horizon, and the *Victoria* serenely continued her journey at a lower altitude.

chapter **23**

Joe's anger—the death of a righteous man—vigil
over the body—arid conditions—the burial—chunks
of quartz—Joe's delusion—precious ballast—
coordinates of the gold-bearing mountains—Joe
starts to despair.

A magnificent night spread over the earth. The priest slept in a state of peaceful collapse.

"He isn't going to recover!" Joe said. "Poor young fellow! Barely thirty years old!"

"He'll die in our arms!" the doctor said despairingly. "His breathing was already weak, and it's getting weaker still—I can't do a thing to save him!"

"Those filthy scoundrels!" Joe exclaimed, bursting into sudden

The volcano

anger as he sometimes did.[1] "And to think that worthy priest still found words to pity them, excuse them, forgive them!"

"Heaven has arranged a lovely night for him, Joe, maybe his last. He'll suffer very little from now on, and his death will be simply a peaceful sleep."

His patient spoke a few halting words; the doctor went up to him; the dying man's breathing grew labored; he asked for air; they opened the flaps all the way, and he contentedly inhaled the mild breezes of that translucent night; the stars shared their shimmering brilliance with him, and the moon enfolded him in the white shroud of her rays.

"My friends," he said in a feeble voice, "I'm going now! May God reward you and lead you to port! May He pay my debt of gratitude in my place!"

"Don't give up hope," Kennedy answered him. "Your weakened condition is just temporary. You won't die! How could anybody die on this beautiful summer night?"

"My death is at hand," the missionary went on. "I'm certain! Let me look it in the eye! Death, the beginning of things eternal, is only the ending of our earthly cares. Set me on my knees, my brothers, I beg you!"

Kennedy lifted him; it filled them with pity to see his failing limbs buckle beneath him.

"My God! My God!" exclaimed the dying cleric. "Take pity on me!"

His features were luminous. Already he seemed to live again in a new existence—far from this earth where he had never known any joys, in the heart of this night that cast its gentlest radiance over him, on the road to that heaven now lifting him and miraculously taking him in.

His last action was to bless for all time his friends of one day. And he sank back into Kennedy's arms, while great tears bathed the hunter's face.

"Dead!" the doctor said, bending over him. "Dead!"

And the three friends knelt in unison and prayed silently.

"Tomorrow morning," Fergusson said soon after, "we'll bury him in that African earth his blood has watered."

For the rest of the night, the doctor, Kennedy, and Joe took turns keeping vigil over the body, and not a word disturbed that devout silence; each man wept.

The next day the wind was southerly, and the *Victoria* floated slowly across a huge mesa in the mountains; over there, craters that were now extinct . . . over here, ravines that had never been tilled; not a drop of water was visible among these parched ridges; just piles of rocks, occasional boulders, pits of whitish shale, all pointing to an absolutely barren environment.

Around noontime, looking to bury the body, the doctor decided to drop down into a ravine surrounded by plutonic rock many ages old; the nearby mountains would shelter him and let him lower his gondola to the ground, since there were no trees that could offer him a hitching post.

But as he reminded Kennedy, he had dropped all his ballast while saving the priest, so now he could descend only if he released a commensurate amount of gas; so he opened the valve of his outer balloon. Hydrogen spurted out, and the *Victoria* settled quietly into the ravine.

The doctor shut off the valve as soon as the gondola touched down; Joe jumped out of it, one hand holding onto its rim, the other picking up a number of stones that soon replaced his weight; then he could use both hands and soon piled more than 500 pounds of stones inside the gondola; then the doctor and Kennedy could disembark in their turn. The *Victoria* was in a state of buoyancy but didn't have the lifting power to rise any higher.

Even so, there was no need to gather a large number of these stones, because the chunks Joe had picked up were tremendously heavy, which aroused Fergusson's attention for a moment. The soil was littered with quartz and crystal-filled rocks.

"What a very odd discovery," the doctor noted to himself.

Meanwhile Kennedy and Joe were a few paces off, picking a site for the grave. The ravine was boxed in like a sort of furnace, and it was tremendously hot. The noonday sun poured searing rays straight into it.

First they had to clear away the rock fragments cluttering the ground; then they dug a grave deep enough that wild animals couldn't unearth the corpse.

They reverently laid the martyr's body inside.

After throwing soil over his mortal remains, they arranged big rock fragments on top, fashioning a tombstone.

But the doctor stood still, lost in thought. He didn't hear his companions calling, and he didn't go back with them to look for shelter from the heat of the day.

"What's on your mind, Samuel?" Kennedy asked him.

"A strange natural irony, an odd quirk of fate. Do you know the kind of land that's providing the burial site for this man of self-denial, this man so poor in life?"

"Samuel, what are you going on about?" the Scot asked.

"This priest took a vow of poverty, and now he's at rest in a gold-field!"

"A goldfield!" Kennedy and Joe exclaimed.

"A goldfield," the doctor replied quietly. "These chunks you're trampling underfoot like worthless stones—they're ore of great purity."

"It can't be!" Joe said over and over.

"Search those crevices of slaty shale—you'll soon find some sizable nuggets."

Joe pounced on the scattered fragments like a madman. Kennedy came close to doing the same.

"Steady there, my gallant, Joe," his master told him.

"Easy for you to say, sir."

"Dear me! A philosophical chap like you—"

"Aw, master, this beats philosophy any day!"

"Come now, think for a minute! What good would all this wealth do us? We can't bring it along."

"Can't bring it along? Applesauce!"

"It's a little heavy for our gondola! I actually hesitated to let you in on this discovery, for fear of disappointing you."

"What!" Joe said. "Leave all this treasure behind! Our own fortune! Ours alone! Just kick it aside!"

"Be careful, my friend. Are you coming down with gold fever? Didn't that dead man you've just buried teach you what human commodities are worth?"

"Course he did," Joe replied. "But c'mon—this is gold! Mr. Kennedy, will you help me pick up a few handfuls of these riches?"

"Poor old Joe," said the hunter, who couldn't help grinning. "What'll we do with it all? We aren't here to seek our fortunes, we should just let it lie."

"They're a little heavy, these riches," the doctor resumed, "and they'll be difficult to stick in your pocket."

"But at least," Joe replied, driven to his last line of defense, "couldn't we bring some of this ore along as ballast, instead of sand?"

"All right, I'll agree to that!" Fergusson said. "But go easy on the scowling when we dump thousands of guineas overboard."

"Thousands of guineas!" Joe went on. "There's that much gold here?"

"Yes, my friend; it's a treasury where nature has been accumulating wealth for centuries; there's enough in these parts to make entire countries rich! It's the goldfields of Australia and California side by side in the same wilderness!"

"And it'll all go to waste!"

"Maybe! In any event here's what I'll do to make it up to you."

"I doubt if you can," Joe remarked, looking dejected.

"Hear me out. I'll fix the exact position of this lode, I'll give it to you, and when you get back to England, you'll share it with your fellow citizens, if you think all this gold can bring them happiness."

"Fine, master, it's plain you're in the right; I give up, there's no other way to go about it. We'll fill our gondola with this precious ore. If any ballast is left at the end of the trip, we'll come out ahead."

And Joe got to work; he went at it with a will; soon he had piled up nearly a thousand pounds of quartz fragments, which encased the gold in stony sheaths of great hardness.

The doctor watched him with a smile; as the work proceeded, he took his sights and found that these graveside deposits were in longitude 22° 23′ and latitude 4° 55′ north.

Then, taking one last look at the mound where the poor Frenchman's body lay in the earth, he went back to the gondola.

He would have set up a modest, makeshift cross over that grave, left behind in the heart of Africa's wastelands; but not a single tree was growing in the area.

"God will know where he is," he said.

Another concern just as serious ran through Fergusson's mind; he would have given a good deal of that gold to find a little water; he wanted to replace the tankful heaved overboard when they lifted off with the Negro, but it wasn't possible in these arid lands; his uneasiness didn't let up; forced to continually service his burner, he began running out of water for quenching their thirst; so he swore he wouldn't miss any opportunity to replenish his supply.

Returning to the gondola, he found it jam-packed with greedy Joe's stones; he climbed inside without saying anything, Kennedy took his usual place, and Joe followed them both, casting avaricious glances at the riches he had left in the ravine.

The doctor lit his burner; the coil warmed up, after a few minutes the hydrogen began flowing, the gas expanded, but the balloon didn't budge.

Joe watched these developments uneasily, not saying a word.

"Joe," the doctor said.

Joe didn't answer.

"Joe, do you hear me?"

Joe nodded, then played dumb.

"Kindly do me the favor," Fergusson went on, "of dumping some of that ore out on the ground."

"But sir, you let me—"

"I let you replace the ballast, that's all."

"But—"

"Would you like to stay in this desert forever?"

Joe threw a desperate look at Kennedy; but the hunter gave him a helpless shrug.

"Well, Joe?"

"Isn't your burner working?" he continued stubbornly.

"My burner is lit as you can plainly see! But the balloon won't lift off until you've lightened her a little."

Joe scratched his ear, took the smallest quartz fragment of the lot, weighed it in his hand, reweighed it, juggled it; it came in at three or four pounds; he tossed it out.

The *Victoria* didn't budge.

"Huh?" he said. "Aren't we rising yet?"

"Not yet," the doctor replied. "Pray continue."

Kennedy snickered. Joe tossed out another ten pounds or so. The balloon stayed put. Joe turned white.

"My poor boy," Fergusson said, "if I'm not mistaken, you, Dick, and I weigh about 400 pounds; so you'll need to get rid of a weight at least equal to ours, since you replaced us with that much."

"Toss out 400 pounds!" Joe exclaimed piteously.

"And something else as well so we can lift off. Come on, chin up!"

Heaving deep sighs, the worthy lad set about lightening the balloon. From time to time he stopped:

"We're rising!" he said.

"We're not rising," was the invariable reply.

"She's moving," he finally said.

"Keep at it," Fergusson repeated.

"She's rising! I'm sure she is."

"Keep going," Kennedy countered.

Then, desperately picking up one last rock, Joe dumped it out of the gondola. The *Victoria* rose about a hundred feet, and with the burner's help, she soon climbed higher than the surrounding peaks.

"Now, Joe," the doctor said, "if we manage to keep this much until our journey's end, it still means a handsome fortune for you, and you'll be rich the rest of your days!"

Joe didn't answer but stretched out sumptuously on his bed of ore.

"My dear Dick," the doctor went on, "look at the power this metal can exert over the world's most decent lad! Think of the passions, the rapacity, the crimes that could result if this goldfield became common knowledge! It's heartbreaking."

By evening the *Victoria* had gone 90 more miles to the west; at which point she was 1,400 miles from Zanzibar as the crow flies.

chapter **24**

The wind drops—outskirts of the desert—calculating the water supply—equatorial nights—Samuel Fergusson's uneasiness—their current situation—upbeat replies from Kennedy and Joe—one more night.

Hitched to a solitary and largely withered tree, the *Victoria* spent the night in perfect tranquility; the travelers could enjoy a little badly needed sleep; the excitements of the preceding days had left them with melancholy memories.

Toward morning the sky regained its warmth and sparkling clarity. The balloon rose into the air; after several fruitless attempts she met up with a current that carried her to the northwest, although not very quickly.

"We aren't making any headway," the doctor said. "If I'm not mistaken, we've accomplished half of our journey in roughly ten days; but at our present rate, we'll take months to finish it. What's even more troubling, there's a danger we'll run out of water."

"But we'll find more," Dick replied. "There's no way we won't bump into some river, brook, or pond in this huge stretch of country."

"That's all I ask."

"Could it be that Joe's cargo is slowing us down?"

Kennedy brought this up to tease the gallant lad; he had been itching to, since Joe's delusions had taken him in for an instant; but since he hadn't acted on them, he could play the critic, tongue in cheek, of course.

Joe gave him a piteous glance. But the doctor didn't answer. With deep misgivings he was thinking about the Sahara's huge, lonely expanses; there caravans travel weeks on end without finding a well for quenching their thirst. Accordingly he was keeping a very close eye on the tiniest dips in the terrain.

These measures and their recent experiences had noticeably changed the attitudes of our three travelers; they talked less; they were increasingly wrapped up in their own thoughts.

Since his eyes had plunged into that ocean of gold, our worthy Joe wasn't the same anymore; he kept still; he stared greedily at those stones piled up in the gondola—worthless today, priceless tomorrow.

What's more, this part of Africa had a worrisome appearance. Little by little it was changing into a desert. No more villages, not even a cluster of shacks. Vegetation was getting scarce. Just a few scrubs looking like heather on some Scottish moor, the beginnings of whitish sand and gray flint, a few mastic trees and thornbushes. Out in this barren environment, our globe's primitive skeleton is on view in the jagged ridges of the exposed rock. Seeing these signs of arid conditions, Dr. Fergusson got to thinking.

Apparently not one caravan had ever faced this wilderness area; it would have left visible traces of its campsites, the bleached bones of its men or animals. There wasn't a thing. And you felt that a vast realm of sand would soon overpower this desolate district.

But they couldn't turn back; it was crucial to forge ahead; the doctor asked for nothing better; he kept hoping a storm would take him out

of this country. But there wasn't a cloud in the sky! By day's end the
Victoria hadn't gone thirty miles.

If only their water wasn't running short! But three gallons[1] were
all they had left! Fergusson set one gallon aside for quenching their
thirst, which could rage unbearably in a 90° temperature;[2] that left
two gallons for the burner's needs; these could produce only 480 cubic
feet of gas; and yet the burner used up some 9 cubic feet per hour, so
they couldn't keep going for more than fifty-four hours. It was strictly
a matter of arithmetic.

"Fifty-four hours!" he told his companions. "Yet I'm bound and determined not to travel at night, for fear of missing a brook, spring, or pool, so we have just 3½ travel days left to us, and during that time we need to find water at any cost. I felt I should warn you about this serious state of affairs, my friends, because I'm saving just one gallon for us to drink, and we'll need to ration it stringently."

"We'll ration it," the hunter replied. "But it's too early to give up hope; we've got three days ahead of us, right?"

"Yes, my dear Dick."

"Well, no use crying before we're hurt, and in three days it'll be time for a decision; till then, let's be extra watchful."

At their evening meal they doled out the water meticulously; grogs featured higher dosages of brandy; but they had to be careful with this liqueur, which is more apt to increase your thirst than quench it.

During the night the gondola rested on an immense mesa that featured a sizable hollow. Its elevation was barely 800 feet above sea level. This circumstance offered the doctor a ray of hope; it reminded him of the theories by geographers that a huge expanse of water existed in central Africa. But if this lake *did* exist, he needed to get to it; and yet nothing was happening in that motionless sky.

The placid night with its starlit magnificence gave way to the unchanging day and its fierce sunlight; at the crack of dawn, the temperature turned boiling hot. At five o'clock that morning, the doctor gave the signal to set out, and for a longish time the *Victoria* stood stockstill in the leaden air.

The doctor could have escaped that blazing heat by rising into higher zones; but this called for using up a greater amount of water, which was out of the question by then. So he settled for keeping his vehicle a hundred feet off the ground; there a feeble current nudged her toward the western horizon.

Their breakfast consisted of a little dried meat and pemmican. By noon the *Victoria* had traveled barely a few miles.

"We can't go any faster," the doctor said. "We aren't in command, we take what we're given."

"Hang it all," the hunter said, "this is one of those times, my dear Samuel, when I wouldn't look down on a propeller!"

"No doubt, Dick, always assuming it doesn't need water to get going, because then we'd be in the exact same pickle; besides, nothing functional has been invented as yet. Balloons are still at the point where ships were before steam was discovered. It took six thousand years to conjure up paddlewheels and propellers; so we'll be waiting a while."

"Ruddy heat!" Joe said as he mopped his dripping brow.

"If we had more water, this heat would be of real service to us, because it causes the hydrogen in our balloon to expand; then the flame in the coil needn't burn as high! The truth is, if we weren't down to the last of our liquid, we wouldn't have to be so frugal. We lost our precious tank because of that blasted savage!"

"You aren't sorry you acted as you did, Samuel?"

"No, Dick, since we managed to snatch that poor man from a horrible death. But we certainly could use that hundred pounds of water we dumped; it guaranteed us another twelve or thirteen days of travel, definitely enough to get us across this desert."

"Isn't our trip at least half over?" Joe asked.

"In terms of distance, yes; but not in terms of time if the wind dies. Right now it's showing a tendency to give out completely."

"Come on, sir," Joe continued, "no need to complain; so far we've scraped through pretty well, and I'm not the sort to give up hope, no matter what fix I'm in. Take it from me, we'll find water."

But the ground kept sinking mile after mile; the gold-bearing mountains quit rolling and simply died away into the plain; they were the last assertions of a depleted nature. Sparse weeds replaced the lovely trees to the east; a few strips of degraded greenery still fought off the invading sand; big rocks had fallen from distant summits, were crushed in their descent, got scattered around as sharp pebbles, soon turned into coarse-grained sand, and then intangible dust.

"This is Africa as you've pictured it, Joe; I was right in telling you to be patient!"

"Well, sir," Joe remarked, "at least it's perfectly natural! Heat and sand! It'd be silly to expect anything else in a country like this. Look here," he added with a grin, "I've never had any faith in your forests and meadows; they don't add up! A bloke doesn't take the trouble to come all this way just to see an English countryside. For the first time I feel like I'm in Africa, and I don't mind sampling a little of it."

Toward evening the doctor noted that the *Victoria* hadn't gone

twenty miles during that boiling day. After the sun vanished below the horizon, which was as clean-cut as a straight line, a sultry darkness surrounded him.

The next morning was Thursday, May 1; but the days went by with discouraging monotony; each morning was like the one before; the noonday sun shed the same lavish, constant, unending rays, and the darkness at night distilled the diffuse heat that the next morning would hand off again to the next evening. The wind was now barely notice-able, more like an exhalation than a breeze, and you could foresee the time when this wind would run out of breath itself.

The doctor fought against the dreariness of these circumstances; he still had the calm and composure that come from steely courage. Spyglass in hand, he examined every corner of the horizon; he saw its last hills shrinking little by little, its last vegetation fading away; in front of him stretched the desert in all its vastness.

The responsibilities on his shoulders affected him a good deal, although he kept his feelings to himself. These two men, Dick and Joe, were both his friends—he had dragged them far away, almost solely on the grounds of friendship or duty. Was this defensible behavior? Wasn't he trying to go down forbidden ways? Wasn't his journey attempting to go beyond the bounds of the impossible? Wasn't God saving this thankless continent for the scholars of much later centuries?

As happens in times of discouragement, all these ideas mushroomed in his brain, turning into an irresistible train of thought that took Samuel to an irrational and unreasonable place. Acknowledging that he shouldn't do this to himself, he then wondered what he *should* do.[3] Wouldn't it be possible to retrace his steps? Weren't there higher currents that would take him back to less arid regions? Confident of the countries he had traveled over, he wasn't too sure about the countries to come; accordingly, prodded by his conscience, he decided to have a candid talk with his two companions; he clearly laid out the situation for them; he showed them the things that had been done and the things left to do; in a pinch they could backtrack, or at least try to; what were their views?

"My views are the same as my master's," Joe replied. "I can put up with anything he can and then some. Wherever he goes, I go."

"What about you, Kennedy?"

"My dear Samuel, I'm not a fellow who gives in to despair; nobody's more at home than I am with the dangers of this undertaking; but that doesn't mean I want to see you facing 'em. So I'm with you body and soul. The way things stand, I think we should keep at it, carry on to the finish. Anyhow I figure it's just as risky to backtrack. So follow your nose, we're behind you all the way."

"Thank you, my worthy friends," the doctor replied, genuinely touched. "I expected this kind of dedication, but I needed the encouraging words. Once again, thank you."

And the three friends shook hands heartily.

"Give me your attention," Fergusson resumed. "According to my last position fix, we're no more than 300 miles from the Gulf of Guinea; the desert can't go on indefinitely, since the coast is populated and the region explored a good way inland. If necessary we'll head for that coast, and I can't believe we won't find some oasis or well where we could replenish our water supply. But what we lack is a wind, and without one, we're stalled up here in a flat calm."

"Let's wait and see what happens," the hunter said.

During that never-ending day, they took turns examining the sky, to no avail; nothing came in sight that raised their hopes. Swelling one last time, the terrain vanished into the setting sun, whose horizontal rays stretched in long fiery lines over an immense flatland. It was the desert.

Our travelers hadn't covered even fifteen miles—yet, as they had done the day before, they used up 135 cubic feet of gas to run the burner, plus they had to sacrifice two pints of water out of eight to quench their raging thirst.

The night went by quietly, too quietly! The doctor didn't fall asleep.

chapter 25

A little philosophy—a cloud on the horizon—inside a fog bank—the surprise balloon—signals—spitting image of the Victoria—*palm trees—traces of a caravan—the well in the middle of the desert.*

The next day, same clear sky, same motionless air. The *Victoria* climbed to an altitude of 500 feet; but she made little noticeable progress into the west.

"We're in the heart of the desert," the doctor said. "Look at that vast expanse of sand! What a strange sight! What an odd quirk of nature! Why is there such extravagant vegetation elsewhere and such a barren wasteland here, yet both are in the same latitude and under the same sunlight?"

"My dear Samuel, I couldn't care less about why," Kennedy replied. "The reason doesn't worry me as much as the reality. It is what it is, and nothing else matters."

"It's helpful to be a little philosophical, my dear Dick; it can't do any harm."

"Let's philosophize, I'm all for it; we've got the time; we're barely moving. The wind hasn't the gumption to start blowing, it's dozed off."

"Not for long," Joe said. "Some cloud layers look like they're forming in the east."

"Joe's right," the doctor replied.

"Fine," Kennedy said. "Will we get our kind of cloud, with a good rain plus a good wind to splash it in our faces?"

"We'll see, Dick, we'll see."

"It's Friday though, master, and Fridays are unlucky for me."

"Well, this particular Friday I hope you'll get over being superstitious."

"I'd like to, master. Whew!" he said, daubing his face. "Heat's nice to have, especially in the winter; but no need to overdo it in the summer."

"Aren't you afraid of the hot sunlight on our balloon?" Kennedy asked the doctor.

"No, the gutta-percha that coats her taffeta can stand much higher temperatures. Using my coil, I've sometimes gotten her as hot inside as 158°,[1] but the envelope doesn't seem to have suffered."

"A cloud! An actual cloud!" Joe yelled just then, his keen eyesight rivaling any spyglass.

In essence a heavy cloud layer, now distinctly visible, was rising slowly above the horizon; it had such depth that it seemed inflated; it was an assemblage of little clouds that always kept their original shapes, from which the doctor concluded that the cluster didn't have any air currents inside.

This densely packed mass had come in sight around eight o'clock in the morning, and it wasn't until eleven o'clock that it rose as high as the sun's disk, which vanished completely behind that heavy curtain; at the same moment, the cloud's bottom layer broke free of the horizon line, which burst into full light.

"It's only one isolated cloud," the doctor said. "We mustn't put too much stock in it. Look, Dick, it's still the exact shape it was this morning."

"In short, Samuel, there won't be any rain or wind, for us at least."

"I'm afraid not, because it's staying at quite an altitude."

"Well, Samuel, how about we chase down that cloud, since it doesn't want to burst over us?"

"I don't imagine that will help a great deal," the doctor replied. "We'd use up gas and considerably more water as a result. But in our circumstances we mustn't overlook a thing; we'll go higher."

Turning his burner up all the way, the doctor shot its flame into the loops of the coil; the heat grew intense, and soon the balloon started climbing as her hydrogen expanded.

Around 1,500 feet up she came to the opaque cloud mass, then went inside a heavy fog lingering at that altitude; but she didn't find the tiniest puff of wind; this fog actually seemed free of moisture, and objects coming in contact with it barely got damp. Engulfed by that vapor, the *Victoria* may have moved forward in a more noticeable manner, but that was all she accomplished.

The doctor was gloomily verifying the modest results of this maneuver, when he heard Joe exclaim in a tone of tremendous surprise:

"Well, strike me dead!"

"What is it, Joe?"

"Master! Mr. Kennedy! This is fantastic!"

"What's going on?"

"We aren't the only ones in the sky! Somebody's up to no good! They've stolen our contraption from us!"

"Is he losing his mind?" Kennedy asked.

Joe was the picture of astonishment! He didn't move a muscle.

"Could the poor boy be suffering from sunstroke?" the doctor said, turning to him. "What are you talking about?"

"Take a look, sir," Joe said, pointing to a spot in the air.

"By St. Patrick!" Kennedy exclaimed in his turn. "It's unbelievable! Samuel, Samuel, look at this!"

"I'm looking," the doctor replied quietly.

"Another balloon! And other travelers like us!"

Sure enough, floating in the air 200 feet away, there was another

lighter-than-air vehicle, complete with gondola and travelers; she was following the exact same course as the *Victoria*.

"Well," the doctor said, "all we have to do is signal her; get the flag, Kennedy, and let's show our colors."

Apparently the travelers in that second balloon had the same idea at the same moment, because they raised the very same banner, put it through the exact same paces, and reproduced the identical greeting.

"What's the meaning of this?" the hunter asked.

"They're monkeys," Joe exclaimed. "They're mimicking us!"

"It means," Fergusson replied with a chuckle, "that you, my dear Dick, are the one sending that signal; in other words, we ourselves are the people in that second gondola, and that balloon is quite simply our own *Victoria*."

"With all due respect, master," Joe said, "you'll never convince me of such a thing."

"Climb up on the rim, Joe, wave your arms, and you'll see."

Joe did so: he saw his gestures instantly and accurately duplicated.

"It's merely that visual effect known as a mirage, nothing more," the doctor said. "A simple optical phenomenon; it's caused by the unequal densities of these layers of air, that's all."

"It's marvelous," Joe kept saying, unable to leave off and continuing to fool around with different arm movements.

"What a fetching sight!" Kennedy went on. "It's a treat to see our good old *Victoria*! Did you realize how smart she looks and how grandly she carries herself?"

"You can put it any fancy way you like," Joe remarked. "It's one for the books all right."

But it wasn't long before that image gradually faded away; the clouds deserted the *Victoria*—who didn't try to keep up—and climbed to a higher altitude, vanishing an hour later into the wild blue yonder.

The wind was barely noticeable, yet it seemed to grow even weaker. Desperate, the doctor dropped closer to the ground.

Yanked out of their worries by that incident, the travelers sank back into their gloomy thoughts, overwhelmed by the ravenous heat.

Around four o'clock Joe sighted something that stood out against

The surprise balloon

the immense sandy flatlands, and soon he could confirm that two palm trees were growing a short distance away.

"Palm trees!" Fergusson said. "But does that mean there's a spring nearby, or a well?"

He took a spyglass and made sure Joe wasn't seeing things.

"Water! Water at last!" he repeated. "And we're saved—although we're barely moving, we're still going forward, and we'll ultimately reach it!"

"Fine, master!" Joe said. "How about we drink some beforehand? The air's positively stifling."

"Let's drink some, my boy!"

Nobody had to be coaxed. They put away a whole pint, which reduced their water supply to just 3½ pints.

"Ooh, that hit the spot!" Joe said. "It went down so good! Barclay Perkins never brewed a beer that gave me more pleasure."

"That's one of the benefits of doing without," the doctor replied.

"But the others don't amount to much," the hunter said. "In exchange for never having to do without, I'll give up the pleasure any day."

By six o'clock the *Victoria* was soaring over the palm trees.

The two trees were scrawny, sickly, dried up—two ghost trees without foliage, more dead than alive. Fergusson viewed them with dismay.

Beneath their feet they made out the half-worn stonework of a well; but under the sun's fiery heat, it seemed those stones were crumbling into intangible dust. There wasn't any semblance of moisture. Samuel's heart constricted, and he was about to share his fears with his companions, when their exclamations caught his attention.

Westward as far as the eye could see, there stretched a long trail of bleached bones; fragments of skeletons surrounded the wellhead; a caravan had pushed on to this point, its progress marked by that extended boneyard; one by one its weaker members had collapsed on the sand; reaching the long-sought spring, the stronger had faced horrible deaths at the edge of it.

The travelers looked at each other and turned white.

"Let's not disembark," Kennedy said, "let's get away from this ghastly place! We won't turn up a drop of water here!"

"Not so fast, Dick, we don't want to be conscience-stricken because

we overlooked something. We can spend the night here as well as anywhere else. We'll search that well to the very bottom; there used to be
a spring; maybe something remains."

The *Victoria* touched down; Joe and Kennedy filled the gondola
with an amount of sand equaling their weight, then they disembarked.
They ran to the well and descended some steps that had nearly disinte-
grated. It looked like the spring had given out many years before. They
dug into the dry, crumbling sand, the most arid sand possible; there
wasn't a trace of any moisture.

The doctor watched them climb back to the desert above, sweating,
disheveled, covered with dust particles, beaten, discouraged, desperate.

He knew that their search had been futile; he had expected as much
and said nothing. From that day forward he felt he had to summon the
courage and strength for three.

Joe had brought back the shriveled remains of a goatskin flask,
which he angrily tossed among the bones scattered over the ground.

During supper the travelers didn't exchange a word; they forced
themselves to eat.

And yet they still hadn't endured the genuine agonies of thirst, and
they despaired for the future.

chapter **26**

---

*113° — the doctor's thoughts — a desperate search —
the burner goes out — 140°[1] — gazing at the desert — a
nighttime stroll — solitude — collapse — Joe's plans — he
gives himself one more day.*

The course that the *Victoria* had traveled the previous day didn't take
her more than ten miles, and to keep her going, they used up 162 cubic
feet of gas.

Saturday morning the doctor gave the signal to set out.

"We can run the burner for just another six hours," he said. "If we haven't discovered a well or a spring in those six hours, God only knows what will happen to us."

"Not much wind this morning, master!" Joe said. "But maybe it'll pick up," he added, seeing how dejected Fergusson felt and how badly he concealed the fact.

It was hopeless! The skies lay in the grip of a flat calm, like those stubborn doldrums that handcuff ships in the tropical seas. The heat became unbearable, and the thermometer inside the tent said it was 113° in the shade.[2]

Stretched out next to each other, Joe and Kennedy tried to forget their circumstances, if not in sleep at least in idleness. This forced inertia gave them some painful leisure time. The man most to be pitied is the one who can't tear himself away from his thoughts with chores or physical activity; but here they had nothing to watch over, nor anything to work on; they had to put up with the situation without being able to improve it.

They started to experience the cruel agonies of thirst; brandy, far from pacifying this urgent need, did the opposite and made it worse, richly deserving that nickname of "tiger's milk" given it by African natives. They had barely two pints of overheated liquid left. Each man kept a protective eye on those oh-so-precious drops, and nobody dared touch his lips to them. Two pints of water in the heart of a desert!

Deep in thought, Dr. Fergusson was wondering at this point if he had acted wisely. To keep going in the air, he had fruitlessly broken that water down—wouldn't he have been better off holding onto it? He had traveled a little way, true, but had he really accomplished anything? He had ended up short of water to get where he was—what difference would it make if his latitude were sixty miles back? If the wind finally picked up, it would blow there as well—and with even more speed if it were easterly! But Samuel's hopes spurred him on! And yet those two squandered gallons of water would have been ample for a nine-day layover in this desert! And what changes might have come about in nine days! Then again, if he had held onto that water, he might have been forced to ascend by dropping ballast, paying for it later by releasing gas in order to come back down! Yet the balloon's gas was her blood, her life!

These myriad thoughts jostled each other in his head, which he held in his hands, and for whole hours he didn't lift it again.

"We need to make one last effort!" he told himself around ten in the morning. "We need to try one last time to discover an air current that will take us away! We need to risk our last resources."

And while his companions dozed, he drastically increased the temperature of the hydrogen in his lighter-than-air vehicle; as the gas expanded, the balloon grew rounder, then climbed straight into the sun's vertical rays. From altitudes of a hundred feet to five miles, the doctor searched in vain for a puff of wind; his liftoff point stayed stubbornly beneath him; an absolute calm seemed to reign all the way to the uppermost reaches of breathable air.

Finally there was no water left for the burner; without any gas, the instrument quit running; the Bunsen battery stopped working, then the *Victoria* shrank and gently landed on the sand, at the same spot her gondola had gouged out before.

It was noon; Fergusson's sights gave longitude 19° 35′ and latitude 6° 51′, roughly 500 miles from Lake Chad, and more than 400 miles from Africa's west coast.

When he touched down, Dick and Joe shook off their lead-footed idleness.

"We've come to a stop," the Scot said.

"We had to," Samuel replied in a glum voice.

His companions understood. The ground had been continually sinking, consequently they were at sea level by then; thus the balloon remained in a perfect state of buoyancy and stayed absolutely still.

Our travelers replaced their weight with an equivalent load of sand, then they stepped onto the ground; each man was wrapped up in his thoughts, and for several hours they didn't talk. Joe fixed a supper consisting of crackers and pemmican, which they barely touched; a mouthful of steaming water topped off this dismal meal.

During the night nobody was awake, but nobody was asleep either. The heat was stifling. The next day no more than half a pint of water remained; the doctor set it aside, and they vowed they wouldn't touch it until the bitter end.

"It's stifling, the heat's getting worse!" Joe soon exclaimed. Then he checked the thermometer: "Well, that doesn't surprise me—it says 140°."[3]

"The sand's as red-hot as if it came out of an oven," the hunter replied. "And there isn't a cloud in that boiling sky! It's enough to drive you insane!"

"Let's not give in to despair," the doctor said. "At this latitude these intense heat waves are certain to be followed by storms, and they arrive with lightning speed; the sky's oppressively calm, yet it can change dramatically in less than an hour."

"But surely," Kennedy went on, "we'd get some sort of hint!"

"Well," the doctor said, "I think the barometer's showing a tendency to drop slightly."

"May heaven hear your prayers, Samuel! Because we're stuck on the ground here like a bird with broken wings."

"But the difference, my dear Dick, is that our wings are in one piece, and I have high hopes we'll put them to use again."

"Oh, for a wind!" Joe exclaimed. "Anything that'll take us to a brook or a well, then we'd have all we need; we've got enough provisions, and if we had water we could sit tight for a month without hurting! But it's a cruel fate to go thirsty."

In addition to thirst, gazing endlessly at that desert also sapped their spirits; there wasn't a bit of variety in the terrain—not a sand dune, not a pebble, caught the eye. This debilitating flatness led to that disorder known as fear of deserts.[4] That arid blue sky and that sandy yellow vastness were so placid, it was ultimately terrifying. In this blazing air the heat seemed to quiver, as it does over a white-hot fireplace; your mind grew desperate at seeing this immense stillness, at not discovering any reason why this state of things should ever come to an end, because vastness is itself a kind of eternity.

Going without water in this scorching temperature, the poor fellows consequently began to show signs of delusional behavior; their eyes were swollen, their vision blurred.

At nightfall the doctor decided to fight off this disturbing condition by taking a brisk walk; he wanted to roam that sandy plain for a few hours, not scouting around, simply walking.

"Join me," he told his companions. "Believe me, it'll be good for you."

"No way," Kennedy replied. "I couldn't take a step."

*Night in
the desert*

"I'd much rather sleep," Joe said.

"But sleeping or lounging will do you harm, my friends. So put an end to this idleness. Come on now, join me."

The doctor couldn't get a rise out of them and went off by himself into the starry translucence of the night. His first steps were painful, the steps of a man grown weak and no longer used to walking; but soon he saw that these exertions would be beneficial to him; he forged ahead for several miles into the west, and his spirits were already lifting, when he suddenly got dizzy; he thought he was leaning over a chasm; he felt

his knees buckle; that huge, lonely realm terrified him; he was a decimal point, the center dot of an infinite circumference, in other words, nothing! In that darkness the *Victoria* had vanished completely. The doctor was filled with invincible terror—he, the cool, daring traveler! He tried to return in his tracks, but without success; he called out; not even an echo answered him, and his voice plummeted into the void like a pebble into a bottomless pit! Then he collapsed onto the sand, all by himself, out in the immense stillness of the desert.

At midnight he came to in the arms of his loyal Joe; uneasy over his master's extended absence, the lad had set out on his clearly marked trail across the plain; he found the doctor unconscious.

"What happened to you, master?" he asked.

"It's nothing, my gallant Joe; a momentary weakness, that's all."

"Of course it's nothing, master; but get up again; lean on me, and let's go home to the *Victoria*."

On Joe's arm, the doctor went back the way he came.

"That wasn't smart, sir, it's no good taking risks like that. You might've been ambushed," he added with a grin. "Look here, sir, let's talk seriously."

"Go on, I'm listening!"

"We positively have to make up our minds. This situation can't drag on longer than a few more days, and if we don't get a wind, we're done for."

The doctor didn't reply.

"Well, one of us needs to go out on a limb for the good of everybody, and if I'm the one, that'd be perfectly natural!"

"What are you saying? What's your plan?"

"A very simple plan: I'll take some provisions and walk straight ahead till I arrive someplace, which I can't help doing. Meantime, if the heavens send you a favorable wind, you aren't to wait for me, you're to get going. As for me, if I reach some village, I'll make do with a few Arabic words you'll give me in writing, and I'll bring you help or you can have my hide! That's my idea, what do you say?"

"It's insane, Joe, but worthy of your gallant heart. The thing's impossible, you're not leaving us."

"Come on, sir, we've got to try something; as I said, you aren't to wait for me, so it can't hurt any—and in a pinch I might pull it off!"

"No, no, Joe! Let's not separate! That would be another woe on top of the rest. The fates have decreed that this is how things will be, and most likely they've decreed that things will be otherwise later on. Therefore let's wait and practice acceptance."

"So be it, master; but I give you fair warning: you can have one more day; I won't wait any longer than that; today's Sunday—or Monday rather, since it's one in the morning; if we aren't out of here by Tuesday, I'll give my plan a try; that's the decision I've made, and it's final."

The doctor didn't reply; before long he was back inside the gondola, taking his place next to Kennedy. The hunter was plunged in an abject silence that wouldn't be turning into sleep.

chapter **27**

Dreadful heat—delusions—the last drops of water—
night of despair—suicide attempt—a simoom—the
oasis—lion and lioness.

The doctor's first priority the next day was to check their barometer. Its mercury column registered a drop that was barely noticeable.

"Nothing!" he told himself. "Nothing!"

He got out of the gondola and sized up the weather; same heat, same blank sky, same relentless conditions.

"So should we give in to despair?" he exclaimed.

Wrapped up in his thoughts, Joe didn't say a word and chewed over his plan to go exploring.

Kennedy woke up quite ill and in a state of alarming excitability. He suffered horribly from thirst. His swollen tongue and lips could barely form a sound.

A few drops of water were still left; each man knew this, each man thought about them and felt drawn to them; but nobody dared to take a step.

These three companions, these three friends, gave each other wild-eyed stares as if they were greedy animals, a change especially visible in Kennedy; his strapping frame yielded sooner to these unbearable hardships; that whole day he was in a delirious state; he paced around, let out hoarse yells, and chewed his knuckles, all set to open his veins and drink his own blood.

"Land of thirst, eh?" he snarled. "I call it the land of despair!"

Then he sank down and passed out completely; all you could hear was the breath whistling between his parched lips.

Toward evening Joe started to go insane in his turn; that huge plot of sand looked to him like an immense pond with limpid, sparkling waves; more than once he took a dive into the scorched earth trying to drink it, then got up with his mouth full of dust.

"Bugger!" he yelled in fury. "It's salt water!"

Then, while Fergusson and Kennedy were still stretched out and not moving, he was gripped by the irresistible desire to drink up those last few drops of water they had been saving. It proved too powerful for him; dragging himself on his knees, he approached the gondola, his eyes never left the bottle where that liquid was simmering, he focused on it with outrageous intensity, he grabbed it and lifted it to his lips.

Just then these words burst out in a heartrending voice: "Water! Water!"

Kennedy had dragged himself up beside him; the poor man was pathetic, he was begging on his knees, he was weeping.

Weeping in his turn, Joe handed him the bottle, and Kennedy drained every drop of its contents.

"Thank you," he rasped.

But Joe didn't hear him; he had collapsed on the sand as well.

As for what went on during that frightful night, none of them knew. But on Tuesday morning, under that firestorm pouring from the sun, the poor fellows felt their limbs withering little by little. When Joe tried to stand, it was impossible for him; he couldn't carry out his plan.

He looked around him. In the gondola the doctor stared with lunatic intensity at some imaginary point in space, downcast, arms folded over his chest. Kennedy was frightening to see; he swung his head from right to left like a wild animal in a cage.

All at once the hunter's eyes darted to his rifle, its butt jutting past the edge of the gondola.

"Hah!" he exclaimed, getting up with a superhuman effort.

He pounced on the weapon, distraught, insane, and he pointed the barrel toward his mouth.

"Sir! Sir!" Joe yelled, pouncing back.

"Let go of me! Get away!" the Scot said, gasping.

The two men struggled furiously.

"Get away, or I'll kill you!" Kennedy said again.

But Joe clung to him tenaciously; they thrashed around this way for nearly a minute, the doctor not seeming to notice; in their struggles the rifle suddenly went off; at the sound of the shot, the doctor stood erect like a ghost; he looked around him.

But all at once his eyes lit up, his hand pointed to the horizon, and in a voice that had nothing human left in it, he croaked:

"There! There! Over there!"

His gesture had such force that Kennedy and Joe broke apart, then both of them looked.

The plain was as agitated as a raging sea on a stormy day; waves of sand were rolling over each other in the intense dust; an immense column came whirling out of the southeast with tremendous speed; the sun vanished behind a dense cloud whose outrageously long shadow reached as far as the *Victoria*; the fine-grained sand glided past with the ease of liquid molecules, and that rising tide was coming closer little by little.

A powerful look of hope gleamed in Fergusson's eyes.

"A simoom!"[1] he exclaimed.

"A simoom!" Joe echoed, not sure what this was about.

"Bully!" Kennedy exclaimed with the fury of despair. "We're going to die!"

"Bully indeed!" the doctor countered. "Because, on the contrary, we're going to live!"

He quickly started throwing out the sand that helped ballast the gondola.

His companions finally understood, climbed in, and went to his side.

"And now, Joe," the doctor said, "dump about fifty pounds of your ore!"

Joe didn't hesitate, although he felt something like a twinge of regret. The balloon lifted off.

"Just in time," the doctor exclaimed.

In fact the simoom had arrived with lightning speed. In another instant the *Victoria* would have been crushed, smashed to pieces, demolished. That immense whirlwind was almost on top of her; she vanished under a hailstorm of sand.

"Drop more ballast!" the doctor shouted to Joe.

"Out it goes," the lad replied, ditching an enormous piece of quartz.

The *Victoria* climbed swiftly above the whirlwind; but she got caught up in those immense exchanges of air, and they carried her over that foaming sea with incalculable speed.

Samuel, Dick, and Joe didn't speak; they looked, they hoped, they were actually revitalized by these swirling gusts.

At three o'clock the turbulence died away; falling back to the earth, the sand formed countless dunes; the sky resumed its earlier tranquility.

Motionless again, the *Victoria* hovered in sight of an oasis, an island covered with green trees that rose above the surface of that sandy ocean.

"Water! There's water!" the doctor called.

Opening the valve on top, he immediately let some hydrogen out and made a gentle landing 200 feet from the oasis.

In four hours the travelers had covered a distance of 240 miles.[2]

Immediately replacing their weight in the gondola, Kennedy jumped to the ground, Joe at his heels.

"Your shotguns!" the doctor said. "Take your shotguns, and be careful."

Dick pounced on his rifle, and Joe grabbed one of the shotguns. They swiftly reached the trees and went under the fresh greenery, which announced the presence of generous springs; they paid no attention to the wide areas that had been trampled, the fresh tracks marking the moist soil here and there.

Suddenly they heard a roar twenty paces away.

"That's a lion roaring!" Joe said.

"Bully!" the hunter shot back, riled up. "We'll battle the brute! It gets my juices flowing to do a little battling."

"Careful, Mr. Dick, careful! Our lives depend on *your* life."

But Kennedy didn't hear him; he forged ahead, eyes glowing, rifle cocked, scary in his recklessness. Under a palm tree an enormous black-maned lion was crouching, ready to attack. The instant he saw the hunter, he sprang; but he hadn't touched the ground before a bullet got him in the heart; he dropped in his tracks.

"Hooray! Hooray!" Joe yelled.

Kennedy rushed to the well, skidded down the damp steps, lay on his face in front of a cool spring, and greedily plunged his lips into it; Joe did likewise, and all you heard were the lapping tongues of human animals quenching their thirst.

*They hear
a roar.*

"Watch out, Mr. Dick," Joe said, pausing to breathe. "Don't overdo it!"

Kennedy didn't reply but kept drinking. He dunked his head and his hands in that bounteous water; he got tipsy on it.

"What about Dr. Fergusson?" Joe said.

At these words Kennedy came to; he filled a bottle he had brought along, then dashed up the steps of the well.

You can imagine his astonishment! An enormous solid object blocked the opening. Following Dick, Joe shrank back too.

"We can't get out!"

"Rubbish! What's the meaning of . . . ?"

Dick didn't finish; a dreadful roar told him he had a new enemy to deal with.

"Another lion!" Joe exclaimed.

"Not quite, it's a lioness! Hold on, you ruddy brute," the hunter said, quickly reloading his rifle.

He fired a second later, but the animal had vanished.

"After her!" he shouted.

"No, Mr. Dick, no! Your shot didn't kill her; the body would've tumbled down here; she's outside, ready to spring on the first one of us she sees, and he'll be a dead man!"

"But what can we do? We have to get out! Samuel's waiting for us!"

"Let's lure the critter; take my shotgun and hand me your rifle."

"What's the idea?"

"Watch."

Removing his canvas jacket, Joe arranged it over the tip of the weapon and offered it as bait above the opening. The furious beast pounced on it. Waiting in the passageway, Kennedy shattered her shoulder with a single bullet. With a roar the lioness tumbled down the stair, knocking Joe over. Already the lad thought he could feel the beast's enormous paws crashing down on him, then a second discharge rang out, and Dr. Fergusson appeared in the opening, the shotgun in his hand still smoking.

Joe got nimbly to his feet, climbed over the animal's body, and handed his master the bottle of water.

Fergusson took just an instant to raise it to his lips and half empty it, then our three travelers thanked Providence from the bottoms of their hearts for saving them so miraculously.

chapter 28

Delectable evening—Joe's cuisine—disquisition on raw meat—anecdote about James Bruce—making camp—Joe's dreams—the barometer drops—the barometer rises again—preparing to set out—the hurricane.

The evening was delightful, and they spent it in the cool shade of the mimosas after a nurturing meal; they didn't skimp on the tea and grog.

Kennedy had scoured this little domain in every direction; he had beaten the bushes; our travelers were the only living creatures in this paradise on earth; stretched out on their bedclothes, they spent a peaceful night that helped them forget their past afflictions.

The next morning, May 7, the sun shone in all its radiance, but its beams couldn't pierce that heavy curtain of shade. Since he had ample provisions, the doctor decided to wait at this locality for a favorable wind.

Joe had transferred his portable kitchen to the oasis, and he tinkered around with all kinds of culinary schemes, using water with carefree extravagance.

"What a strange mix of pain and pleasure!" Kennedy exclaimed. "All these good things after such hardships! All this luxury following such misery! Gad, I nearly went insane!"

"My dear Dick," the doctor told him, "here you are, discussing life's ups and downs, but without Joe you wouldn't be here at all."

"My good friend!" Dick said, holding his hand out to Joe.

"It was nothing," the lad replied. "You'd do the same in return, Mr. Dick, though if I have my druthers, there'll never come a time when you need to!"

"What poor creatures we are," Fergusson went on, "to lose heart over so little!"

Siesta time in the oasis

"You mean over so little water, master? It's an ingredient pretty necessary to life—that must be why!"

"No question, Joe, and people with nothing to eat hold out longer than people with nothing to drink."

"I believe it; anyway, in a pinch you can eat whatever turns up, even your fellow man, though that kind of meal must upset your tummy for a spell."

"But the savages don't balk at it," Kennedy said.

"Right, because they *are* savages, so they're used to eating raw meat; which is a custom that would put me off!"

"It's off-putting enough," the doctor resumed. "In fact, nobody gave any credence to the accounts by Africa's earliest explorers; they reported that several tribes dined on raw meat, and people mostly refused to accept the fact. It was in this regard that James Bruce had a unique experience."

"Tell us about it, sir; we've got the time," Joe said, stretching out luxuriantly on the cool grass.

"Gladly. James Bruce was a Scot from the County of Stirling, and from 1768 to 1772 he combed all Ethiopia as far as Lake Tana, searching for the Nile's headwaters; then he went back to England, where his journeys didn't appear in print until 1790. His accounts met with tremendous skepticism, a skepticism that probably lies in store for our own. The customs in Ethiopia seemed so different from the habits and manners of the English that nobody was willing to believe him. Among other details, James Bruce had asserted that tribes in east Africa ate raw meat. This fact stirred up wholesale opposition. He could say anything he liked, nobody would be going there to see! Bruce was a very courageous man and a very hot-tempered one. These misgivings aroused his ire to a fever pitch. Raw meat became a running joke, and in an Edinburgh sitting room one day, a Scot brought the topic up in his presence, flatly stating that it was neither possible nor factual. Bruce said nothing; he left and came back in a few moments with a piece of raw steak sprinkled with salt and pepper in the African style. 'Sir,' he told the Scot, 'you've expressed misgivings about something I've asserted, and you've seriously insulted me; in calling it undoable, you're completely mistaken. And to prove this to the world, you're immediately going to eat this raw steak, or you'll answer to me for your words at swordpoint.' Frightened, the Scot did as he was told, although not without plenty of scowling. Then, with the greatest composure, James Bruce added: 'Even if the thing weren't factual, sir, at least you'll no longer claim it isn't possible.'"

"Good comeback," Joe said. "If that Scot got a touch of indigestion, he asked for it. And when we're back home in England, if folks express misgivings about our own journey . . ."

"Well, Joe, what would you do?"

"I'd make the skeptics eat pieces of the *Victoria* without salt and pepper!"

And the other two laughed at Joe's machinations. Then they spent the day in this kind of easygoing chitchat; along with strength, hope returned; along with hope, courage. The past faded out with miraculous speed and gave way to the future.

Joe would have been happy to stay forever in this enchanting sanctuary; it was the kingdom of his dreams; he felt at home here; he made his master give him its exact bearings, and with great solemnity he wrote in his travel diary: longitude 15° 43′ and latitude 8° 32′.

Kennedy had just one regret, the fact that he couldn't go hunting in that undersized forest; he found the setup a bit lacking in wildlife.

"But your memory's so short, my dear Dick," the doctor remarked. "What about that lion and lioness?"

"Oh, them!" he said, with the true hunter's scorn for beasts already bagged. "But anyhow their being in this oasis goes to show that we aren't very far from more fertile regions."

"Shaky proof, Dick; when those animals are driven by hunger or thirst, they often travel considerable distances; tonight we'd better stand watch more alertly and light some fires."

"In this temperature?" Joe asked. "Well, if we must, we must. But it'd really bother me to burn down this lovely grove that's come in so handy for us."

"We'll be especially careful not to let the flames spread," the doctor replied, "so that others can someday find this haven out in the desert!"

"I'll make sure, sir; but do you think folks know about this oasis?"

"Certainly. It's a rest stop for the caravans that operate in central Africa, and a visit from them could well be unpleasant for you, Joe."

"Are there still some of those awful Nyam-Nyams around?"

"Of course, because that's the general label for all of these peoples — and in the same climate, the same races are bound to have identical customs."

"Ugh!" Joe commented. "Anyhow it's perfectly natural! If savages had the same tastes as aristocrats, how could we tell 'em apart? At least, by jingo, you wouldn't have to coax these fine folks to eat the Scot's raw steak — or the Scot himself on top of it."

After this very sensible observation, Joe went to build his pyres for the night, making them as small as possible. Luckily these precautions weren't needed, and each man in his turn fell sound asleep.

The next day the weather still hadn't changed; it remained obstinately fair. The balloon stayed motionless, not a shake or shiver indicating the tiniest puff of wind.

The doctor started to feel uneasy again: if the journey were to drag on this way, they wouldn't have enough provisions. After nearly perishing from lack of water, would they now be reduced to dying of starvation?

But his confidence came back when he saw the mercury drop quite visibly in the barometer; there were clear signs of an impending change in the air; so in order to take advantage of the earliest opportunity, he decided to make preparations for setting out; he topped off the water tanks for both the burner and themselves.

After that Fergusson had to restore his vehicle's buoyancy, and Joe was obliged to jettison a substantial part of his precious ore. As his health returned, so did his ambitious notions; he scowled more than once before obeying his master, but the doctor showed him that he couldn't heft such a significant weight; he offered him a choice between water and gold; Joe quit dithering and tossed a good number of his precious rocks out on the sand.

"That's for people who'll come along after us," he said. "They'll be pretty amazed to find a fortune in a place like this."

"Huh?" Kennedy said. "What if some traveling scientist runs across these specimens?"

"Make no mistake, my dear Dick, he'll be highly surprised and he'll write about his surprise in many oversized volumes! Someday we'll hear about a wondrous deposit of gold-bearing quartz out in the African desert!"

"And it'll all be Joe's doing!"

The idea of possibly bamboozling some expert tickled the gallant lad and made him grin.

The rest of that day, the doctor waited in vain for the atmosphere to change. The temperature went up, and it would have been intolerable without the shade at the oasis. The thermometer registered 149° in the sun.[1] Fire fell from the sky in an honest-to-goodness downpour. It was a record heat, their highest reading to date.

As he had the night before, Joe made camp that evening, and there were no new incidents while the doctor and Kennedy stood watch.

But at around three in the morning on Joe's watch, the temperature suddenly dropped, clouds covered the sky, and the darkness deepened.

"Everybody up!" Joe shouted, rousing his two companions. "We have a wind!"

"Finally!" the doctor said, checking the sky. "It's a storm! Head for the *Victoria*!"

They weren't a second too soon. Under the stress of the hurricane, the *Victoria* was leaning sideways, dragging the gondola along, leaving streaks in the sand. If part of her ballast had happened to fall overboard, the balloon would have lifted off, and any hope of recovering her would be gone for good.

But fast-moving Joe raced at top speed and halted the gondola, while the balloon, in danger of ripping, settled onto the sand. Back in his usual place, the doctor lit the burner and dropped the extra weight.

The travelers took one last look at the storm-bent trees of the oasis, picked up an easterly wind at 200 feet, and soon vanished into the night.

chapter 29

Signs of vegetation — a French author's flight of fancy — magnificent country — the kingdom of Adamawa — Speke and Burton's exploring linked to Barth's — the Atlantika Mountains — the Benue River — the town of Yola — Mt. Bagélé — Mt. Mendif.

From the moment they set out, our travelers made excellent time; it took them a while to leave that desert so nearly fatal to them.

Around 9:15 in the morning, they glimpsed a few signs of vegetation, grass floating on this sea of sand and informing them, as it had Christopher Columbus, that land was nearby; green shoots poked up timidly between the stones, which themselves would become the reefs of this ocean.

On the horizon there were rolling hills, not yet very high; blurred by the mist, their outlines were dimly taking shape; things were getting less monotonous.

The doctor greeted this new region with delight, and like a seaman on watch, he was on the verge of calling:

"Land ho!"

An hour later the landmass lay under his eyes, still wild-looking but less flat, less bare, a few trees outlined against the gray sky.

"Are we in civilized country?" the hunter said.

"Civilized, Mr. Dick? Well, so to speak; I don't see any people yet."

"It won't be long," Fergusson replied, "at the rate we're traveling."

"Are we still in Negro country, Mr. Samuel?"

"Still, Joe, but coming up on Arab country."

"Arabs, sir, real Arabs with camels?"

"No, without camels; those animals are scarce, not to say unknown, in these regions; we need to go a few more degrees north to find them."

"What a shame!"

"Why is that, Joe?"

"Because if the wind reversed direction, they'd be helpful to us."

"How so?"

"Sir, it's an idea that just came to me: we could harness 'em to the gondola and get 'em to tow us. What do you think?"

"My poor Joe, somebody else had that idea before you; a very witty French author* made use of it . . . in a work of fiction, it's true. His travelers are in a balloon hauled along by camels; enter a lion who devours the camels, swallows the tow rope, and hauls the balloon in their place; then he's devoured in turn, etc. As you can see, the whole thing's an outlandish flight of fancy and has nothing in common with our method of propulsion."

A bit mortified to hear that his idea wasn't original, Joe tried to think of an animal that might have devoured the lion; but he didn't come up with one and went back to inspecting the countryside.

A lake of middling expanse spread out under his eyes, with a natural amphitheater formed by hills that hadn't yet earned the right to be called mountains; there were many fertile, winding valleys, also a hopelessly tangled assortment of the most varied trees; oil palms towered over the whole works, sporting fifteen-foot leaves on their stems, which were dotted with sharp thorns; red cotton trees filled the passing breezes with their delicate, fluffy seed; screw pines, which Arabs call *kenda*, perfumed the air with their lively aroma up to the zone where the *Victoria* was traveling; papaya trees with hand-shaped leaves, skunk trees that supply Sudan with chestnuts, baobab trees, and banana trees rounded out the luxuriant flora of these intertropical districts.

"Superb country!" the doctor said.

"Here come the animals," Joe added. "Humans can't be far behind."

"Gad, what magnificent elephants!" Kennedy exclaimed. "Any way to get in a little hunting?"

"And how, my dear Dick, could we halt in such a strong air current? No, you'll have to resign yourself to being tantalized! You'll make up for it later."

* Monsieur Méry.

In fact there was plenty to arouse a hunter's imagination; Dick's heart gave a leap in his chest, and his fingers tightened over the butt of his Purdey rifle.

The country's fauna was on a par with its flora. Wild oxen wallowed in the heavy grass, their entire bodies vanishing inside it; the most enormous gray, black, and yellow elephants swept through the forests like a cyclone, breaking, chewing, trashing, marking their progress with total devastation; waterfalls and streams ran northward down the wooded slopes; families of hippopotamus bathed in them noisily, while twelve-foot manatees sprawled over the banks, their bodies fish-shaped, their round udders swollen with milk and raised to the sky.

It was a complete, one-of-a-kind menagerie inside a marvelous greenhouse, where countless birds and a thousand colors shimmered through the treelike plants.

All this natural abundance told the doctor that he had reached the superb kingdom of Adamawa.

"We're converging on modern discoveries," he said. "I've rejoined the interrupted trail of travelers in our era; we've had a piece of luck, my friends; we'll be able to connect the efforts of Captains Burton and Speke with the exploring of Dr. Barth; we've moved on from the two Englishmen to the Hamburg scholar, and we'll soon arrive at the farthest point reached by that daring scientist."

"It seems to me," Kennedy said, "that there's a huge stretch of country between these two exploring parties, judging from how far we've come."

"It's easy to calculate; take the map and find the longitude of Lake Victoria's southern tip, the point reached by Speke."

"It's roughly 37°."

"What about the town of Yola that Barth got to, which we'll raise this evening—what's its position?"

"About longitude 12°."

"So that leaves 25 degrees between the two; at 60 miles per degree, that makes 1,500 miles."[1]

"A nice little jaunt," Joe noted, "for folks who'll be on foot."

"But they'll manage it. Livingstone and Moffat are still heading inland; they've discovered Lake Malawi, which isn't very far from Lake Tanganyika, Burton's find; these immense regions will certainly be explored before the turn of the century. But I'm sorry the wind's taking us so much to the west," the doctor added, checking his compass. "I wanted to head north again."

After a twelve-hour run, the *Victoria* reached the boundaries of Nigritia. Shuwa Arabs, who were the first to populate this land, were putting their migrant flocks out to graze. With an estimated elevation of some 7,800 feet, the huge summits of the Atlantika Mountains rose above the horizon, mountains where Europeans still haven't set foot. Their western slopes see to it that the waters in this part of Africa all run off into the ocean; they are the Mountains of the Moon for this district.

Finally a true river appeared under our travelers' eyes, and thanks to the immense anthills nearby, the doctor identified it as the Benue River, that major tributary of the Niger that natives have nicknamed "Wellspring of the Waters."

"This river," the doctor told his companions, "will one day become the natural connecting link with Nigritia's interior; under the command of one of our gallant captains, the steamboat *Pleiad* has already ascended to the town of Yola; you can see that we're in charted territory."

Working in the fields, many slaves were busy raising sweet sorghum, a type of grain that's a basic ingredient in their menus; when the *Victoriu* appeared and shot past like a meteor, they watched her with dazed astonishment. In the evening she pulled up forty miles outside Yola, and ahead of her in the distance stood the two sharp pinnacles of Mt. Mendif.

The doctor tossed out his anchors and hitched up to a tall treetop; but a very harsh wind jostled the *Victoria* until she keeled over sideways, sometimes leaving the gondola in a tremendously precarious position. Fergusson didn't shut his eyes that night; often he was on the verge of cutting his mooring line and running before the wind. Finally the storm died down, and the shakes and shivers of their lighter-than-air vehicle were no longer a cause for concern.

The next day they had a more moderate wind, but it took the travelers far from the town of Yola, which had been newly rebuilt by Fula tribesmen and which Fergusson was keen on seeing; nevertheless he had to resign himself to heading north, and even a little east.

Kennedy proposed that they lay over in these hunting grounds; Joe claimed that their need for fresh meat was getting urgent; but the country's savage customs, the population's attitudes, and a few gunshots fired the *Victoria*'s way encouraged the doctor to keep on going. At this point they were crossing a region that was the setting for arson and mass murder, for furious battles that never cease, for conflicts where sultans stake their very kingdoms in the thick of the most appalling bloodshed.

The many populous villages had long huts, which stretched between great pasturelands of heavy grass scattered with violet flowers; looking like huge beehives, these shacks were protected by spiked fences. The wild hillsides recalled the "glens" in the Scottish Highlands, as Kennedy kept pointing out.

Despite his efforts, the wind took the doctor straight northeast toward Mt. Mendif, which vanished up into the clouds; the lofty summits of these mountains separate the Niger and Lake Chad basins.

A peak soon appeared, eighteen villages clinging to its flanks like a

*Crater on
Mt. Mendif*

litter of babies to their mama's bosom—it was Mt. Bagélé, a magnificent sight for eyes that look down and take in the whole picture; they
would see that the ravines were covered with fields of rice and peanuts.

At three o'clock the *Victoria* hovered in front of Mt. Mendif. They
couldn't dodge around it, they had to rise over it. By increasing his
temperature to 180°,[2] the doctor gave his balloon an added lifting
power of nearly 1,600 pounds; she climbed more than 8,000 feet. This
was the highest altitude they had attained during the journey, and the
temperature dropped so sharply, the doctor and his companions had
to wrap themselves in their bedclothes.

Fergusson descended in a hurry because the balloon's envelope was strained to the breaking point; but he had time to note the mountain's volcanic origin, its extinct craters that now were only deep chasms. Huge accumulations of bird droppings made Mcndif's flanks look like limestone, and they offered enough manure for all the soil in the United Kingdom.

At five o'clock, sheltered from southerly winds, the *Victoria* gently skirted the mountain slopes and halted in a wide glade far from any dwellings; the instant she touched down, they took pains to secure her firmly, and Kennedy set out over the sloping plain, shotgun in hand; before long he was back with half a dozen wild duck and a species of snipe, which showcased Joe's talents at their best. They enjoyed that meal and slept soundly the whole night through.

chapter 30

Mosfeia—the sheik—Denham, Clapperton, Oudney—Vogel—Loggoum's capital—Toole—calm over Kernak—the governor and his court—the attack—pyromaniac pigeons.

The next day, May 11, the *Victoria* resumed her adventurous course; our travelers trusted her the way a seaman trusts his ship.

At any time or place, during dreadful hurricanes, tropical heat waves, dangerous liftoffs, or even more dangerous landings, she had come through triumphantly. Fergusson guided her by sleight of hand, you might say; consequently, even though he didn't know his final destination, the doctor had no other worries about his journey's outcome. But in this country of barbarians and fanatics, common sense dictated that he take the strictest precautions; so he advised his companions to keep watch around the clock for anything and everything.

The wind led them a little more to the north, and around nine o'clock they glimpsed the big town of Mosfeia, built on a knoll that was itself boxed in between two lofty mountains; it occupied an invulnerable location; the only means of access was a narrow road between a marsh and some woods.

Just then a sheik made his entrance into town, dressed in bright-colored clothing, accompanied by an escort on horseback, and preceded by trumpeters and heralds who parted the tree branches for him as he went.

The doctor dropped down to get a closer look at these natives; but as the balloon grew bigger before their eyes, signs of sheer terror spread among them, and in no time they were scampering away as fast as their legs and horses could move.

Only the sheik stayed put; he took his long musket, cocked it, and waited proudly. The doctor got within 150 feet of him, then in his most dulcet tones greeted him in Arabic.

But when these words dropped from the sky, the sheik dismounted, fell prostrate in the dust of the road, and the doctor couldn't get him to leave off his adoring.

"These people," he said, "can't help but see us as supernatural beings—when the first Europeans came among them, the natives thought they were a race of supermen. And when this sheik mentions our encounter in the future, he won't fail to exaggerate things with all the resources of his Arabic imagination. You can easily guess how their legends will portray us someday."

"That might be a problem," the hunter replied. "From a civilizing standpoint it would be better if we were viewed as plain human beings; that would give these Negroes quite a different idea of what Europeans are capable of."

"Agreed, my dear Dick, but what can we do? You could spend hours explaining how a balloon works to the wisest men in the country, but it would be too much for them, and they'd still think it was a supernatural apparition."

"Sir," Joe asked, "you mentioned the first Europeans who explored this country; could you please tell us who they were?"

"My dear boy, we're on Major Denham's exact route; right here in Mosfeia he was welcomed by the Sultan of Mandara; he'd come from Bornu, he went with the sheik on a sortie against the Fulas, and he was present at the attack on the town, which gallantly withstood the Arabs' bullets with its arrows and drove off the sheik's troops; all this was only a prelude to murder, raids, and pillaging; they stripped the major of everything he had and left him naked, so if he hadn't slipped under a horse's belly and fled from his conquerors at a frantic gallop, he never would have reentered Kouka, Bornu's capital."

"But who was this Major Denham?"

"A courageous Englishman; from 1822 to 1824 he commanded an expedition into Bornu along with Captain Clapperton and Dr. Oudney. They left Tripoli during the month of March, got to Murzuk, the capital of Libya's Fezzan region, used the route Dr. Barth would later take back to Europe, and reached Kouka near Lake Chad on February 16, 1823. Denham went on various exploratory outings in Bornu, in the Mandara Kingdom, and along the lake's east bank; meanwhile, on December 15, 1823, Captain Clapperton and Dr. Oudney pushed into Sudan as far as Sokoto, and Oudney died of exhaustion and deprivation in the town of Murmur."

"So this part of Africa," Kennedy asked, "has sacrificed many lives on the altar of science?"

"Yes, this region is deadly! We're traveling straight to the kingdom of Bagirmi, which Vogel crossed in 1856 on his way to Wadaï, where he vanished. This young man—he was only twenty-three—had been sent to assist Dr. Barth with his work; the two of them met up on December 1, 1854; then Vogel began to explore the country; his last letters, toward 1856, announced that he planned to scout out the kingdom of Wadaï, which no European had entered at that time; apparently he got to its capital city of Wara, where some say he was held captive and others say he was put to death for trying to climb one of the area's sacred mountains; but we mustn't be too quick to accept the deaths of travelers, because that does away with having to search for them; Dr. Barth, for example, was officially declared dead on many occasions, which he rightly found aggravating! So it's entirely possible the Sultan of Wadaï is holding Vogel captive in hopes of getting ransom money. Baron von Neimans was about to leave Cairo for Wadaï when he died in 1855. We now know that Herr von Heuglin has started on Vogel's trail with an expedition arriving from Leipzig. Accordingly we soon should have the facts about the fate of that interesting young traveler."*

Mosfeia had vanished below the horizon a good while earlier. The Mandara Kingdom unfolded its amazing fertility under our travelers' eyes—its forests of acacia trees, its locust trees with red flowers, the herbaceous plants in its fields of cotton and indigo; the Chari River rolled along its impetuous course, emptying into Lake Chad eighty miles farther on.

The doctor had his companions follow it on Barth's maps.

"You see the tremendous exactitude," he said, "with which this scholar did his work; we're heading straight to the Loggoum district and maybe even to Kernak, its capital. That's where poor Toole died when he was barely twenty-two: he was a young Englishman, a sub-lieutenant in the 80th Regiment who had joined Major Denham in Africa a few weeks earlier, and it wasn't long before he met his death there. By Jove, you'd be right in calling this immense region the European's graveyard!"

Fifty-foot barges were coming down the Chari's course. A thousand feet up, the *Victoria* scarcely attracted the natives' attention; but the wind—which had been blowing with some force until then—was showing a tendency to die down.

"Are we going to get caught again in a flat calm?" the doctor said.

"Oh great! At least, master, we won't have to worry about the desert and running out of water."

"No, but the people are even more threatening."

"Now here," Joe said, "is something like a town."

"That's Kernak. The last puffs of wind are taking us to it, and if we like, we'll be able to draft an exact ground plan."

"Aren't we going to pull in closer?" Kennedy asked.

"Nothing could be easier, Dick; we're right over the town; let me give the spigot on our burner a partial turn, and we'll soon be descending."

Half an hour later the *Victoria* stood stock-still, 200 feet in the air.

---

* Following the doctor's departure, letters sent from El Obeid by Herr Munzinger, the expedition's new leader, unfortunately leave no further doubts about Vogel's death.

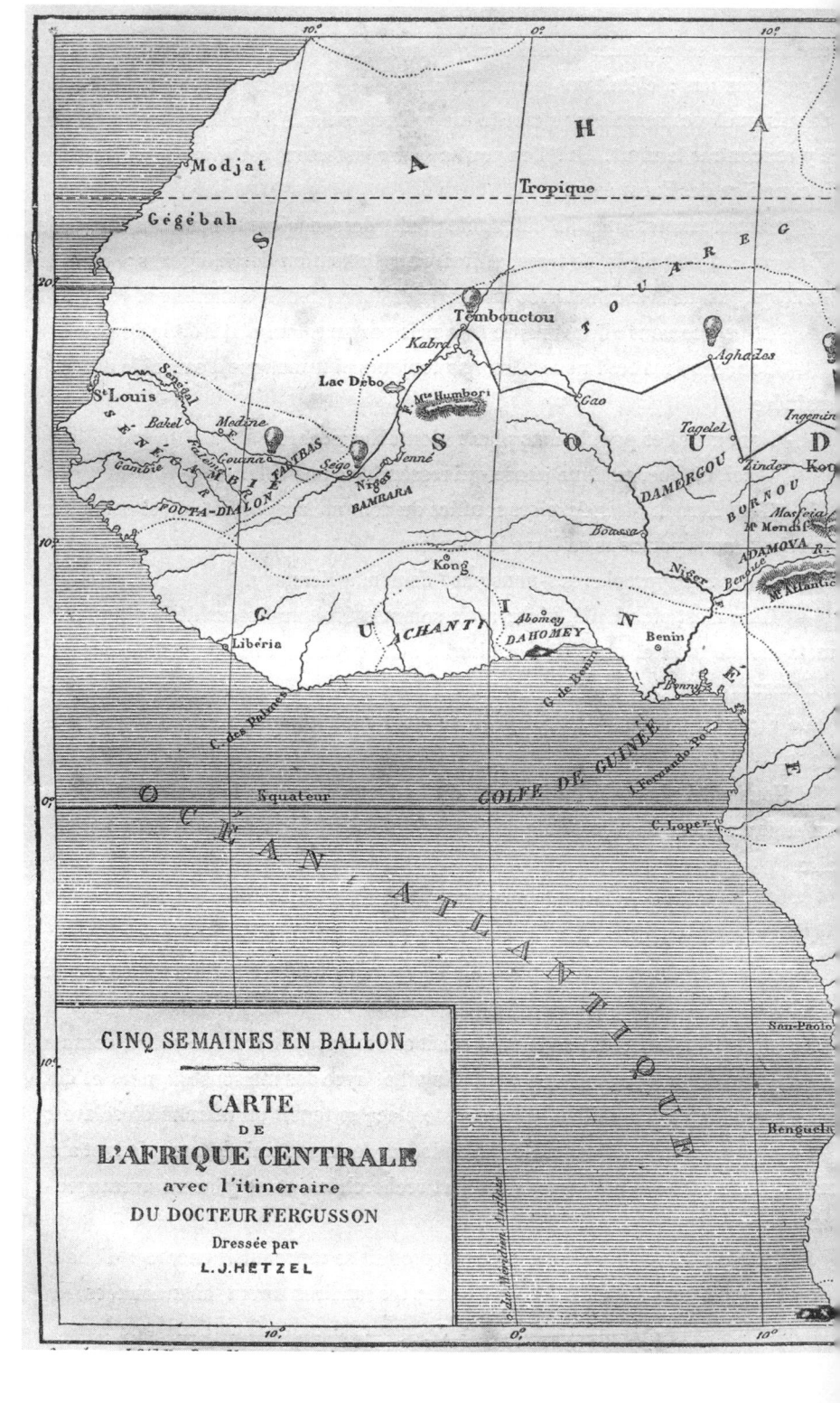

CINQ SEMAINES EN BALLON

CARTE
DE
L'AFRIQUE CENTRALE
avec l'itineraire
DU DOCTEUR FERGUSSON
Dressée par
L.J.HETZEL

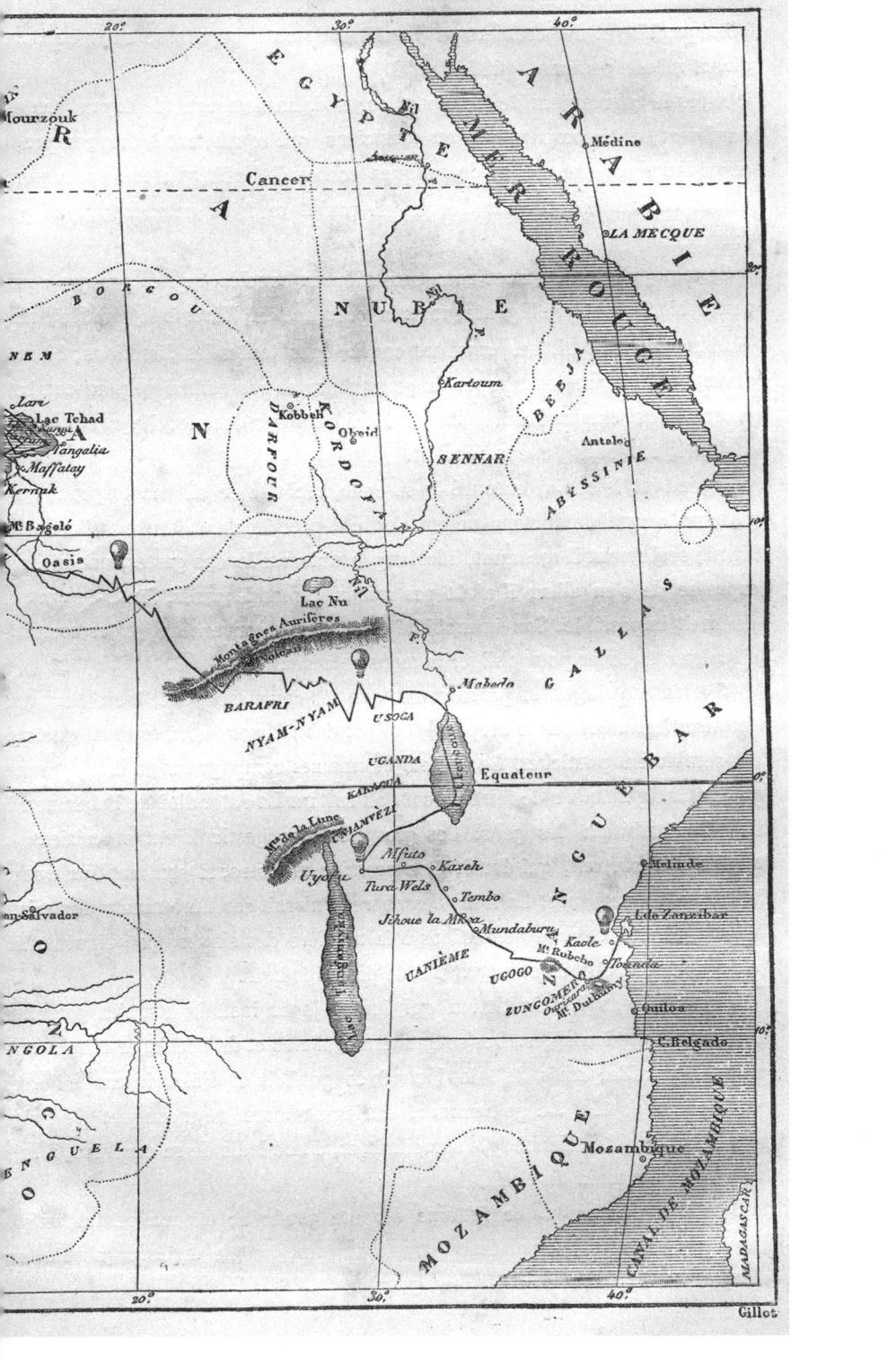

Gillot

"At this point we're closer to Kernak," the doctor said, "than a man on top of St. Paul's steeple is to London. So we can sightsee at our leisure."

"What's that pounding noise all around us?"

Joe looked closely and saw that the noise came from many weavers beating pieces of fabric, which were stretched over huge tree trunks in the open air.

By then you could take in the full expanse of Loggoum's capital, as if you had unrolled its ground plan; it was an honest-to-goodness town with rows of houses and tolerably wide streets; a slave auction was under way in the middle of a huge square; there were multitudes of customers, because Mandara women have exceptionally small hands and feet, are much in demand, and fetch excellent prices.

When the *Victoria* came in sight, the effect produced so often was reproduced once more: first there was shouting, then deep astonishment; business dealings came to a halt; work stopped; noises died out. The travelers stayed perfectly still, not missing one detail of that populous city; they actually dropped as low as sixty feet from the ground.

Then Loggoum's governor emerged from his mansion, his green banner unfurled and followed by musicians blowing buffalo horns raucously enough to burst your eardrums, or anything else except their own lungs. The crowd gathered around him. Dr. Fergusson tried to make himself heard; he wasn't successful.

With their high foreheads, curly hair, and nearly aquiline noses, these people seemed proud and intelligent; but they found the *Victoria*'s presence unusually upsetting; you saw riders racing in from every direction; it soon became clear that the governor's troops were mobilizing to do battle with this extraordinary enemy. Joe did a nice job waving white handkerchiefs, plus every other color, but to no effect.

Meanwhile the sheik gathered his court around him, called for silence, and delivered a speech without a single word that the doctor could understand; it was a mix of Arabic and Baghirmi; only, thanks to the universal language of hand gestures, Samuel did grasp that he was being cordially invited to go someplace else; he asked for nothing better, but given the lack of wind, this wasn't a possibility. His inaction exasperated the governor, and the courtiers let out a chorus of howls to shoo the monster away.

They were odd characters, these courtiers, with five or six multi-colored shirts over their bodies; they had enormous bellies, some of which looked artificially stuffed. The doctor surprised his companions when he told them this was how the sultan's subjects paid homage to him. The abdomen's rotundity indicated a person's ambition. These fat men shouted and flailed about, especially one who must have been prime minister, assuming his proportions had been suitably rewarded by the present administration. The crowds of Negroes added their howls to the shouts of the court, aping their body language and producing a single instantaneous movement of ten thousand arms.

These methods of intimidation were judged insufficient, so others more daunting took their place in the mix. Soldiers packing bows and arrows fell into battle formation; but the *Victoria* had already expanded and climbed serenely out of range. Then the governor grabbed a musket and pointed it at the balloon. But Kennedy had his eye on him, and a bullet from his rifle shattered the weapon in the sheik's hands.

At this bolt from the blue, there was a mad scramble; they all rushed inside their huts at top speed, and the town remained absolutely deserted the rest of the day.

Night fell. Not a puff of wind anywhere. They had no choice but to remain stationary 300 feet off the ground. Not a light gleamed in the darkness; a deathly silence reigned. The doctor was extra cautious; this calm could be a trap.

And Fergusson was right to be on his guard. Around midnight the whole town seemed to go up in flames; hundreds of blazing streaks crisscrossed in the air like rockets, forming a tangle of fiery lines.

"How very odd!" the doctor said.

"Lord almighty!" Kennedy responded. "You'd think that bonfire was heading up our way!"

Sure enough, while muskets went off and frightful shrieks rang out, that mass of flame *was* rising toward the *Victoria*. Joe got ready to drop ballast. Before long Fergusson found the explanation for this phenomenon.

The town had turned thousands of pigeons loose against the *Victoria*, their tails garnished with flammable material; as they climbed, the terrified birds scrawled incandescent zigzags in the air. Kennedy was ready to fire every one of his weapons into the heart of that blazing mass; but what could he do against those endless battalions? The pigeons had already surrounded the gondola and the balloon, whose walls reflected their light as if they were encircled by a network of fire.

The doctor didn't hesitate, chucked out a quartz fragment, and stayed beyond the reach of those dangerous birds. For two hours you could see them race here and there in the night; then, one by one, their numbers shrank and their lights went out.

"Now we can sleep in peace," the doctor said.

"Not a bad trick for savages to dream up!" Joe noted.[1]

"Yes, they employ pigeons pretty routinely to set thatched roofs on

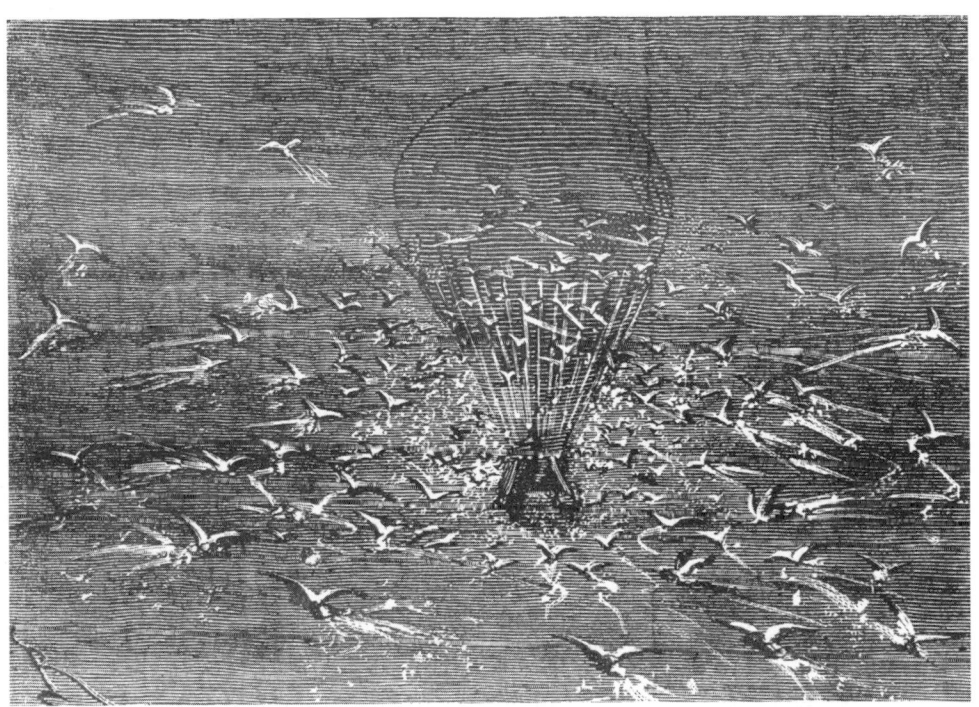

fire in rival villages; but this time the village flew higher than their pyromaniac poultry!"

"Which proves," Kennedy said, "that a balloon doesn't have any enemies worth worrying about."

"Oh yes it does," the doctor countered.

"So who are they?"

"The careless people riding in her gondola; therefore, my friends, be vigilant always and everywhere."

During his watch at around three in the morning, Joe finally saw the
town move off beneath his feet. The *Victoria* had resumed her travels.
Kennedy and the doctor woke up.

Samuel checked the compass and was pleased to note that the wind
was taking them north-northeast.

"A stroke of luck," he said. "Everything's in our favor; we'll find our
way to Lake Chad before the day is out."

"Is it a good-sized lake?" Kennedy asked.

"Substantial, my dear Dick; its maximum length and breadth both
measure about 120 miles."

"It'll add a little variety to our trip to take a jaunt over a body of
water."

"Yet I don't think we have any reason to complain; we've had ample
variety, and more significantly, we've had it under the best possible
conditions."

"No question, Samuel; except for those hardships out in the desert,
we haven't run any serious risks."

"The fact is, our good *Victoria* has always conducted herself marvelously. Today's May 12; we left on April 18; that makes twenty-five days
of travel. Another ten days or so and we'll reach the coast."

"Where exactly?"

"I have no idea; what difference does it make?"

"You're right, Samuel; we'll leave it to Providence to guide us and
keep us in our current good shape! We don't look like we've been crossing the world's most infected countries!"

"We were able to rise above it all, and we have."

"Let's hear it for journeys through the air!" Joe exclaimed. "After twenty-five days we're still fit, well fed, and perfectly rested—maybe too rested, because my limbs are starting to feel rusty, and I wouldn't mind doing thirty miles to shake out the kinks!"

"You'll have that pleasure in the streets of London, Joe; but I'll finish by saying that we set out from there as a trio like Denham, Clapperton, and Overweg, or Barth, Richardson, and Vogel—and we've been luckier than our predecessors, so we're still a trio! But it's vitally important that we don't separate. If one of us were on the ground, then suddenly the *Victoria* had to lift off to dodge an unforeseen danger, who knows if we'd ever meet up again? That's why I'm quick to tell Kennedy that I don't like him going too far when he's out hunting."

"Kindly let me have my little fun, Samuel my friend; it can't hurt to replenish our provisions; besides, before our departure you painted me a picture of all sorts of superb hunting, and so far I haven't given Andersson or Gordon-Cumming much of a run for their money."

"But my dear Dick, either your memory's failing, or your modesty makes you forget your achievements; it seems to me you already have an antelope, an elephant, and two lions on your conscience, not to mention various small fry."

"Phooey! What's that to an African hunter who sees the whole animal kingdom pass in front of his sights? Well, I'll be! Look at that herd of giraffes!"

"Those are giraffes?" Joe said. "They're the size of my fist!"

"Because we're a thousand feet overhead; but if you were beside them, you'd see that they're three times your height!"

"And how about that herd of gazelle," Kennedy went on, "and those ostriches racing like the wind?"

"Those are ostriches?" Joe said. "They look like chickens . . . well-built chickens!"

"See here, Samuel, can't we get closer to 'em?"

"We can get closer, Dick, but not touch down. Seriously, what's the point of shooting animals you can't make use of? If it was a matter of exterminating a lion, a wildcat, or a hyena, I could understand; we'd have one less predator on the loose; but to slay an antelope or gazelle for no good reason other than to satisfy your everyday hunting urges, that really isn't justified.[1] Even so, my friend, we're going to stay a hundred feet up, so if you spot some fierce predator, do us the favor of putting a bullet in its heart."

The *Victoria* dropped down little by little, nevertheless staying at a comforting altitude. In that hostile, heavily populated region, they had to be wary of unexpected perils.

So our travelers faithfully followed the Chari's course; the delightful banks of this river vanished under the variously colored shade trees; clinging vines and creepers were winding every which way, creating the oddest tangles of color. As lively as lizards, crocodiles were romping in the bright sunlight or diving into the water; while at play they pulled alongside the many green islands that impeded the river's current.

Consequently it was in the midst of this lush rural greenery that the district of Maffatay went by. Around nine o'clock in the morning, Dr. Fergusson and his friends finally reached the south shore of Lake Chad.

So this was Africa's answer to the Caspian Sea, a huge lake whose existence had long been relegated to the realm of tall tales, an inland sea visited only by the expeditions under Denham and Barth.

The doctor tried to pin down its current layout, already quite different from what it had been in 1847; in essence there's no way to draft an accurate map of this lake; it's surrounded by viscous marshes that are virtually impossible to cross, marshes in which Barth felt sure he would perish; they're covered with reeds and fifteen-foot papyrus plants, and in a year's time they become part of the lake itself; often, too, the towns spreading along its edges end up half submerged (as happened to Ngornu in 1856), and now gators and hippopotamuses swim in the same spots where many Bornu dwellings used to stand.

The sun poured its blinding rays over those tranquil waves, and to the north the two elements of fire and water merged into a single horizon.

The doctor wanted to confirm the nature of the lake's contents, long thought to be salt water; its surface wasn't dangerous to approach, and their gondola skimmed over it like a bird, just five feet up.

Joe dipped a bottle in and drew it out half full; sampling the water, they found it wasn't fit to drink and tasted a little like baking soda.

While the doctor was jotting down the results of his experiment,

a gunshot rang out next to him. Kennedy couldn't resist firing a bullet at a monstrous hippopotamus; the animal had been lazing on the surface, then had vanished underwater at the sound of the shot—although the hunter's conical bullet didn't seem to have troubled the beast otherwise.

"It'd be better to harpoon him," Joe said.

"How?"

"With one of our anchors. They come with the right size hook for that sort of animal!"

"Hmm," Kennedy said, "Joe's onto something there . . ."

"Which I beg you not to put into practice!" the doctor fired back. "The animal would promptly drag us someplace we aren't interested in going."

"Especially now that we've figured out the water quality in Lake Chad. Is this thing good eating, Dr. Fergusson, this fish that got away?"

"Your fish, Joe, is quite simply a mammal belonging to the pachyderm order; its meat is excellent, they say, and the lakeside tribes do a booming business in these creatures."

"Then I'm sorry Mr. Kennedy's gunshot wasn't up to snuff."

"The animal is vulnerable only in the belly and between the haunches; Dick's bullet wouldn't even have broken its skin. But if the terrain strikes me as promising, we'll lay over at the north end of the lake; there Kennedy will have a whole menagerie to choose from, and he'll be able to make up for lost time."

"Well," Joe said, "let's hope Mr. Dick gets in a little hippo hunting! I'd like to sample the meat of that amphibious beast. It doesn't exactly seem natural to visit the heart of Africa, then dine on woodcock and partridge as if we were back in England!"

chapter 32

Bornu's capital—the islands of the Biddiomahs— bearded vultures—the doctor's worries—his precautions—an attack in midair—the ripped envelope—falling out of the sky—supreme dedication—the lake's north shore.

After arriving at Lake Chad, the *Victoria* met up with an air current that was more inclined to head west; a couple of clouds tempered the daytime heat; what's more, you could feel a little air circulating over that huge expanse of water; but around one o'clock, the balloon cut diagonally across that part of the lake, then proceeded overland again for a distance of seven or eight miles.

At first the doctor was a bit annoyed by this change of heading, but he no longer felt like complaining when he spotted the town of Kouka, Bornu's famous capital; he got a momentary glimpse of it, girded round by its walls of white clay; a couple of rather crudely built

View of the town of Kouka

mosques loomed awkwardly above its neighborhoods of Arabic homes, which looked like tabletops covered with dice. In the courtyards of these homes and in the public squares, palm trees and rubber trees were growing, crowned by domes of foliage over a hundred feet wide. Joe pointed out that these immense parasols were an appropriate defense against the hot sunlight, and he credited this to good thinking on the part of Providence.

Kouka actually consists of two distinct towns separated by the *dendal*, a wide boulevard eighteen hundred feet long and clogged just then with pedestrians and riders. The wealthy section is ensconced on one side, showing off its tall, airy huts; the poor section is crammed into the other side, a sorry assemblage of low, cone-shaped shanties where a native population twiddles its thumbs, since Kouka is neither a mercantile nor a manufacturing center.

The place reminded Kennedy of Edinburgh—but an Edinburgh where its two clear-cut sections, Old Town and New Town, were spread out over a plain.

Yet our travelers were barely able to glance at it, because the region's air currents are unstable by nature, and a contrary wind abruptly laid hold of them, carrying them some forty miles back across Lake Chad.

There they had something new to look over; they could count up the many islands in the lake where the Biddiomahs resided—fearsome, bloodthirsty pirates as much dreaded in these parts as the Tuaregs in the Sahara. These savages were all set to welcome the *Victoria* with stouthearted volleys of stones and arrows, but she soon left these islands behind, flitting over them like some gigantic beetle.

Just then Joe looked at the horizon, turned to Kennedy, and told him:

"Criminy, Mr. Dick, since you're always up for hunting, that's just your cup of tea."

"What is, Joe?"

"And this time my master won't make you hold your fire."

"What are you talking about?"

"Over there, you see that flock of large birds heading our way?"

"Birds!" the doctor repeated, grabbing his spyglass.

"I see 'em," Kennedy remarked. "There are at least a dozen."

"Fourteen, with all due respect," Joe replied.

"I hope to heaven they're a species vicious enough that softhearted Samuel doesn't feel like objecting!"

"I won't say a thing," Fergusson replied, "but I'd prefer to see those birds from farther away!"

"You're afraid of critters with feathers?" Joe asked.

"They're bearded vultures, Joe, the largest kind;[1] and if they attack us . . ."

"Well, we'll defend ourselves, Samuel! We have a whole arsenal ready to welcome 'em! Trust me, those creatures aren't all that fearsome!"

"Think so?" the doctor responded.

Ten minutes later the flock had gotten within shotgun range; the air echoed with the raucous shrieking of those fourteen birds; they headed for the *Victoria*, more irritated than frightened by her presence.

"Listen to that squawking!" Joe said. "What a racket! It probably doesn't sit well if you trespass on their territory and have the nerve to fly around like they do!"

"They look awful enough in all honesty," the hunter said, "and I think they'd be pretty fearsome if they were packing Purdey Moore rifles!"

"They don't need to," Fergusson replied, now very grim.

The bearded vultures were sweeping in immense circles as they flew, and little by little their orbits closed in around the *Victoria*; they streaked through the sky with fantastic speed, sometimes shooting along as fast as a bullet, then brazenly veering from their line of fire by making sharp turns.

Worried, the doctor decided to go higher in the air and get out of this dangerous neighborhood; he set about making the hydrogen expand, and soon the balloon started to climb.

But the bearded vultures climbed along with him, in no mood to let him go.

"They seem to have it in for us!" the hunter said, cocking his rifle.

In fact those birds kept coming closer, and more than one got within fifty feet, as if daring Kennedy to open fire.

"I've a good mind to let 'em have it," the Scot said.

"No, Dick, don't! Let's not infuriate them needlessly! It will provoke them to attack us."

"But I'll finish 'em off in nothing flat."

"You're mistaken, Dick."

"We have a bullet for every one of those birds."

"And what if they lunge at the upper part of the balloon, how would you get at them? Just imagine you were facing a pride of lions on the ground, or a school of sharks out in the ocean! For a balloonist this situation is fully as dangerous."

"You're serious, Samuel?"

"Very serious, Dick."

"So we wait."

"We wait. Stay on the alert in case of attack, but don't fire unless I say so."

By then the birds had assembled a little way off; you clearly saw their bare-skinned necks stretching out with the exertions of their shrieking, their crests made of cartilage that were dotted with purple warts and bristling in anger. These specimens were as big as they came; their bodies measured more than a yard long, and the undersides of their white wings gleamed in the sun; you would have taken them for airborne sharks, so fearsome was the resemblance.

"They're following us," the doctor said, watching them ascend along with him. "No matter how quickly we climb, they can fly even higher!"

"Well, what should we do?" Kennedy asked.

The doctor didn't answer.

"Listen, Samuel," the hunter continued, "there are fourteen of those birds; if we fire all our weapons, we have seventeen rounds at our disposal. Isn't that enough to wipe the brutes out or drive 'em off? I'll see to a good number of 'em personally."

"I don't doubt your skills, Dick; I'll gladly concede that if they fly in front of your rifle, they're as good as dead; but I repeat, if they simply attack the top half of the balloon, you won't be able to get them in your sights; they'll puncture this envelope keeping us in the air, and we're 3,000 feet up!"

At that moment one of the fiercest birds swooped right down on the *Victoria*, beak and claws wide open, ready to bite, ready to rip into her.

"Fire! Fire!" the doctor shouted.

He barely got the words out before the bird fell spinning into the void, dead as a doornail.

Kennedy grabbed one of the double-barreled shotguns. Joe was sighting down the other.

Startled by the shot, the bearded vultures swerved away for an instant; but almost immediately they went back on the offensive with heightened fury. Kennedy's first bullet completely beheaded the closest one. Joe shattered the wing of another.

"Eleven to go," he said.

But then the birds changed tactics, and they rose in unison above the *Victoria*. Kennedy looked at Fergusson.

Despite his composure and inner strength, the doctor turned white. There was a terrifying moment of silence. Then they heard a shrill ripping noise, the sound of silk under assault, and the gondola gave way beneath our travelers' feet.

"We're done for!" Fergusson yelled as his eyes darted to the barometer, now swiftly rising.

Then he added: "Out with the ballast!"

All the quartz fragments were gone in a few seconds.

"We're still falling! We're plunging into the lake! Joe, do you hear me? Empty the water tanks!"

Joe did so. The doctor leaned over the side. The lake seemed to be coming at him like a rising tide; objects grew bigger before his eyes; the gondola wasn't 200 feet above the surface of Lake Chad.

"The provisions! The provisions!" the doctor shouted.

And the container holding them vanished into space.

That slowed their descent, but the poor devils were still falling!

"Throw something out! Anything!" the doctor shouted one final time.

"There's nothing left," Kennedy said.

"Wrong!" Joe replied tersely, giving a quick wave of the hand.

And he vanished over the side of the gondola.

"Joe! Joe!" The doctor called out, horrified.

But Joe couldn't hear him anymore. Lightened, the *Victoria* began to ascend again and climbed a thousand feet into the skies, where the wind rushed into the deflated envelope, taking them toward the lake's north shore.

"Gone!" the hunter said with a gesture of despair.

"Gone, to save our lives!" Fergusson replied.

And these courageous men felt two great teardrops slide from their eyes. They leaned over the side, trying to find some trace of poor Joe, but already they were far away.

"What's the plan?" Kennedy asked.

"Get down on the ground as quickly as possible, Dick, and then wait."

After traveling sixty miles the *Victoria* made a bumpy landing on a deserted shore to the north of the lake. They hitched the anchors to a stunted tree, and the hunter secured them firmly.

Night fell, but neither Fergusson nor Kennedy could sleep for a second.

chapter 33

Conjectures—restoring the Victoria's *buoyancy—
Dr. Fergusson's new calculations—Kennedy goes
hunting—thoroughly exploring Lake Chad—
Tangalia—heading back—Lari.*

The next day, May 13, the travelers immediately scouted out the part of the coast they were occupying. It was like an island of solid ground in the middle of an immense marsh. Around this piece of firm terrain there were reeds as far as the eye could see, reeds that stood as tall as trees in Europe.

Impossible to cross, these swamps fortified the *Victoria*'s position; you needed to keep watch only along the lakeshore; that huge sheet of water widened farther out, especially to the east, and nothing was visible on the horizon, neither islands nor the opposite shore.

The two friends still hadn't dared to talk about their unfortunate companion. Kennedy broke down first and shared his conjectures with the doctor.

"Maybe Joe isn't a goner," he said. "He's a sharp lad and a swimmer like few others. He had no problem going across the Firth of Forth in Edinburgh. We'll see him again, though I haven't a clue when or how; but as for you and me, we mustn't overlook anything that'll give him a chance to get back to us."

"May heaven hear your prayers, Dick," the doctor replied, his voice full of emotion. "We'll do everything on earth to find our friend again! First let's take stock. And above all let's get rid of the *Victoria*'s outer envelope, which is no longer of any use; this will free us of a considerable weight, 650 pounds, so it's well worth the trouble."

The doctor and Kennedy went to work; they had a tremendously difficult time; the highly resilient taffeta needed to be torn away piece by piece, then cut into thin strips so they could pull it through the meshes of the netting. The beaks on those birds of prey had produced a rip several feet long.

This operation took a good four hours; but at last the inner balloon was fully liberated, and apparently it hadn't suffered in any way. At this point the *Victoria* was 20% smaller. This difference was noticeable enough to surprise Kennedy.

"Will she do the job?" he asked the doctor.

"No need to worry on that score, Dick; I'll restore her buoyancy, and if poor Joe comes back, we'll be quite able to resume our previous course."

"If I remember right, Samuel, at the time we were falling, we should've been close to an island."

"I have the same recollection, but like all the islands in Lake Chad, that one's undoubtedly occupied by a clan of pirates and murderers; surely those savages would have witnessed our calamity, and if Joe falls into their hands, what are his chances if they aren't superstitious and in awe of him?"

"I'd swear by his shrewdness and dexterity. I'll say it again, he's a fellow who always pulls through."

"I hope so. Now, Dick, go do some hunting in this area, but stay close nevertheless; we have an urgent need to replenish our provisions, since we jettisoned most of what we had."

"Fine, Samuel; I won't be gone long."

Kennedy cut through the tall grass to a nearby thicket, packing a double-barreled shotgun; he fired it frequently, and the doctor quickly gathered that his hunting would be productive.

Meanwhile Samuel got busy with inventorying the items left in the gondola, then with determining the buoyancy of this second lighter-than-air vehicle; there were still some thirty pounds of pemmican, quantities of tea and coffee, about 1½ gallons of brandy, and a totally empty water tank; all the dried meat was gone.

Having lost the hydrogen in the first balloon, the doctor knew that his lifting power was some 900 pounds less; so he needed to use this difference as the basis for reworking his buoyancy. This new *Victoria* had a capacity of 67,000 cubic feet and held 33,480 cubic feet of gas;

The hunter gets in some good hunting.

the expansion mechanism seemed in good shape; neither the battery nor the coil had been damaged.

So the new balloon's lifting power was about 3,000 pounds; adding up the respective weights of the mechanism, the travelers, the water supply, the gondola and its accessories—plus taking aboard fifty gallons of water and a hundred pounds of fresh meat—the doctor arrived at a total of 2,830 pounds. So he could bring along 170 pounds of ballast for unexpected developments, and their lighter-than-air vehicle would be in a state of buoyancy with the atmosphere around her.

He saw to his arrangements accordingly, compensating for Joe's absence with extra ballast. These various preparatory measures took up the whole day, and he had completed them by the time Kennedy returned. The hunter had gotten in some good hunting; he brought back a sterling cargo of geese, wild duck, snipe, teal, and plover. He set about processing and smoking this game. Skewered on a thin stick, each piece hung over a fire of green wood. Kennedy knew his stuff, and when he had completed these procedures to his satisfaction, he stowed the full results in the gondola.

The hunter would round out his provisions the next day.

Evening crept up on our travelers in the midst of these labors. Their supper consisted of pemmican, crackers, and tea. Their exertions had left them both hungry and sleepy. But during their spells on watch, they each combed the darkness, sometimes thinking they had caught snatches of Joe's voice; but no such luck—it wasn't anywhere near them, that voice they longed to hear!

The doctor woke Kennedy up at the crack of dawn.

"For a good while," he told the Scot, "I've been pondering what we should do to find our companion again."

"Whatever your plan is, Samuel, I'm all for it; keep talking."

"More than anything it's important that Joe hears from us."

"Of course! What if the dear laddie starts to think we've ditched him?"

"He wouldn't! He knows us too well! The idea would never enter his head; but it's crucial for him to learn where we are."

"Learn how?"

"We'll climb back in the gondola and rise into the air."

"But what if the wind gets hold of us?"

"Luckily it won't have any effect. See, Dick—the breeze will carry us back over the lake, and this circumstance would have been an aggravation yesterday, but it's a blessing today. So we'll confine our efforts to staying over this huge expanse of water for the entire day. Joe can't fail to see us up there, and he's bound to be continually watching. Maybe he'll even manage to let us know where he's hiding."

"If he's by himself and on the run, he's sure to."

"And if he's being held prisoner," the doctor resumed, "the natives don't normally lock up their captives, so he'll see us and understand why we're on the lookout."

"But we still have to make every allowance," Kennedy went on. "Suppose we don't find any clues, suppose he hasn't left any traces of his movements—what'll we do?"

"We'll attempt to get back to the north end of the lake, staying in sight as much as possible; we'll wait there, we'll explore the banks, we'll scour those shores that Joe will surely try to reach, and we won't leave the place without doing everything we can to find him."

"Then let's get going," the hunter replied.

The doctor took the exact bearings of that piece of solid ground they were leaving; based on his map and position fix, he estimated that he was north of Lake Chad between the town of Lari and the village of Ingemini, both of them visited by Major Denham. Meanwhile Kennedy rounded out his supply of fresh meat. However, even though the surrounding marshes showed signs of rhinoceroses, manatees, and hippopotamuses, he didn't run into a single one of those enormous animals.

At seven o'clock in the morning, they unhooked the anchor from the tree—not without many difficulties of the sort poor Joe managed to perfection. The gas expanded, and the new *Victoria* rose 200 feet into the air. At first she hesitated, turning round and round; but finally she caught a tolerably brisk current, proceeded over the lake, and soon took off at a speed of twenty miles per hour.

The doctor stayed continually at an altitude that fluctuated between 200 and 500 feet. Kennedy often fired his rifle. Over islands our travelers got quite recklessly close, their eyes scouring the thickets, the bushes, the shrubbery, especially where some shadow, some crevice in the rock, might have given their companion a refuge. They dropped down near some long dugout canoes that were crisscrossing the lake. The fishermen on board took one look, jumped into the water, and swam back to their island in undisguised terror.

"We aren't finding anything," Kennedy said after two hours of searching.

"Let's wait, Dick, and not lose heart; we must be close to the scene of the accident."

By eleven o'clock the *Victoria* had gone ninety miles; then she fell in with another air current that went nearly at a right angle, propelling her some sixty miles east. She soared over a very large and well-populated island that the doctor figured must be Farram, site of the Biddiomahs' capital. He kept expecting to see Joe burst from some bush, running for his life, calling out to him. If he was free, they could pick him up without difficulty; if he was a prisoner, they could resort again to the tactic they had used with the missionary, and he would soon be back with his friends; but nothing was visible, nothing stirred! They were in despair.

At 2:30 the *Victoria* arrived in sight of Tangalia, a village located on Lake Chad's east shore and marking the farthest point reached by Denham when he explored the region.

The doctor grew uneasy at the persistent wind direction. He felt it was tossing him back to the east, pushing him to central Africa again, to its endless deserts.

"We absolutely must call a halt," he said, "and even disembark; for Joe's sake particularly we should go back over the lake; but beforehand let's try to find an air current heading the opposite way."

For over an hour he searched the different zones. The *Victoria* always drifted above dry land; but at a thousand feet up, fortunately, a powerful gust took her back to the northwest.

It wasn't possible that Joe was being held on one of the islands in the lake; he certainly would have found a way to make his presence known; maybe he had been dragged overland. That's how the doctor was reasoning it out when he got back in sight of Lake Chad's north shore.

As for thinking that Joe had drowned, this was out of the question. One horrible thought *did* occur to both Fergusson and Kennedy: crocodilians are common in these parts![1] But neither of them had the gumption to spell out this fear. Yet it was so clearly on their minds, the doctor said without any further preamble:

"Crocodiles are found only on the lakeshore or the shores of the islands; Joe will be crafty enough to keep out of their way; what's more, they aren't very dangerous, and Africans bathe with impunity without any fear of being attacked."

Kennedy didn't reply; he preferred to say nothing rather than discuss such a dreadful possibility.

The doctor sighted the town of Lari around five o'clock in the evening. Its citizens were at work harvesting the cotton in front of their shacks, which were made of interwoven reeds and sat in the middle of tidy, carefully kept enclosures. This congregation of some fifty huts occupied a slight dip in the terrain, a valley stretching between low mountains. The strong wind carried the doctor farther than he would have liked; but it shifted a second time and took him right back to his starting point, that island of solid ground where he had spent the preceding night. Instead of connecting with tree branches, their anchor got caught in some masses of reeds, which merged with the thick sludge of the marsh and put up considerable resistance.

The doctor had a lot of trouble restraining his lighter-than-air vehicle; but the wind finally died out at nightfall, and the two friends stood watch together, close to despair.

chapter 34

The hurricane—forced departure—loss of an anchor—gloomy thoughts—making a decision—twister—the sunken caravan—contrary and favorable winds—heading back south—Kennedy on the job.

At three o'clock in the morning, the wind raged and blew with such force, the *Victoria* couldn't remain near the ground without danger to herself; the reeds were scraping against her envelope, threatening to rip it.

"We need to go, Dick," the doctor said. "We can't stay on under these conditions."

"But Samuel, what about Joe?"

"I'm not deserting him! Absolutely not! Even if this hurricane carries me a hundred miles north, I'll come back! But right now everybody's safety is in jeopardy."

"Go without him?" the Scot exclaimed in real anguish.

"Don't you realize I'm as heartsick as you are?" Fergusson went on. "Can't you see I'm acting out of urgent necessity?"

"Whatever you say," the hunter replied. "Let's get going."

But they had great difficulty setting out. The anchor was hopelessly stuck and withstood all their efforts, while the balloon pulled the opposite way and wedged it even more tightly. Kennedy wasn't able to wrench it loose; what's more, in their current circumstances his task had become downright dangerous, because there was a chance the *Victoria* would lift off before he had gotten on board again.

The doctor wasn't willing to run this risk, ordered the Scot back in the gondola, and resigned himself to cutting the anchor rope. The *Victoria* leaped 300 feet into the air and followed a course due north.

Fergusson had no choice but to ride out the storm; arms folded, he was wrapped up in his gloomy thoughts.

After a few seconds of intense silence, he turned to Kennedy, who was just as tight-lipped.

"Maybe we've been tempting fate," he said. "Human beings aren't meant to undertake such a journey!"

And a melancholy sigh broke from his chest.

"Just a few days ago," the hunter replied, "we congratulated each other on escaping so many dangers! All three of us shook hands!"

"Poor Joe! So decent and good-natured! So gallant and openhearted! His riches blinded him temporarily, yet he willingly jettisoned his wealth! And now he's far away from us! And the wind's carrying us off with unstoppable speed!"

"Look here, Samuel, assuming he's taken refuge among the lakeside tribes, couldn't he do what travelers did who visited 'em before us, men like Denham or Barth? Those fellows saw their countries again."

"Oh, my poor Dick! Joe doesn't know a word of the local language! He's alone and without means! The explorers you mention proceeded only after sending the chieftains many gifts, and they traveled in the midst of escorts armed and ready for such expeditions. Even so, they couldn't avoid the worst kinds of suffering and adversity! What do you think will happen to our poor companion? It's horrifying to consider, and this is one of the greatest griefs I've been given to experience!"

"But we'll come back, Samuel."

"We'll come back, Dick, even if we have to leave the *Victoria* behind, return to Lake Chad on foot, and get in contact with the Sultan of Bornu! The Arabs can't have bad memories of the first Europeans."

"I'm right behind you, Samuel," the hunter replied firmly, "you can count on me! If need be, we'll forget about finishing this journey! Joe proved his dedication to us, we'll make sacrifices for him!"

That decision heartened these two courageous men. They clearly were of one mind. Fergusson tried every trick in the book to get into a countercurrent that could take him back toward Lake Chad; but it was impossible at that point, and in such barren terrain and such a violent hurricane, it was no longer feasible even to land.

Consequently the *Victoria* crossed over the country of the Tibbous; she cleared Belad-el-Djérid, a wilderness of brambles that forms the Sudan border, then entered a wilderness of sand crisscrossed by the long trails of caravans; the last rows of vegetation soon merged with the sky on the southern horizon, not far from the main oasis in this part of Africa, whose fifty wells sit in the shade of magnificent trees; but it was impossible to stop. Featuring tents of striped cloth and a few camels stretching their viper-shaped heads over the sand, an Arab campsite brought some life to the solitude; but the *Victoria* went by like a shooting star, covering a distance of sixty miles in three hours, although Fergusson had no control over her course.

"We can't call a halt!" he said. "We can't disembark! Not a tree! Not an outcrop! Are we heading clear across the Sahara? Heaven is definitely against us!"

He was going on like this with the rage of despair, when he saw the desert sands to the north rise up in the midst of heavy dust, then swirl around under the impetus of the countercurrents.

In the middle of the whirlwind, there was an entire caravan, battered, broken up, toppling over, vanishing underneath an avalanche of sand; scattered camels let out pathetically muffled groans; shouts and shrieks came from that stifling fog. At times the bright hues of a multicolored garment stood out in the chaos, and the roar of the storm held sway over this scene of destruction.

The sand soon collected into compact piles, and where a smooth plain had recently stretched, a trembling hill rose up, the immense grave of that sunken caravan.

The doctor and Kennedy witnessed that dreadful sight, their faces white; they couldn't maneuver their balloon anymore, and she swirled in the midst of the countercurrents, no longer heeding their various

efforts to make the gas expand. Clutched by these eddies in the air, she spun around with dizzying speed; the gondola rocked back and forth, shaking and shivering; the instruments that hung under the tent were banging against each other and in danger of breaking, the pipes of the coil were bent over to the snapping point, the water tanks clattered as they shifted around; our travelers were only two feet apart but couldn't hear each other, and they clung tightly to the rigging, trying to bear up under the hurricane's fury.

His hair flying about, Kennedy watched without a word; in the face of danger, the doctor had recovered his courage, and his features gave no sign of his intense feelings, not even when the *Victoria* gave a last whirl and suddenly halted in an unexpected calm; then a northerly wind took charge, driving her backward over the same course she had followed that morning, and with just as much speed.

"Where are we going?" Kennedy exclaimed.

"My dear Dick, leave that to Providence, a better source than we are for knowing what's needed; I was wrong to doubt, because here we are, returning to places we never thought we'd see again."

The ground had looked so flat and uniform when they came over it earlier, but now it seemed as agitated as waves after a storm; a sequence of low knolls, barely in place, punctuated the wilderness; the wind blew fiercely, and the *Victoria* flew through space.

The balloon's heading was slightly different from the one our travelers had followed that morning; therefore, nearing nine o'clock, they weren't back alongside Lake Chad but instead saw the desert still stretching in front of them.

Kennedy pointed this out.

"It makes little difference," the doctor replied. "The main thing is to return south; we'll meet up with the towns of Bornu, Wouddie, or Kouka, and I wouldn't hesitate to halt thereabouts."

"If you're pleased, I am too," the hunter responded. "But heaven help us if we're reduced to crossing the desert like those poor Arabs! What we saw was horrifying!"

"And often repeated, Dick. Crossing a desert has different dangers than crossing a body of water; a desert offers every peril an ocean does, even sinking from sight—plus you face unbearable exhaustion and hardship."

"I think the wind's showing a tendency to die down," Kennedy said. "The dust over the sand is thinning out, the surface isn't heaving as much, and the horizon's clearing up."

"Better and better—we need to keep watch with our spyglass and make sure nothing gets by us!"

"Leave it to me, Samuel; when the first tree shows up, you'll hear about it."

And Kennedy parked himself in the front of the gondola, spyglass in hand.

chapter **35**

*Joe's story—the island of the Biddiomahs—being
adored—the sunken island—the lakeshore—the tree
of snakes—journey on foot—afflictions—mosquitoes
and ants—hunger—the* Victoria *flies past—the*
Victoria *vanishes—despair—the marsh—last call.*

What had happened to Joe while his master vainly searched for him?

After he leaped into the lake and came back to the surface, his first move was to look up at the sky; he saw that the *Victoria* was already quite high above the lake, climbing swiftly, growing smaller and smaller, soon catching a quick current, then vanishing into the north. His master and his friend were safe.

"Good thing," he told himself, "that I thought of jumping into Lake Chad; it didn't occur to Mr. Kennedy, though he certainly wouldn't have balked at doing the same, because it's perfectly natural to lay down your life to save two others. That's simple arithmetic."

Comforted on this point, Joe gave some thought to himself; he was in the middle of an immense lake surrounded by unknown and probably ferocious tribes. It was one more reason for pulling through on his own steam; otherwise he wasn't alarmed.

Before the attack by those birds of prey—who, in his view, were acting like proper bearded vultures—he had noticed an island on the horizon; so he decided to head toward it, and after getting rid of his more restrictive items of clothing, he tapped into everything he had mastered in the sport of swimming; it didn't bother him in the least to do a run of five or six miles; accordingly, so long as he was far from shore, he thought only of swimming straight ahead with everything he had.

After an hour and a half, he had sharply reduced the distance separating him from the island.

But as he got closer to land, a thought flitted through his brain, took hold, and stayed in the forefront of his mind. He knew that those lakeshores were the haunts of huge gators, and he had heard how voracious the animals were.

Despite his mania for finding everything on earth perfectly natural, the worthy lad felt powerfully concerned; he feared his white flesh would be especially appealing to crocodiles, and so he proceeded with tremendous caution, keenly alert. He was no more than 200 yards from a shoreline of green shade trees, when he caught a whiff of a pungent musky odor in the air.

"Right!" he told himself. "Just what I was afraid of! There's a croc around."

And he made a quick dive, but not quick enough to avoid contact with an enormous body whose scaly skin grazed him in passing; he thought he was done for and started swimming with desperate speed; he shot back to the surface, took a breath, and vanished again. It was more than his philosophical outlook could handle—he went through fifteen minutes of unspeakable anxiety, thinking he could hear the whoosh of that huge maw behind him, ready to snap him up. He was proceeding in midwater, making as little noise as possible, when he felt something grab him by the arm, then around the waist.

Poor Joe! He thought of his master one last time and began struggling desperately, but instead of being dragged to the bottom, as crocodiles normally do with their prey before gobbling them up, he felt himself yanked back to the surface.

He had barely managed to take a breath and open his eyes, when he saw that he was flanked by two Negroes as black as ebony; these Africans had a tight grip on him and were letting out strange shouts.

"Well, I'll be!" Joe couldn't help exclaiming. "Negroes instead of crocodilians! Crikey, that's a step up in my book! But how do these gents dare to go for a dip around here?"

Joe didn't know that island dwellers in Lake Chad—like many Blacks—swim with impunity in these waters, never worrying their heads over the gators that infest them; the amphibious saurians in this lake have a reputation for being basically harmless, and it isn't undeserved.

But had Joe jumped out of the frying pan and into the fire? He left that for future events to determine, and since he had no choice in the matter, he went along quietly when they took him ashore.

"Obviously," he told himself, "these blokes saw the *Victoria* skim over the waves of their lake like some airborne monster; they watched from far away when I jumped, and they can't help respecting a man who falls out of the sky! I say let 'em!"

Joe had gotten to this point in his cogitating, when he stepped ashore in the midst of a howling crowd—both sexes, all ages, just one color. He was surrounded by a tribe of superbly black Biddiomahs. He didn't even have to blush because of his skimpy clothing; he was in step with the country's latest "styles of undress."

But before he had time to figure out where he stood, it became clear that he was the subject of wholesale adoration. This couldn't help but reassure him, although he was reminded of that episode in Kazeh:

"I have a hunch I'm about to turn back into a god, another son of the moon or some such. Well, it's as good a rank as any when you haven't any say-so. The main thing is to play for time. If the *Victoria* happens to come by again, I'll make the most of my new status and give my admirers the miraculous sight of an ascension into heaven."

While Joe was musing along these lines, the crowd closed around him; they fell prostrate, they wailed, they touched him, they got overfamiliar; but at least they had the thoughtfulness to offer him a magnificent feast consisting of sour milk and ground rice in honey; always looking out for himself, the worthy lad put away one of the best meals he had consumed in his life, giving his devotees an exalted notion of how the gods pack it in on special occasions.

When evening arrived, the island's witch doctors took him reverently by the hand and led him to a sort of hut surrounded by amulets; before going inside, Joe nervously eyeballed the piles of bones heaped around this sanctuary; after they locked him in his shack, however, he had plenty of time to ponder his predicament.

During that evening and part of the night, he heard ceremonial chanting, the thumping of some sort of drum, and that clanking of scrap metal African ears find so euphonious; choruses of shrieks accompanied squirming, scowling dances that went on forever around the sacred shack.

Through the mud-and-reed walls of his hut, Joe could catch the whole earsplitting performance; under other circumstances he might have been quite entertained by these strange solemnities; but his mind was soon troubled by a highly uncomfortable idea. Even taking a positive view of things, he found it senseless and even sad for somebody to wander through this savage region among such tribes. Out of all the travelers who dared venture into these regions, few had seen their countries again. Besides, how reliable was his status as the subject of all this adoring? Pride goeth before a fall, as he had good reason to know! He wondered if, in this country, being adored led to being eaten!

For a few hours Joe mulled over these upsetting prospects, then exhaustion got the better of his gloomy thoughts and he fell into a reasonably deep sleep, which undoubtedly would have continued until daybreak, if an unexpected dampness under the sleeper hadn't woken him up.

The dampness soon changed into water, and the water rose all the way to Joe's waist.

"What's going on?" he said. "A flood? A waterspout? Have those Negroes invented a new torture? Blimey, I'm not hanging around till it's up to my neck!"

With that he hit the wall with his shoulder, staved it in, and found himself . . . in the middle of the lake! The island was no more! It had sunk during the night! The vast waters of Lake Chad were taking its place!

"Nasty country for real estate developers!" Joe told himself. And he devoted his energies to doing some more swimming.

The gallant lad had been saved by a phenomenon that's fairly common in Lake Chad; more than one island has vanished in this way, although seeming as solid as a rock, and the waterside communities have often had to take in the hapless survivors of these dreadful catastrophes.

Joe hadn't known about this local idiosyncrasy, but he was quick to take advantage of it. He spotted a small craft drifting around and quickly pulled up to it. It was a tree trunk that had been crudely hollowed out. Luckily two paddles were inside, and Joe went with the flow, making the most of a fairly swift current.

"Let's see where we stand," he said. "It's the polestar's job to point the way north anywhere on earth—that'll be a help to me."

He was pleased to find that the current was carrying him toward Lake Chad's north shore, and he let it. Around two in the morning, he set foot on a headland covered with thorny reeds that were a real nuisance even to a philosophical chap; but a tree grew there, offering him an obvious bed in its branches. Joe climbed into it as a safety measure, didn't sleep much, and waited for the crack of dawn.

Morning came with that speed characteristic of the equatorial regions. Joe glanced over the tree that had sheltered him during the night; his terrified eyes took in a pretty shocking sight. The branches of that tree were literally crawling with snakes and chameleons; their intertwining bodies completely hid its foliage; you would have sworn it was a new species of tree that sprouted reptiles; the whole thing was creeping and writhing in the early morning sunlight! Joe felt a sharp thrill of terror mixed with disgust, and the horde hissed at him as he jumped to the ground.

"Nobody will ever believe it," he said.

He didn't know that Dr. Vogel's final letters had revealed this peculiarity of the Lake Chad shoreline, which has more reptiles than any country on earth. After what he had just seen, Joe was determined to be more cautious in the future, and he started off to the northeast, getting his bearings from the sun. He very carefully avoided any shacks, huts, shanties, or hideouts—in a nutshell, anything that could function to contain members of the human race.

How many times he examined the sky! He hoped to see the *Victoria*, and although he looked in vain that whole travel day, he still had complete faith in his master; it took great strength of character for him to accept his circumstances so philosophically. He faced not only exhaustion but hunger, because it's hard to charge your batteries on a diet of roots, the marrow from shrubs such as the *mêlé*, or fruit from that palm called the gingerbread tree; and yet he estimated that he had gone some thirty miles farther west. His body had scratches in twenty places from the thousands of thorns that garnish the reeds, acacias, and mimosas by the lake, and his bleeding feet made walking tremendously painful. But in the end he managed to bear up under these afflictions, and when night fell, he decided to spend it on the shores of Lake Chad.

There he had to endure the agonizing bites of thousands of insects: flies, mosquitoes, and half-inch ants literally covered the ground. After two hours Joe wasn't wearing a stitch of the few clothes left to him; the insects had devoured them! It was a dreadful night, and our weary traveler didn't get an hour of sleep; meanwhile boars, wild buffaloes, and a dangerous type of manatee called the *ajoub* thrashed around in the bushes and underwater; this wildlife concert blared throughout the night. Joe didn't dare to even fidget. He had a tough time practicing patience and acceptance under these conditions.

Finally it was daylight again; Joe got up in a hurry, and you can imagine the disgust he felt on seeing the vile creature he had shared his bed with—a toad! But it was a toad five inches wide, a monstrous, repulsive creature that looked him over with big round eyes. Joe felt sick to his stomach, and energized by his revulsion, he ran at top speed and did a nosedive into the lake. This swim took the edge off the itching that tormented him, and after chewing a few leaves, he took to the trail again with a persistence and doggedness he couldn't explain; he no longer felt in touch with his own actions, and yet the feeling inside him was more powerful than despair.

But he was tormented by dreadful pangs of hunger; his belly complained bitterly, being less accepting than he was; he had to tie a creeper tightly around his body; fortunately he could quench his thirst every step of the way, and when he recalled what he had suffered in the desert, he felt comparatively lucky that he wasn't facing the agonies caused by that urgent need.

"What's keeping the *Victoria* . . . ?" he wondered. "The wind's blowing from the north! She'll have to come back over the lake! Probably Mr. Samuel will have worked out some new arrangement to restore her buoyancy; but he had all day yesterday to finish the job; so today it might be possible for him to. . . . But I'd better act as if I'll never see him again. After all, if I manage to reach one of the big lake towns, I'll be in the same position as travelers my master told us about. Why wouldn't I pull through like they did? What the hell, some of 'em made it back! Come on! Chin up!"

And so our courageous Joe talked as he walked—then he stumbled on a gathering of savages in midforest. He stopped in time, and nobody spotted him. The Negroes were busy poisoning their arrows with spurge sap, a major concern for tribes in these parts and carried out with a kind of solemn pageantry.[1]

Motionless, holding his breath, Joe was hiding deep in a thicket, when he looked up through a gap in the foliage and spied the *Victoria*—the *Victoria* herself, heading toward the lake, barely a hundred feet above him. But it was impossible to call out! Impossible to get her attention!

A tear came to his eye, not out of despair but gratitude: his master was looking for him, his master hadn't deserted him! He needed to wait until these Blacks were gone; then he could leave his hiding place and run down to the water's edge.

But the *Victoria* had already vanished into the distant skies. Joe was determined to wait for her: she was sure to fly back over! She indeed flew back, but more to the east. Joe ran, waved, and shouted . . . it was no use! A strong wind carried the balloon off with unstoppable speed!

For the first time there were no strength and hope left in the poor fellow's heart; he felt he was done for; he believed his master was gone for good; he didn't dare think anymore, he wanted to turn off his brain.

That whole day and part of the night, he walked on like a madman, feet bloody, body bruised. He dragged himself along, sometimes on his knees, sometimes on his hands; he saw the moment coming when his strength would fail him and it would be time to die.

Pushing on this way, he ended up in front of a marsh—or rather what he soon learned was a marsh, because night had set in a few hours back; without warning he fell into a viscous mire; despite his efforts, despite his desperate resistance, he felt himself gradually sinking into the depths of that swampy terrain; a few minutes later it was up to his waist.

"Well, I'm at death's door!" he told himself. "And some death this is . . . !"

He struggled furiously; but his efforts only managed to bury him deeper in that grave the poor fellow was digging for himself. There wasn't a single piece of wood to buoy him up, a single reed to hang onto . . . ! He could see that it was all over . . . ! His eyes closed!

"Master . . . master . . . help!" he called out.

Despairing, alone, already stifled, his voice died away in the night.

chapter 36

Hordes on the horizon — a band of Arabs — the chase — it's him! — fall from a horse — the throttled Arab — a bullet from Kennedy — stratagem — airlift — Joe safe.

When Kennedy went back on the lookout in the front of the gondola, he kept a very careful eye on the horizon.

After a while he turned to the doctor and said:

"If I'm not mistaken, that's a band of men or animals on the move out there; you still can't see 'em clearly. Anyhow they're causing quite a commotion, because they're kicking up a cloud of dust."

"Could it be another contrary wind," Samuel said, "a twister coming to drive us back to the north?"

He stood up and examined the horizon.

"I doubt it, Samuel," Kennedy replied. "It's a herd of gazelle or wild oxen."

"Maybe, Dick; but those hordes are at least nine or ten miles away, and speaking for myself, I can't identify a thing, not even with a spyglass."

"Anyhow I won't let 'em out of my sight; they're up to something unusual, and it has me stumped; at times you'd think they were on horseback doing field exercises. By George, that's it! They really *are* horsemen! Look!"

The doctor carefully studied the figures in question.

"I think you're right," he said. "It's a detachment of Arabs or Tibbous;

they're hurrying in the same direction we are; but we're faster and we'll easily gain on them. In half an hour they'll be in view, and we'll see what we're up against."

Kennedy had grabbed his spyglass again and was carefully eyeing them. The body of horsemen grew more visible; some of them had separated from the rest.

"Apparently they're doing a field exercise," Kennedy went on, "or it's a hunting party. You'd think those fellows were chasing something down. I'd really like to find out what."

"Patience, Dick. If they continue heading that way, we'll overtake them shortly and leave them far behind; we're doing twenty miles per hour, and no horse can keep up that kind of pace."

Kennedy stayed on the lookout, and a few minutes later he said:

"They're Arabs charging at top speed. I can make 'em out perfectly. There are about fifty. I can see their burnooses[1] billowing in the wind. It's a field exercise; their commander's a hundred paces out in front, and they're rushing to close ranks."

"Whoever they are, Dick, they aren't a concern, and I'll go higher when we need to."

"Hold on! Hold on a second, Samuel!" After looking again, Dick added, "That's odd. There's something that puzzles me; from the way they're forcing the pace, from their ragged formation, those Arabs seem more like they're chasing him than following him."

"You're certain of that, Dick?"

"No question. I'm absolutely right! It's a hunt—a manhunt! That's not their commander out in front, it's somebody on the run."

"On the run?" Samuel said excitedly.

"Yes!"

"Let's keep him in sight and see what happens."

The balloon promptly gained three or four miles on the horsemen, even though they were moving with phenomenal speed.

"Samuel! Samuel!" Kennedy exclaimed in a trembling voice.

"What's the matter, Dick?"

"Am I hallucinating? Is this possible?"

"What do you mean?"

"Hold on."

And the hunter quickly wiped the lenses in his spyglass, then took another look.

"Well?" the doctor asked.

"It's him, Samuel!"

"Him?" the doctor exclaimed.

That *him* said it all! There was no need to supply a name!

"He's on horseback! Barely a hundred paces ahead of his enemies! He's running from 'em!"

"It's Joe all right!" the doctor said, turning white.

"He's too busy running to see us!"

"He'll see us," Fergusson replied, cutting back the flame in his burner.

"How?"

"In five minutes we'll be fifty feet off the ground; in fifteen we'll be right above him."

"We need to alert him with a gunshot!"

"No! He can't come back toward us, they'll cut him off."

"What should we do?"

"Wait."

"Wait! What about those Arabs?"

"We'll overtake them! We'll pass them by! We aren't two miles behind, and so long as Joe's horse still holds up—"[2]

"Good God!" Kennedy interrupted.

"What's wrong?"

Kennedy had let out a despairing yell as Joe hurtled to the ground. His horse had just collapsed, apparently spent.

"He saw us!" the doctor exclaimed. "He waved to us as he got back on his feet!"

"But the Arabs will catch up with him! What's he waiting for? I say, that took real backbone! Bravo!" the hunter added, beside himself.

After falling, Joe had instantly gotten to his feet just as one of the swiftest horsemen rushed at him; he ducked and dodged, leaped like a panther onto the horse's rump, grabbed the Arab from behind, throttled him with his wiry, steel-fingered hands, toppled the man onto the sand, and resumed his hair-raising escape.

An immense shout from the Arabs rose into the air; but they were all caught up in the chase and hadn't spotted the *Victoria*, which was some 500 paces to the rear and barely thirty feet off the ground; their fastest horsemen weren't twenty lengths behind the escapee.

One of their lancers had gotten appreciably closer to Joe and was about to run him through, when Kennedy drew a clear, steady bead on the fellow, stopped him cold with a bullet, and knocked him to the earth.

Joe didn't even look back at the sound. When they saw the *Victoria*, part of the band pulled up short and fell face down in the dust; the others continued the chase.

"But what's Joe doing?" Kennedy exclaimed. "He isn't stopping!"

"He's doing better than that, Dick; I see what he's up to! He keeps riding in the same direction as the balloon. He's counting on us to use our heads! Ah, the gallant lad! We'll carry him off under the Arabs' noses! We aren't more than 200 paces back!"

"What should we do?" Kennedy asked.

"Set your shotgun aside."

"Right," the hunter said, putting down his weapon.

"Could you hold 150 pounds of ballast in your arms?"

"Even more."

"No, that will be enough."

And the doctor piled bags of sand into Kennedy's arms.

"Stay in the rear of the gondola and get ready to drop this ballast in one fell swoop. But for God's sake, don't do it before I give the word!"

"Relax!"

"Otherwise we'll let Joe down, and he'll be done for!"

"You can count on me!"

By then the *Victoria* was almost directly above that band of horsemen who were so hot on Joe's heels. In the front of the gondola, the doctor unrolled the ladder, ready to toss it out at the critical moment. Joe had kept a distance of fifty feet between his pursuers and himself. The *Victoria* overtook them.

"Get ready!" Samuel told Kennedy.

"All set."

"Joe, save yourself!" the doctor yelled in a ringing voice as he tossed out the ladder, its bottom rungs scraping the ground and stirring up dust.

When the doctor called to him, Joe looked back without reining in

Joe is carried off.

his steed; the ladder flopped down next to him, and just as he caught hold of it:

"Drop away," the doctor snapped to Kennedy.

"Done."

And relieved of a weight greater than Joe's, the *Victoria* climbed 150 feet into the air.

Joe clung tightly to the ladder while it shook and shivered from side to side; gesturing something unprintable to the Arabs, he climbed on board with clownlike agility and joined his companions, who gave him a hearty welcome.

The Arabs let out a howl of surprise and fury. The runaway had just been airlifted out of their clutches, and the *Victoria* shot off into the distance.

"Master! Mr. Dick!" Joe had said.

And he had fainted dead away in his excitement and exhaustion, while Kennedy yelled in a state of near delirium:

"He's safe! He's safe!"

"Of course!" the doctor answered, serenely composed once more.

Joe was nearly naked; his bloody arms and bruised body all testified to what he had suffered. The doctor dressed his wounds and laid him under the tent.

Joe soon recovered from his fainting spell and asked for a glass of brandy, which the doctor felt shouldn't be denied him, since Joe deserved special treatment and wasn't just anybody. After downing his drink, he shook hands with his two companions and announced he was ready to tell his story.

But they wouldn't let him talk, and the gallant lad fell sound asleep again, something he seemed to desperately need.

By then the *Victoria* had gone off at an angle into the west. Thanks to the efforts of a bit too much wind, she crossed over palm trees bent or uprooted by the storm, then sighted the wilderness of brambles again; and after managing a run of nearly 200 miles in the wake of Joe's airlift, she crossed over longitude 10° as evening drew on.

chapter 37

Course to the west—Joe wakes up—his stubbornness—end of Joe's story—Tagelel—Kennedy's uneasiness—northern route—a night near Agadez.

During the night the wind recuperated from its daytime exertions, while the *Victoria* was peacefully at rest above the crown of a big sycamore; the doctor and Kennedy took turns standing watch, and Joe benefited by falling sound asleep and dozing for a good twenty-four hours.

"That's the medicine he needs," Fergusson said. "Nature will take care of his recovery."

At daybreak the wind was erratic but gathering strength again; it lurched both north and south, but finally it carried the *Victoria* to the west.

Map in hand, the doctor identified the kingdom of Damergou, rolling lands of great fertility, the shacks in its villages built from long reeds interwoven with milkweed boughs; out in the tilled fields, seed grinders were mounted on little platforms to protect them from intrusive mice and termites.

They soon reached the town of Zinder, identifiable from its huge square for public executions; the gallows tree stands in the center; the hangman keeps watch at the foot of it, and anybody who passes under its shadow is immediately strung up!

Checking the compass, Kennedy couldn't help saying:

"It's blowing us north again!"

"What difference does it make? If it takes us to Timbuktu, we'll have no reason to complain! We couldn't carry out a grander journey, or under finer conditions . . ."

". . . or in better health," Joe remarked, sticking his cheery face triumphantly through the tent flaps.

"Our gallant friend! Our rescuer!" the hunter exclaimed. "How goes it?"

"Why, perfectly naturally, Mr. Kennedy! Couldn't be better! Nothing perks a fellow up like a leisurely spin after a dip in Lake Chad! Right, master?"

"My worthy boy!" Fergusson replied, shaking his hand. "What distress and anxiety you caused us!"

"And you caused me! Do you think I was in a state of bliss over what happened to you? You can give yourself credit for scaring me silly!"

"We'll never get anywhere, Joe, if that's the way you view things."

"Looks like his fall didn't change him any," Kennedy added.

"You've shown supreme dedication, my boy, and that rescued us; if the *Victoria* had fallen into the lake, nobody could have pulled her out."

"But if my dedication—as you like to call my somersault—is what rescued you, didn't it rescue me too? All three of us are in the pink of health! Consequently we have nothing to blame ourselves for in this whole business."

"Nobody *ever* gets anywhere with this boy," the hunter said.

"The best policy for us," Joe shot back, "is to quit talking about it. What's done is done! For better or for worse, we can't do it over again."

"Stubborn as ever!" the doctor said with a chuckle. "Will you at least be kind enough to tell us your story?"

"If it means so much to you! But beforehand I'm going to turn this plump goose into something properly cooked, because I notice Mr. Dick didn't waste any time."

"Quite true, Joe."

"All right, we'll see how this African game takes to a European stomach."

With the help of the burner, the goose got roasted quickly and devoured instantly. Joe polished off his share like a man who hasn't eaten in days. After tea and grog he brought his companions up to date on his adventures; he spoke with some emotion, describing what happened with his usual philosophical outlook. Time and again the doctor couldn't keep from shaking his hand, when he saw his worthy servant more concerned for his master's safety than his own; as for that moment when the island of the Biddiomahs sank underwater, Samuel explained to him that this phenomenon is common in Lake Chad.

Finally, moving right along, Joe came to the part where he fell into the marsh and called out in despair one last time.

"I figured I was done for, master," he said, "and I thought of you. I put up a struggle. How? I won't go into details; I had no intention of being swallowed without an argument . . . then, two paces away, I see—get this—the end of a freshly cut mooring line; I make one last try and somehow I reach the rope; I pull on it; it resists; I haul myself up, and there I am on solid ground at last! At the end of that line I find an anchor . . . ! Wow, master, if you don't mind my saying so, that was a 'safety anchor' if there ever was one! I recognize it! It's one of the *Victoria*'s anchors! You'd touched down around there! I follow where the line goes, which tells me where you've gone, and after additional efforts I pull myself out of the bog. I'd recovered my strength along with my nerve, so I walked for part of the night and put some distance between the lake and me. Finally I reached the edge of an immense forest. Some horses were in an enclosure, where they were grazing without a worry in their heads. Anybody can get on a horse with enough motivation, agreed? I don't give it a moment's thought—I hop on the back of one of those quadrupeds, and off we go full speed ahead to the north. I won't mention the towns I didn't see or the villages I ducked around. Naw. I cross through seeded fields, I jump over shrubbery, I clear fences, I spur my animal on, I get him worked up, I make him fly! I reach the end of the farmland. Good, there's the desert! Suits me; I'll see farther and clearer. I keep hoping I'll find the *Victoria* waiting for me to dash up and jump in. Not a sign of her. Three hours later I blunder like a fool into an Arab campsite! Cripes, some hunting party that was . . . ! You see, Mr. Kennedy, a hunter doesn't know what hunting really is till he's the one being hunted! Even so, I recommend passing up the opportunity where possible! My horse had collapsed from exhaustion; they corner me; I fight back; I jump behind an Arab on his horse! I have nothing against him, so I sincerely hope he doesn't resent me throttling him! But I'd spotted you . . . and you know the rest! The *Victoria* races after me, and you snatch me up like a knight tilting at the ring.[1] Wasn't I right to count on you? Well, Mr. Samuel, you see how simple it all is. Nothing in the world could be more natural! I'd do it all again if it would help you any! Otherwise, as I told you, master, it isn't worth talking about."

"My gallant Joe!" the doctor replied with feeling. "So we weren't wrong to trust in your shrewdness and skill!"

"Phooey, sir, just stay on top of developments and you'll pull through! The surest way, you see, is always to take things as they come."

During Joe's story the balloon had swiftly covered a long stretch of country. Soon Kennedy pointed out a cluster of huts on the horizon that looked like a town. The doctor checked his map and identified the hamlet of Tagelel in Damergou.

"We've found Barth's route again," he said. "This is where he separated from his two companions Richardson and Overweg. The first was to take the Zinder route, the second the route to Maradi, and you remember that Barth was the only one of those three travelers who saw Europe again."

"Therefore," the hunter said, tracing the *Victoria*'s heading on the map, "we're going due north."

"Due north, my dear Dick."

"And that doesn't make you a little uneasy?"

"Why?"

"Because this way leads us to Tripoli and over the big desert."

"Oh, we won't be going that far, my friend; at least I hope not."

"But where do you expect to halt?"

"Look here, Dick, aren't you interested in visiting Timbuktu?"

"Timbuktu?"

"Positively," Joe said. "You can't take a trip to Africa without dropping by Timbuktu!"

"You'll only be the fifth or sixth European to see that mystery town."

"Timbuktu it is!"

"Then let's get up between latitude 17° and 18°, and there we'll find a favorable wind to take us west."

"Fine," the hunter replied. "But we still have to go a good way north?"

"At least 150 miles."

"Then," Kennedy remarked, "I'll grab a little shut-eye."

"Sweet dreams," Joe replied. "And you should make like Mr. Kennedy, master; you've got to be in need of rest, because I made you keep some ungodly hours."

The hunter stretched out inside the tent; but Fergusson rarely gave in to exhaustion and stayed on the lookout.

Three hours later, going at tremendous speed, the *Victoria* passed over a rocky landscape with rows of tall, bare mountains on granite foundations; a few isolated peaks had elevations as high as 4,000 feet; giraffes, antelopes, and ostriches leaped with marvelous agility through forests of acacias, mimosas, souahs,[2] and date palms; after the barren wilderness, vegetation was regaining the upper hand. This was the country of the Kailouas, who wrap their faces in lengths of cotton cloth, like their dangerous neighbors the Tuaregs.

At ten o'clock that evening, after a mighty 250-mile crossing, the *Victoria* came to a halt over a major town: the moon gave you a glimpse of a subdivision that lay half in ruins; a few tips of mosques shot up here and there, highlighted by the white glow from above; the doctor took some star sights and found he was at the latitude of Agadez.

Formerly an immense trade center, this town was already in ruins by the time Dr. Barth paid it a visit.

Nobody spotted the *Victoria* in the dark, and she touched down in a huge field of millet[3] two miles beyond Agadez. The night was fairly tranquil and lasted until around five in the morning, when a light wind wooed the balloon westward and even a little to the south.

Fergusson jumped at this piece of good luck. He quickly ascended and headed off into the spreading sunlight.

chapter 38

The day of May 17 was serene and totally uneventful; the desert was back again; a moderate wind led the *Victoria* to the southwest; she didn't veer either right or left; her shadow drew a perfectly straight line over the sand.

Before setting out, the doctor took care to replenish his water supply; he was afraid that he might not be able to touch down in these regions, which were teeming with Aulliminden Tuaregs. The mesa rose 1,800 feet above sea level, sinking lower to the south. Our travelers cut across the route from Agadez to Murzuk — a route often pummeled by the feet of camels — and arrived that evening in latitude 16° and longitude 4° 55′, having covered 180 long, monotonous miles.

During that day Joe fixed their last pieces of game, which required only minimal preparation; he served up quite a tasty supper of snipe shish kebab. The wind was blowing well, so the doctor decided to continue on through the night, which featured a radiant moon that was nearly full. The *Victoria* climbed to an altitude of 500 feet, and during the sixty-odd miles of this nighttime crossing, she wouldn't have troubled the gentle slumber of a baby.

On Sunday morning the wind changed direction again; it blew to the northwest; a few crows flew through the air, and a flock of vultures soared closer to the horizon, fortunately keeping their distance.

The sight of those birds led Joe to compliment his master on his idea of using two balloons.

"Where would we be," he said, "with just one envelope? This second balloon is like a ship's lifeboat; in case of a wreck, we can still use it to get to safety."

"You're right, my friend; only I'm a trifle worried about my lifeboat; it isn't as good as the vessel herself."

"What do you mean?" Kennedy asked.

"I mean that our new *Victoria* isn't as good as the old one; whether her fabric is starting to wear through, or her gutta-percha is melting from the heat of the coil, I'm aware that she's definitely leaking gas; so far it's nothing major, but it adds up in the long run; we're tending to lose altitude, and to stay aloft, I have to work harder to make the hydrogen expand."

"Bloody hell!" Kennedy said. "I don't see any way to fix that."

"There isn't any, my dear Dick; which is why we'd be wise to press on and avoid halting even at night."

"Are we still far from the coast?" Joe asked.

"Which coast, my boy? If only we knew where chance will guide us; all I can tell you is that Timbuktu still lies 400 miles to the west."

"And how long will it take us to get there?"

"If the wind doesn't lead us too far astray, I figure on coming into town toward Tuesday evening."

"Then we'll arrive quicker than that caravan," Joe said, pointing to a long line of animals and men winding through the middle of the desert.

Fergusson and Kennedy leaned over the side and saw a huge array of all sorts of creatures; there were more than 150 camels, the type that tote a 500-pound load from Timbuktu to Tafilet for twelve gold mutkals;[1] under the tail each carried a little bag to catch its excrement, the only campfire fuel you can count on in the desert.

These Tuareg camels are the species of choice; they can go three to seven days without water and two without food; the speed of these dromedaries is greater than a horse's, and they intelligently obey the voice of the *khabir*, the caravan guide. They are known locally by the name *mehari*.

These were the details the doctor gave his companions as they studied that community of men, women, and children, who were walking carefully over sand that was in semimotion, sand barely held in place by a few thistles, shriveled weeds, and puny shrubs. The wind erased their footprints almost immediately.

Joe asked how Arabs managed to find their way in the desert and reach the wells scattered over those immense wastes.

"Arabs," Fergusson answered, "have been given a marvelous path-finding instinct by nature; where a European would lose his bearings, they never hesitate; a nondescript rock, a pebble, a tuft of grass, a different shade of sand are enough to point them the right way; during the night they steer by the polestar; they don't go over two miles per hour and rest during the blazing noonday heat; you can gather from this how long they take to cross the Sahara, a desert more than 900 miles wide."

But the *Victoria* had already vanished before the astonished eyes of those Arabs, who must have envied her speed. By evening she had crossed longitude 2° 20′,* then that night she traveled another degree and a fraction.

The weather changed completely on Monday; rain fell with great intensity; they had to bear up under this deluge and the added weight it gave the balloon and gondola; this ongoing cloudburst explained the marshes and swamps that exclusively make up the country's surface; plant life reappeared thereabouts, along with mimosa, baobab, and tamarind trees.

This was the Songhai Empire, its villages topped by upside-down roofs like Armenian hats; there were few mountains but just enough hills to form ravines and preserves where guinea fowl and snipe criss-crossed in the air; here and there an impetuous stream cut across the routes; the natives cross over by clinging to a creeper that stretches from one tree to another; the forests gave way to jungles bustling with gators, hippopotamuses, and rhinoceroses.

"We'll soon come in sight of the Niger," the doctor said. "The region changes as it nears a big river. These moving roadways, as they're aptly called, brought vegetation with them initially, just as they'll bring civilization later on. Thus the seeds of Africa's leading cities have been sown along the banks of the Niger's 2,500-mile course."

"You know," Joe said, "that reminds me of the pious bloke who felt

* Using the meridian of Paris as longitude 0°.

it was so thoughtful of Providence to always run rivers through big towns!"

At noon the *Victoria* passed over a hamlet, Gao, an assemblage of rather squalid shacks that used to be a teeming metropolis.

"This is where Barth crossed the Niger coming back from Timbuktu," the doctor said. "It's a river that has been famous since ancient times, the Nile's rival, a river of heavenly origin according to pagan superstitions; like the Nile it has captured the attention of geographers down through the ages; and even more than the Nile, its exploration has cost many lives."

The Niger flowed between its two well-separated banks; its waters rolled southward with distinct force; but our fast-moving travelers could barely catch its intriguing contours.

"I wanted to tell you about this river," Fergusson said, "and already we've left it behind! Under the names of *Dhiouleba, Mayo, Egghirreuu,* and *Quorra* among others, it runs through an immense stretch of country, almost rivaling the Nile in length. These names quite simply mean 'river' in the different regions it crosses."

"Did Dr. Barth take this route?" Kennedy asked.

"No, Dick; after leaving Lake Chad, he traveled through the chief towns in Bornu and cut across the Niger at Say, four degrees below Gao; then he went deep into those unexplored regions found in the Niger bend, and after eight months of additional exertions, he made it to Timbuktu—which we ourselves will reach in under three days, with a wind as brisk as this."

"Did anybody discover the Niger's source?" Joe asked.

"Quite a while ago," the doctor answered. "Many exploring parties were motivated to scout out the Niger and its tributaries, and I can list the main ones for you. From 1749 to 1758,[2] Adanson inspected the river and visited Gorée Island; from 1785 to 1788 Golbéry and Geoffroy Saint-Hilaire traveled over the deserts of Senegambia and went as far up as the country of the Moors, who murdered Saugnier, Brisson, Adams, Riley, Cochelet, and so many other unfortunates. Then came the famous Mungo Park, Sir Walter Scott's friend and also Scottish himself. Sent in 1795 by the Royal African Society of London, he reached the Bambara Empire, sighted the Niger, covered 500 miles with a slave trader, scouted out the Gambia River, and after going back to England in 1797, he left again on January 30, 1805, along with his brother-in-law Anderson, the draftsman Scott, and a crew of hired hands; he reached Gorée Island, took on a detachment of thirty-five soldiers, and sighted the Niger again on August 19; but by that point, due to exhaustion, hardships, ill-treatment, foul weather, and the country's unsanitary conditions, no more than eleven Europeans were left out of forty; on November 16 Mungo Park's final letters reached his wife, and a year later a peddler from those parts stated that on December 23, when the unfortunate Park reached Bussa on the Niger, his small craft overturned in the river's waterfalls, and he himself was slaughtered by the natives."

"And his dreadful fate didn't keep explorers away?"

"Quite the contrary, Dick; because by that point they had to do more than scout out the river, they had to recover the traveler's papers. In 1816 London organizers put together an expedition in which Major Gray took part; it arrived in Senegal, entered Fouta Djallon, visited the Fula and Mandingo peoples, then went back to England without accomplishing anything further. In 1822 Major Laing explored all of west Africa bordering on England's possessions, and he was the first to reach the Niger's headwaters; according to his records, the wellspring of this immense river is less than two feet across."

"No problem to jump over," Joe said.

"Excuse me? No problem?" the doctor countered. "If we're to believe tradition, any individual attempting to jump across that spring is immediately swallowed up; anybody who tries to draw water out of it feels an invisible hand push him back."

"And is it acceptable to not believe tradition?" Joe asked.

"It's acceptable. Five years later it was Major Laing's destiny to cross the Sahara, to enter Timbuktu, and a few miles farther to be garroted by the Oulad-Shiman,[3] who tried to force him to turn Muslim."

"Another life lost!" the hunter said.

"It was at this juncture that a valiant young man of slender means undertook to carry out the most amazing journey of the modern era; I'm referring to the Frenchman René-Auguste Caillié. After various attempts in 1819 and 1824, he again left the Rio Nuñez on April 19, 1827; he arrived in Timé on August 3, so exhausted and ill that he couldn't resume his journey until January 1828, six months later; then, protected by his oriental clothing, he joined a caravan, reached the Niger on March 10, entered the town of Djenné, and boated down the river as far as Timbuktu, where he arrived on April 30. Paul Imbert, another Frenchman, may have seen that intriguing town in 1670, likewise the Englishman Robert Adams in 1810; but René-Auguste Caillié would be the first European to bring back exact information; on May 4 he left this queen city of the desert; on the 9th he inspected the very place where Major Laing was murdered; on the 19th he arrived in Araouane, then left that mercantile town to run a thousand dangers in the huge wastes lying between Sudan and Africa's northernmost regions; finally he got to Tangier and on September 28 set sail for Toulon; in nineteen months, despite 180 days of illness, he'd crossed Africa west to north. By Jove, if Caillié had been born in England, he would have been honored as the most courageous traveler of modern times, the equal of Mungo Park! But in France his achievements weren't fully appreciated."*

"He was a bold companion," the hunter said. "And what happened to him?"

"He died from his exertions at age thirty-nine; the Paris Geographical Society thought it had done enough by awarding him a cash prize in 1828; England would have given him the highest honors! Meanwhile, as he was carrying out this marvelous journey, an Englishman had envisioned the same undertaking and was attempting it with just as much courage if not quite as much luck. This was Captain Clapperton, Denham's companion. In 1829 he went back to Africa, landing on the west coast in the Bight of Benin; he picked up the trails of Mungo Park and Laing, in Bussa recovered the records of Park's death, and on August 20 arrived in Sokoto, where, held captive, he breathed his last in the arms of his loyal assistant Richard Lander."

"And what happened to this Lander?" Joe asked with great interest.

"He managed to get back to the coast and then home to London, bringing along the captain's papers and an accurate report of his own journey; then he offered to help the government finish scouting out the Niger; he joined forces with his brother John, the second child of poor Cornwall parents, and from 1829 to 1831 these two men went back down the river from Bussa to its mouth, describing it village by village, mile by mile."

"So both brothers escaped the usual fate?" Kennedy asked.

"Yes, during that expedition at least—because in 1833 Richard undertook a third journey to the Niger and was struck down near the river's mouth by a bullet from an unknown musket. So you see, my friends, this country we're crossing has witnessed the noblest kinds of dedication, for which, all too often, death has been the reward!"

* Dr. Fergusson speaks from an Englishman's viewpoint and perhaps is exaggerating; nevertheless we must acknowledge that out of France's travelers, René-Auguste Caillié didn't enjoy the fame his dedication and courage deserved.

chapter 39

*The countryside in the Niger bend—phantasmagoric
view of the Hombori Mountains—Kabra—
Timbuktu—Dr. Barth's ground plan—loss of glory—
wherever heaven wants.*

During that bleak Monday Dr. Fergusson was happy to give his companions a thousand details on the region they were crossing. The terrain was fairly level and offered no obstacles to their progress. The doctor's only worry came from that bloody northeasterly wind, which was blowing furiously and took him farther from the latitude of Timbuktu.

After running north to that town, the Niger curves around like an immense jet of water and falls back into the Atlantic Ocean, fanning out at the delta; the countryside in this bend is quite varied, sometimes luxuriantly fertile, sometimes exceptionally barren; cornfields give way to undeveloped plains, which turn into wide expanses covered with broom.[1] Numerous flocks of all sorts of aquatically inclined birds (pelican, teal, kingfisher) live along the banks of the streams and backwaters.

Now and again they saw a campsite of Tuaregs taking refuge under their animal-skin tents, while their wives were outside attending to chores, milking the camels, and puffing up a storm as they smoked their pipes.

Toward eight in the evening, the *Victoria* had gone some 200 miles farther west, at which point our travelers witnessed a magnificent sight.

A few shafts of moonlight had made their way through a rift in the clouds, glided between the streaks of rain, and fallen on the Hombori mountain chain. Nothing could have looked more eerie than those basaltic peaks; their phantasmagoric profiles stood out against the dark-

ening sky; you would have sworn they were the fabled ruins of some immense town in the Middle Ages, the same thing ice barriers suggest to an amazed onlooker during a dark night in the polar seas.[2]

"That's scenery out of *The Mysteries of Udolpho*," the doctor said.[3] "Ann Radcliffe couldn't have cut those mountains into a more frightening shape."

"Cor," Joe replied, "I wouldn't take an evening stroll by myself in that spooky country! Look here, master, if it wasn't so heavy, I'd pack the whole landscape off to Scotland. It would look spiffy on the shores of Loch Lomond, and tourists would flock there in droves."

"Our balloon isn't big enough for that dream to come true. But it seems to me we're changing direction. Good! The hobgoblins in this locality are kindly souls; they're blowing a little southeasterly breeze that will put us back on track."

In essence the *Victoria* was resuming a course more to the north, and on the morning of the 20th, she passed over a hopelessly tangled network of channels, streams, and rivers, the whole mishmash of the

Niger's tributaries. Covered with dense weeds, several of these channels looked like lush meadows. There the doctor picked up the route Barth took when he boated down the river to Timbuktu. The Niger was 4,800 feet wide at this point, flowing between two banks rich in leafy vegetables and tamarind trees; herds of gazelle were leaping about, their annulated horns[4] blending with the tall weeds where gators lay silently in wait.

Loaded with merchandise from Djenné, long lines of donkeys and camels plunged under the lovely trees; soon an amphitheater of low houses appeared in a curve of the river; all the fodder gathered thereabouts lay heaped on their terraces and roofs.

"It's Kabra!" the doctor exclaimed delightedly. "It's the harbor for Timbuktu; the town isn't five miles from here!"

"So you're happy, sir?" Joc asked.

"Ecstatic, my boy."

"Well, this too shall pass."

By two o'clock, in fact, the queen city of the desert was unfolding beneath our travelers' eyes—secretive Timbuktu, which used to have its schools of learned men and its chairs of philosophy just like Athens and Rome.

Fergusson tracked its tiniest details on the ground plan drafted by Barth himself, confirming the German's exceptional accuracy.

The town forms a huge triangle drawn on an immense plain of white sand; its apex points north and pierces a corner of the desert; nothing's nearby, just a few grasses, some dwarf mimosas, and some scrawny shrubs.

As for Timbuktu's appearance, imagine a pile of marbles and dice; that's the bird's-eye view; the streets are pretty narrow and lined with one-story houses of sunbaked brick plus huts of straw or reeds, the first square, the second cone-shaped; a few townspeople were negligently reclining on the terraces, draped in bright robes, lance or musket within reach; however no women were out at that time of day.

"But they're said to be beautiful," the doctor added. "You'll notice the three towers of the three mosques—they're all that remain of a great many. The town has definitely deteriorated since its glory days! Sankore Mosque stands at the peak of the triangle, its rows of hallways supported by arches of classic design; farther on, near the Sanegungu quarter, are Sidi Yahya Mosque and a few two-story houses. Don't go looking for palaces or monuments. The sheik is a mere peddler, and his royal home is a trading post."

"Seems like those ramparts have just about collapsed," Kennedy said.

"They were destroyed by Fula tribesmen in 1826; at that time the town was over a third larger, because, since the eleventh century, Timbuktu has been universally lusted after and has belonged consecutively to Tuareg, Songhai, Moroccan, and Fula invaders; in the sixteenth century a local scholar such as Ahmad Baba al Masufi could own a library of sixteen hundred manuscripts, but today this great hub of civilization is nothing more than a commercial warehouse for central Africa."

In fact the town seemed to have lapsed into total indifference; it radiated that negligence so widespread in cities on their last legs; its outskirts were cluttered with immense trash heaps, the only things standing out from the terrain aside from the marketplace hill.

As the *Victoria* went by, she aroused a little activity below, a drumbeat or two; but the last scholar in the place barely had time to study this new phenomenon; driven off by the desert wind, our travelers continued to follow the river's winding course, and soon Timbuktu was nothing more than one of their trip's fleeting memories.

"And now," the doctor said, "we'll go wherever heaven wants!"

"Provided it's to the west," Kennedy shot back.

"Phooey!" Joe commented. "Even if we backed up all the way to Zanzibar, or crossed the ocean to America, I wouldn't feel a bit alarmed!"

"First we must be able to, Joe."

"And what's keeping us from being able to?"

"Gas, my boy; our balloon's lifting power has noticeably decreased, and we'll need to do some major economizing if we're to make it to the coast. I'll even have to drop some ballast. We're too heavy."

"That's what comes of just twiddling your thumbs, master! If you lie down and loaf all day like a slacker in a hammock, you'll fill out and get overweight. This is a lazy man's journey that we're on, and when we get back, they'll find us big and fat."

"More choice thoughts from Joe," the hunter replied. "But let's see how it all works out; do we know what heaven has in store for us? Our journey's still far from over. Where do you figure we'll come down on the African coast, Samuel?"

"I'd be hard pressed to answer you, Dick; we're at the mercy of highly variable winds; but ultimately I'd feel lucky if I landed between Sierra Leone and Portendick; that's a stretch of country where we'll meet up with friends."

"And it'll be a pleasure to shake hands with 'em; but are we at least heading the way we want?"

"Not really, Dick; look at the magnetic needle on our compass; we're running south and going up the Niger toward its headwaters."

"A first-rate opportunity to discover 'em," Joe remarked. "Too bad somebody already has. Does that mean we couldn't find new ones in a pinch?"

"No, Joe; but don't worry, I honestly don't expect to go that far."

At nightfall the doctor dropped his last bags of ballast; the *Victoria* climbed again; the burner was going full blast but could barely keep him aloft; by that point he was sixty miles south of Timbuktu, and the next morning he woke up over the banks of the Niger, not far from Lake Debo.

chapter 40

Dr. Fergusson's uneasiness—stubbornly heading south—a cloud of locusts—view of Djenné—view of Ségo—the wind shifts—Joe's regrets.

At this point large islands divided the riverbed into narrow branches with very swift currents. A few shepherd huts stood on one of these islands; but it wasn't possible to get its exact bearings, because the *Victoria* kept picking up speed. Unfortunately she was still trending south, going over Lake Debo in a matter of seconds.

Forcing the envelope to expand all it could, Fergusson searched for other air currents at different altitudes, but in vain. He quickly gave up this strategy, which increased his chances of losing gas by putting pressure on the weakened walls of his lighter-than-air vehicle.

He didn't say anything, but he was growing quite uneasy. By pushing him back toward Africa's southern parts, the wind's stubbornness upset his calculations. He didn't know who or what to count on anymore. If he didn't reach English or French territories, what would happen in the midst of those barbaric people overrunning the Guinea coast? How could he wait there for a ship to take him back to England? And the wind's present heading was driving him over the kingdom of Dahomey, populated by one of the fiercest tribes and at the mercy of a king who sacrificed thousands of human victims at public festivities! There, they would be done for.

On the other hand the balloon was visibly weakening, and the doctor felt she would give out on him! But the weather was brightening a little, and he hoped that when the rain let up, it would lead to a change in the air currents.

So he got an unpleasant reminder of where things stood when Joe made this comment:

"Great!" the lad said. "Now we'll have twice as much rain, a real deluge this time, judging from that cloud moving in!"

"Another cloud?" Fergusson asked.

"And a prize winner!" Kennedy replied.

"I've never seen anything to match it," Joe remarked. "The edges look like they were drawn with a chalk line."

"I can breathe again," the doctor said, putting down his spyglass. "That isn't a cloud."

"Get along with you!" Joe said.

"No, it's a swarm!"

"Excuse me?"

"It's a swarm of locusts."

"Those are locusts?"

"Thousands of locusts that will sweep through the sky like a whirlwind, and God help this countryside if they land, because they'll wreak havoc!"

"I'd be curious to see that!"

"Wait a bit, Joe; in ten minutes that cloud will be upon us, and you'll assess it with your own two eyes."

Fergusson spoke the truth; several miles in extent, that dense, heavy cloud arrived with an earsplitting racket, parading its immense shadow across the ground; there were incalculable legions of those locusts, also known as grasshoppers when they aren't migrating. A hundred paces from the *Victoria*, they swooped down on the lush green countryside; a quarter of an hour later, the pack of them took to the air again, and even from far away our travelers could tell that the trees and bushes had been stripped bare, the meadows scalped. You would have sworn that winter had suddenly descended on that landscape and left it utterly barren.

"Well, Joe?"

"Well, sir, it's very interesting but perfectly natural. What one locust does in a small way, thousands do in a big way."

"A rain of terror so to speak," the hunter said. "It's even more dreadful than a hailstorm when you add up the damage."

"And it's impossible to guard against," Fergusson replied. "Sometimes the natives have thought to burn the forests down, even crops in the field, in order to halt the flights of those insects; but when the front lines rush into the fire, they put it out with their sheer mass, so there's no stopping the rest of the horde. In these regions, luckily, they make a sort of restitution for the destruction they cause; the natives gather great numbers of these insects and eat them with pleasure."

"They're like airborne shrimp," Joe said, adding he was sorry he had never tasted one for his "continuing education."

The countryside grew swampier as evening drew on; the forests gave way to solitary clumps of trees; alongside the river you could make out tobacco plantations and marshes full of fodder. Sitting on a large island, the town of Djenné turned up, including the two towers of its earthen mosque and the rank odor from those millions of swallows nests accumulating on its walls. The crowns of a few baobabs, mimosas, and date palms poked up between the houses; even at night the place seemed quite busy. In fact Djenné is a major commercial town; it caters to all of Timbuktu's needs; its varied industrial output is shipped there aboard small craft sailing downriver or caravans traveling the shady lanes.

"If it wouldn't prolong our journey," the doctor said, "I'd be tempted to land in that town; surely more than one Arab there has gone to France or England and might be acquainted with our method of propulsion. But it wouldn't be wise."

"Let's put that visit off till our return trip," Joe said with a grin.

"Besides, my friends, the wind is showing a slight tendency to blow from the east, if I'm not mistaken; it wouldn't do to miss such an opportunity."

The doctor tossed out a few items that were now useless, a few empty bottles and a meat carton that no longer served any purpose; he managed to keep the *Victoria* in a zone more conducive to his plans. At four in the morning, the first rays of sunlight fell on Ségo, capital of the Bambara Empire, easy to recognize from the four towns that comprise it, from its Moorish mosques, and from the ferryboats constantly coming and going, transferring residents to its various quarters. But our travelers barely managed to see or be seen; they were flying on a quick, direct course to the northwest, and the doctor's uneasiness subsided little by little:

"Another two days in this direction at this speed, and we'll reach the Senegal River."

"And will it be friendly country?" the hunter asked.

"Not exactly; if the *Victoria* should fail us though, we could get to the French settlements in a pinch! But if she can hold up for a few hundred miles, we'll make it to the west coast safe, sound, and in good spirits."

"And that'll be that!" Joe said. "Oh well, too bad! If I wasn't so keen on talking about this trip, I'd never set foot on the ground again! Do you think they'll put any stock in our story, master?"

"Who knows, my gallant Joe! Ultimately there will always be one undeniable fact—a thousand witnesses will have seen us set out from one side of Africa; a thousand witnesses will see us arrive on the other side."

"In which event," Kennedy replied, "I think it'll be hard to say we didn't go all the way across!"

"Aw, Mr. Samuel," Joe continued with a heavy sigh, "there'll be times when I'll regret not having my solid gold rocks! They would've given *weight* to our assertions and *persuasiveness* to our reports! At a gram of gold per listener, I could put together a nice crowd to hear me out . . . and even to adore me!"

chapter 41

Nearing the Senegal River—the Victoria *continues to lose altitude—they keep dumping and dumping— Messrs. Pascal, Vincent, and Lambert[1]—the marabout El-Hadj Umar Tall—Muhammad's rival— difficult mountains—Kennedy's weapons—Joe's stratagem—layover above a forest.*

On May 27 at around nine in the morning, the countryside took on a new guise: the long, sprawling slopes changed into hills that heralded the arrival of mountains; the balloon would have to go over the range separating the Niger and Senegal basins, the range that determines whether their waters run off into the Gulf of Guinea or the Cape Verde bay.

The territory leading to the Senegal River is on the books as a dangerous part of Africa. Dr. Fergusson knew this from the accounts of his predecessors; they had suffered a thousand hardships and run a thousand dangers among those primitive Negroes; this deadly climate consumed the majority of Mungo Park's companions. So Fergusson was more determined than ever to not set foot in this unfriendly land.

But he didn't get a moment's peace; the *Victoria* was noticeably losing altitude; whenever he went over a mountaintop, he had to dump additional amounts of things that were more or less useless. And that's what they faced for more than 120 miles; they were worn out from all the climbing and descending; the balloon kept going back down as if she were Sisyphus's rock;[2] their lighter-than-air vehicle was already so deflated, she looked like a bag of bones; her shape grew leaner and leaner, and the wind dug huge pockets in her flabby envelope.

Kennedy couldn't help commenting on this.

"Did the balloon split somewhere?" he said.

"No," the doctor answered. "But obviously the heat has softened or

Joe detaching the tent from the gondola

melted the gutta-percha, and the hydrogen is seeping through the taffeta."

"How can we stop this seepage?"

"We can't. We'll lighten her; that's the only way; anything we can discard, we'll discard."

"What's next?" the hunter asked as he looked around the gondola, already well cleaned out.

"The tent weighs a substantial amount, let's get rid of it." This order was Joe's responsibility, and he climbed onto the hoop that kept the strands of netting in place; from there he had no problem detaching the tent's heavy folds and heaving them overboard.

"That'll cheer up a whole tribe of Negroes," he said. "It's enough to deck out a thousand natives—with them, a little cloth goes a long way."

The balloon had risen a little, but it soon became clear she was sinking toward the ground again.

"Let's disembark," Kennedy said, "and see what we can do about that envelope."

"I repeat, Dick, that we haven't any way to repair it."

"Then what should we do?"

"We'll jettison everything that isn't absolutely indispensable; I want to avoid stopping in these parts at any cost; these forests we're now skimming over have their share of dangers."

"What! Lions? Hyenas?" Joe asked with a sneer.

"Worse than that, my boy—human beings, and the most vicious in Africa."

"Says who?"

"Travelers who have come here before us; also the French occupying the colony of Senegal—they've inevitably entered into relations with the neighboring tribes; under Colonel Faidherbe's administration, they've scouted out more and more of this country; officers such as Messrs. Pascal, Vincent, and Lambert have brought back valuable documentation from their expeditions. They've explored the regions formed by the bend of the Senegal River, areas left in ruins by war and looting."

"So how did that happen?"

"This way. In 1854 El-Hadj Umar Tall, a marabout[3] in the Fouta region of Senegal, claimed to be inspired like Muhammad, and he urged all the tribes to wage war on the infidels, in other words, on Europeans. He brought destruction and devastation to the lands between the Senegal River and its tributary the Falémé River. Under his guidance three hordes of fanatics crisscrossed the country, looting and slaughtering, not sparing a village or even a hut; he pushed into the Niger valley as far as the town of Ségo, threatening it a good while. In 1857 he went farther north and laid siege to the fort of Médine, which the French had built on the riverbank; the hero defending this settlement was Paul Holl, who stood his ground for several months, nearly without food or ammunition until Colonel Faidherbe came to his rescue. Then El-Hadj and his forces went back over the Senegal River, reentering the kingdom of Kaarta to continue their thievery and slaughter; now then, the regions below us are where he and his bandit hordes fled and found refuge, and I assure you it wouldn't be good to fall into his hands."

"We won't fall into 'em," Joe said. "We'll lighten the *Victoria* if we have to jettison everything down to our shoes."

"We aren't far from the river," the doctor said. "But I anticipate that our balloon won't be able to carry us beyond it."

"If we just reach its banks," the hunter remarked, "it'll be a step up."

"That's what we're trying to do," the doctor said. "Except one thing worries me."

"What?"

"We'll have mountains to go over, which will be difficult since I can't increase our vehicle's lifting power, not even by generating the greatest heat possible."

"Then," Kennedy added, "let's wait and see."

"Poor *Victoria!*" Joe said. "I've gotten attached to her like a seaman to his ship; it'll be hard to part with her! Who cares if she's not the same as when we set out! But I won't hear a word against her! She's done an honorable job for us, and it'll break my heart to leave her behind."

"Don't worry, Joe; if we leave her, it will happen because we have no choice. She'll stay on the job until she's at the end of her strength. All I ask from her is another twenty-four hours."

"She has nothing left," Joe commented, studying her. "She's wasting away, she's going fast. Poor balloon!"

"If I'm not mistaken, Samuel," Kennedy said, "those mountains you mentioned are on the horizon."

"They are indeed," the doctor said after examining them with his spyglass. "They strike me as quite high—we'll have a hard time clearing them."

"Can't we dodge around 'em?"

"I doubt it, Dick; see the immense area they take up: nearly half the horizon!"

"They even look like they're closing in around us," Joe said. "They're gaining on both the right and left."

"We absolutely must go over them."

That ultra dangerous obstacle seemed to be coming on with tremendous speed, but in actuality a very brisk wind was sweeping the *Victoria* toward those sharp peaks. She had to go higher at any cost or risk crashing into them.

"Empty our water tank," Fergusson said. "Keep enough for just one day."

"Done!" Joe said.

"Are we rising again?" Kennedy asked.

"A little, fifty feet or so," the doctor answered, his eyes never leaving the barometer. "But it isn't enough."

In essence that lofty mountain range was bearing down on the travelers as if planning to pounce on them; they weren't even close to rising above it; they needed to go more than 500 feet higher. Accordingly they dumped out the water supply for the burner; they kept only a few pints; but it still didn't do the trick.

"But we must get over," the doctor said.

"Since the tanks are empty, let's ditch 'em," Kennedy said.

"Go ahead."

"Out they go!" Joe said. "It's sad to see us crumbling away a piece at a time."

"As for you, Joe, don't go demonstrating your dedication the way you did the other day! Whatever happens, swear to me you won't leave us."

"Relax, master, nobody's going anywhere."

The *Victoria* was back around 120 feet up, but the mountain peak still loomed over her. This was a moderately steep ridge that culminated in a genuinely sheer wall. It was still more than 200 feet higher than the travelers.

"In ten minutes," the doctor told himself, "our gondola will smash into those rocks if we don't manage to rise over them!"

"Well, Mr. Samuel?" Joe asked.

"Keep only our supply of pemmican, and drop all the meat with any weight."

The balloon got lighter by another fifty pounds or so; she rose quite noticeably, but it would make little difference if she didn't climb to a higher level than the mountains. They were in a terrifying predicament; the *Victoria* was racing at great speed; they knew in their hearts she would be dashed to pieces; the impact would be truly dreadful.

The doctor looked around the gondola.

It was almost empty.

"Just in case, Dick, get ready to jettison your weapons."

"Jettison my weapons!" the hunter replied in alarm.

"My friend, if I ask you to, that will mean it's necessary!"

"Samuel! Samuel!"

"Your weapons and your supplies of shot and powder could cost us our lives."

"We're getting close!" Joe exclaimed.

Sixty feet! The mountain was still sixty feet higher than the *Victoria*.

Joe took the bedclothes and heaved them overboard. Without a word to Kennedy, he also ditched several bags of bullets and shot.

The balloon climbed again; she rose higher than that hazardous peak, and her upper half gleamed in the sunlight. But the gondola still hung slightly below some slabs of rock, doomed to crash into them.

"Kennedy! Kennedy!" the doctor shouted. "Throw out your weapons or we're done for!"

"Hold it, Mr. Dick!" Joe said.

Turning around, Kennedy saw him vanish over the side of the gondola.

"Joe! Joe!" he yelled.

"That poor devil!" the doctor exclaimed.

The mountain's summit may have been some twenty feet wide at that spot, and its opposite side featured a gentler incline. The gondola rose right to the level of this flattish mesa; it slid across ground made up of sharp pebbles that screeched on the way.

"We're going over . . . going over . . . we're over the whole thing!" yelled a voice that made Fergusson's heart give a leap.

The courageous lad had held onto the gondola's lower rim; he had sprinted across that summit on foot, in this way relieving the balloon of his total weight; he actually had to keep a firm grip on her, because she was tending to pull away from him.

When he reached the opposite slope and the void was in front of him, Joe hauled himself up with a burst of energy, clung to the rigging, and climbed in next to his companions.

"Nothing to it," he remarked.

"My gallant Joe! My friend!" the doctor said warmly.

"Pshaw, I didn't do it for you!" the lad replied. "It was for Mr. Dick's rifle! I owed him one after that business with the Arab lancer! I like to pay off my debts, and now we're even," he added, handing the hunter his weapon of choice. "I'd hate to see you without it."

Speechless, Kennedy shook his hand heartily.

The *Victoria* had nothing left to do but descend; this was easy; soon she was 200 feet off the ground and in a state of buoyancy. The terrain had a contorted appearance; it featured many irregularities that would be very hard to dodge at night in a balloon that no longer followed orders. Evening was coming on fast, and despite his unwillingness, the doctor had to call a halt until the following day.

"We'll look for a promising place to lay over," he said.

"Aha!" Kennedy replied. "You've finally made up your mind?"

"Yes, for some while I've been pondering a plan that we'll go ahead and carry out; it's still only six o'clock in the evening, so we'll have time. Drop anchor, Joe."

Joe did so, and the two anchors dangled under the gondola.

"I see some huge forests," the doctor said. "We'll ride over their tree-tops and hook up to one of them. I wouldn't spend a night on the ground for anything in the world."

"Can't we disembark?" Kennedy asked.

"What for? Let me remind you that it will be dangerous for us to separate. Besides, I require your help with a difficult task."

The *Victoria* skimmed over those immense forests and before long came to a sudden stop; her anchors caught hold; the wind died out as evening drew on, and she stood nearly stock-still over a huge field of greenery, which was formed by the treetops in a forest of sycamores.

Nothing to it!

chapter **42**

===

Generosity contest—last to be jettisoned—the
expansion mechanism—Joe's dexterity—midnight—
the doctor's watch—Kennedy's watch—he dozes off—
the blaze—shrieks—out of range.

Right off Dr. Fergusson took some star sights and fixed his position; he was barely twenty-five miles from the Senegal River.

"All we have to do, my friends," he said after tapping his map, "is to cross the river; but there are no bridges or rowboats, so we must cross by balloon at any cost; therefore we need to lighten her still more."

"But I'm not too clear on how we'll manage that," the hunter replied, worried about his weapons. "Unless one of us agrees to be jettisoned and left to bring up the rear . . . and it's my turn to claim that honor."

"Blimey!" Joe replied, "Haven't I gotten good at—"

"This isn't about jumping overboard, my friend, but reaching the African coast on foot; I'm an expert hiker, an expert hunter—"

"I'll never go along with it!" Joe shot back.

"My gallant friends, you aren't in a competition to see who's the most generous," Fergusson said. "Hopefully such an extreme measure won't be necessary; but if it is, we won't separate—we'll cross this country together."

"Now you're talking," Joe said. "It wouldn't hurt us to go for a little stroll."

"But beforehand," the doctor went on, "we'll do one last thing to lighten our *Victoria*."

"What?" Kennedy asked. "You've got my curiosity up."

"We need to get rid of the tanks for the burner, the Bunsen battery, and the coil; they're a weight of nearly 900 pounds that we've had to carry through the air."[1]

"But Samuel, how will you get your gas to expand?"

"I won't; we'll manage without it."

"Oh come now—"

"Hear me out, my friends; I've meticulously calculated the lifting power we'll have left; it's enough to carry all three of us plus the few items still remaining; we'll weigh barely 500 pounds including our two anchors, which I want to hold onto."

"My dear Samuel," the hunter replied, "you're better informed on these matters than we are; you're the only one who can assess the situation; tell us what we should do, and we'll do it."

"Just say the word, master."

"I repeat, my friends—no matter how serious this decision may be, we need to jettison our mechanism."

"We'll jettison it!" Kennedy shot back.

"Let's get going!" Joe urged.

It wasn't an easy task; they had to dismantle the mechanism piece by piece; first, they took out the mixing tank, then the tank for the burner, and finally the tank in which the water was broken down; it required nothing less than the combined strength of all three travelers to wrench these containers from the bottom of the gondola where they had been tightly fitted in; but Kennedy was so muscular, Joe so crafty, and Samuel so ingenious, they prevailed in the end; the different pieces vanished consecutively over the side and into the sycamores below, making huge gaps in the foliage.

"Those Negroes will be pretty startled," Joe said, "to bump into things like that in the woods; they could turn 'em into idols!"

Next they had to deal with the pipes running from the coil up inside the balloon. Joe managed to sever their rubber joints a few feet above the gondola; but as for the pipes themselves, they were more trouble because they were secured at the upper end, and brass wires fastened them right to the valve wheel.

That's when Joe put on a marvelous display of dexterity; in his bare feet so he wouldn't scratch the envelope, he clung to the netting and managed to climb all the way up the outside of the balloon, despite her shaking and shivering; after a thousand difficulties he got to the very top, hung on by one hand to that slippery surface, and undid the outside bolts that held the pipes in place. The latter were easy to remove, and they drew them out the lower appendix, which they tied off tightly so it was hermetically sealed.

Freed of this considerable weight, the *Victoria* rose straight into the air and pulled the anchor rope taut.

By midnight they had successfully finished these various tasks and were seriously exhausted; they ate a quick meal of pemmican and cold grog, since the doctor no longer had any heat to put at Joe's disposal.

In any case the lad and Kennedy were dropping from exhaustion.

"Lie down and get some sleep, my friends," Fergusson told them. "I'll take the first watch; at two o'clock I'll wake Kennedy up; at four Kennedy will wake Joe up; at six we'll set out, and heaven protect us during this last travel day!"

The doctor's two companions needed no coaxing, stretched out in the bottom of the gondola, and immediately fell sound asleep.

It was a peaceful night; a few clouds crowded against the moon in her final quarter, her tentative rays barely breaking through the darkness. Leaning an elbow on the gondola's rim, Fergusson looked all around him; he kept a careful eye on the dark curtain of foliage that spread beneath his feet and hid the ground from his view; the tiniest noise aroused his suspicions, and every time the leaves rustled, he launched a full investigation.

He was in that frame of mind, intensified by solitude, in which nebulous terrors flood the brain. At the end of such a journey, after a fellow has overcome so many obstacles and right when his goal is within reach, his fears are more vivid, his feelings become more intense, his destination seems to recede before his eyes.

What's more, their current circumstances were anything but comforting—out in a barbaric country, using a means of transportation that, when all was said and done, could fail him at any moment. The doctor no longer relied wholeheartedly on his balloon; gone were the days when he could do daredevil maneuvers because he had confidence in her.

While processing these feelings, the doctor thought he detected muffled noises down in those huge forests; he even thought he saw a flame flare up momentarily between the trees; he looked intently and aimed his night glass in that direction; but nothing was visible, and the silence seemed to grow even deeper.

No doubt Fergusson was having hallucinations; he listened without detecting the tiniest sound; his spell on watch ending at that point, he woke Kennedy up, urged the hunter to be exceptionally vigilant, and took his place next to Joe, who was sleeping with all his might and main.

Kennedy placidly lit his pipe and rubbed his eyes, which he had trouble keeping open; he leaned on an elbow in one corner and puffed energetically to drive his sleepiness away.

The most abject silence reigned around him; a mild breeze stirred in the treetops and gently rocked the gondola, lulling the hunter into a sleep that was coming over him in spite of himself; trying to resist, he blinked his eyelids several times, peered into the night with a couple of those glances that don't really see anything, then finally yielded to exhaustion and dozed off.

How long was he plunged in that state of inertia? He couldn't answer this question when he woke up, a development abruptly caused by an unexpected crackling sound.

He rubbed his eyes, got to his feet. Intense heat struck him in the face. The forest was in flames.

"Fire! Fire!" he yelled, not at all clear on what was happening.

His two companions got up again.

"What's the matter?" Samuel asked.

"It's a major blaze!" Joe said. "But who could've—"

Just then there was an outburst of shrieking beneath the starkly lit foliage.

"Lumme, savages!" Joe exclaimed. "They set the forest on fire to make sure we burn up!"

"Talibas!" the doctor said. "Probably marabouts serving El-Hadj Umar Tall!"

A ring of fire surrounded the *Victoria*; the crackling of deadwood mingled with the fizzing of green branches; creepers, leaves, and every living piece of vegetation were writhing in that lethal fire; your eyes saw only an ocean of flames; tall trees were outlined in black against the inferno, their branches covered with blazing coals; that cluster of flames, that conflagration, reflected off the clouds, and the travelers felt they were trapped inside a fireball.

"Run for it!" Kennedy yelled. "Climb down! It's the only chance we have!"

But Fergusson held him back firmly, rushed to the anchor rope, and chopped it through with a single swing of the axe. Stretching up

toward the balloon, flames were already licking at her glowing walls; but the *Victoria* had been released from her bonds, and she climbed over a thousand feet into the skies.

Fearsome shouts rang out in the forest below, then sharp cracks from firearms; caught in an air current that sprang up with the dawn, the balloon headed west.

It was four o'clock in the morning.

chapter 43

The Talibas — the chase — a devastated country — not much wind — the Victoria *loses altitude* — the last provisions — the Victoria *leaps around — fighting back with gunfire* — the wind picks up — the Senegal River — Gouina Falls — hot air — crossing the river.

"If we hadn't taken the precaution of lightening our balloon last evening," the doctor said, "we would've been done for, there's no getting around it."

"A stitch in time saves nine," Joe remarked. "Nothing could be more natural."

"We're still in danger," Fergusson countered.

"Why are you worried?" Dick asked. "The *Victoria* can't descend without your say-so, and what if she does?"

"What if she does? Dick, take a look!"

Our travelers had just passed the edge of the forest when some thirty horsemen came in sight, dressed in bulky pants and fluttering burnooses; they were armed, some with lances, others with long muskets; keeping their speedy, spirited horses to a canter, they were going the same way as the *Victoria*, which by then was moving at a moderate pace.

Seeing the travelers, they let out wild yells and shook their weapons; you could read anger and menace in their dusky faces, which looked even fiercer with their sparse but bristly beards; they crossed effortlessly over the low mesas and mild gradients leading down to the Senegal River.

"Here they come!" the doctor said. "They're cruel Talibas, ferocious marabouts serving El-Hadj Umar Tall! I'd rather be surrounded by wild animals in midforest than fall into the hands of those bandits."

"They don't look very neighborly!" Kennedy said. "And they're strapping brutes!"

"Luckily their animals can't fly," Joe replied. "That's a point for our side."

"Look at those ruined villages," Fergusson said, "those shacks burned to the ground! That's their handiwork; and here, in place of huge tracts of tilled land, they've left drought and devastation."

"For now they can't get at us," Kennedy remarked, "and if we make it to the far side of the river, we'll be safe."

"Completely safe, Dick; but we mustn't go lower," the doctor replied, his eyes darting to the barometer.

"Anyhow, Joe," Kennedy went on, "it won't hurt to get our weapons ready."

"Can't do any harm, Mr. Dick; good thing we didn't sprinkle 'em down the road behind us."

"My rifle!" the hunter exclaimed. "Here's hoping we never part."

And Kennedy loaded it with the greatest care; he had an ample supply of powder and bullets left.

"What's our altitude?" he asked Fergusson.

"About 750 feet; but we no longer can look for favorable currents by climbing or descending. We're at the balloon's mercy."

"That's a nuisance," Kennedy continued. "There isn't much of a wind, and if we'd run into a hurricane like the ones earlier, we would've lost sight of those wretched bandits hours ago."

"The rascals are following us at a canter," Joe said. "They're taking it easy, they're out for a stroll."

"If they were in range," the hunter said, "I'd have fun unhorsing 'em one after the other."

"I daresay!" Fergusson replied. "But we'd be in range as well, and our *Victoria* would offer an all-too-easy target for bullets from their long muskets; and if they punctured her, just imagine the predicament we'd be in."

The Talibas chased them all morning long. Approaching eleven o'clock, our travelers had gone barely fifteen miles farther west.

The doctor kept an eye out for the tiniest clouds on the horizon. He lived in constant dread of changes in the atmosphere. If he should be tossed back toward the Niger, what would happen to him? Furthermore he noted that the balloon was visibly tending to lose altitude; since setting out he'd already dropped more than 300 feet, and the Senegal River had to be a dozen or so miles away; at his present speed he was bound to be traveling for another three hours.

Just then a new round of yells caught his attention; the Talibas were frantically urging their horses onward.

The doctor checked his barometer and learned the reason for all the shrieking:

"We're descending," Kennedy said.

"Yes," Fergusson replied.

"Bloody hell!" Joe thought.

After a quarter of an hour, the gondola wasn't 150 feet off the ground, but the wind was blowing with more energy.

The Talibas reared up on their horses, and soon a barrage from their muskets exploded in the sky.

"You're too far off, you morons!" Joe called. "We'd better make sure those scoundrels keep their distance."

He drew a bead on one of the closer horsemen and fired; the Taliba tumbled to the ground; his companions came to a stop, and the *Victoria* pulled farther ahead.

"They're playing it safe," Kennedy said.

"Because they're convinced they'll catch us," the doctor replied. "And they'll succeed if we keep descending! We absolutely must go higher!"

"What can we dump?" Joe asked.

"Our entire remaining stock of pemmican! That's an additional thirty pounds we can dispense with!"

"It's gone!" Joe said, following orders.

The gondola had nearly touched down, then it rose again in the midst of howls from the Talibas; but half an hour later the *Victoria* was swiftly dropping again; her gas was seeping through the envelope's pores.

Soon the gondola was skimming over the ground; El-Hadj's Negroes rushed toward it; but as happens in such circumstances, the *Victoria* had barely touched down when she gave a leap into the air, only to swoop again a mile farther on.

"So we aren't going to get away!" Kennedy said.

"Toss out our brandy stores, Joe," the doctor snapped, "our instruments, everything that has any weight whatever—and our last anchor, since we have no choice!"

Joe snatched up the barometers and thermometers; but they didn't amount to much, and after the balloon climbed for an instant, she soon fell back toward the earth. The Talibas were hard on her heels, just 200 paces behind her.

"Throw out the two shotguns!" the doctor shouted.

"Not without firing 'em at least," the hunter replied.

And he squeezed off four consecutive rounds into the crowd of horsemen; four Talibas fell, to frenzied shouts from the rest of the band.

The *Victoria* went higher again; she made several enormously long leaps, like an immense rubber ball bouncing over the ground. Our poor travelers were a strange sight, trying to get away by taking gigantic strides, seeming to gain new energy as soon as they touched the earth, like the giant wrestler Antaeus![1] But this situation couldn't go on. It was almost noon. The *Victoria* was tiring, emptying out, getting leaner; her envelope grew flabby and fluttery; the spreading folds of its taffeta squealed against each other.

"Heaven's abandoning us," Kennedy said. "We're riding for a fall!"

Joe didn't reply but looked at his master.

"No!" Fergusson said. "We have over 150 additional pounds left to drop."

"Just what exactly?" Kennedy asked, thinking the doctor was losing his mind.

"The gondola!" Samuel replied. "Let's get up in the netting! We can hold onto the meshes and make it to the river! Hurry! Hurry!"

And the daredevils didn't hesitate to clutch at this last straw. They clung to the meshes of the netting as the doctor had instructed, and while Joe held on with one hand, he cut the ropes attaching the gondola; it dropped away just as their vehicle was going down for good.

Fighting back with gunfire

"Hooray! Hooray!" he shouted as the balloon, lighter again, climbed back to 300 feet.

The Talibas spurred their horses; they were racing at full gallop; but the *Victoria* found a livelier wind, increased her lead, and swiftly headed for a hill that blocked the western horizon. This was a promising circumstance for our travelers—they could fly over it, while El-Hadj's horde had to turn north in order to get around this latest obstacle.

The three friends held on tight to the netting; they had managed to tie it together underneath them, and it formed a sort of fluttering pocket.

Suddenly, after they had cleared the hill, the doctor exclaimed:

"The river! The Senegal River!"

Sure enough, the river was rolling along two miles away, quite a broad expanse of water; low and fertile, the opposite bank offered a safe refuge and a promising place to come in for a landing.

"Another quarter of an hour," Fergusson said, "and we'll be out of danger!"

But it wasn't to be; the empty balloon gradually dropped down over terrain almost completely devoid of vegetation. There were long slopes and rocky plains, just a few shrubs and some coarse grass dried out by the hot sun.

The *Victoria* touched down several times and rose again; her leaps got shorter and lower; ultimately she sat still, and the top part of her netting brushed the high branches of a baobab, the only tree left standing out in that deserted countryside.

"It's over," the hunter said.

"Just a hundred paces from the river," Joe added.

Our hapless trio stepped down onto the ground, and the doctor led his two companions toward the banks of the Senegal.

At this location the river was making a thunderous racket that didn't let up; reaching its edge, Fergusson realized they were at Gouina Falls! Not a rowboat at waterside, not a sign of life.

Two thousand feet wide, the Senegal River rushed down from a height of 150 feet, making a deafening noise. It flowed from east to west, and the row of rocks that blocked its course ran north to south. The rocks standing in the middle of the falls had strange shapes, like immense prehistoric animals turned to stone in the midst of the waters.

Clearly this chasm was impossible to cross; Kennedy couldn't help throwing up his hands.

But Dr. Fergusson exclaimed in a bold, forceful voice:

"It's *not* over!"

"I didn't think so," said Joe, who never lost confidence in his master.

The sight of that dried-up grass had given the doctor a daring idea. It was their only chance. He quickly led his friends over to the vehicle's envelope.

"We have at least an hour's head start on those bandits," he said. "Let's not waste a second, my friends; gather up a huge load of this dry grass; I need at least a hundred pounds' worth."

"To do what?" Kennedy asked.

"I haven't any more gas; all right, I'll cross the river using hot air!"

"Ah, my gallant Samuel!" Kennedy exclaimed. "You're truly a man among men!"

Joe and Kennedy got to work, and an enormous haystack soon sprang up next to the baobab tree.

Meanwhile the doctor had enlarged the throat of his lighter-than-air vehicle, cutting a wider opening at the bottom; he took care beforehand to expel any remaining hydrogen through the valve; then he piled a load of dry grass under the envelope and set it on fire.

It doesn't take long to inflate a balloon with hot air; a temperature of 180°° is enough to thin the air inside and reduce its weight by 50%; so the *Victoria* began to get noticeably rounder again; there was no shortage of grass; the fire increased thanks to the doctor's attentions, and his lighter-than-air vehicle fattened up before their eyes.

By that point it was twelve forty-five.

Just then, two miles to the north, the band of Talibas came in sight; you could hear their yells and the hoofbeats of horses racing at top speed.

"They'll be here in twenty minutes!" Kennedy said.

"More grass, Joe, more grass! In ten minutes we'll be high in the sky!"

"There you go, sir."

The *Victoria* was two-thirds inflated.

"My friends, hold onto the netting as we did before!"

"Righto," the hunter replied.

After ten minutes the balloon gave a lurch or two, indicating she

was set to lift off. The Talibas were closing in; they were barely 500 paces away.

"Hold on tight," Fergusson shouted.

"Not to worry, master!"

With his foot the doctor pushed another load of grass into the blaze.

Fully inflated by the rise in temperature, the balloon lifted off, rubbing against the baobab's branches.

"We're on our way!" Joe exclaimed.

A barrage of musket fire replied to him; a bullet actually scraped

his shoulder; but Kennedy leaned over the side, fired his rifle with one hand, and laid another enemy low.

Indescribable shouts of rage greeted the ascension of their lighter-than-air vehicle, which climbed to nearly 800 feet. A fast moving wind took hold of her, she shook and shivered alarmingly, and meanwhile the courageous doctor and his companions gazed at the chasm of waterfalls opening up beneath their eyes.

Ten minutes later, without a word spoken, our courageous travelers were gradually descending toward the river's other bank.

Dressed in French military uniforms, a group of about ten men stood there, astounded, marveling, awestruck. You can imagine their amazement when they saw that balloon lift off from the river's right bank. They were close to thinking it was some astronomical phenomenon; but their officers, a naval lieutenant and sublieutenant, knew about Dr. Fergusson's daring endeavor from Europe's newspapers, and they instantly realized what was going on.

Gradually deflating, the balloon dropped lower and lower while the bold balloonists held onto her netting; but there wasn't much chance she could make it ashore; so the Frenchmen dashed into the river and gave the three Englishmen a warm welcome, just as the *Victoria* splashed down several yards from the Senegal's left bank.

"Dr. Fergusson!" the lieutenant exclaimed.

"The same," the doctor replied serenely, "along with his two friends."

The Frenchmen led the travelers away from the river, while a swift current carried off the half-deflated balloon, which looked like an immense bubble as she went over Gouina Falls and sank into the waters of the Senegal River.

"Poor *Victoria*!" Joe said.

The doctor couldn't keep back a tear; he spread his arms, and his two friends rushed into them under the sway of deep emotion.

chapter 44

Conclusion—the signed statement—the French settlements—the outpost in Médine—the Basilisk*—Saint-Louis—the English frigate—return to London.*

That military expedition on the riverbank had been sent by Senegal's governor; its two officers were Lieutenant of Marines Dufraisse and Sublieutenant Rodamel; plus it also included a sergeant and seven enlisted men. For two days they had been busy scouting out the most promising location for an outpost in Gouina, and then they witnessed Dr. Fergusson's arrival.

You can easily imagine the backslaps and congratulations lavished on our three travelers.[1] The Frenchmen could vouch for the completion of this daring project and naturally became Samuel Fergusson's witnesses.

Accordingly the doctor asked them right off if they would officially verify his arrival at Gouina Falls.

"Would you be willing to sign a statement to that effect?" he asked Lieutenant Dufraisse.

"We're at your service!" the officer answered.

He led the Englishmen to a temporary outpost built on the river-bank; there they received the most attentive care and lavish hospitality. And at this location they drew up a statement that resides today in the archives of the Royal Geographical Society of London, a statement that reads as follows:

TO WHOM IT MAY CONCERN—

We the undersigned declare that on the date given below, we watched Dr. Fergusson and his two companions Richard Kennedy and Joseph Wilson* arrive while holding onto the netting of a balloon; said balloon fell a few paces from us into the very heart of the river, rode off with the current, and vanished over Gouina Falls. In witness whereof we have signed the present statement independently of the above named. — Executed at Gouina Falls, May 24, 1862.

SAMUEL FERGUSSON, RICHARD KENNEDY, JOSEPH WILSON;
Lieutenant of Marines DUFRAISSE; Sublieutenant RODAMEL;
Sergeant DUFAYS; Privates FLIPPEAU, MAYOR, PELISSIER,
LOROIS, RASCAGNET, GUILLON, and LEBEL.

Dr. Fergusson and his gallant companions had completed their wondrous crossing, as unimpeachable witnesses could confirm; they were now among friends and in the midst of exceptionally cordial tribes who dealt regularly with the French settlements.

They had arrived in Senegal on Saturday, May 24, and on the 27th of the same month, they reached the outpost in Médine, located on the river a little farther north.

French officers there welcomed them with open arms plus a full range of services and resources; the doctor and his companions were able to ship out almost immediately on a small steamboat, the *Basilisk*, which runs downriver to the Senegal's mouth.

Two weeks later on June 10, they arrived in Saint-Louis, whose governor gave them a magnificent welcome; they had completely recovered from their stress and exhaustion. What's more, Joe told anybody willing to listen:

"All in all that was a pretty tame journey we went on, and if a bloke's hungry for excitement, I'd advise him to skip it; it got very tedious toward the end, and if we hadn't run a few risks on Lake Chad and the Senegal River, I honestly think we would've died of yawning!"

An English frigate was ready to leave; our three travelers made their way on board; they reached Portsmouth on June 25, London the next day.

We won't describe the welcome they received at the Royal Geographical Society nor the enthusiasm that greeted them elsewhere.

* Dick is short for Richard and Joe for Joseph.

Kennedy left right away for Edinburgh, packing his notorious rifle; he lost no time assuring his old housekeeper that all was well.

Dr. Fergusson and his loyal Joe remained the same men we're acquainted with. But unbeknownst to the two, something in them had changed.

They had become friends and equals.

Newspapers all over Europe never tired of praising the daring explorers, and the *Daily Telegraph* chalked up a print run of 977,000 copies the day it published the journey's highlights.

During a public gathering at the Royal Geographical Society, Dr. Fergusson gave a report on his airborne expedition, winning for himself and his two companions the gold medal awarded to the most notable feat of exploration in the year 1862.

First and foremost, Dr. Fergusson's journey confirmed in the most meticulous fashion the geographical facts and figures determined by Messrs. Barth, Burton, Speke, and others. Thanks to current expeditions under Messrs. Speke and Grant, Heuglin and Munzinger (respectively going up to the Nile's headwaters and pushing into central Africa), it won't be long before we can validate Dr. Fergusson's *own* discoveries in that immense region, which stretches from longitude 14° all the way to longitude 33°.

THE END

Note on the Translation

Five Weeks in a Balloon was first published as *Cinq semaines en ballon* by J. Hetzel et Cie. in January 1863; Hetzel issued its first illustrated edition in January 1865. Full scans of both editions can be accessed from the Bibliothèque nationale de France at http://gallica.bnf.fr.

This English rendering adheres to the paragraphing in the French original and is complete down to the smallest substantive detail. I've used the Livre de Poche red-cover reissue (2000) as a working text, but since no edition seems entirely free of typos or other production slips, I've double-checked the Livre de Poche reissue against the 1863 and 1865 Hetzel editions as well as later reprints and online texts.

My translation is intended for the U.S. public. Consequently I've worked to create an English text that's both faithful and communicative—faithful in mirroring the content, effect, and priorities of the original French, communicative in its overall wording, in its efforts to suggest Verne's comic and narrative styles, and in its presentation of historical, cultural, and specialized detail. Where the text refers to people, places, things, or concepts that may be unfamiliar to a twenty-first-century American, I've sometimes added a clarifying endnote. As for the footnotes in this new translation, they all derive from the French original.

Since Verne's novel cites an unusually large number of true-life explorers, scientists, and other historical personages, I precede the endnotes with a glossary of thumbnail biographies entitled "Gallery of Heroes." When rendering proper names, whether personal or geographical, the translation favors spellings in regular use today.

Among the many numerical citations in the French, there are repeated references to the *league*, a unit of measurement that seems surprisingly capricious, its sense changing from place to place and period to period. *Five Weeks in a Balloon* employs the "4-kilometer league," which equals 2.484 statute miles but which the novel often rounds down to 2.4 miles. In addition, the French original sometimes reckons weights in *tonneaux* or in metric tons, which my renderings convert to short tons. As for currency, I take the Victorian pound sterling as roughly equivalent to five U.S. dollars, the nineteenth-century franc as equivalent to twenty U.S. cents. The purchasing power of one nineteenth-century dollar seems to have been equivalent to some twenty modern dollars.

Otherwise American readers will have little difficulty with units of measure in *Five Weeks in a Balloon*, since the novel favors the Imperial system of feet, pounds, gallons, and miles used in both Victorian England and today's United States. For Gallic readers, however, the French original often adds footnotes giving metric equivalents—I've kept these for the sake of completeness but have shifted them to the endnotes.

No critical edition exists of *Cinq semaines en ballon*, therefore the translation also makes adjustments where the French original appears to contain production errors or other problematic details; these instances are likewise given in the notes.

FPW

Gallery of Heroes

Abbadie, Antoine Thomson d' (1810–1897). French geographer; explored Ethiopia.

Adams, Robert (1785?–1837?). U.S. sailor; shipwrecked and sold into slavery in northwestern Africa; published *The Narrative of Robert Adams* in 1816.

Adanson, Michel (1727–1806). French naturalist; studied the flora and fauna of Senegal.

Ahmad Baba al Masufi (1556–1627). West African author and activist; Timbuktu's most admired scholar, he wrote over forty books on legal and historical topics.

Anderson, Alexander (1769?–1805). Surgeon, brother-in-law of Mungo Park, and second in command on the latter's expedition up the Niger River; died of dysentery en route.

Arnaud, Joseph-Pons d' (1812–1884). French civil engineer; searched for the source of the White Nile.

Avanchers, Father Léon des (1809–1879). French missionary and geographer; bought and freed slaves in Ethiopia.

Baikie, William (1824–1864). Scottish physician; explored the Niger River.

Baldwin, William Charles (1826–1903). British sportsman; hunted big game around the Cape.

Barnum, Phineas Taylor (1810–1891). American showman; promoter of circuses, sideshows, traveling museums, and assorted hoaxes.

Barral, Jean Augustin (1809–1884). French physicist, agronomist, and balloonist; studied clouds and ice crystals.

Barth, Heinrich (1821–1865). German explorer, linguist, and cultural historian; author of the still-esteemed *Travels and Discoveries in North and Central Africa*.

Battuta, Ibn (1304–1368?). Wide-ranging Moroccan traveler; scoured north and west Africa, the Somali Peninsula, and points east as far as China.

Beke, Charles (1800–1874). English geographer; charted the Blue Nile.

Beltrame, Giovanni (1824–1906). Italian missionary; explored central Africa.

Belzoni, Giovanni (1778–1823). Italian explorer; collected Egyptian antiquities.

Bimbashi, Selim (?–?). Turkish naval commander; searched for the Nile's source over the years 1839–1842.

Bixio, Jacques Alexandre (1808–1865). French physician and balloonist of Italian origin; studied the formation and composition of clouds.

Blanchard, Sophie (1778–1819). French balloonist, the profession's first female; carried off sixty-seven successful ascensions before perishing in an accident over Paris.

Bonnemain, François-Louis de (1817?–1867). Corsican cavalryman based in Algiers; explored Libya, in 1857 issuing *A Report on a Mission to Ghadames*.

Bou Derba, Ismaël (1823–1878). Linguist and interpreter for military expeditions in the Sahara.

Bowdich, Thomas Edward (1791–1824). British traveler; explored western Africa, publishing an account in 1919, *Mission from Cape Coast Castle to Ashantee*; died of malaria.

Bright, John (1811–1889). English Liberal statesman; joined with Richard Cobden in opposing Britain's Corn Laws.

Brioschi, Carlo (1782–1833). Neapolitan astronomer and balloonist; nearly perished while trying to set an altitude record.

Brisson, Pierre-Raymond de (1745–1820?). Frenchman sold into slavery in Senegal; with Saugnier published *Voyages to the Coast of Africa* in 1792.

Browne, William (1768–1813). English traveler; explored Darfur.

Bruce, James (1730–1794). Controversial Scottish explorer; traced the origins of the Blue Nile.

Brun-Rollet, Antoine (1807–1858). French explorer from Savoy; claimed the Misselad River was the true Nile.

Burchell, William (1781–1863). English naturalist; collected a huge number of tropical specimens, as described in his *Travels in the Interior of Southern Africa*.

Burckhardt, Johann (1784–1817). Swiss traveler; explored Nubia in disguise.

Burton, Richard (1821–1890). Illustrious English explorer, translator, and Renaissance man; searched for the Nile's headwaters.

Cailliaud, Frédéric (1787–1869). French geologist; explored Egypt and penned *A Trip to Meroe on the White River*.

Caillié, René-Auguste (1799–1838). French explorer; first European to come back alive from Timbuktu.

Campbell, John (1766–1840). Scottish preacher; developed and refurbished mission sites in South Africa.

Castel-Bolognesi, Angelo (1836–1874). Italian traveler and trader from Ferrara; wrote *Journey to the Gazelle River*.

Chaillu, Paul du (1831?–1903). Franco-American anthropologist; studied gorillas and pygmy culture.

Chapman, James (1831–1872). Hunter and explorer born in Cape Town; took the first 3D photos of African scenes.

Clapperton, Hugh (1788–1827). Scottish mariner and explorer; headed two expeditions into west and central Africa.

Clot Bey. Egyptian title of French physician Antoine Clot (1793–1868); founder of a hospital and medical school near Cairo.

Cobden, Richard (1804–1865). English manufacturer and Liberal statesman; joined with John Bright in opposing Britain's Corn Laws.

Cochelet, Charles (?–?). French castaway held captive in the Sahara; published an account of the experience in 1821, *Shipwreck of the French Brig* Sophia.

Colonieu, Victor-Martin (1826–1902). French commander and antislaver; published *Journey into the Algerian Sahara.*

Courval, Arthur Constant Collas de (1832–1873). French explorer and physician; in 1860 studied malarial cases in Khartoum.

Cuny, Charles (1811–1858). French physician; explored Egypt and Sudan, as described in his *Journal of a Trip from Siout to El Obeid.*

Debono, Andrea (1821–1871). Maltese traveler and trader; explored the upper reaches of the White Nile.

Decken, Karl Klaus von der (1833–1865). German explorer; first Westerner to attempt the ascent of Mt. Kilimanjaro.

Denham, Dixon (1786–1828). English army officer; contentious explorer of Nigeria, Chad, and the Sahara.

Dickinson, John (1832–1863). British physician; volunteered as doctor to the UK's Mission in Central Africa; died of blackwater fever in Malawi.

Dickson, Thomas (1785?–1825?). Scottish surgeon; accompanied Clapperton on his second African expedition, vanishing early on.

Dochard, Duncan (?–1818). British army surgeon; died during the early stages of Gray's expedition down the Gambia and Niger rivers, as described in their *Travels in Western Africa.*

Duncan, John (1805–1849). Scottish cavalryman; master-of-arms on a Niger steamship expedition.

Durand, Jean-Baptiste Léonard (1742–1812). French administrator; published *Journey to Senegal in 1785 and 1786.*

Duroulé, François Janus Le Noir (1665–1705). French diplomat stationed in Egypt; sent by Louis XIV to establish diplomatic relations with Ethiopia; killed in Sudan.

Duveyrier, Henri (1840–1892). French traveler; explored the northern Sahara as a teenager and frequently thereafter to study Tuareg customs.

El-Hadj Umar Tall (1797?–1864). Muslim religious and political leader; established a short-lived empire in Senegal and Guinea.

El-Tounsy, Mohammed ibn-Omar (1789–1857). Arab medical administrator based in Cairo; from 1810 to 1811 explored east Chad, as described in his *Journey to Wadaï*.

Erhardt, Jakob (1823–1901). German missionary; drafted a rough map of north Africa's major lakes.

Escayrac de Lauture, Stanislas d' (1826–1868). French linguist and seeker of the Nile's headwaters; published *Memories of Sudan*.

Faidherbe, Louis (1818–1889). French officer and administrator; as governor of Senegal, he fortified its river to protect French trade interests.

Ferret, Pierre (1814–1882). French traveler; explored Ethiopia with Joseph Galinier, the two publishing *Journey to Abyssinia* in 1847.

Fresnel, Fulgence (1795–1855). French consul at Jidda; described the slave market in his *Memoir of Wadaï*.

Galinier, Joseph (1814–1888). French traveler; explored Ethiopia with Pierre Ferret, the two publishing *Journey to Abyssinia* in 1847.

Galton, Sir Francis (1822–1911). English savant and traveler; penned *Narrative of an Explorer in Tropical South Africa*.

Garnerin, André-Jacques (1769–1823). French balloonist and parachute developer; named Official Aeronaut of France.

Gay-Lussac, Louis Joseph (1778–1850). French chemist and pioneering investigator of the earth's atmosphere.

Geoffroy Saint-Hilaire, Étienne (1772–1844). French naturalist; member of Napoleon's 1798 expedition to Egypt.

Golbéry, Sylvain de (1742–1822). French geographer and military engineer; published *Travels in Africa*.

Gordon-Cumming, Roualeyn (1820–1866). Scottish sportsman; wrote *Five Years of a Hunter's Life in the Far Interior of South Africa*.

Grant, James (1827–1892). Scottish officer; explored the White Nile with Speke.

Gray, William (?-?). British army officer; from 1818 to 1821 explored the Gambia and Niger rivers with Duncan Dochard, as described in their *Travels in Western Africa*.

Hahn, Carl Hugo (1818–1895). German linguist and Lutheran missionary; brokered peace between warring tribes in Namibia.

Halm, Hugo (?-1866?). German missionary; explored the Okavango River in southwest Africa during the 1860s.

Harnier, Wilhelm von (1836–1861). German explorer of the Blue Nile; killed during a buffalo hunt.

Hecquard, Louis Hyacinthe (1814–1866). French officer based in Senegal; published *Coastal and Inland Travels in West Africa*.

Heuglin, Theodor von (1824–1876). German explorer, ornithologist, and mining engineer; published *Travels in Northeast Africa*.

Holl, Paul (?–?). French officer; in 1857 successfully defended the outpost of Médine during an extended siege led by El-Hadj Umar Tall.

Hornemann, Friedrich (1772–1801). Pioneering German explorer; hired by the English to cross north Africa from Cairo to the Niger.

Houghton, Daniel (1740–1791). Irish army officer; set out for Timbuktu and Hausa but vanished without a trace.

Imbert, Paul (1580?–1640?). Sailor captured and enslaved by Moroccans; first Frenchman to visit Timbuktu (around 1618).

Kaufmann, Father Anton (1821?–1882). Austrian missionary and ethnographer; worked with tribes in the White Nile Valley.

Kepler, Johannes (1571–1630). German astronomer; studied planetary motion.

Knoblecher, Ignatius (1819–1858). Slovenian missionary in central Africa; compiled glossaries of Denka, Bari, and other inland languages.

Koner, Wilhelm David (1817–1887). German geographer and historian; published *About the Latest Discoveries in Africa*.

Krapf, Johann (1810–1881). German missionary and linguist; established a mission in Kenya and translated portions of the Bible into African tongues.

Kummer, Adolphus (1786?–1817). German naturalist; visited west Africa with Dochard and Peddie in 1816; died of fever.

Lafargue, Ferdinand. (1800?–1872?). French trader and administrator in south Sudan.

Laing, Alexander (1793–1826?). Scottish officer and explorer; first Westerner to cross the Sahara north to south and reach Timbuktu.

La Jaille, André-Charles, Marquis de (1749–1815). French traveler; published *Journey to Senegal over the Years 1784 and 1785*.

Lambert, Arsène (1828?–1859?). French officer; explored Senegal during Faidherbe's administration.

Lamiral, Dominique Harcourt (1751–1800). French slave trader based in Senegal; published *Metamorphoses of the Aristocracy*.

Lander, John (1807–1839). English adventurer and younger brother of Richard Lander; the two explored the Niger River.

Lander, Richard (1804–1834). English adventurer and elder brother of John Lander; explored West Africa with Clapperton, then the Niger with his brother.

Lefebvre, Charlemagne Théophile (1811–1860). French explorer; led a scientific expedition to Ethiopia, coauthoring *Travels in Abyssinia*.

Lejean, Guillaume (1828–1871). French ethnographer and ambassador to Ethiopia; explored the Nile and Senegal rivers.

Lemprière, William (?–1834). British physician; from 1789 to 1790 tended to the son and wives of the Moroccan monarch Sidi Mohammed ben Abdallah.

Levaillant, François (1753–1824). French explorer and ornithologist; collected specimens in the Cape area, penning a six-volume *Natural History of African Birds*.

Livingstone, David (1813–1873). Famed Scottish missionary; explored the Zambezi, Shire, and Ruvuma rivers.

MacCarthy, Charles (1768–1824). Irish brigadier-general; variously governor of Senegal, Gorée Island, and Sierra Leone.

Mackenzie, Charles (1825–1862). Scottish missionary; consecrated bishop in Cape Town, he worked with Livingstone in central Africa.

McClure, Robert (1807–1873). Irish polar explorer; traveled the Northwest Passage by boat and sled.

Maestlin, Michael (1550–1631). German astronomer; mentor of Johannes Kepler.

Magyar, Laszlo (1818–1864). Hungarian mariner and explorer; published *Journeys in South Africa*.

Maizan, Eugène (1816–1845). French naval officer; notorious for being brutally tortured, dismembered, and murdered by Wakamba tribesmen.

Malte-Brun, Victor Adolphe (1816–1889). French geographer and mapmaker; secretary-general of the Paris Geographical Society.

Malzac, Alphonse de (1822?–1860). French slave trader, ivory hunter, and White Nile expert; deemed a scoundrel by Heuglin and others.

Mehemet Ali (1769–1849). Ottoman commander; founded a ruling dynasty in Egypt.

Méry, Joseph (1797–1866). French tale spinner, scriptwriter, and satirist; Verne cites his short story "Lion Fishing" in chapter 29.

Meusnier, Jean-Baptiste (1754–1793). French chemist and engineer; experimented with regulating a balloon's buoyancy.

Miani, Giovanni (1810–1872). Venetian musician and scholar; searched for the Nile's headwaters.

Moffat, Robert (1795–1883). Scottish missionary; spent forty-nine years with the peoples of the Kalahari Desert, writing *Missionary Labors and Scenes in Southern Africa*.

Mollien, Gaspard-Théodore (1796–1872). French traveler and diplomat; explored Senegal and Guinea, publishing *Journey into the African Interior*.

Monteiro, Joachim John (1833–1878). Portuguese geologist and engineer; explored Angola, the Congo River, and Africa's slave trade.

Montgolfier, Joseph-Michel (1740–1810) and Jacques-Étienne (1745–1799). French balloonists and inventors; launched the first manned balloon in 1783.

Morrison, Robert (1773?–1825). English naval surgeon and naturalist; explored
Nigeria with Clapperton.

Munzinger, Werner (1832–1875). Swiss administrator; explored central Africa
with Heuglin.

Neimans, Baron von (1832?–1855). Bavarian explorer; died in Cairo while
organizing a search for Vogel.

Oudney, Walter (1790–1824). Scottish physician and naturalist; explored
Nigeria and the Sahara.

Overweg, Adolf (1822–1852). German scientist and explorer; mapped the Lake
Chad region.

Palmerston, Lord (1784–1865). British statesman; twice elected prime minister.

Panet, Léopold (1819?–1859). Senegalese explorer; first to cross the Mauri-
tanian Sahara, as described in his *Report of a Journey from Senegal to
Mogador*.

Park, Mungo (1771–1806). Scottish surgeon; first Westerner to explore the
Niger River.

Partarrieu, Adrien (1791?–1860). Senegalese guide and interpreter; assisted the
British in west Africa over the years 1818–1824.

Pascal, S. L. (1834?–1861?). French officer; explored Gambia's Bambouk district
c. 1860.

Pearce, Nathaniel (1779–1820). English naval officer; spent a decade in Ethiopia,
describing the experience in *The Life and Adventures of Nathaniel Pearce*.

Peddie, John (1778?–1817). British officer and herbologist based in Natal; led
an expedition into eastern Senegal, dying of fever while on the Rio Nuñez.

Peney, Alfred (1817–1861). French physician and medical administrator in
Egypt; explored the White Nile with Debono.

Petermann, August (1822–1878). German mapmaker; directed a geographical
institute in Gotha, there publishing his famed journal *Petermann's
Mitteilungen*.

Petherick, John (1813–1882). Welsh explorer, trader, and mining engineer;
prospected for coal in Egypt and Nubia, traded ivory in Sudan.

Poncet, Ambroise (1835–1868) and Jules (1838–1873). Brothers from
Marseilles; established trading posts along the Nile.

Prax, Jean Bonaventure François (1807–1859). French naval officer and
amateur ethnographer; in 1847 penned a study of Tunisian trade practices.

Radcliffe, Ann (1764–1823). English novelist; pioneering writer of Gothic
romances.

Raffenel, Anne-Jean-Baptiste (1809–1858). French naval officer and
administrator; published an atlas, *Travels to West Africa Including
Exploration of Senegal*.

Rath, Johannes (1816–1903). Austrian missionary and linguist; pioneering settler of Namibia.

Rebmann, Johannes (1820–1876). German missionary; first European to reach Mt. Kilimanjaro and Mt. Kenya.

Richardson, James (1806–1851). English explorer; led two expeditions across the Sahara, others to Sudan and Lake Chad.

Riley, James (1777–1840). U.S. merchant seaman; enslaved on the west Sahara coast by marauding natives, as described in his *Sufferings in Africa*.

Ritchie, Joseph (1788?–1819). English surgeon and naturalist; explored the Niger River while searching for Timbuktu.

Rochet d'Héricourt, Charles François Xavier (1801–1854). French geologist and geographer; explored the African shores of the Red Sea.

Roungawi, Ibrahim (?–?). In 1844 provided information on the Nile's headwaters to Fresnel; explored Sudan in the 1850s.

Roscher, Albrecht (1836–1860). German geographer; explored Tanzania.

Rüppell, Wilhelm Peter Eduard (1794–1884). German naturalist; explored Nubia and Ethiopia.

Saugnier, François (1754–?). French explorer captured by Moroccans; in 1792 published *Voyages to the Coast of Africa* with Brisson.

Schlagintweit, Hermann (1826–1882), Adolf (1829–1857), Robert (1833–1885). German geographers and mountaineers; explored India, Tibet, and the Himalayas.

Scott, Sir Walter (1771–1832). Famed Scottish novelist; Verne was a fan.

Selkirk, Alexander (1676–1721). Scottish sailor, the model for Defoe's Robinson Crusoe; marooned for four years on the Juan Fernández Islands off Chile.

Speke, John Hanning (1827–1864). English army officer; discovered Lake Victoria and the Nile's source.

Steudner, Carl Theodor Hermann (1832–1863). German botanist; member of Heuglin's 1861 expedition to Ethiopia and Sudan.

Sturt, Charles (1795–1869). British army officer; led three expeditions into Australia's interior.

Thibaut, Georges (1795–1869). French trader; explored the White Nile.

Thompson, Thomas Richard Heywood (1813–1876). British explorer and naturalist; ascended the Niger River in 1841.

Thornton, Richard (1838–1863). English geologist; worked with Livingstone and Decken in east Africa.

Toole, Ernest (1802?–1824). English sublieutenant; explored the Lake Chad area with Denham but died of fever almost immediately.

Trotter, Henry Dundas (1802–1859). Scottish naval officer; led a trade expedition up the Niger River.

Tuckey, James Hingston (1776–1816). Irish-born officer in the Royal Navy; explored the Congo River.

Tyrwhitt, John (?–1824). English midshipman; traveled with Clapperton and Denham in Libya, Chad, and Nigeria.

Van Hecke, Dr. ——— (?–?). Brussells inventor; in 1847 experimented with using wings and vanes to steer balloons.

Vaudey, Alexandre (1814?–1854). French trader in ivory and gum; coauthored *The First French Explorers of Equatorial Sudan.*

Vayssière, Alexandre (1817–1860). French hunter and explorer; published *Memoir of a Journey to High Nubia in 1851.*

Vincent, Alfred Henri Joseph (1820–1911). French officer; explored Senegal and mapped Mauritania during Faidherbe's administration.

Vinco, Angelo (1819–1853). Italian explorer and priest; opened a mission in Sudan.

Vogel, Eduard (1829–1856). German astronomer and explorer of central Africa; clubbed to death by Wadaï natives.

Wahlberg, Johan August (1810–1856). Swedish naturalist; killed by a wounded elephant while exploring the Limpopo River.

Warrington, Hanmer George (1776–1847). British army officer and consul general in Tripoli; promoted three separate expeditions up the Niger River.

Washington, John (1801–1863). British naval officer and hydrographer; official planner of Livingstone's expedition up the Zambezi River.

Werne, Ferdinand (1800–1874). German physician and explorer; in 1849 published *Expedition to Discover the Sources of the White Nile.*

Wild, Gottlieb (1840?–1920?). Swiss traveler; explored the Horn of Africa with Munzinger; published *From Cairo to Massawa: Recollections of Werner Munzinger* in 1879.

Notes

1. English translations in this introduction are my own, with the exception of quotes from the U.S. edition of Jean Jules-Verne's biography.

2. A full scan of "Un voyage en ballon" is accessible at http://www.truescans .com/Verne.htm, likewise a scan of Anne T. Wilbur's 1852 English translation, "A Voyage in a Balloon," possibly the first English translation of anything by Verne. The story made its first book appearance in a collection of his short fiction, *Dr. Ox* (1874), where it was mildly revised and retitled "A Drama in the Skies" ("Un Drame dans les airs").

3. The third paragraph of the 1874 revision, retitled "A Drama in the Skies," replaces hydrogen with *gaz d'éclairage* (coal gas). Even so, other hydrogen references remain, including a later allusion to the balloon's gas *as* hydrogen: *La raréfaction de l'air dilatait considérablement l'hydrogène du ballon* (As the air grew thinner, the balloon's hydrogen expanded considerably).

4. Hetzel's original 1853 edition and some later reprints add a qualifier to the novel's subtitle: *Drafted from Dr. Fergusson's Notes.*

CHAPTER 1

1. French editions add a footnote converting this to 62,500 francs—equivalent to about $250,000 in today's dollars.

2. Latin: "Onward and upward!"

3. French editions add a footnote translating this for Gallic readers: *Bulletins de la Société royale géographique de Londres.*

4. The name is spelled "Kokburn" in French editions—apparently a fictional character. A later Verne novel, *A Floating City* (1870), includes a similarly named American statistician, one "Cokburn."

5. This foreshadows another oblivious Englishman in Verne's fiction, Phileas Fogg of *Around the World in Eighty Days*, a man who could travel down "the whole wonderful valley of the Ganges without even thinking to look at it."

6. Details of their achievements can be found in the "Gallery of Heroes" at the back of the book.

7. To jibe with standard spellings and to aid access in the "Gallery of Heroes," the translation sometimes tweaks Verne's spelling and alphabetizing.

CHAPTER 2

1. Curiously, French editions read: "*découvreur* (discoverer)."
2. German: "Newsletter."
3. German: "Journal of General Geography."

CHAPTER 3

1. A footnote in French editions gives the Gallic equivalent: about five feet eight inches.

CHAPTER 4

1. A footnote in French editions gives the equivalent in 4-kilometer leagues: 172.
2. A footnote in French editions gives the equivalent in 4-kilometer leagues: 625.
3. The novel is consistently admiring of Barth's professionalism, praising the "tremendous exactitude" of his maps in chapter 30 and their "exceptional accuracy" down to the "tiniest details" in chapter 39. Modern commentators agree, Hazel Mary Martell calling him "more scientific and methodical than earlier explorers" (26).
4. French editions use just two terms for blacks in Africa: *Nègre* (Negro) and *Noir* (Black). They're always capitalized, as are other nationalities and ethnicities in the novel: Scot, Arab, American, Frenchman, Englishman, German, etc. Unfortunately, early British translations often substituted pejorative slang terms.
5. Today known as Tabora.
6. Called Lake Ukéréoué (or Oukéréoué) in French editions.

CHAPTER 5

1. Dialects used along the upper Niger.
2. A footnote in French editions gives the equivalent in 4-kilometer leagues: 50.
3. Muslim nomad.

CHAPTER 6

1. A favorite destination back then for aeronauts in fiction and satire—as in Cyrano de Bergerac's *States and Empires of the Moon* (1657) or Edgar Allan Poe's "The Unparallelled Adventure of One Hans Pfaall" (1835).
2. Spelled "Mittchell" in French editions; apparently they're fictional characters.

CHAPTER 7

1. A footnote in French editions gives the equivalent of 1,661 cubic meters.
2. French editions give continental equivalents in the footnote attached to

this paragraph: for 340,000 cubic feet, 20,000 cubic meters; for 22 tons, 20,000 kilograms.

3. A footnote in French editions gives equivalents for Gallic readers: "roughly 100 liters—a gallon contains 8 pints and equals 4.453 liters."

CHAPTER 8
1. In French editions this item follows "Kennedy's arsenal" in the chapter heading, unlike the sequence in the chapter itself.

2. These are U.S. tons ("short tons"). French editions give *800 tonneaux*.

3. A footnote in French editions gives a rough equivalent in 4-kilometer leagues: about 1,400.

4. A footnote in French editions gives the equivalent in 4-kilometer leagues as follows: "100 leagues. The doctor always rounds his statute miles to the nearest sixtieth of a degree."

5. Kennedy is a Scot, and it seems improbable that he would swear by an Irish saint, but so he does in French editions, both here and in chapter 25. At the time of writing Verne had visited Scotland only once. NB: earlier English translations sometimes substitute St. Andrew or St. James.

CHAPTER 9
1. Ancient Greek: "Eureka!" Or in English, "I've got it!"

2. The planet is named after the Roman god Mercury, patron of thieves, trickery, and financial gain.

CHAPTER 10
1. A footnote in French editions gives the equivalent of 1.5 cubic meters.

2. Oddly, the 1863 and 1865 Hetzel editions give "concave," as do many reprints. Likewise with the reference to a "convex cone" four paragraphs later.

3. Both the 1863 and 1865 Hetzel editions give 1/481, a discrepancy corrected in reissues.

4. A footnote in French editions gives the equivalent of 10° centigrade, adding: "The gases increase in volume by 1/267 per 1° centigrade."

5. A footnote in French editions gives the rough equivalent of 62 cubic meters. NB: many French editions feature a printer error here—1,614 instead of 1,674.

6. Or 100° centigrade, per a footnote in French editions.

7. In French editions footnotes give equivalents for Gallic readers: 70 cubic meters of oxygen . . . 140 cubic meters of hydrogen . . . 210 cubic meters in all.

8. A footnote in French editions gives the equivalent of 1 cubic meter.

9. A footnote in French editions gives the equivalent of ⅓ of a cubic meter.

CHAPTER 11
1. A footnote in French editions gives the equivalent in 4-kilometer leagues: 12½.

2. Tube at the bottom of the envelope.

3. Footnotes in French editions give these equivalents: 3,250 liters . . . more than 8 metric tons of iron.

4. In both the 1863 and 1865 Hetzel editions, a footnote gives this equivalence: 9,166 gallons = nearly 41,250 liters. However, reissues often fudge these figures. Some, including the Rencontre and Livre de Poche texts, give 966 gallons = nearly 41,250 liters, possibly a printer error that has been handed down through the years. The 1965 Lidis edition attempts a questionable fix, giving 966 gallons = 4,347 liters. In short, there seems to be a need for French scholars to undertake more aggressive textual work with Verne's novels.

CHAPTER 12

1. In French editions this item follows "the doctor's maps" in the chapter heading, unlike the sequence in the chapter itself.

2. A footnote in French editions gives an equivalent: "About 5 centimeters. The drop in pressure is almost 1 centimeter for every 100 meters of altitude."

3. In place of "nonsense syllables," the French reads *onomatopées* — onomatopoeias, or words deriving from the sounds associated with their meanings. It could be argued that Joe's "oohs, ahs, and wows" aren't onomatopoeias but simply familiar interjections.

4. In place of "arabica" and "robusta," the French original gives synonyms in use at the time: *bourbon* and *rio-nuñez*.

5. A footnote in French editions gives the equivalent of 10° centigrade.

6. German: *The Newest Discoveries in Africa*.

7. A footnote in French editions gives the equivalent in 4-kilometer leagues: 50.

CHAPTER 13

1. Fever-reducing drug from the bark of the cinchona tree. It proves a lifesaver in part 3 of Verne's novel *The Mysterious Island*.

2. Well into the nineteenth century, many physicians believed that epidemics were caused by "miasmas," or toxic air. In theory, then, patients could recover by rising above the bad air, i.e., by relocating to some mountain resort—or, in Dick Kennedy's case, by heading skyward in a balloon. In the 1880s, however, germ theory replaced miasmatic theory, and researchers soon established that mosquito-borne microorganisms were the cause of malaria.

CHAPTER 14

1. German: "blue buck."

2. Guild in the City of London.

3. Per the Fahrenheit scale. A footnote in French editions gives the centigrade equivalent: fourteen degrees.

4. A footnote in French editions gives the equivalent in 4-kilometer leagues: nearly 200.

CHAPTER 15
1. Plazas surrounded by huts.
2. Medicine men.
3. From Myanga, a region in Kenya.
4. Hardened resin.
5. It's brewed from corn.

CHAPTER 16
1. Verne may be alluding to the *chat-tigre* (wildcat), as he does in chapter 31. True tigers aren't native to Africa.

CHAPTER 17
1. "Get a move on!"
2. French texts give *camaldores,* apparently stemming from chapter 10 in the French edition of Gordon-Cumming's memoirs, *La vie au desert: cinq ans de chasse.* The English original, *Five Years of a Hunter's Life,* gives "cameel-dorn," a Dutch synonym for camel thorn trees.
3. Equivalent to about $3,500 in today's dollars.

CHAPTER 18
1. On the map in chapter 30, Lake Victoria is called "Lake Ukéréoué."

CHAPTER 19
1. In French editions the chapter heading places this item after "ascensions in lighter-than-air vehicles," unlike the sequence in the chapter itself.
2. A footnote in French editions gives the equivalent in 4-kilometer leagues: over 125.

CHAPTER 20
1. The translation follows the 1863 and 1865 Hetzel editions. However, some online texts and print reissues (e.g., the Rencontre, Livre de Poche, and 1965 Lidis editions) substitute thirty *leagues*—meaning that the *Victoria* would be doing a good seventy-five miles per hour.
2. Better known to tourists as Big Ben.

CHAPTER 21
1. In French editions this item follows "Help! Help!" in the chapter heading, unlike the sequence in the chapter itself.
2. French editions give *notre langue.* However, Joe would actually be coping

with two languages: although his native tongue is English, he would be calling out in French.

CHAPTER 22

1. The translation follows the 1863 and 1865 Hetzel editions. However, some online texts and print reissues (e.g., the Rencontre, Livre de Poche, and 1965 Lidis editions) give "compassionate *lips*," almost certainly an error.

CHAPTER 23

1. Compare Joe's introduction early in chapter 6, which claims he "never grumbled or got in a bad mood."

CHAPTER 24

1. A footnote in French editions gives an equivalent for Gallic readers: about 13½ liters.

2. Per the Fahrenheit scale. A footnote in French editions gives the centigrade equivalent: 50°.

3. Early on Fergusson is described as a "fatalist," but here and in chapter 26 he seems more given to soul-searching than many of Verne's leading men. In tight spots he examines his own role, his own contributions to the crisis, rather than simply blaming destiny, the fates, or his luck.

CHAPTER 25

1. Per the Fahrenheit scale. French editions also give the centigrade equivalent for Gallic readers: 70°.

CHAPTER 26

1. French editions give 122° in the chapter heading, although the chapter itself gives 140°, and a footnote supplies its centigrade equivalent.

2. Per the Fahrenheit scale. A footnote in French editions supplies the centigrade equivalent: 45°.

3. Per the Fahrenheit scale. A footnote in French editions gives the centigrade equivalent: 60°.

4. Xerophobia.

CHAPTER 27

1. Sandstorm that spins like a cyclone.

2. A footnote in French editions gives the rough equivalent in 4-kilometer leagues: 100.

CHAPTER 28

1. Per the Fahrenheit scale. A footnote in French editions gives the centigrade equivalent: 69°.

CHAPTER 29

1. A footnote in French editions gives the rough equivalent in 4-kilometer leagues: 625.

2. Per the Fahrenheit scale. A footnote in French editions gives the centigrade equivalent: 100°.

CHAPTER 30

1. This curious tactic resurfaces in *The Dog, the General, and the Birds* (2003), an animated film from French director Francis Nielsen. The film offers a fanciful explanation for the 1812 burning of Moscow: a Russian general sets hundreds of birds on fire, sends them through the town, and drives off Napoleon's troops.

CHAPTER 31

1. In *Twenty Thousand Leagues under the Seas*, Captain Nemo gives harpooner Ned Land a similar rebuke. The *Nautilus* encounters a pod of whales in part 2 of the novel, and Land wants to pursue them "just to keep my hand in." Speaking for Verne, Nemo replies: "It would be killing just for the sake of killing. I'm well aware that's a privilege reserved for mankind, but I won't tolerate such bloodthirsty pastimes. When your colleagues, Mr. Land, destroy decent, harmless creatures like the southern right whale or the bowhead whale, they're guilty of criminal behavior. Consequently they've already eradicated the stock in Baffin Bay, and they'll ultimately wipe out a whole class of beneficial animals."

Verne's ecological worries were well founded. Today, according to worldwildlife .org, barely three hundred bowheads remain, and "seven out of the thirteen great whale species are classified as endangered or vulnerable, even after decades of protection." As for African fauna, the same website lists elephants as currently vulnerable, with black rhinos, gorillas, and chimpanzees cited as endangered.

CHAPTER 32

1. *Gypaetus barbatus*, the only species in the genus. Although some Victorian translations may feature condors or gyrfalcons, the only accurate English rendering is "bearded vulture."

CHAPTER 33

1. In nineteenth-century French usage, alligator and cayman *(caïman)* were synonyms for crocodile, per Abel Boyer and G. Harmonière's *Nouveau dictionnaire* (1834) at http://books.google.com. Accordingly, Verne's text uses the three terms loosely and interchangeably. Even so, many American readers are well aware that alligators and caymans are New World fauna and not native to Africa. Therefore, to reduce confusion, the translation favors more generic terms: "gator" for *alligator*, "croc" or "crocodilian" for *caïman*.

CHAPTER 35

1. They used the arrows in hunting, fishing, and warfare. The latex, or milky fluid, from several species of spurge *(Euphorbia candelabrum, E. cereiformis, E. heptagone, E. mauritanica, E. striata,* and *E. virosa)* served as a traditional source of poison throughout central and southern Africa.

CHAPTER 36

1. Cloaks with hoods.

2. The 1863 and 1865 Hetzel editions, plus the print reissues from Rencontre, Lidis, and Livre de Poche, all use a question mark here instead of an em dash. Many online texts omit punctuation entirely at this point.

CHAPTER 37

1. Jousting competition where a rider snags a dangling ring with a lance.

2. Unable to trace; from the context "souahs" are a breed of tropical tree.

3. Weeds cultivated as a foodstuff.

CHAPTER 38

1. About $25.00. A footnote in French editions gives an equivalent for Gallic readers: 125 francs.

2. The year 1758 is historically correct and is so given in the 1863 and 1865 Hetzel editions. However, some French reissues (including the Rencontre and Livre de Poche texts) give 1753, a printer error.

3. Tuareg clansmen.

CHAPTER 39

1. Shrubs belonging to the pea family.

2. Verne recycles this metaphor shortly after the *Nautilus* cuts the Antarctic Circle in *Twenty Thousand Leagues under the Seas.*

3. Gothic romance published in 1794; its setting is a creepy castle in the Apennine Mountains.

4. Horns composed of ringlike segments.

CHAPTER 41

1. In French editions this item follows "the marabout El-Hadj Umar Tall" in the chapter heading, unlike the sequence in the chapter itself.

2. In Greek myth Sisyphus was eternally doomed to push a boulder up a hill, only to have it roll down again.

3. Muslim holy man.

CHAPTER 42

1. Earlier, in chapter 7, Fergusson twice gives the weight of this equipment as just 700 pounds.

CHAPTER 43

1. In Greek myth he grew weaker when lifted into the air, stronger when back on the ground.

2. Per the Fahrenheit scale. A footnote in French editions gives the centigrade equivalent: 100°.

CHAPTER 44

1. The translation follows the Livre de Poche text, which gives *les félicitations et les embrassements dont furent accablés les trois voyageurs.* However, the 1863 Hetzel edition gives *qui furent réservés aux trois voyageurs* [in store for the three travelers], and the 1865 Hetzel edition offers a slight modification, *dont réservés aux trois voyageurs.* Even so, Arthur B. Evans reports that his copy of an 1867 Hetzel edition agrees with the Livre de Poche text—which, in turn, agrees with all other reissues and online texts that I've seen. Evidently *furent accablés* was a deliberate revision by Verne or his publisher. Again, there seems to be a need for French scholars to undertake more aggressive textual work with Verne's novels.

Bibliography

WORKS OF JULES VERNE

All works were published in Paris by J. Hetzel unless otherwise indicated. Most novels by Verne were first published in serial format in Hetzel's *Magasin d'éducation et de récréation*, then as octodecimo books (normally unillustrated), and finally as octavo illustrated "luxury" editions in red and gold. The date given is that of the first book publication. Many entries have been gleaned from the excellent bibliographical studies of Volker Dehs, Jean-Michel Margot, François Raymond, Olivier Dumas, Edward Gallagher, Judith A. Mistichelli, and John A. Van Eerde, and especially those of Piero Gondolo della Riva and Brian Taves and Stephen Michaluk Jr.

Works in the Series Extraordinary Voyages *(Voyages extraordinaires)*

Novels marked by an asterisk were published after Jules Verne's death in 1905. It is important to understand that most of these post-1905 works were either substantially revamped or, in some cases, almost totally written by Jules Verne's son, Michel. For each novel listed, information about its first English-language edition is provided (date of publication, publisher, and translator) as well as the alternate English titles sometimes used. Also included are recommendations about the translation quality of certain English-language editions.

Cinq semaines en ballon (1863, illus. Edouard Riou and Henri de Montaut).
    Five Weeks in a Balloon (1869, New York: Appleton, trans. William Lackland). Recommended: translation by Frederick Paul Walter. Not recommended: Chapman and Hall edition (reprint 1995, Sutton "Pocket Classics"), the Routledge edition (reprint 1911, Parke), as well as translations by Arthur Chambers (1926, Dutton; reprint 1996, Wordsworth Classics) and by I. O. Evans (1958, Bernard Hanison, "Fitzroy Edition").

Voyage au centre de la Terre (1864, illus. Edouard Riou). *A Journey to the Centre of the Earth* (1871, Griffith and Farran, translator unknown). Alternate titles: *A Journey to the Interior of the Earth, Journey to the Center of the Earth*. Recommended: translations by Robert Baldick (1965, Penguin Books, *Journey to the Center of the Earth*), by William Butcher (1992, Oxford University Press, *Journey to the Centre of the Earth*), and by Frederick Paul Walter (2010, Excelsior, *Amazing Journeys: Five Visionary Classics*). Not recommended: all reprints of the Griffith and Farran ("Hardwigg") edition, which begin "Looking back to all that has occurred to me since that eventful day . . ." (1965, Airmont; 1986, Signet Classics; 1992, Tor Books; among many others).

De la Terre à la Lune (1865, illus. Henri de Montaut). *From the Earth to the Moon* (1867, Gage, translator unknown). Alternate titles: *From the Earth to the Moon Direct, in Ninety-seven Hours Twenty Minutes; The Baltimore Gun Club; The American Gun Club; The Moon Voyage*. Recommended: translations by Harold Salemson (1970, Heritage Books, *From the Earth to the Moon*), by Walter James Miller (1978, Crowell, *The Annotated Jules Verne: From the Earth to the Moon*), by Ron Miller (2006, Black Cat Press, *From the Earth to the Moon*), and by Frederick Paul Walter (2010, Excelsior, *Amazing Journeys: Five Visionary Classics*). Not recommended: translations by Louis Mercier and Eleanor King (1873, Sampson Low, *From the Earth to the Moon Direct, in Ninety-seven Hours Twenty Minutes*; reprint 1967, Airmont; 1983, Avenel; among many others), by Edward Roth (1874, King and Baird, *The Baltimore Gun Club*; reprint 1962, Dover), and by Lowell Bair (1967, Bantam, *From the Earth to the Moon*).

Voyages et aventures du capitaine Hatteras (1866, illus. Edouard Riou and Henri de Montaut). *At the North Pole: The Voyages and Adventures of Captain Hatteras* and *The Desert of Ice: The Voyages and Adventures of Captain Hatteras* (1874–1875, Osgood, translator unknown). Alternate titles: *The English at the North Pole* and *The Field of Ice, The Adventures of Captain Hatteras*. Recommended: translation by William Butcher (2005, Oxford University Press). Not recommended: I. O. Evans's "Fitzroy Edition" translation (1961, *The Adventures of Captain Hatteras: At the North Pole* and *The Adventures of Captain Hatteras: The Wilderness of Ice*).

Les Enfants du capitaine Grant (1867–1868, illus. Edouard Riou). *In Search of the Castaways* (1873, Lippincott, translator unknown). Alternate titles: *The Mysterious Document/On the Track/Among the Cannibals, The Castaways, or A Voyage around the World, Captain Grant's Children*. Recommended: Routledge edition (1876, translator unknown, *Voyage Round the World: South America/Australia/New Zealand*). Not recommended: the Lippincott edition or the I. O. Evans's "Fitzroy Edition" translation (1964, Arco, *The Children of Captain Grant: The Mysterious Document* and *The Children of Captain Grant: Among the Cannibals*).

Vingt mille lieues sous les mers (1869–1870, illus. Edouard Riou and Alphonse-Marie de Neuville). *Twenty Thousand Leagues under the Seas* (1872, Sampson Low, trans. Louis Mercier). Alternate titles: *Twenty Thousand Leagues under the Sea, 20,000 Leagues under the Sea, At the Bottom of the Deep, Deep Sea.* Recommended: translations by Walter James Miller and Frederick Paul Walter (1993, Naval Institute Press, *Jules Verne's Twenty Thousand Leagues under the Sea*) and by William Butcher (1998, Oxford University Press, *Twenty Thousand Leagues under the Seas*). Not recommended: translation by Louis Mercier cited previously (reprint 1963, Airmont; 1981, Castle; 1995, Tor Books; among many others).

Autour de la Lune (1870, illus. Emile-Antoine Bayard and Alphonse-Marie de Neuville). *Round the Moon* (1873, Sampson Low, trans. Louis Mercier and Eleanor King). Alternate titles: *All Around the Moon, Around the Moon, Circling the Moon, A Moon Voyage.* Recommended: translations by Jacqueline and Robert Baldick (1970, Dent, *Around the Moon*), by Harold Salemson (1970, Heritage Books, *Around the Moon*), and by Frederick Paul Walter (2010, Excelsior, *Amazing Journeys: Five Visionary Classics*). Not recommended: translations by Louis Mercier and Eleanor King (cited previously) and by Edward Roth (1874, Catholic, *All Around the Moon*; reprint 1962, Dover Books).

Une Ville flottante (1871, illus. Jules-Descartes Férat). *A Floating City* (1874, Sampson Low, translator unknown). Alternate title: *The Floating City.* Recommended: translation by Henry Frith (1876, Routledge, *The Floating City*). Not recommended: I. O. Evans's "Fitzroy Edition" translation (1958, Hanison, *A Floating City*). Also of note: a 2011 online critical edition of *Une Ville flottante* prepared by Dr. Tim Unwin for the University of Liverpool Online Series and available at http://www.liv.ac.uk/soclas/los/Une%20ville%20flottante.pdf.

Aventures de trois Russes et de trois Anglais dans l'Afrique australe (1872, illus. Jules-Descartes Férat). *Meridiana: The Adventures of Three Englishmen and Three Russians in South Africa* (1872, Sampson Low, trans. Ellen E. Frewer). Alternate titles: *Adventures of Three Englishmen and Three Russians in Southern Africa, Adventures in the Land of the Behemoth, Measuring a Meridian.* Recommended: translation by Henry Frith (1877, Routledge, *Adventures of Three Englishmen and Three Russians in Southern Africa*). Not recommended: Shepard edition (1874, translator unknown, *Adventures in the Land of the Behemoth*) and I. O. Evans's "Fitzroy Edition" translation (1964, Arco, *Measuring a Meridian*).

Le Pays des fourrures (1873, illus. Jules-Descartes Férat and Alfred Quesnay de Beaurepaire). *The Fur Country* (1873, Sampson Low, trans. N. D'Anvers). Alternate title: *Sun in Eclipse/Through the Behring Strait.* Recommended: translation by Edward Baxter (1987, NC Press, *The Fur Country*). Not recommended: I. O. Evans's "Fitzroy Edition" (1966, Arco, *The Fur Country: Sun in Eclipse* and *The Fur Country: Through the Behring Strait*).

Le Tour du monde en quatre-vingts jours (1873, illus. Alphonse-Marie de Neuville and Léon Benett). *A Tour of the World in Eighty Days* (1873, Osgood, trans. George M. Towle). Alternate titles: *The Tour of the World in Eighty Days, Around the World in Eighty Days, Around the World in 80 Days, Round the World in Eighty Days*. Recommended: translation by William Butcher (1995, Oxford University Press, *Around the World in Eighty Days*) and by Frederick Paul Walter (2010, Excelsior, *Amazing Journeys: Five Visionary Classics*). Not recommended: translations by Lewis Mercier (1962, Collier/Doubleday) and by K. E. Lichtenecker (1965, Hamlyn).

Le Docteur Ox (1874, illus. Lorenz Froelich, Théophile Schuler, Emile-Antoine Bayard, Adrien Marie, Edmond Yon, and Antoine Bertrand). *Doctor Ox* (1874, Osgood, trans. George M. Towle). Short story collection. Alternate titles: *From the Clouds to the Mountains, A Fancy of Doctor Ox, Dr. Ox and Other Stories, Dr. Ox's Experiment and Other Stories, A Winter amid the Ice and Other Stories, A Winter amid the Ice and Other Thrilling Tales*. Collection contains the following short stories and nonfiction: "Une Fantaisie du docteur Ox" (Doctor Ox), "Maître Zacharius" (Master Zacharius), "Un Hivernage dans les glaces" (A Winter amid the Ice), "Un Drame dans les airs" (A Drama in the Air), and "Quarantième ascension du Mont-Blanc" (Fortieth French Ascent of Mont Blanc, written by Verne's brother, Paul). Recommended: translation by Towle cited previously and translation by Andrew Brown (2003, Hesperus Press, *A Fantasy of Doctor Ox*). Not recommended: translation by Abby L. Alger (1874, Gill, *From the Clouds to the Mountains*) and I. O. Evans's "Fitzroy Edition" translation (1964, Arco, *Dr. Ox and Other Stories*).

L'Île mystérieuse (1874–1875, illus. Jules-Descartes Férat). *The Mysterious Island: Dropped from the Clouds/The Abandoned/The Secret of the Island* (1875, Sampson Low, trans. W. H. G. Kingston). Alternate titles: *The Mysterious Island: Dropped from the Clouds/Marooned/Secret of the Island, Mysterious Island*. Recommended: translations by Sidney Kravitz (2001, Wesleyan University Press) and by Jordon Stump (2001, Modern Library).

Le Chancellor (1875, illus. Edouard Riou and Jules-Descartes Férat). *The Wreck of the Chancellor* (1875, Osgood, trans. George M. Towle). Alternate titles: *The Survivors of the Chancellor, The Chancellor*. Recommended: translation by Towle cited previously. Not recommended: I. O. Evans's "Fitzroy Edition" translation (1965, Arco, *The Chancellor*).

Michel Strogoff (1876, illus. Jules-Descartes Férat). *Michael Strogoff* (1876, Leslie, trans. E. G. Walraven). Alternate titles: *Michael Strogoff: From Moscow to Irkoutsk; Michael Strogoff, or the Russian Courier; Michael*

Strogoff, or the Courier of the Czar. Recommended: translation by W. H. G. Kingston as "revised" by Julius Chambers (1876, Sampson Low).

Hector Servadac (1877, illus. Paul Philippoteaux). *Hector Servadac* (1877, Sampson Low, trans. Ellen E. Frewer). Alternate titles: *To the Sun?* and *Off on a Comet!, Hector Servadac: Travels and Adventures through the Solar System, Anomalous Phenomena/Homeward Bound, Astounding Adventures among the Comets*. Recommended: translation by Adam Roberts (2007, Solaris, *Off on a Comet*). Not recommended: translations by Edward Roth (1877–1878, Claxton et al., *To the Sun?* and *Off on a Comet!*; reprint 1960, Dover Books) and by I. O. Evans (1965, Arco, *Hector Servadac: Anomalous Phenomena* and *Hector Servadac: Homeward Bound*).

Les Indes noires (1877, illus. Jules-Descartes Férat). *The Black Indies* (1877, Munro, translator unknown). Alternate titles: *The Child of the Cavern, The Underground City, Black Diamonds*. Recommended: translation by Sarah Crozier (2005, Luath Press, *The Underground City*). Not recommended: I. O. Evans's "Fitzroy Edition" translation (1961, Arco, *Black Diamonds*).

Un Capitaine de quinze ans (1878, illus. Henri Meyer). *Dick Sand; or a Captain at Fifteen* (1878, Munro, translator unknown). Alternate titles: *Dick Sands, The Boy Captain, A Fifteen Year Old Captain, Captain at Fifteen*. Recommended: Munro edition cited previously. Not recommended: translation by Forlag (1976, Abelard-Schuman, *Captain at Fifteen*).

Les Cinq Cents Millions de la Bégum (1879, illus. Léon Benett). *The 500 Millions of the Begum* (1879, Munro, translator unknown). Alternate titles: *The Begum's Fortune, The Begum's Millions, The Five Hundred Millions of the Begum*. Recommended: Stanford L. Luce translation (2005, Wesleyan University Press, *The Begum's Millions*). Not recommended: Munro edition cited previously, W. H. G. Kingston translation (1879, Sampson Low, *The Begum's Fortune*), and I. O. Evans's "Fitzroy Edition" translation (1958, Hanison/Arco, *The Begum's Fortune*).

Les Tribulations d'un Chinois en Chine (1879, illus. Léon Benett). *The Tribulations of a Chinaman in China* (1879, Lee and Shepard, trans. Virginia Champlin [Grace Virginia Lord]). Alternate titles: *The Tribulations of a Chinese Gentleman, The Tribulations of a Chinaman*. Recommended: translation by Champlin cited previously. Not recommended: I. O. Evans's "Fitzroy Edition" translation (1963, Arco, *The Tribulations of a Chinese Gentleman*).

La Maison à vapeur (1880, illus. Léon Benett). *The Steam House, or A Trip across Northern India* (1880, Munro, trans. James Cotterell). Alternate titles: *The Steam House, The Demon of Cawnpore/Tigers and Traitors*.

Recommended: translation by Agnes D. Kingston (1880, Sampson Low, *The Steam House*). Not recommended: I. O. Evans's "Fitzroy Edition" translation (1959, Hanison, *The Steam House: The Demon of Cawnpore* and *The Steam House: Tigers and Traitors.*

La Jangada (1881, illus. Léon Benett and Edouard Riou). *The Jangada, or 800 Leagues over the Amazon* (1881, Munro, trans. James Cotterell). Alternate titles: *The Giant Raft, The Jangada, The Giant Raft: Down the Amazon/ The Cryptogram.* Recommended: translation by W. J. Gordon (1881–1882, Sampson Low, *The Giant Raft*). Not recommended: I. O. Evans's "Fitzroy Edition" translation (1967, Arco, *The Giant Raft: Down the Amazon* and *The Giant Raft: The Cryptogram*).

Le Rayon vert (1882, illus. Léon Benett). *The Green Ray* (1883, Munro, trans. James Cotterell and Sampson Low, trans. Mary de Hauteville). Recommended: translation by Karen Loukes (2009, Luath Press, *The Green Ray*).

L'Ecole des Robinsons (1882, illus. Léon Benett). *Robinson's School* (1883, Munro, trans. James Cotterell). Alternate titles: *Godfrey Morgan: A California Mystery, An American Robinson Crusoe, The School for Crusoes.* Recommended: translation by J. C. Curtin (1883, Redpath's Weekly, *An American Robinson Crusoe*). Not recommended: I. O. Evans's "Fitzroy Edition" translation (1966, Arco, *The School for Crusoes*).

Kéraban-le-têtu (1883, illus. Léon Benett). *The Headstrong Turk* (1883–1884, Munro, trans. James Cotterell). Alternate titles: *Kéraban the Inflexible: The Captain of the Guidara* and *Kéraban the Inflexible: Scarpante, the Spy.* Recommended: translation by J. C. Curtin (1883, Redpath's Weekly, *The Headstrong Turk*).

L'Archipel en feu (1884, illus. Léon Benett). *Archipelago on Fire* (1885, Munro, translator unknown). Alternate title: *The Archipelago on Fire.* Recommended: Sampson Low edition (1885, trans. anonymous).

L'Etoile du Sud (1884, illus. Léon Benett). *The Southern Star* (1885, Munro, translator unknown). Alternate titles: *The Vanished Diamond: A Tale of South Africa, The Southern Star Mystery, The Star of the South.* Recommended: translation by Stephen Gray (2003, Pretoria: Protea Book House, *The Star of the South*). Not recommended: I. O. Evans's "Fitzroy Edition" translation (1966, Arco, *The Southern Star Mystery*).

Mathias Sandorf (1885, illus. Léon Benett). *Mathias Sandorf* (1885, Munro, trans. G. W. Hanna). Recommended: translation by Edward Brumgnach (2005, available as an e-book through Amazon or Barnes and Noble).

L'Epave du Cynthia (1885, with André Laurie, illus. George Roux). *Waif of the "Cynthia"* (1885, Munro, translator unknown). Alternate title: *Salvage from the Cynthia*. Recommended: Munro edition cited previously. Not recommended: I. O. Evans's "Fitzroy Edition" translation (1964, Arco, *Salvage from the Cynthia*).

Robur-le-conquérant (1886, illus. Léon Benett). *Robur the Conqueror* (1887, Munro, translator unknown). Alternate titles: *The Clipper of the Clouds, A Trip Round the World in a Flying Machine*. Recommended: *Clipper of the Clouds* (1887, Sampson Low, translator unknown). Not recommended: the Munro edition cited previously, the translation edited by Charles E. Horne (1911, Vincent Park, *Robur the Conqueror*), and the I. O. Evans "Fitzroy Edition" translation (1962, Arco, *The Clipper of the Clouds*).

Un Billet de loterie (1886, illus. George Roux). *Ticket No, "9672"* (1886, Munro, trans. Laura E. Kendall). Alternate title: *The Lottery Ticket*. Recommended: translation by Kendall.

Le Chemin de France (1887, illus. George Roux). *The Flight to France, or The Memoirs of a Dragoon* (1888, Sampson Low, and 1889, Munro, translator unknown).

Nord contre Sud (1887, illus. Léon Benett). *Texar's Vengeance, or North versus South* (1887, Munro, translator unknown). Alternate titles: *Texar's Revenge, or North against South, North against South: A Tale of the American Civil War, North against South: Burbank the Northerner/Texar the Southerner*. Recommended: Sampson Low edition (1887, trans. anonymous, *Texar's Revenge, or North against South*). Not recommended: I. O. Evans's "Fitzroy Edition" translation (1965, Arco, *North against South: Burbank the Northerner* and *North against South: Texar the Southerner*).

Deux Ans de vacances (1888, illus. Léon Benett). *A Two Years' Vacation* (1889, Munro, translator unknown). Alternate titles: *Adrift in the Pacific, Adrift in the Pacific/Second Year Ashore, Two Years' Holiday, A Two Years' Vacation*. Recommended: Munro edition cited previously. Not recommended: I. O. Evans's "Fitzroy Edition" translation (1965, Arco, *Two Years' Holiday: Adrift in the Pacific* and *Two Years' Holiday: Second Year Ashore*) and translation by Olga Marx (1967, Holt, Rinehart and Winston, *A Long Vacation*).

Sans dessus dessous (1889, illus. George Roux). *The Purchase of the North Pole* (1890, Sampson Low, translator unknown). Alternate titles: *Topsy-Turvy, The Earth Turned Upside Down*. Recommended: Sophie Lewis translation (2012, Hesperus Press, *The Earth Turned Upside Down*). Not recommended: Ogilvie edition (1890, trans. anonymous, *Topsy-Turvy*) and I. O. Evans's "Fitzroy Edition" translation (1966, Arco, *The Purchase of the North Pole*).

Famille-sans-nom (1889, illus. Georges Tiret-Bognet). *A Family without a Name* (1889, Munro, Lovell, translator unknown). Alternate titles: *A Family without a Name: Leader of the Resistance/Into the Abyss; Family without a Name*. Recommended: translation by Edward Baxter (1982, NC Press, *Family without a Name*). Not recommended: I. O. Evans's "Fitzroy Edition" translation (1963, Arco, *Family without a Name: Leader of the Resistance* and *Family without a Name: Into the Abyss*).

César Cascabel (1890, illus. George Roux). *Caesar Cascabel* (1890, Cassell, trans. A. Estoclet). Alternate title: *The Travelling Circus/The Show on Ice*. Recommended: translation by Estoclet cited previously. Not recommended: I. O. Evans's "Fitzroy Edition" translation (1970, Arco, *César Cascabel: The Travelling Circus* and *César Cascabel: The Show on Ice*).

Mistress Branican (1891, illus. Léon Benett). *Mistress Branican* (1891, Cassell, trans. A. Estoclet). Alternate titles: *Mystery of the Franklin, The Wreck of the Franklin*. Recommended: translation by Estoclet cited previously.

Le Château des Carpathes (1892, illus. Léon Benett). *The Castle of the Carpathians* (1893, Sampson Low, translator unknown). Alternate title: *Carpathian Castle*. Recommended: translation by Charlotte Mandel (2010, Melville House, *The Castle in Transylvania*). Not recommended: I. O. Evans's "Fitzroy Edition" translation (1963, Arco, *Carpathian Castle*).

Claudius Bombarnac (1893, illus. Léon Benett). *The Special Correspondent, or the Adventures of Claudius Bombarnac* (1894, Lovell, translator unknown). Alternate title: *Claudius Bombarnac* (same translation).

P'tit-Bonhomme (1893, illus. Léon Benett). *Foundling Mick* (1895, Sampson Low, translator unknown). Literal translation: *Li'l-Fellow*.

Mirifiques Aventures de Maître Antifer (1894, illus. George Roux). *Captain Antifer* (1895, Sampson Low, translator unknown).

L'Île à hélice (1895, illus. Léon Benett). *The Floating Island* (1896, Sampson Low, trans. W. J. Gordon; reprint 1990, Kegan Paul). Alternate title: *Propeller Island*. Recommended: none.

Face au drapeau (1896, illus. Léon Benett). *Facing the Flag* (1897, Neely, translator unknown). Alternate titles: *For the Flag, Simon Hart: A Strange Story of Science and the Sea*. Recommended: Cashel Hoey translation (1897, Sampson Low, *For the Flag*). Not recommended: I. O. Evans's "Fitzroy Edition" translation (1961, Arco, *For the Flag*).

Clovis Dardentor (1896, illus. Léon Benett). *Clovis Dardentor* (1897, Sampson Low, translator unknown).

Le Sphinx des glaces (1897, illus. George Roux). *An Antarctic Mystery* (1898, Sampson Low, trans. Mrs. Cashel Hoey). Alternate title: *The Sphinx of the Ice*. Recommended: Frederick Paul Walter translation (2012, Excelsior, *The Sphinx of the Ice Realm*). Not recommended: Basil Ashmore "Fitzroy Edition" translation (1961, Arco, *The Mystery of Arthur Gordon Pym by Edgar Allan Poe and Jules Verne*).

Le Superbe Orénoque (1898, illus. George Roux). *The Mighty Orinoco* (2002, Wesleyan University Press, trans. Stanford L. Luce).

Le Testament d'un excentrique (1899, illus. George Roux). *The Will of an Eccentric* (1900, Sampson Low, translator unknown).

Seconde patrie (1900, illus. George Roux). *Their Island Home* and *The Castaways of the Flag* (1923, Sampson Low, trans. Cranstoun Metcalfe).

Le Village aérien (1901, illus. George Roux). *The Village in the Treetops* (1964, "Fitzroy Edition," Arco, trans. I. O. Evans). Literal translation: *The Aerial Village*.

Les Histoires de Jean-Marie Cabidoulin (1901, illus. George Roux). *The Sea Serpent: The Yarns of Jean-Marie Cabidoulin* (1967, "Fitzroy Edition," Arco, trans. I. O. Evans).

Les Frères Kip (1902, illus. George Roux). *The Kip Brothers* (2007, Wesleyan University Press, trans. Stanford L. Luce).

Bourses de voyage (1903, illus. Léon Benett). *Travel Scholarships* (2013, Wesleyan University Press, trans. Teri J. Hernández).

Un Drame en Livonie (1904, illus. Léon Benett). *A Drama in Livonia* (1967, "Fitzroy Edition," Arco, trans. I. O. Evans).

Maître du monde (1904, illus. George Roux). *The Master of the World* (1911, Parke, translator unknown). Recommended: translation by Cranstoun Metcalfe (1914, Sampson Low). Not recommended: Parke edition cited previously and I. O. Evans's "Fitzroy Edition" translation (1962, Arco).

L'Invasion de la mer (1905, illus. Léon Benett). *Invasion of the Sea* (2001, Wesleyan University Press, trans. Edward Baxter).

*Le Phare du bout du monde (1905, illus. George Roux). *The Lighthouse at the Edge of the World* (1923, Sampson Low, trans. Cranstoun Metcalfe).

*Le Volcan d'or (1906, illus. George Roux). *The Golden Volcano: The Claim on the Forty Mile* and *The Golden Volcano: Creek Flood and Famine* (1962, "Fitzroy Edition," Arco, trans. I. O. Evans).

*L'Agence Thompson and Co. (1907, illus. Léon Benett). *The Thompson Travel Agency: Package Holiday* and *The Thompson Travel Agency: End of the Journey* (1965, "Fitzroy Edition," Arco, trans. I. O. Evans).

*La Chasse au météore (1908, illus. George Roux). *The Chase of the Golden Meteor* (1909, Grant Richards, trans. Frederick Lawton). Alternate title: *The Hunt for the Meteor*.

*Le Pilote du Danube (1908, illus. George Roux). *The Danube Pilot* (1967, "Fitzroy Edition," Arco, trans. I. O. Evans).

*Les Naufragés du Jonathan (1909, illus. George Roux). *The Survivors of the Jonathan: The Masterless Man* and *The Survivors of the Jonathan: The Unwilling Dictator* (1962, "Fitzroy Edition," Arco, trans. I. O. Evans).

Le Secret de Wilhelm Storitz (1910, illus. George Roux). *The Secret of Wilhelm Storitz* (1963, "Fitzroy Edition," Arco, trans. I. O. Evans).

Hier et demain (1910, illus. Léon Benett, George Roux, and Félicien Myrbach-Rheinfeld). *Yesterday and Tomorrow* (1965, "Fitzroy Edition,"Arco, trans. I. O. Evans). Short story collection. Original French collection contains the following short stories: "La Famille Raton" (The Rat Family), "M. Ré-Dièze et Mlle Mi-Bémol" (Mr. Ray Sharp and Miss Me Flat), "La Destinée de Jean Morénas" (The Fate of Jean Morénas), "Le Humbug" (The Humbug), "Au XXIXème siècle: La Journée d'un journaliste américain en 2889" (In the Twenty-ninth Century: The Diary of an American Journalist in 2889), and "L'Eternel Adam" (The Eternal Adam). The 1965 Arco English translation does not contain the same stories as the original French edition: "La Famille Raton" (The Rat Family) and "Le Humbug" (The Humbug) were deleted and replaced with "Une Ville idéale" ("An Ideal City"), "Dix heures de chasse" ("Ten Hours Hunting"), "Frritt-Flacc" ("Frritt-Flacc"), and "Gil Braltar" ("Gil Braltar"). Recommended: *Adventures of the Rat Family* (1993, Oxford University Press, trans. Evelyn Copeland).

L'Etonnante Aventure de la mission Barsac (Hachette, 1919, illus. George Roux). *The Barsac Mission: Into the Niger Bend* and *The Barsac Mission: The City in the Sahara* (1960, "Fitzroy Edition," Arco, trans. I. O. Evans).

Novellas and Short Stories

In Hetzel's original editions of Verne's *Extraordinary Voyages* series, some novels were supplemented with a novella or a short story that had often been previously published in a journal (e.g., *Musée des familles*) or a newspaper (e.g., *Le Figaro*). Only two short story collections were published as part of the *Extraordinary Voyages*—*Le Docteur Ox* (*Doctor Ox*) and *Hier et demain* (*Yesterday and Tomorrow*)—and most of the stories contained therein also had appeared earlier. The latter collection was published only after Verne's death in 1905, and many of the short stories in it were either significantly revamped or entirely written by Jules Verne's son, Michel.

"Un Drame au Mexique. Les premiers navires de la marine mexicaine" (1876, illus. Jules-Descartes Férat) with *Michel Strogoff*. First published as "L'Amérique du Sud. Etudes historiques. Les premiers navires de la marine mexicaine" in the *Musée des familles* (July 1851, illus. Eugène Forest and Alexandre de Bar): 304–12. "The Mutineers: A Romance of Mexico" with *Michel Strogoff, the Courier of the Czar* (1877, Sampson Low, trans. W. G. Kingston). Alternate titles: "A Drama in Mexico," "The Mutineers, or A Tragedy in Mexico," "The Mutineers."

"Un Drame dans les airs" (1874, illus. Emile-Antoine Bayard) in *Le Docteur*

Ox. First published as "La science en famille. Un voyage en ballon" in the *Musée de familles* (Aug. 1851, illus. Alexandre de Bar): 329–36. "A Voyage in a Balloon" in *Sartain's Union Magazine of Literature and Art* (May 1852, trans. Anne T. Wilbur): 389–95. Alternate titles: "A Drama in the Air," "Balloon Journey," "A Drama in Mid-Air." This was the first Verne story to be translated into English.

"Martin Paz" (1875, illus. Jules-Descartes Férat) with *Le Chancellor*. First published as "L'Amérique du Sud. Moeurs péruviennes. Martin Paz, nouvelle historique" in the *Musée des familles* (July–Aug.1852, illus. Eugène Forest and Emile Berton): 301–13, 321–35. "The Pearl of Lima. A Story of True Love" in *Graham's Magazine* (April 1853, trans Anne T. Wilbur): 422–45. "Martin Paz" in *The Survivors of the Chancellor; and Martin Paz* (1876, Sampson Low, trans. Ellen E. Frewer). Alternate title: "The Pearl of Lima."

"Maître Zacharius" (1874, illus. Théophile Schuler) in *Le Docteur Ox*. First published as "Maître Zacharius, ou l'horloger qui avait perdu son âme. Tradition génevoise" in the *Musée des familles* (Apr.–May 1854, illus. Alexandre de Bar and Gustave Janet): 193–200, 225–31. "Master Zacharius" in *Dr. Ox and Other Stories* (1874, Osgood, trans. George M. Towle). Alternate titles: "Master Zachary," "The Watch's Soul."

"Un Hivernage dans les glaces" (1874, illus. Adrien Marie) in *Le Docteur Ox*. First published in the *Musée des familles* (Apr.–May 1855, illus. Jean-Antoine de Beauce): 161–72, 209–20. "Winter in the Ice" in *Dr. Ox and Other Stories* (1874, Osgood, trans. George M. Towle). Alternate titles: "A Winter amid the Ice," "A Winter among the Ice-Fields," "Winter on Ice."

"Le Comte de Chanteleine." Published as "Le Comte de Chanteleine. Épisode de la révolution" in the *Musée des familles* (Oct. –Nov. 1864, illus. Edmond Morin, Alexandre de Bar, and Jean-Valentin Foulquier): 1–15, 37–51. *The Count of Chanteleine* (2011, BearManor Media, trans. Edward Baxter).

"Les Forceurs de blocus" (1871, illus. Jules-Descartes Férat) with *Une Ville flottante*. First published in the *Musée des familles* (Oct. –Nov. 1865, illus. Léon Morel-Fatio, Evrémond Bérard, Fréderic Lixe, and Jean-Valentin Foulquier): 17–21, 35–47. "The Blockade Runners" in *The Floating City, and the Blockade Runners* (1874, Sampson Low, translator unknown) and *The Blockade Runners* (2011, Luath Press, trans. Karen Loukes).

"Le Docteur Ox" (1874, illus. Lorenz Froelich) in *Le Docteur Ox*. First published in the *Musée des familles* (Mar.–May 1872, illus. Ulysse Parent and Alexandre de Bar): 65–74, 99–107, 133–41. "Doctor Ox's Experiment" in *Dr. Ox and Other Stories* (1874, Osgood, trans. George M. Towle). Alternate titles: "A Fancy of Doctor Ox," "Dr. Ox," "Dr. Ox's Hobby."

"Les Révoltés de la Bounty" (1879, illus. S. Drée) with *Les Cinq Cents Millions de la Bégum*. First published in the *Magasin d'éducation et de récréation* (Oct.–Dec. 1879, illus. S. Drée): 193–98, 225–30, 257–63. "The Mutineers of the Bounty" in *The Begum's Fortune, with an account of The Mutineers of the Bounty* (1880, Sampson Low, trans. W. H. G. Kingston).

"Dix heures en chasse" (1882, illus. Gédéon Baril) with *Le Rayon vert*. First published in the *Journal d'Amiens, Moniteur de la Somme* (Dec. 19–20, 1881): 2–3. "Ten Hours Hunting" in *Yesterday and Tomorrow* (1965, "Fitzroy Edition," Arco, trans. I. O. Evans).

"Frritt-Flacc" (1886, illus. George Roux) with *Un Billet de loterie*. First published in *Le Figaro illustré* (1884–1885): 6–7. "Dr. Trifulgas: A Fantastic Tale" in *Strand Magazine* 4 (July–Dec. 1892, translator unknown): 53–57. Alternate titles: "Fritt-Flacc," "The Ordeal of Dr. Trifulgas," "Fweeee—Splash!"

"Gil Braltar" (1887, illus. George Roux) with *Le Chemin de France*. "Gilbraltar" (1938, Hurd and Walling, trans. Ernest H. De Gay).

"Un Express de l'avenir." Written by Verne's son, Michel, and first published in *Le Figaro* (Sept. 1, 1888). Translated and published (under his father's name) as "An Express of the Future" in *Strand Magazine* 10 (July–Dec. 1895): 638–40.

"La Journée d'un journaliste américain en 2889" (1910, illus. George Roux) in *Hier et demain*. Written by Verne's son, Michel, and first published in English (under his father's name) as "In the Year 2889" in *The Forum* 6 (Sept. 1888–Feb. 1889, illus. George Roux): 662–77. Later modified by Jules Verne and published as "La Journée d'un journaliste américain en 2890" in *Mémoires de l'Académie d'Amiens* 37 (1890): 348–70. The latter version was then published as "Au XXIXème siècle: La Journée d'un journaliste américain en 2889" in *Hier et demain* (Paris: Hetzel, 1910). It was then translated and reprinted as "In the Twenty-ninth Century: The Diary of an American Journalist in 2889" in *Yesterday and Tomorrow* (1965, "Fitzroy Edition," Arco, trans. I. O. Evans).

"La Famille Raton" (1910, illus. Félicien Myrbach-Rheinfeld) in *Hier et demain*. First published as "Aventures de la famille Raton. Conte de fées" in *Le Figaro illustré* (Jan. 1891): 1–12. *Adventures of the Rat Family*, trans. Evelyn Copeland (1993, Oxford University Press).

"La Destinée de Jean Morénas" (1910, illus. Léon Benett) in *Hier et demain*. Written by Verne's son, Michel, from his father's unpublished short story "Pierre-Jean" (see under "Rediscovered Works"). "The Somber Fate of Jean Morénas" in *Vice, Redemption and the Distant Colony* (2011, BearManor Media, trans. Kieran M. O'Driscoll).

"Le Humbug" (1910, illus. George Roux) in *Hier et demain*. "Humbug: The

American Way of Life" (1991, Acadian, trans. William Butcher) and "The Humbug" in *The Jules Verne Encyclopedia*, ed. Brian Taves and Stephen Michaluk Jr. (1996, Scarecrow, trans. Edward Baxter).

"Monsieur Ré-Dièze et Mademoiselle Mi-Bémol" (1910, illus. George Roux) in *Hier et demain*. First published in *Le Figaro illustré* (Dec. 25, 1893): 221–28. "Mr. Ray Sharp and Miss Me Flat" in *Yesterday and Tomorrow* (1965, "Fitzroy Edition," Arco, trans. I. O. Evans).

"L'Eternel Adam" (1910, illus. Léon Benett) in *Hier et demain*. Written by Verne's son, Michel, as "Edom" from his father's unfinished short story (see under "Rediscovered Works") and first published in *La Revue de Paris* (Oct. 1, 1910): 449–84. Translated as "Eternal Adam" in *Saturn* 1, no. 1 (Mar. 1957, trans. Willis T. Bradley): 76–112.

Rediscovered Works: Unpublished Early Novels, Short Stories, and Original Manuscripts

Un Prêtre en 1835 (A Priest in 1835, written in 1846–1847). Published as *Un Prêtre en 1839* (1992, Cherche Midi).

"Jédédias Jamet" (Jedediah Jamet, written in 1847). Published as "Jédédias Jamet" in *San Carlos et autres récits inédits*, 177–206 (1993, Cherche Midi), translated as "Jédédias Jamet, or The Tale of an Inheritance" in *The Marriage of a Marquis*, 91–119 (2011, BearManor Media, trans. Kieran M. O'Driscoll).

"Pierre-Jean" (written ca. 1852). Published as "Pierre-Jean" in Olivier Dumas, *Jules Verne*, 205–34 (1988, La Manufacture). Original manuscript of "La Destinée de Jean Morénas." Translated as "Pierre-Jean" in *Vice, Redemption and the Distant Colony* (2011, BearManor Media, trans. Kieran M. O'Driscoll).

"Le Siège de Rome" (The Siege of Rome, written ca. 1853). Published as "Le Siège de Rome" in *San Carlos et autres récits inédits*, 81–146 (1993, Cherche Midi), translated as "The Siege of Rome" in *Bandits & Rebels* (2013, BearManor Media, trans. Edward Baxter).

"Le Mariage de Monsieur Anselme des Tilleuls" (The Marriage of M. Anselme des Tilleuls, written ca. 1855). Published as "Le Mariage de M. Anselme des Tilleuls. Souvenirs d'un élève de huitième" (1991, Olifant) and as "Le Mariage de M. Anselme des Tilleuls. Souvenirs d'un élève de huitième" in *San Carlos et autres récits inédits*, 47–80 (1993, Cherche Midi), translated as *The Marriage of a Marquis* (2011, BearManor Media, trans. Edward Baxter).

"San Carlos" (San Carlos, written ca. 1856). Published as "San Carlos" in *San Carlos et autres récits inédits*, 147–76 (1993, Cherche Midi), translated as "San Carlos" in *Bandits & Rebels* (2013, BearManor Media, trans. Edward Baxter).

Voyage en Angleterre et en Ecosse—Voyage à reculons (A Trip to England and Scotland—A Backwards Trip, written in 1859–1860). Published as *Voyage à reculons en Angleterre et en Ecosse* (1989, Cherche Midi), translated as *Backwards to Britain* (1992, Chamber, trans. Janice Valls-Russell).

Joyeuses misères de trois voyageurs en Scandinavie (Joyous Miseries of Three Travelers in Scandinavia, written in 1861). Published as *Joyeuses misère de trois voyageurs en Scandinavie* (2003, Géo), translated as *Joyous Miseries of Three Travellers in Scandinavia* (2011, www.ibiblio.org/julesverne /JoyousMiseriescompact.pdf, trans. William Butcher).

Paris au XXème siècle (written in 1863). Published as *Paris au XXème siècle* (1994, Hachette), translated as *Paris in the Twentieth Century* (1996, Random House, trans. Richard Howard).

L'Oncle Robinson (Uncle Robinson, written in 1870–1871). Original manuscript of *L'Île mystérieuse* (1874–1875). Published as *L'Oncle Robinson* (1991, Cherche Midi), translated as *Shipwrecked Family: Marooned with Uncle Robinson* (2011, BearManor Media, trans. Sidney Kravitz).

Le Phare du bout du monde (The Lighthouse at the End of the World, written from 1901 to 1905). Original manuscript of *Le Phare du bout du monde* (1905). Published as *Le Phare du bout du monde* (1999, Montréal: Stanké), translated as *Lighthouse at the End of the World* (2007, University of Nebraska Press, Bison Books, trans. William Butcher).

Le Beau Danube jaune (The Beautiful Yellow Danube, written in 1896–1897). Original manuscript of *Le Pilote du Danube* (1908). Published as *Le Beau Danube jaune* (1988, Société Jules Verne), translated as *Golden Danube* (2014, BearManor Media, trans. Kieran M. O'Driscoll).

En Magellanie—Au bout du monde (In the Magellanes—At the End of the World, written from 1896 to 1899). Original manuscript of *Les Naufragés du Jonathan* (1909). Published as *En Magellanie* (1987, Société Jules Verne), translated as *Magellania* (2002, Welcome Rain, trans. Benjamin Ivry).

Le Volcan d'or—Le Klondyke (The Golden Volcano—The Klondyke, written in 1899–1900). Original manuscript of *Le Volcan d'or*. Published as *Le Volcan d'or. Version originale* (1989, Société Jules Verne), translated as *The Golden Volcano* (2008, University of Nebraska Press, Bison Books, trans. Edward Baxter).

Le Secret de Wilhelm Storitz—L'Invisible, L'Invisible fiancée, Le Secret de Storitz (The Secret of Wilhelm Storitz, written in 1901). Original manuscript of *Le Secret de Wilhelm Storitz*. Published as *Le Secret de Wilhelm Storitz* (1985, Société Jules Verne), translated as *The Secret of Wilhelm Storitz* (2011, University of Nebraska Press, Bison Books, trans. Peter Schulman).

La Chasse au météore—Le Bolide (The Hunt for the Meteor—The Bolide,

written in 1901). Original manuscript of *La Chasse au météore* (1908).
Published as *La Chasse au météore. Version originale* (1986) and as *La
Chasse au météore (Version originale) suivi de Edom* (1994, Société Jules
Verne), translated as *The Meteor Hunt* (2006, University of Nebraska Press,
Bison Books, trans. Frederick Paul Walter and Walter James Miller).

"Voyage d'études" (Study Trip, written in 1903–1904). Unfinished manuscript,
completed and published by Michel Verne as *L'Etonnante Aventure de la
mission Barsac* (1919). Original version published in *San Carlos et autres
récits inédits*, 207–60 (1993, Cherche Midi) and translated as "Fact-Finding
Mission" in *Vice, Redemption and the Distant Colony* (2011, BearManor
Media, trans. Kieran M. O'Driscoll).

"Edom." (Edom, written from 1903 to 1905). Unfinished manuscript, rewritten
and published in *Hier et demain* (1910) by Michel Verne as "L'Eternel
Adam." Proofs published in the *Bulletin de la Société Jules Verne* 100 (1991):
21–48.

Theater Plays and Operettas
(Performed or Published, in Chronological Order)

Les Pailles rompues (Broken Straws, 1849). First performed at the Théâtre
Historique on June 12, 1850. Published by Beck (Paris) in 1850.

Monna Lisa (Mona Lisa, 1852). Published posthumously in *Jules Verne*, ed.
Pierre-André Touttain, 1974.

Les Châteaux en Californie (Castles in California, 1852). Published in the *Musée
des familles*, June 1852.

Le Colin-Maillard (Blind Man's Bluff, 1852). First performed at the Théâtre
Lyrique on April 28, 1853. Published by Michel Lévy (Paris) in 1853.

Les Compagnons de la Marjolaine (The Companions of the Marjolaine, 1853).
First performed at the Théâtre Lyrique on June 6, 1855. Published by Michel
Lévy (Paris) in 1855. Translated as *The Knights of the Daffodil* in *Mr. Chimp
and Other Plays by Jules Verne* (2011, BearManor Media, trans. Frank
Morlock).

Monsieur de Chimpanzé (Mister Chimpanzee, 1857). First performed at the
Bouffes-Parisiennes on February 17, 1858. Published in the *Bulletin de la
Société Jules Verne* 57 (1981, ed. Robert Pourvoyeur). Translated as *Mr.
Chimpanzee* in *Mr. Chimp and Other Plays by Jules Verne* (2011, BearManor
Media, trans. Frank Morlock).

Le Page de madame Marlborough (The Page of Mrs. Marlborough, attributed
operetta signed E. Vierne, music by Frédéric Barbier, 1858). First performed
at the Folies Nouvelles on October 28, 1858. Published posthumously, ed.
V. Dehs, in *Bulletin de la Société Jules Verne*, no. 160 (2006): 5–28.

L'Auberge des Ardennes (The Ardennes Inn, 1859). First performed at the
Théâtre Lyrique on September 1, 1860. Published by Michel Lévy (Paris) in
1860.

Onze jours de siège (Eleven Days of Siege, 1854–1860). First performed at the
Théâtre du Vaudeville on June 1, 1861. Published by Michel Lévy (Paris) in
1861. Translated as *Eleven Days of Siege* in *Mr. Chimp and Other Plays by
Jules Verne* (2011, BearManor Media, trans. Frank Morlock).

Un Fils adoptif (An Adopted Son, with Charles Wallut, 1860). Published
posthumously, ed. V. Dehs, in *Bulletin de la Société Jules Verne*, no. 140
(2001): 15–48. Translated as *The Adoptive Son* in *Mr. Chimp and Other
Plays* by Jules Verne (2011, BearManor Media, trans. Frank Morlock).

Un Neveu d'Amérique, ou Les Deux Frontignac (A Nephew from America, or
the Two Frontignacs, 1872). First performed at the Théâtre Cluny on April
17, 1873. Published by Hetzel (Paris) in 1873.

Le Tour du monde en 80 jours (Around the World in Eighty Days, version by
Edouard Cadol and Jules Verne, 1873). Published posthumously, ed. V. Dehs,
in *Bulletin de la Société Jules Verne*, no. 152 (2004): 5–80.

Le Tour du monde en 80 jours (Around the World in Eighty Days, 1874). First
performed at the Théâtre de la Porte Saint-Martin, November 7, 1874.
Published in *Les Voyages au théâtre* by Jules Verne and Adolphe d'Ennery
(Paris, J. Hetzel, 1881). *Around the World in Eighty Days — The 1874 Play*
(2013, BearManor Media).

Le Docteur Ox (Doctor Ox, operetta with Philippe Gille and Arnold Mortier,
music by Offenbach, 1877). First performed at the Théâtre des Variétés on
January 26, 1877. Published by Choudens père et fils, 1877.

Les Enfants du capitaine Grant (The Children of Captain Grant, 1878). First
performed at the Théâtre de la Porte Saint-Martin on December 26, 1878.
Published in *Les Voyages au théâtre* by Jules Verne and Adolphe d'Ennery
(Paris, J. Hetzel, 1881).

Michel Strogoff (Michael Strogoff, 1880). First performed at the Théâtre de
Châtelet on November 17, 1880. Published in *Les Voyages au théâtre* by
Jules Verne and Adolphe d'Ennery (Paris, J. Hetzel, 1881).

Voyage à travers l'impossible (Journey through the Impossible, 1882). First
performed at the Théâtre de la Porte Saint-Martin on November 25, 1882.
Published by Jean-Jacques Pauvert (Paris) in 1981. Translated as *Journey
through the Impossible* (2003, Prometheus, trans. Edward Baxter).

Kéraban-le-têtu (Keraban the Stubborn, 1883). First performed at La Gaîté-
Lyrique on September 3, 1883. Published in the *Bulletin de la Société Jules
Verne* 85–86 (1988).

Mathias Sandorf (Mathias Sandorf, 1887). Written by William Busnach and

Georges Maurens, authorized by Verne. First performed at the Théâtre de l'Ambigu on November 26, 1887. Published by the Société Jules Verne (1992), translated as *Mathias Sandorf: A Play in Three Acts*, (2010, Borgo Press, trans. Frank Morlock).

(For an anthology of Verne's other plays, see Christian Robin, ed., *Jules Verne: Théâtre inédit*. Paris: Cherche Midi, 2006.)

Poetry and Song Lyrics

Collected in *Poésies inédites*, ed. Christian Robin (1989, Paris: Cherche Midi) and in *Textes oubliés*, ed. Francis Lacassin (1979, Paris: UGE, Collection 10/18) and in *Chansons de Jules Verne, l'univers musical dans les récits de voyages*, ed. Frédéric-Gaël Theuriau (2011, Saarbrücken: Editions universitaires européennes) with the full scores of the compositions.

Literary Criticism, Nonfiction, Speeches, and Other Prose

For an anthology of different speeches and articles, see Volker Dehs, ed., *Bulletin de la Société Jules Verne*, no. 120 (1994).

"Salon de 1857" (The Parisian Salon of 1857). *Revue des Beaux-Arts. Tribune des Artistes* (June–Sept. 1857): 231–34, 249–55, 269–76, 285–92, 305–13, 325–30, 345–49. Reprint ed. William Butcher (Acadien, 2008); online ed. Volker Dehs. http://www.jules-verne.eu/Salon_1857.pdf.

"A propos du 'Géant'" (Concerning the "Giant"). *Musée des familles* (Dec. 1863): 92–93. Reprinted in *Textes oubliés*, ed. Francis Lacassin (1979, UGE, Collection 10/18). "Edgard Poë [*sic*] et ses oeuvres" (Edgar Poe and His Works). *Musée des familles* (Apr. 1864): 193–208. Reprinted in *Textes oubliés*, ed. Francis Lacassin (1979, UGE, Collection 10/18). Translated by I. O. Evans as "The Leader of the Cult of the Unusual" in *Edgar Allan Poe Scrapbook*, ed. Peter Haining (1978, Schocken).

Géographie illustrée de la France et de ses colonies (Illustrated Geography of France and Its Colonies, 1867–1868, illus. Edouard Riou, Hubert Clerget), coauthored with Théophile Lavallée.

"Une Ville idéale" (An Ideal City). *Mémoires de l'Académie des sciences, belles-lettres, et arts d'Amiens* 22 (1874–1875): 347–78. Reprinted in *Textes oubliés*, ed. Francis Lacassin (1979, UGE, Collection 10/18). Translated by I. O. Evans as "An Ideal City" and included in *Yesterday and Tomorrow* (1965, Arco).

Histoire des grands voyages et des grands voyageurs: Découverte de la terre (1870, not illustrated). Original version of the first volume, written only by Verne, whereas the second version in six volumes (1878–1880, not illustrated) was written by Gabriel Marcel and corrected by Verne. *Les Grands Navigateurs du XVIIIème siècle* (1879, illus. Léon Benett and Paul

Philippoteaux), and *Les Voyageurs du XIXème siècle* (1880). Translated by
Dora Leigh as *The Exploration of the World: Famous Travels and Travellers,
The Great Navigators of the Eighteenth Century, The Exploration of the
World* (1879, Scribner's).

"The Story of My Boyhood." *The Youth's Companion* (Apr. 9, 1891): 221. Verne's
original autobiographical essay, "Souvenirs d'enfance et de jeunesse"
(Memories of Childhood and Youth), was published in French for the first
time in *Jules Verne*, ed. Pierre-André Touttain (1974, Cahiers de l'Herne).

"Discours de distribution des prix au Lycée de Jeunes Filles d'Amiens" (July
29, 1893). Reprinted in *Textes oubliés*, ed. Francis Lacassin (1979, UGE,
Collection 10/18). Translated by I. O. Evans as "The Future for Women: An
Address by Jules Verne," in *The Jules Verne Companion*, ed. Peter Haining
(1978, Souvenir).

"Future of the Submarine." *Popular Mechanics* 6 (June 1904): 629–31.

"Solution of Mind Problems by the Imagination." *Hearst's International
Cosmopolitan* (Oct. 1928): 95, 132. Written in 1903.

(For an anthology of different speeches and articles, see Volker Dehs, ed.,
Bulletin de la Société Jules Verne, no. 120 (1994).

SELECTED INTERVIEWS

Belloc, Marie A. "Jules Verne at Home." *Strand Magazine* (Feb. 1895): 207–13.

Compère, Daniel, and Jean-Michel Margot. *Entretiens avec Jules Verne 1873–
1905*. Geneva: Slatkine, 1998.

De Amicis, Edmondo. "A Visit to Jules Verne and Victorien Sardou."
Chautauquan (Mar. 1897): 702–707.

Jones, Gordon. "Jules Verne at Home." *Temple Bar* 129 (1904): 664–70.

Sherard, Robert H. "Jules Verne at Home." *McClure's Magazine* (Jan. 1894):
115–24.

———. "Jules Verne Revisited." *T.P.'s Weekly* (Oct. 9, 1903): 589.

CORRESPONDENCE AND OTHER
AUTOBIOGRAPHICAL WRITINGS

Bottin, André. "Lettres inédites de Jules Verne au lieutenant colonel
Hennebert." *Bulletin de la Société Jules Verne* 18 (1971): 36–44.

Dumas, Olivier. *Jules Verne, avec la correspondance inédite de Jules Verne avec
sa famille*. Lyon: La Manufacture, 1988.

Dumas, Olivier, Piero Gondolo della Riva, and Volker Dehs. *Correspondance
inédite de Jules Verne et de Pierre-Jules Hetzel (1863–1886)*. Vol. 1 (1863–
1874). Geneva: Slatkine, 1999.

———. *Correspondance inédite de Jules Verne et de Pierre-Jules Hetzel* (1863–1886). Vol. 2 (1875–1878). Geneva: Slatkine, 2001.

———. *Correspondance inédite de Jules Verne et de Pierre-Jules Hetzel* (1863–1886). Vol. 3 (1879–1886). Geneva: Slatkine, 2002.

———. *Correspondance inédite de Jules et Michel Verne avec l'éditeur Louis-Jules Hetzel* (1886–1914). Vol. 1 (1886–1896). Geneva: Slatkine, 2004.

———. *Correspondance inédite de Jules et Michel Verne avec l'éditeur Louis-Jules Hetzel* (1886–1914). Vol. 2 (1897–1914). Geneva: Slatkine, 2006.

Martin, Charles-Noël. *La Vie et l'oeuvre de Jules Verne*. Paris: Michel de l'Ormeraie, 1978.

Parménie, A. "Huit lettres de Jules Verne à son éditeur P.-J. Hetzel." *Arts et Lettres* 15 (1949): 102–107.

Parménie, A., and C. Bonnier de la Chapelle. *Histoire d'un éditeur et de ses auteurs, P.-J. Hetzel (Stahl)*. Paris: Albin Michel, 1953.

Turicllo, Mario. "Lettre de Jules Verne à un jeune Italien." *Bulletin de la Société Jules Verne* 1 (1936): 158–61.

Verne, Jules. "Correspondance." *Bulletin de la Société Jules Verne* 49 (1979): 31–34.

———. "Correspondance avec Fernando Ricci," *Europe* 613 (1980): 137–38.

———. "Correspondance avec Mario Turicllo." *Europe* 613 (1980): 108–35.

———. "Deux lettres à Louis-Jules Hetzel." In *Jules Verne*, ed. Pierre-André Touttain, 73–74. Paris: Cahiers de l'Herne, 1974.

———. "Deux lettres inédites." *Bulletin de la Société Jules Verne* 48 (1978): 253–54.

———. "Jules Verne: 63 lettres." *Bulletin de la Société Jules Verne* 11–13 (1938): 47–129.

———. "Lettre à Nadar." *L'Arc* 29 (1966): 83.

———. "Lettre à Paul, à propos de Turpin." In *Jules Verne*, ed. Pierre-André Touttain, 81–82. Paris: Cahiers de l'Herne, 1974.

———. "Lettres à Nadar." In *Jules Verne*, ed. Pierre-André Touttain, 76–80. Paris: Cahiers de l'Herne, 1974.

———. "Lettres diverses." *Europe* 613 (1980): 143–51.

———. "Quelques lettres." *Livres de France* 6 (May–June, 1955): 13–15.

———. "Sept lettres à sa famille et à divers correspondants." In *Jules Verne*, ed. Pierre-André Touttain, 63–70. Paris: Cahiers de l'Herne, 1974.

———. "Souvenirs d'enfance et de jeunesse." In *Jules Verne*, ed. Pierre-André Touttain, 57–62. Paris: Cahiers de l'Herne, 1974.

———. "Spécial Lettres No. 1." *Bulletin de la Société Jules Verne* 65–66 (1983): 4–50.

―――. "Spécial Lettres No. 2." *Bulletin de la Société Jules Verne* 69 (1984): 3–25.

―――. "Spécial Lettres No. 3." *Bulletin de la Société Jules Verne* 78 (1986): 3–52.

―――. "Spécial Lettres No. 4." *Bulletin de la Société Jules Verne* 83 (1987): 4–27.

―――. "Spécial Lettres No. 5." *Bulletin de la Société Jules Verne* 88 (1988): 8–18.

―――. "Spécial Lettres No. 6." *Bulletin de la Société Jules Verne* 94 (1990): 10–33.

―――. "Trente-six lettres inédites." *Bulletin de la Société Jules Verne* 68 (1983): 4–50.

―――. "Vingt-deux lettres de Jules Verne à son frère Paul." *Bulletin de la Société Jules Verne* 69 (1984): 3–25.

SECONDARY SOURCES ON JULES VERNE AND HIS WORKS

Bibliographies and Bibliographical Studies

Angenot, Marc. "Jules Verne and French Literary Criticism, I." *Science Fiction Studies* 1, no. 1 (1973): 33–37.

―――. "Jules Verne and French Literary Criticism, II." *Science Fiction Studies* 1, no. 2 (1973): 46–49.

Butcher, William. "Jules and Michel Verne." In *Critical Bibliography of French Literature: The Nineteenth Century*, ed. David Baguley, 923–40. Syracuse, NY: Syracuse University Press, 1994.

Compère, Daniel. "Le Monde des études verniennes." *Magazine Littéraire* 119 (1976): 27–29.

Decré, Françoise. *Catalogue du fonds Jules Verne*. Nantes: Bibliothèque Municipale, 1978. Updated by Colette Gaillois in *Catalogue du fonds Jules Verne*, Supplément 1 (1978–1983). Nantes: Bibliothèque Municipale, 1984.

Dehs, Volker. *Bibliographischer Führer durch die Jules-Verne-Forschung / Guide bibliographique à travers la critique vernienne, 1872–2001*. Wetzlar, DE: Phantastische Bibliothek, 2002.

Dumas, Olivier, et al. "Bibliographie des oeuvres de Jules Verne." *Bulletin de la Société Jules Verne* 1 (1967): 7–12. Additions and updates: *BSJV* 2 (1967): 11–15; *BSJV* 3 (1967): 13; *BSJV* 4 (1967): 15–16. Reprinted in Dumas, *Jules Verne*, 160–67. Lyon: La Manufacture, 1988.

Evans, Arthur B. "A Bibliography of Jules Verne's English Translations." *Science Fiction Studies* 32, no.1 (Mar. 2005): 87–123.

―――. "Jules Verne in English: A Bibliography of Modern Editions and Scholarly Studies." *Verniana* 1 (2008–2009): 9–22. http://www.verniana.org/volumes/01/HTML/ArtBiblio.html.

Gallagher, Edward J., Judith A. Mistichelli, and John A. Van Eerde. *Jules Verne: A Primary and Secondary Bibliography*. Boston: G. K. Hall, 1980.

Gondolo della Riva, Piero. *Bibliographie analytique de toutes les oeuvres de Jules Verne.* Vols. 1 and 2. Paris: Société Jules Verne, 1977, 1985.

Margot, Jean-Michel. *Bibliographie documentaire sur Jules Verne.* Amiens: Centre de Documentation Jules Verne, 1989.

Raymond, François, and Daniel Compère. *Le Développement des études sur Jules Verne.* Paris: Minard, Archives des Lettres Modernes, 1976.

BIOGRAPHIES

Allott, Kenneth. *Jules Verne.* London: Crescent Press, 1940.

Allotte de la Fuÿe, Marguerite. *Jules Verne, sa vie, son oeuvre.* Paris: Simon Kra, 1928. Published in English as *Jules Verne,* trans. Erik de Mauny. London: Staples, 1954.

Avrane, Patrick. *Jules Verne.* Paris: Stock, 1997.

Butcher, William. *Jules Verne: The Definitive Biography.* New York: Thunder's Mouth Press, 2006. Revised edition, Acadian, 2008.

Claretie, Jules. *Jules Verne.* Paris: A. Quantin, 1883.

Costello, Peter. *Jules Verne: Inventor of Science Fiction.* London: Hodder and Stoughton, 1978.

Dehs, Volker. *Jules Verne. Eine kritische Biographie.* Düsseldorf: Artemis and Winkler, 2005.

Dumas, Olivier. *Jules Verne.* Lyon: La Manufacture, 1988.

———. *Voyage à travers Jules Verne.* Montreal: Stanké, 2000.

Dusseau, Joëlle. *Jules Verne.* Paris: Perrin, 2005.

Jules-Verne, Jean. *Jules Verne.* Paris: Hachette, 1973. Published in English as *Jules Verne: A Biography,* trans. Roger Greaves. New York: Taplinger, 1976.

Lemire, Charles. *Jules Verne.* Paris: Berger-Levrault, 1908.

Lottman, Herbert R. *Jules Verne: An Exploratory Biography.* New York: St. Martin's Press, 1996. Published in French as *Jules Verne,* trans. Marianne Véron. Paris: Flammarion, 1996.

Lynch, Lawrence. *Jules Verne.* New York: Twayne, 1992.

Martin, Charles-Noël. *La Vie et l'oeuvre de Jules Verne.* Paris: Michel de l'Ormeraie, 1978.

Soriano, Mark. *Jules Verne.* Paris: Julliard, 1978.

Valetoux, Philippe. *Jules Verne en mer et contre tous.* Paris: Magellan, 2005.

Other Selected Critical Studies

Alkon, Paul. *Science Fiction before 1900.* New York: Twayne, 1994.

Angenot, Marc. "Jules Verne: The Last Happy Utopianist." In *Science Fiction: A Critical Guide,* ed. Patrick Parrinder, 18–32. New York: Longman, 1979.

————. "Science Fiction in France before Verne," *Science Fiction Studies* 5, no. 1 (Mar. 1978): 58–66.

L'Arc 29 (1966). Special issue devoted to Jules Verne.

Arts et Lettres 15 (1949). Special issue devoted to Jules Verne.

Barthes, Roland. "Nautilus et Bateau Ivre." In Barthes, *Mythologies*, 90–92. Paris: Seuil, 1957, 1970. Published in English as "The Nautilus and the Drunken Boat," trans. A. Lavers, in Barthes, *Mythologies*, 65–67. New York: Hill and Wang, 1972.

————. "Par où commencer?" *Poétique* 1 (1970): 3–9. Reprinted in Barthes, *Nouveaux essais critiques*, 145–51. Paris: Seuil, 1972.

Behrmann, Bridget. "Éclat: Duality and the Absolute in *Voyages et aventures du capitaine Hatteras*." *Verniana* 7 (2014–2015): 1–16.

Bellemin-Noël, Jean. "Analectures de Jules Verne." *Critique* 26 (1970): 692–704.

Benford, Gregory. "Verne to Varley: Hard SF Evolves." *Science Fiction Studies* 32, no. 1 (March 2005): 163–71.

Berri, Kenneth. "Les *Cinq cents millions de la Bégum* ou la technologie de la fable." *Stanford French Review* 3 (1979): 29–40.

Boia, Lucien. "Un Ecrivain original: Michel Verne." *Bulletin de la Société Jules Verne* 70 (1984): 90–95.

————. *Jules Verne: les paradoxes d'un mythe*. Paris: Belles Lettres, 2005.

Bradbury, Ray. "The Ardent Blasphemers." Foreword to Jules Verne, *Twenty Thousand Leagues under the Sea*, trans. Anthony Bonner, 1–12. New York: Bantam Books, 1962.

Bridenne, Jean-Jacques. *La Littérature française d'imagination scientifique*. Lausanne, CH: Dassonville, 1950.

Buisine, Alain. "Circulations en tous genres." *Europe* 595–96 (1978): 48–56.

————. "Repères, marques, gisements: à propos de la robinsonnade vernienne." *Revue des Lettres Modernes* 523–29 (Apr.–June 1978). Special issue devoted to Jules Verne.

Bulletin de la Société Jules Verne (1967–2000). Edited by Olivier Dumas. The official publication of the Jules Verne Society in France and one of the best sources for up-to-date and reliable information on Jules Verne.

Burgaud, Philippe, and Jean-Michel Margot. "Jules Verne chez Hachette de 1914 à 1950." *Verniana* 6 (2013–2014): 1–42. http://www.verniana.org/volumes/06/index.en.html.

Butcher, William. "Crevettes de l'air et baleines volantes." *La Nouvelle Revue Maritime* 386–87 (May–June 1984): 35–40.

————. "L'Écrivain à découvert." *Bulletin de la Société Jules Verne* 101 (1992): 43–45. http://jv.gilead.org.il/butcher/.

———. "Les Épisodes fantômes de *Vingt mille lieues*." *Europe* 909–10 (2005): 119–34

———. "Graphes et graphie." In Butcher, *Regards sur la théorie des graphes*, 177–82. Lausanne, CH: Presses polytechniques romandes, 1980.

———. "Hidden Treasures: The Manuscripts of *Twenty Thousand Leagues*." *Science Fiction Studies* 32, no. 1 (Mar. 2005): 132–49. http://jv.gilead.org.il /sfs/.

———. "L'Incompris, ou la propagation d'un mythe." *Bulletin de la Société Jules Verne* 102 (1992): 14–16.

———. "Journey without End: On Translating Verne." *Babel* 40, no. 2 (1994): 131–36. http://jv.gilead.org.il/butcher/.

———. "Long-Lost Manuscript." *Modern Language Review* 93, no. 4 (Oct. 1998): 961–71.

———. "Mysterious Masterpiece." In *Jules Verne: Narratives of Modernity*, ed. Edmund J. Smyth, 142–57. Liverpool: Liverpool University Press, 2000.

———. "La Poésie de l'arborescence chez Verne." *Studi Francesi* 104 (1992): 261–67. http://jv.gilead.org.il/butcher/.

———. "Le Sens de *L'Éternel Adam*." *Bulletin de la Société Jules Verne* 58 (1981): 73–81.

———. "The Tribulations of a Chinese in China: Verne and the Celestial Empire." *Journal of Foreign Languages* 5 (Sept. 2006): 63–79.

———. "Le Verbe et la chair, ou l'emploi du temps." In *Jules Verne 4: Texte, image, spectacle*, ed. François Raymond, 125–48. Paris: Minard, 1983.

———. *Verne's Journey to the Centre of the Self: Space and Time in the* Voyages Extraordinaires. London and New York: Macmillan and St. Martin's Press, 1990.

Butor, Michel. "Homage to Jules Verne." Trans. John Coleman. *New Statesman* (July 15, 1966): 94.

———. "Le Point suprême et l'âge d'or à travers quelques oeuvres de Jules Verne." *Arts et Lettres* 15 (1949): 3–31. Reprinted in Butor, *Répertoire I*, 130–62. Paris: Editions de Minuit, 1960. Reprinted in English as Butor, "The Golden Age in Jules Verne." In Butor, *Inventory*, 114–45. Trans. Patricia Dreyfus. New York: Simon and Schuster, 1961.

Cahiers du Centre d'études verniennes et du Musée Jules Verne (1981–96). Edited by Christian Robin. 13 issues published.

Carrouges, Michel. "Le Mythe de Vulcain chez Jules Verne." *Arts et Lettres* 15 (1949): 32–48.

Chambers, Ross. "Cultural and Ideological Determinations in Narrative: A Note on Jules Verne's *Cinq cents millions de la Bégum*." *L'Esprit créateur* 21, no. 3 (fall 1981): 69–78.

Chatelain, Danièle, and George Slusser. "The Creation of Scientific Wonder: Jules Verne's Dialogue with Claude Bernard." *Verniana* 2 (2009–2010): 89–124. http://www.verniana.org/volumes/02/index.en.html.

Chesneaux, Jean. "L'Invention linguistique chez Jules Verne." In *Langues et techniques, nature et société 1*, ed. J. M. C. Thomas and Lucien Bernot, 345–51. Paris: Klincksieck, 1972.

———. *Jules Verne: Un Regard sur le monde*. Paris: Bayard, 2001.

———. *Une Lecture politique de Jules Verne*. Paris: Maspero, 1971. Published in English as *The Political and Social Ideas of Jules Verne*, trans. Thomas Wikeley. London: Thames and Hudson, 1972.

Clément, Stéphanie. "La double profondeur dans *Vingt mille lieues sous les mers* ou le sens des limites." *Verniana* 6 (2013–2014): 55–66. http://www.verniana.org/volumes/06/index.en.html.

Compère, Daniel. *Approche de l'île chez Jules Verne*. Paris: Lettres Modernes, 1977.

———. "Le Bas des pages." *Bulletin de la Société Jules Verne* 68 (1983): 147–53.

———. "Fenêtres latérales." In *Jules Verne IV: Texte, image, spectacle*, ed. François Raymond, 55–72. Paris: Minard, 1983.

———. *Jules Verne, écrivain*. Geneva: Droz, 1991.

———. *Jules Verne: Parcours d'une oeuvre*. Amiens: Encrage, 1996.

———. "Poétique de la carte." *Bulletin de la Société Jules Verne* 50 (1979): 69–74.

———. *Un Voyage imaginaire de Jules Verne: Voyage au centre de la Terre*. Paris: Lettres Modernes, 1977.

Compère, Daniel, and Volker Dehs. "Taskinar and Co.: Introduction à une étude des mots inventés dans l'oeuvre de Jules Verne." *Bulletin de la Société Jules Verne* 67 (1983): 107–11.

Crovisier, Jacques. "Géodésiens et astronomes reels ou fictifs dans les *Aventures de trois Russes et de trois Anglais dans l'Afrique Australe*." *Verniana* 6 (2013–2014): 93–110. http://www.verniana.org/volumes/06/index.en.html.

———. "Le Storm glass, un instrument de météorologie oublié, présent dans les *Voyages extraordinaires*." *Verniana* 3 (2010–2011): 1–10. http://www.verniana.org/volumes/03/index.en.html.

Davy, Jacques. "A propos de l'anthropophagie chez Jules Verne." *Cahiers du centre d'études verniennes et du Musée Jules Verne* 1 (1981): 15–23.

Dehs, Volker. "La Bibliothèque de Jules et Michel Verne." *Verniana* 3 (2010–2011): 51–118. http://www.verniana.org/volumes/03/index.en.html.

———. "Nemo, Flourens, et quelques autres: Divagations autour de *Ville mille lieues sous les mers*." *Verniana* 3 (2010–2011): 11–32. http://www.verniana.org/volumes/03/index.en.html.

———. "Quelques préfaces de Jules Verne, peu ou pas connues." *Verniana* 5
(2012–2013): 31–52. http://www.verniana.org/volumes/05/index.en.html.
———. "Le Premier Dénouement des *Cinq Cents Millions de la Bégum*."
Bulletin de la Société Jules Verne 123 (1997), 37–41.
———. "Les Tribulations de Dufrénoy: Traces historiques, autobiographiques
et intertextuelles dans *Paris au XXe siècle*." *Bulletin de la Société Jules Verne*
171 (Oct. 2009): 34–44.
De la Cotardière, Philippe, and Jean-Paul Dekiss, eds. *Jules Verne: De la science
à l'imaginaire*. Paris: Larousse, 2004.
Demerliac, Jean. "Futurisme, un faux ami de Verne." *Verniana* 6 (2013–2014):
111–38. http://www.verniana.org/volumes/06/index.en.html.
Diesbach, Ghislain de. *Le Tour de Jules Verne en quatre-vingts livres*. Paris:
Julliard, 1969.
Dumas, Olivier. "La Main du fils dans l'oeuvre du père." *Bulletin de la Société
Jules Verne* 82 (1987): 21–24.
Dupuy, Lionel. *En relisant Jules Verne*. Dole, FR: La Clef d'Argent, 2005.
Escaich, René. *Voyage au monde de Jules Verne*. Paris: Plantin, 1955.
Europe 33 (1955). Special issue devoted to Jules Verne.
Europe 595–96 (1978). Special issue devoted to Jules Verne.
Evans, Arthur B. "The Extraordinary Libraries of Jules Verne." *L'Esprit créateur*
28 (1988): 75–86. http://jv.gilead.org.il/evans/.
———. "Le Franglais vernien (père et fils)." In *Modernités de Jules Verne*, ed.
Jean Bessière, 87–105. Paris: Presses Universitaires de France, 1988.
———. "The Illustrators of Jules Verne's *Voyages Extraordinaires*." *Science
Fiction Studies* 25, no. 2 (July 1998): 241–70. http://jv.gilead.org.il/evans/.
———. "Jules Verne." In *Fifty Key Figures in Science Fiction*, ed. Mark Bould
et al., 235–39. New York: Routledge, 2010.
———. "Jules Verne and the French Literary Canon." In *Jules Verne: Narratives
of Modernity*, ed. Edmund J. Smyth, 11–39. Liverpool: Liverpool University
Press, 2000. http://jv.gilead.org.il/evans/.
———. "Jules Verne et la persistence rétinienne." *Cahiers du centre d'études
verniennes et du Musée Jules Verne* 13 (1996): 11–17.
———. "Jules Verne, visionnaire incompris." *Pour la Science* 236 (June 1997):
94–101.
———. *Jules Verne Rediscovered: Didacticism and the Scientific Novel*.
Westport, CT: Greenwood, 1988.
———. "Jules Verne: Exploring the Limits." *Australian Journal of French
Studies* 42, no. 3 (Sept.-Dec. 2005): 265–75. http://jv.gilead.org.il/evans/.
———. "Jules Verne's America." *Extrapolation* 48 (Spring 2007): 35–43. http://
jv.gilead.org.il/evans/.

————. "Jules Verne's Dream Machines: Technology and Transcendence." *Extrapolation* 54 (summer 2013): 129–46.

————. "Jules Verne's English Translations." *Science Fiction Studies* 32, no. 1 (Mar. 2005): 62–86. http://jv.gilead.org.il/evans/.

————. "Literary Intertexts in Jules Verne's *Voyages Extraordinaires*." *Science Fiction Studies* 23, no. 2 (July 1996): 171–87. http://jv.gilead.org.il/evans/.

————. "The 'New' Jules Verne." *Science Fiction Studies* 22, no. 1 (Mar. 1995): 35–46. http://jv.gilead.org.il/evans/.

————. "Protesting Too Much: The Jules vs. Michel Verne Controversy." *Science Fiction Studies* 36, no. 2 (July 2009): 321–26.

————. "Science Fiction in France: A Brief History and Select Bibliography." *Science Fiction Studies* 16, no. 3 (Nov. 1989): 254–76, 338–68. http://jv.gilead.org.il/evans/.

————. "Science Fiction vs. Scientific Fiction in France: From Jules Verne to J.-H. Rosny Aîné." *Science Fiction Studies* 15, no. 1 (1988): 1–11. http://jv.gilead.org.il/evans/.

————. "Vehicular Utopias of Jules Verne." In *Transformations of Utopia*, ed. George Slusser et al., 99–108. New York: AMS Press, 1999. http://jv.gilead.org.il/evans/.

Evans, Arthur B., and Ron Miller. "Jules Verne: Misunderstood Visionary." *Scientific American* (Apr. 1997): 92–97.

Evans, I. O. *Jules Verne and His Works*. London: Arco, 1965.

————. "Jules Verne et le lecteur anglais." *Bulletin de la Société Jules Verne* 6 (1937): 36.

Fabre, Michel. *Le Problème et l'épreuve: formation et modernité chez Jules Verne*. Paris: Harmattan, 2003.

Foucault, Michel. "L'Arrière-fable." *L'Arc* 29 (1966): 5–13. Published in English as "Behind the Fable," trans. Pierre A. Walker, *Critical Texts* 5 (1988): 1–5; also published as "Behind the Fable," trans. Robert Hurley, in *Aesthetics, Method, and Epistemology*, ed. J. Faubion, 137–45. New York: New Press, 1998.

Frank, Bernard. *Jules Verne et ses voyages*. Paris: Flammarion, 1941.

Gilli, Yves, and Florent Montaclair. *Jules Verne et l'utopie*. Besançon: Presses du Centre Unesco de Besançon, 1999.

Gilli, Yves, Florent Montaclair, and Sylvie Petit. *Le Naufrage dans l'oeuvre de Jules Verne*. Paris: Harmattan, 1998.

Gondolo della Riva, Piero. "A propos des oeuvres posthumes de Jules Verne." *Europe* 595–96 (1978): 73–82.

————. "A propos d'une nouvelle." In *Jules Verne*, ed. Pierre-André Touttain, 284–85. Paris: Cahiers de l'Herne, 1974.

Guillaud, Lauric. *Jules Verne face au rêve américain*. Paris: Michel Houdiard, 2005.

Haining, Peter. *The Jules Verne Companion*. London: Souvenir, 1978.

Harpold, Terry. "Reading the Illustrations of Verne's *Voyages extraordinaires*: The Example of *Le Superbe Orénoque*." *ImageTexT* 3, no. 1 (2006). http://www.english.ufl.edu/imagetext/archives/v3_1/harpold/.

———. "The Providential Grace of Verne's *Le Testament d'un excentrique*." *IRIS* 28 (2005): 157–68.

———. "Verne, Baudelaire et Poe – *La Jangada* et 'Le Scarabée d'or.'" *Revue Jules Verne* 19–20 (2005): 162–68.

———. "Verne's Cartographies." *Science Fiction Studies* 32, no. 1 (Mar. 2005): 18–42. http://jv.gilead.org.il/sfs/.

———. "Verne's Errant Readers: Nemo, Clawbonny, Michel Dufrénoy." *Verniana* 1 (2008–2009): 31–42.

———. "Where is Verne's Mars?" In *Visions of Mars: Essays on the Red Planet in Fiction and Science*, ed. Howard V. Hendrix, George E. Slusser, and Eric S. Rabkin, 29–35. Jefferson, NC: McFarland, 2011.

Hedman, Dag. "The Influence of Jules Verne in Sweden Around 1900." *Verniana* 6 (2013–2014): 43–54. http://www.verniana.org/volumes/06/index.en.html.

Hendrix, Howard V. "Verne Among the Punks, or 'It's Not All Just Victorian Clockwork.'" *Verniana* 2 (2009–2010): 81–88. http://www.verniana.org/volumes/02/index.en.html.

Huet, Marie-Hélène. *L'Histoire des Voyages Extraordinaires: Essai sur l'oeuvre de Jules Verne*. Paris: Minard, 1973.

———. "Naissance d'une nation." *Verniana* 6 (2013–2014): 67–80. http://www.verniana.org/volumes/06/index.en.html.

———. "Notice et Notes." *L'Île mystérieuse*. In Jules Verne, *Voyages extraordinaires*, ed. Jean-Luc Steinmetz et al., 1123–87. Paris: Gallimard, Collection Bibliothèque de la Pléiade, 2012.

———. "Winter Lights: Disaster, Interpretation, and Jules Verne's Polar Novels." *Verniana* 2 (2009–2010): 149–78. http://www.verniana.org/volumes/02/index.en.html.

Jensen, William B. "Captain Nemo's Battery: Chemistry and the Science Fiction of Jules Verne." *Chemical Intelligencer* (Apr. 1997): 23–32.

Joyce, Steve. "*A Trip to the Moon*: Jules Verne, H. G. Wells, and Other Influences." *Extraordinary Voyages* 20, no. 1 (Jan. 2014): 1–16.

Jules Verne écrivain. Nantes: Bibliothèque municipale de Nantes, 2000.

Jules Verne et les sciences humaines. Colloque de Cerisy. Paris: UGE, Collection 10/18, 1979.

Jules Verne—filiations, rencontres, influences. Colloque d'Amiens II. Paris: Minard, 1980.

Jules Verne ou les inventions romanesques. Ed. Christophe Refait and Alain Schaffer. Amiens: Encrage, 2007.

Jules Verne: le roman de la mer. Paris: Seuil/Musée National de la Marine, 2005.

Ketterer, David. "Fathoming *20,000 Leagues under the Sea.*" In *The Stellar Gauge: Essays on Science Fiction Writers*, ed. Michael J. Tolley and Kirpal Singh, 7–24. Carlton, AU: Nostrillia Press, 1981.

Klein, Gérard. "Pour lire Verne (I)." *Fiction* 197 (1970): 137–43.

———. "Pour lire Verne (II)." *Fiction* 198 (1970): 143–52.

Lacassin, Francis. "Du Pavillion noir au Québec libre." *Magazine Littéraire* 119 (1976): 22–26.

———. *Passagers clandestins.* Paris: UGE, Collection 10/18, 1979.

———, ed. *Textes oubliés.* Paris: UGE, Collection 10/18, 1979.

Lengrand, Claude. *Dictionnaire des "Voyages Extraordinaires" de Jules Verne: Cahier Jules Verne, I.* Amiens: Encrage, 1998.

Livres de France 5 (1955). Special issue devoted to Jules Verne.

Macherey, Pierre. "Jules Verne ou le récit en défaut." In Macherey, *Pour une théorie de la production littéraire*, 183–266. Paris: Maspero, 1966. Published in English as "The Faulty Narrative," in Macherey, *A Theory of Literary Production*, trans. G. Wall, 159–240. London: Routledge and Kegan Paul, 1978.

Maertens, James W. "Between Jules Verne and Walt Disney: Brains, Brawn, and Masculine Desire in *20,000 Leagues under the Sea.*" *Science Fiction Studies* 22, no. 2 (July 1995): 209–25. http://jv.gilead.org.il/sfs/.

Magazine littéraire 119 (December 1976). Special issue devoted to Jules Verne.

Marcucci, Edmondo. *Les Illustrations des Voyages Extraordinaires de Jules Verne.* Bordeaux: Société Jules Verne, 1956.

Margot, Jean-Michel. "Un Archétype populaire." *Verniana* 6 (2013–2014): 81–92. http://www.verniana.org/volumes/06/index.en.html.

———. *Jules Verne en son temps.* Amiens: Encrage, 2004.

———. "Jules Verne, Playwright." *Science Fiction Studies* 32, no. 1 (March 2005): 150–62. http://jv.gilead.org.il/sfs/.

———. "Où donc situer le Great-Eyry?" *Verniana* 5 (2012–2013): 1–14. http://www.verniana.org/volumes/05/index.en.html.

Martin, Andrew. "Chez Jules: Nutrition and Cognition in the Novels of Jules Verne." *French Studies* 37 (Jan. 1983): 47–58.

———. "The Entropy of Balzacian Tropes in the Scientific Fictions of Jules Verne." *Modern Language Review* 77 (Jan. 1982): 51–62.

————. *The Knowledge of Ignorance from Genesis to Jules Verne*. Cambridge: Cambridge University Press, 1985.

————. *The Mask of the Prophet: The Extraordinary Fictions of Jules Verne*. Oxford: Clarendon Press, 1990.

Mellot Philippe, and Jean-Marie Embs. *Le Guide Jules Verne*. Paris: Les éditions de l'Amateur, 2005.

Miller, Ron. *Extraordinary Voyages: A Reader's Guide to the Works of Jules Verne*. Fredericksburg, VA: Black Cat, 1994.

Miller, Walter James. "Afterword: Freedom and the Near Murder of Jules Verne." In Jules Verne, *Twenty Thousand Leagues under the Sea*, trans. Mendor T. Brunetti, 448–61. New York: New American Library, 2001.

————. "As Verne Smiles." *Verniana* 1 (2008–2009): 1–8. http://www.verniana.org/volumes/01/index.en.html.

————. *The Annotated Jules Verne: From the Earth to the Moon*. New York: Crowell, 1978; rev. ed., New York: Gramercy, 1995.

————. *The Annotated Jules Verne: Twenty Thousand Leagues under the Sea*. New York: Crowell, 1976.

————. "Jules Verne in America: A Translator's Preface." In Jules Verne, *Twenty Thousand Leagues under the Sea*, trans. Walter James Miller, vii–xxii. New York: Washington Square Press, 1965.

Miller, Walter James, and Frederick Paul Walter, eds. and trans. *Jules Verne's Twenty Thousand Leagues under the Sea*. Annapolis, MD: Naval Institute Press, 1993.

Minerva, Nadia. *Jules Verne aux confins de l'utopie*. Paris: Harmattan, 2001.

Modernités de Jules Verne. Edited by Jean Bessière. Paris: Presses Universitaires de France, 1988.

Mongin, Jean-Louis. "*Hector Servadac*, un vrai faux roman scientifique." *Verniana* 5 (2012–2013): 15–30. http://www.verniana.org/volumes/05/index.en.html.

Moré, Marcel. *Nouvelles Explorations de Jules Verne*. Paris: NRF, 1963.

————. *Le Très Curieux Jules Verne*. Paris: Nouvelle Revue Française, 1960.

Moskowitz, Sam, ed. *Science Fiction by Gaslight*. Cleveland, OH: World, 1968.

Noiray, Jacques. *Le Romancier et la machine: L'Image de la machine dans le roman français (1850–1900)*. Paris: José Corti, 1982.

Nouvelles recherches sur Jules Verne et le voyage. Colloque d'Amiens I. Paris: Minard, 1978.

O'Connor, Robert. "Nemo, the *Nautilus*, and the Triumph of the Instrumented Will." *Verniana* 2 (2009–2010): 125–32. http://www.verniana.org/volumes/02/index.en.html.

O'Driscoll, Kieran. *Retranslation through the Centuries: Jules Verne in English.* Pieterlen, CH: Peter Lang, 2011.

Perschon, Mike. "Finding Nemo: Verne's Antihero as Original Steampunk." *Verniana* 2 (2009–2010): 179–94. http://www.verniana.org/volumes/02/index.en.html.

Picot, Jean-Pierre and Christian Robin, eds. *Jules Verne: Cent Ans Après.* Actes du Colloque de Cerisy. Rennes, FR: Terre de Brume, 2005.

Pourvoyeur, Robert. "De l'invention des mots chez Jules Verne." *Bulletin de la Société Jules Verne* 25 (1973): 19–24.

Raymond, François. "Jules Verne ou le mouvement perpétuel." *Subsidia Pataphysica* 8 (1969): 21–52.

———, ed. *Jules Verne 1: Le Tour du monde.* Paris: Minard, 1976.

———, ed. *Jules Verne 2: L'Écriture vernienne.* Paris: Minard, 1978.

———, ed. *Jules Verne 3: Machines et imaginaire.* Paris: Minard, 1980.

———, ed. *Jules Verne 4: Texte, image, spectacle.* Paris: Minard, 1983.

———, ed. *Jules Verne 5: Émergences du fantastique.* Paris: Minard, 1987.

———, ed. *Jules Verne 6: La Science en question.* Paris: Minard, 1992.

Renzi, Thomas C. *Jules Verne on Film: A Filmography of the Cinematic Adaptations of His Works, 1902 through 1997.* Jefferson, NC: McFarland, 1998.

Revue Jules Verne (1996–2014). Founded by Jean-Paul Dekiss. A scholarly journal sponsored by several Verne-related organizations located in Amiens and Nantes, including the Centre International Jules Verne (Amiens) and the Musée Jules Verne (Nantes), among others. As of November 2014, they have published thirty-eight issues.

Robin, Christian. *Un Monde connu et inconnu.* Nantes: Centre universitaire de recherches verniennes, 1978.

———, ed. *Textes et langages X: Jules Verne.* Nantes: Université de Nantes, 1984.

Rose, Mark. "Jules Verne: Journey to the Center of Science Fiction." In *Coordinates: Placing Science Fiction*, ed. George E. Slusser, 31–41. Carbondale: Southern Illinois University Press, 1983.

———. "Filling the Void: Verne, Wells, and Lem." *Science Fiction Studies* 8, no. 2 (1981): 121–42. http://jv.gilead.org.il/sfs/.

Sadaune, Samuel. "Jules Verne et l'avenir." *Verniana* (2009–2010): 47–72. http://www.verniana.org/volumes/02/index.en.html.

Saucy, Nicolas. "Distraction et écriture mécanique chez Verne: deux exemples." *Verniana* 2 (2009–2010): 133–48. http://www.verniana.org/volumes/02/index.en.html.

Scheinhardt, Philippe. *Jules Verne: Génétique et poïétique (1867–1877)*. Lille, FR: Thèse à la carte, 2006.

Schlitz, Françoise. *The Future Revisited: Jules Verne on Screen in 1950s America*. Gosport, IN: Chaplin Books, 2011.

Schulman, Peter. "Eccentricity as Clinamen: Jules Verne's Error-Driven Geniuses." *Excavatio* 16, nos. 1–2 (2002): 274–84.

———. "Introduction and Notes." In Jules Verne, *The Begum's Millions*. Trans. Stanford L. Luce. Middletown, CT: Wesleyan University Press, 2005.

———. "Introduction and Notes." In Jules Verne, *The Secret of Wilhelm Storitz*. Trans. Peter Schulman. Lincoln: University of Nebraska Press, 2011.

———. "*Paris au XXème siècle*'s Legacy: Eccentricity as Defiance in Jules Verne's Uneasy Relationship with His Era." *Romance Quarterly* 48 (Fall 2001), 257–66.

Serres, Michel. "India (The Black and the Archipelago) on Fire." *SubStance* 8 (1974): 49–60.

———. *Jouvences sur Jules Verne*. Paris: Editions de Minuit, 1974.

———. "Le Savoir, la guerre, et le sacrifice." *Critique* 367 (December 1977): 1067–77.

Slusser, George E. "The Perils of Experiment: Jules Verne and the American Lone Genius." *Extrapolation* 40, no. 2 (1999): 101–15.

———. "Why They Kill Jules Verne: Science Fiction and Cartesian Culture." *Science Fiction Studies* 32, no. 1 (Mar. 2005): 43–61.

Smyth, Edmund J. "Jules Verne, SF and Modernity: An Introduction." In *Jules Verne: Narratives of Modernity*, 1–10. Liverpool: Liverpool University Press, 2000.

———. ed. *Jules Verne: Narratives of Modernity*. Liverpool: Liverpool University Press, 2000.

Stableford, Brian. *Scientific Romance in Britain, 1890–1950*. London: Fourth Estate, 1985.

Sudret, Laurence. *Nature et artifice dans Les Voyages extraordinaires de Jules Verne*. Lille, FR: Thèse à la carte, 2001.

Suvin, Darko. "Communication in Quantified Space: The Utopian Liberalism of Jules Verne's Fiction." *Clio* 4 (1974): 51–71. Reprinted in Suvin, *Metamorphoses of Science Fiction*, 147–63. New Haven: Yale University Press, 1979.

Taves, Brian. "Expedition into a Novel." *Verniana* 1 (2008–2009): 23–30. http://www.verniana.org/volumes/01/index.en.html.

———. "The Making of *20,000 Leagues Under the Sea*." *Filmfax* 58 (Oct. 1996–Jan. 1997): 44–52, 138–39.

————. "The Novels and Rediscovered Films of Michel (Jules) Verne." *Journal of Film Preservation*, no. 62 (April 2001): 25–39.

————. "Opening the Sources of *The Kip Brothers*: A Generic Interpretation." *Verniana* 1 (2008–2009): 51–64. http://www.verniana.org/volumes/01/index.en.html.

————. "'Verne's Best Friend and His Worst Enemy'": I. O. Evans and the Fitzroy Edition of Jules Verne." *Verniana* 4 (2011–2012): 25–54. http://www.verniana.org/volumes/04/index.en.html.

————. "Verne's Forgotten Novel, Youthful Swashbuckler." *Verniana* 3 (2010–2011): 33–50. http://www.verniana.org/volumes/03/index.en.html.

————. "With Williamson, Beneath the Sea." *Journal of Film Preservation* 25 (April 1996): 52–60. http://jv.gilead.org.il/taves/.

Taves, Brian, and Stephen Michaluk Jr. *The Jules Verne Encyclopedia*. Lanham, MD: Scarecrow, 1996.

Terrasse, Pierre. "Jules Verne et les chemins de fer." *Bulletin de la Société Jules Verne* 14 (Apr.–June 1970): 116–21.

Thompson, Ian. "Jules Verne, Geography, and Nineteenth Century Scotland." *La Géographie: Acta Géographica* (Dec. 2003): 48–71. http://jv.gilead.org.il/ithompson/.

————. *Jules Verne's Scotland: In Fact and Fiction*. Edinburgh: Luath Press, 2011.

Touttain, Pierre-André, ed. *Jules Verne*. Paris: Cahiers de l'Herne, 1974.

Unwin, Timothy. "Brunel's *Great Eastern* and the Vernian Imagination: The Writing of *Une Ville flottante*." *Verniana* 2 (2009–2010): 23–46. http://www.verniana.org/volumes/02/index.en.html.

————. "The Fiction of Science, or the Science of Fiction." In *Jules Verne: Narratives of Modernity*, ed. Edmund J. Smyth, 46–59. Liverpool: Liverpool University Press, 2000.

————. *Jules Verne: Journeys in Writing*. Liverpool: Liverpool University Press, 2005.

————. *Jules Verne: Le Tour du monde en quatre-vingts jours*. Glasgow: Glasgow University Press, 1992.

————. "Jules Verne: Negotiating Change in the Nineteenth Century." *Science Fiction Studies* 32, no. 1 (Mar. 2005): 5–17. http://jv.gilead.org.il/sfs/.

————. "Technology and Progress in Jules Verne, or Anticipation in Reverse." *AUMLA* 93 (2000): 17–35.

————. "Vernotopia (Utopia, Ecotopia, Technotopia, Heterotopia, Retrotopia, Textotopia, Dystopia)." *Australian Journal of French Studies* 43, no. 3 (Sept. 2006): 333–41.

Vierne, Simone. "Hetzel et Jules Verne, ou l'invention d'un auteur." *Europe* 619–20 (1980): 53–63.

———. *Jules Verne*. Paris: Balland, 1986.

———. *Jules Verne, mythe et modernité*. Paris: Presses Universitaires de France, 1989.

———. *Jules Verne, une vie, une oeuvre*. Paris: Ballard, 1986.

———. *Jules Verne et le roman initiatique: Contribution à l'étude de l'imaginaire*. Paris: Editions du Sirac, 1973.

Vries-Uiterweerd, Garmt de. "Spherical Geometry in *Mirifiques aventures de maître Antifer*." *Verniana* 2 (2009–2010): 1–10. http://www.verniana.org /volumes/02/index.en.html.

Weissenberg, Eric. *Jules Verne: Un Univers fabuleux*. Lausanne, CH: Favre, 2004.

Wier, Stuart K. "The Design of Jules Verne's Submarine *Nautilus*." *Extraordinary Voyages* 19, no. 3 (June 2013): 1–24.

ADDITIONAL MATERIALS RELATING TO
JULES VERNE'S *FIVE WEEKS IN A BALLOON*

Burgaud, Philippe. "Cinq semaines en ballon en film." *Bulletin de la Société Jules Verne* 47, no. 184 (Dec. 2013): 30–37.

Dehs, Volker. "La bibliographie de *Cinq semaines en ballon*." *Bulletin de la Société Jules Verne* 47, no. 183 (Aug. 2013): 4–10.

———. "*Cinq semaines en ballon* devant la critique de 1863." *Bulletin de la Société Jules Verne* 47, no. 183 (Aug. 2013): 30–39.

Evans, Arthur B. "The English Editions of *Five Weeks in a Balloon*." *Verniana* 6 (2013–2014): 139–68. http://www.verniana.org/volumes/06/HTML /CS2013.html.

———. "Fishing for Lion with Jules Verne and Joseph Méry." *Verniana* 5 (2012–2013): 35–38. http://www.verniana.org/volumes/05/HTML/Mery .html.

McKeithan, D. M. "Mark Twain's Tom Sawyer Abroad and Jules Verne's *Five Weeks in a Balloon*." *University of Texas Studies in English* 28 (1949): 257–70.

Miller, Ron. "Magnificent Jules and His Flying Machines." *Dakar* 1 (1967): 15–16.

Tarrieu, Alexandre. "Cette longue liste d'explorateurs." *Bulletin de la Société Jules Verne* 47, no. 184 (Dec. 2013): 14–29.

Vierne, Simone. "Chronologie, introduction, et jugements critiques." In *Cinq semaines en ballon* by Jules Verne, 25–42. Paris: Garnier-Flammarion, 1979.

Jules Gabriel Verne: A Biography

Jules Verne. Photo by Nadar (Félix Tournachon), ca. 1885.

Jules Gabriel Verne was born on February 8, 1828, to a middle-class family in the port city of Nantes, France. His mother, Sophie, née Allotte de la Fuÿe, was the daughter of a prominent family of shipowners, and his father, Pierre Verne, was an attorney and the son of a Provins magistrate. Jules was the eldest of five children. In addition to his three sisters— Anna, Mathilde, and Marie—he also had a younger brother, Paul, to whom he was very close and who went on to have a career in the navy.

As a child and young man, Jules was a relatively conscientious student. Although far from the top of his class, he apparently did win awards for meritorious performance in geography, music, and Greek and Latin, and he easily passed his *baccalauréat* in 1846. But his true passion was the sea. The shipyard docks of nearby Île Feydeau and the bustling commerce of the Nantes harbor never failed to spark Jules's youthful imagination with visions of far-off lands and exotic peoples. Legend has it that he once ran off to sea as a cabin boy aboard a schooner bound for the Indies, but his father managed to intercept the ship before it reached the open sea and to retrieve his wayward son. According to this story, Jules (probably after a good thrashing) promised his parents that he would travel henceforth only in his dreams. Although this charming tale was most likely invented—or at least heavily embroidered upon—by Verne's family biographer, Marguerite Allotte de la Fuÿe, it nevertheless exemplifies the author's lifelong love for the sea and his yearnings for adventure-filled journeys to distant ports of call.

Young Jules also loved machines. During an interview toward the end of his

349

life, he reminisced about his early formative years: "While I was quite a lad, I used to adore watching machines at work. My father had a country-house at Chantenay, at the mouth of the Loire, and near the government factory at Indret. I never went to Chantenay without entering the factory and standing for hours watching the machines. [. . .] This penchant has remained with me all my life, and today I have still as much pleasure in watching a steam engine or a fine loco-motive at work as I have in contemplating a picture by Raphael or Corregio" (quoted in Robert H. Sherard, "Jules Verne at Home," *McClure's Magazine* [Jan. 1894]: 118).

Intending that Jules follow in his footsteps as a lawyer, Pierre Verne sent him to Paris in 1848 to study law. The correspondence between father and son dur-ing the ensuing ten years shows that Jules took his studies seriously, completing his law degree in just two years. But his letters home also make it quite clear that Jules had renewed his lifelong passion for literature. Inspired by such authors as Victor Hugo, Alfred de Vigny, and Théophile Gautier and introduced (via family contacts on his mother's side) into several high-society Parisian literary circles, the young Romantic Verne began to devote himself as never before to his writ-ing. From 1847 to 1862, he composed poetry, wrote many plays and a novel en-titled *Un Prêtre en 1839* (*A Priest in 1839*, unpublished during his lifetime), and penned a variety of short stories that he published in the popular French maga-zine *Musée des familles* to supplement his meager income: "Les Premiers navires de la marine mexicaine" (1851, The First Ships of the Mexican Navy), "Un Voyage en ballon" (1851, A Balloon Journey), "Martin Paz" (1852, Martin Paz), "Maître Zacharius" (1854, Master Zacharius), and "Un Hivernage dans les glaces" (1855, Wintering in the Ice). Some of his plays were performed in local Parisian the-aters: *Les Pailles rompues* (1850, *Broken Straws*), *Le Colin-Maillard* (1853, *Blind Man's Bluff*), *Les Compagnons de la Marjolaine* (1855, *The Companions of the Marjoram*), *Monsieur de Chimpanzé* (1858, *Mister Chimpanzee*), *L'Auberge des Ardennes* (1860, *The Inn of the Ardennes*), and *Onze jours de siège* (1861, *Eleven Days of Siege*). During this period, Verne also became close friends with Alexan-dre Dumas *père* and Dumas *fils* and, through the former's intervention, even-tually became the secretary of the Théâtre Lyrique in 1852 (leaving this post in 1855).

In 1857 Verne married Honorine Morel, née de Viane, a twenty-six-year-old widow with two daughters. Taking advantage of his new father-in-law's contacts in Paris and a monetary wedding gift from Pierre Verne, Jules decided to dis-continue his work at the Théâtre Lyrique and to take a full-time job as *agent de change* at the Paris Stock Market with the firm Eggly et Cie. He spent his early mornings at home writing (at a desk with two drawers—one for his plays, the other for his scientific essays) and most of his days at the Bourse de Paris doing business and associating with a number of other young stockbrokers who had interests similar to his own.

When not busy writing or working at the stock exchange, Verne spent the rest of his time either seeing his old theater friends (he took trips with Aristide Hignard to Scotland and England in 1859 and to Norway and Denmark in 1861)—the former resulting in a travelogue called *Voyage en Angleterre et en Ecosse* (*Journey to England and Scotland*)—or at the Bibliothèque Nationale, collecting scientific and historical news items and copying them onto note cards for future use, a work habit he would continue throughout his life (by 1895 he had accumulated over twenty-five thousand cards). As at least one biographer has noted, the long weekend sessions he spent in the reading rooms of the library may well have been partly motivated by a simple desire for peace and quiet: in 1861 Verne's son Michel had just been born and greatly annoyed his father with his incessant crying.

It was during this time that Verne first conceived of writing a new type of novel called a *roman scientifique* (scientific novel). It would incorporate the large amounts of scientific material that Verne had accumulated in his library research, as well as that gleaned from essays in the *Musée des familles* and other journals to which he occasionally contributed. It would combine scientific exploration and discovery with action and adventure and be patterned on the novels of Sir Walter Scott, James Fenimore Cooper, and Edgar Allan Poe. Poe's works in particular, which had recently been translated into French by Charles Baudelaire in 1856, strongly interested Verne for their unusual mixture of scientific reasoning and the fantastic (he later wrote his only piece of literary criticism on Poe in 1864). Verne's efforts eventually crystallized into a rough draft of a novel-length narrative, which he tentatively entitled *Un Voyage en l'air* (*A Voyage through the Air*).

Biographers disagree as to the exact date when Verne was introduced to the publisher Pierre-Jules Hetzel (either in 1861 or 1862). How they met seems more certain: Verne showed his "balloon" manuscript to Dumas *père*, who put him in touch with the novelist Alfred de Bréhat, who had published several works with Hetzel. During their first meeting, Verne asked Hetzel if he would consider reviewing for publication the rough draft of his novel—a manuscript that, according to his wife, the author had very nearly destroyed a few weeks earlier after its rejection by another publishing house. Hetzel agreed to the request, seeing in this narrative the potential for an ideal "fit" with his forthcoming family-oriented magazine, the *Magasin d'éducation et de récréation*. A couple of weeks later, Verne and Hetzel began what would prove to be a highly successful author-publisher collaboration. It lasted for more than forty years and resulted in over sixty scientific novels collectively called the *Voyages extraordinaires—Voyages dans les mondes connus et inconnus (Extraordinary Voyages—Journeys in Known and Unknown Worlds).*

Shortly after the publication and commercial success of Verne's first novel in 1863—now retitled *Cinq semaines en ballon: Voyage de découvertes en Afrique par trois Anglais (Five Weeks in a Balloon: Voyage of Discovery in Africa by Three Englishmen)*—Hetzel offered the young writer a ten-year contract for at least two works per year of the same sort. Not long after, Verne quit his job at the stock market and began to write full-time.

Following Verne's historic meeting with Hetzel, the remainder of his life and works can be divided into three distinct periods: 1862–1886, 1886–1905, and 1905–1925.

The first, from 1862 to 1886, might be termed Verne's "Hetzel period." During this time, he wrote his most popular *Extraordinary Voyages*, settled permanently with his family in Amiens, purchased a yacht, collaborated on theater adaptations of several of his novels with Adolphe d'Ennery, and ultimately gained both fame and fortune.

Other notable events in Verne's life during this period include:

Hetzel's rejection of his second novel, *Paris au XXème siècle (Paris in the Twentieth Century)*, in 1863 as well as an early draft of *L'Île mystérieuse (The Mysterious Island)* called *L'Oncle Robinson (Uncle Robinson)* in 1865.

The publication of his nonfiction books *Géographie de la France et de ses colonies* (1867–1868, *Geography of France and Its Colonies*, coauthored with Théophile Lavallée) and the three-volume *Histoire des grands voyages et des grands voyageurs* (1878–1880, *History of Great Voyages and Great Voyagers*).

The unparalleled success of the novels *Voyage au centre de la Terre* (1864, *Journey to the Center of the Earth*), *De la Terre à la Lune* (1865, *From the Earth to the Moon*), *Autour de la Lune* (1870, *Around the Moon*), *Vingt mille lieues sous les mers* (1870, *Twenty Thousand Leagues under the Seas*), *Le Tour du monde en quatre-vingts jours* (1873, *Around the World in Eighty Days*), and *Michel Strogoff* (1876, *Michael Strogoff*), among others.

A brief trip to America in 1867 on the *Great Eastern*, accompanied by his brother Paul, and visits to New York and Niagara Falls—subsequently fictionalized in his novel *Une Ville flottante* (1871, *A Floating City*).

Receiving the *Légion d'honneur* just after the outbreak of the Franco-Prussian War in 1870.

The death of his father, Pierre Verne, on November 3, 1871.

The purchase of his third yacht, the *Saint-Michel III*, in which he sailed to Lisbon and Algiers in 1878; to Scotland in 1879; to Holland, Denmark,

Germany, and the Baltics in 1881; and to Portugal, Algeria, Tunisia, and Italy in 1884 (and, while in Italy, was invited to a private audience with Pope Leo XIII).

In 1879, the publication of *Les Cinq Cents Millions de la Bégum* (*The Begum's Millions*) in collaboration with Paschal Grousset, a.k.a. André Laurie, Verne's only combination utopia/dystopia, which also featured his first "mad scientist," Herr Schultze.

In 1882, his move to a new, larger home at 2 rue Charles-Dubois, Amiens — the famous house with the circular tower, which for many years served as the headquarters of the Centre International Jules Verne, Amiens.

The second phase, from 1886 to 1905, might be called Verne's "post-Hetzel period." During this time, Verne worked with Hetzel's son, Louis-Jules (often called Hetzel *fils*), who succeeded his father as manager and principal editor of the Hetzel publishing house. Verne also entered into politics: he was elected to the municipal council of Amiens in 1888, a post he would occupy for fifteen years. But this period is especially notable because of a gradual change in the ideological tone of his *Extraordinary Voyages*. In these later works, the Saint-Simonian pro-science optimism is largely absent, replaced by a growing pessimism about the true value of progress. The omnipresent scientific didacticism, a trademark of Verne's *romans scientifiques*, is now frequently replaced by romantic melodrama, pathos, and/or tragedy. And the triumphant exploration and conquest of the universe, a leitmotif that seemed to undergird most of Verne's earlier novels, now seems secondary to an increased focus on politics, social issues, and human morality. This dramatic change of tone in Verne's later works parallels a number of personal adversities experienced by the author during this period of his life. For example:

Continual problems with his rebellious son Michel (e.g., repeated bankruptcies, costly amorous escapades, divorce from his first wife, difficulties with the law, etc.)

Severe financial worries, forcing Verne to sell his beloved yacht in 1885

The deaths of two individuals who were very close to him: his editor and mentor Hetzel *père* in 1886, and his mother in 1887

An attack at gunpoint on March 9, 1886, by his mentally disturbed nephew Gaston, who shot Verne in the lower leg, leaving him partially crippled for the rest of his life.

Verne's personal correspondence from this period also reflects his growing pessimism. In a letter dated December 21, 1886, to Hetzel *fils*, for example, Verne confides: "As for the rest, I have now entered into the blackest part of my life." A few years later, in 1894, the author tells his brother Paul: "All that remains to me are these intellectual distractions. [. . .] My character is profoundly changed and I have received blows from which I'll never recover."

Whatever the underlying reasons may have been for this change—the absence of Hetzel *père*'s editorial supervision, Verne's awareness of certain disturbing trends in the world at large (e.g., the growth of imperialism and the military-industrial complex), or the sudden flood of tragedies in his personal life—it is evident that many of Verne's post-1886 *Extraordinary Voyages* tend to portray both scientists and scientific innovation with a heavy dose of cynicism or biting satire, or both. And in contrast to the intrepid "go where no one has gone before" scientific enthusiasm, which characterized most of his earlier and most popular works, the later novels now often foreground, in whole or in part, a broad range of social themes: for example, the potential dangers of technology in *Sans dessus dessous* (1889, *Topsy-Turvy*), *Face au drapeau* (1896, *Facing the Flag*), and *Maître du monde* (1904, *Master of the World*); the cruel oppression of the Québécois in Canada in *Famille-sans-nom* (1889, *Family without a Name*); the evils of ignorance and superstition in *Le Château des Carpathes* (1892, *The Castle of the Carpathians*); the intolerable living conditions in orphanages in *P'tit-Bonhomme* (1893, *Li'l-Fellow*); the destructive influence of religious missionaries on South Sea island cultures in *L'Île à hélice* (1895, *Propeller Island*); the imminent extinction of whales in *Le Sphinx des glaces* (1897, *The Sphinx of the Ice Realm*); the environmental damage caused by the oil industry in *Le Testament d'un excentrique* (1899, *The Last Will of an Eccentric*); the slaughter of elephants for their ivory in *Le Village aérien* (1901, *The Aerial Village*); and the folly of Western colonialist rivalries in *Travel Scholarships* (1903, *Bourses de voyage*).

During his last years, despite increasingly poor health (arthritis, cataracts, diabetes, and severe gastrointestinal problems) as well as ongoing family squabbles, Verne diligently continued to write one to two novels per year. But, with a drawer full of nearly completed manuscripts in his desk, he suddenly fell seriously ill in early March 1905, a few weeks after his seventy-seventh birthday. He told his wife Honorine to gather the family around him, and he died quietly on March 24, 1905. He was buried on March 28 in the cemetery of La Madeleine in Amiens. Two years later, an elaborate marble sculpture by Albert Roze was placed over his grave, depicting the author rising from his tomb and stretching his hand toward the sky.

The third and final phase of the Jules Verne story, following the author's death and extending from 1905 to 1919, might well be called the "Verne *fils* period." During these years Verne's posthumous works were published, but most of them were substantially modified—and, in some instances, authored—by his son, Michel.

In early May 1905, Michel, as executor of his father's estate, published in the Parisian newspapers *Le Figaro* and *Le Temps* a list of Jules Verne's surviving unpublished manuscripts: nine novels both titled and untitled in various stages of completion (including the text of *Paris au XXe siècle* [*Paris in the Twentieth Century*] rejected by Hetzel *père* over forty years earlier), sixteen plays, several short stories, a travelogue of his early trip to England and Scotland, and an assortment of historical sketches, notes, and the like. Hetzel *fils* immediately agreed to publish most of the novels that were originally intended to be part of the *Extraordinary Voyages* as well as Verne's short stories, which were grouped in the collection published in 1910 as *Hier et demain* (*Yesterday and Tomorrow*). Another remaining novel in the series, *L'Etonnante Aventure de la mission Barsac* (*The Amazing Adventure of the Barsac Mission*), would be published first in serial format in the newspaper *Le Matin* and later as a book by the publishing company Hachette, which had bought the rights to Verne's works from Hetzel *fils* in 1914.

In recent years, these posthumous works have become the topic of heated controversy among Verne scholars: how much and in what ways did Michel alter these texts prior to their publication? After a close examination of the available manuscripts (now housed in the Centre d'études verniennes in Nantes) by Piero Gondolo della Riva, Olivier Dumas, and other respected Verne scholars, it is now indisputable that Michel had a much greater hand in the composition of Jules Verne's posthumous works than had ever been suspected:

Le Volcan d'or (1906, *The Golden Volcano*): fourteen chapters by Jules; four more chapters added by Michel as well as four new characters.

L'Agence Thompson and Co. (1907, *The Thompson Travel Agency*): almost entirely written by Michel, but under the direction of his father.

La Chasse au météore (1908, *The Meteor Hunt*): seventeen chapters by Jules; four added by Michel as well as four new characters.

Le Pilote du Danube (1908, *The Danube Pilot*): sixteen chapters by Jules; three added by Michel as well as at least one new character and a new title.

Les Naufragés du Jonathan (1909, *The Survivors of the Jonathan*): sixteen chapters by Jules; fifteen added by Michel, along with many new characters, episodes, and a new title.

Le Secret de Wilhelm Storitz (1910, *The Secret of Wilhelm Storitz*): rewritten by Michel to take place in the eighteenth century instead of at the end of the nineteenth; a different conclusion was also added.

Hier et demain (1910, *Yesterday and Tomorrow*): most of the short stories appearing in this collection had been substantially altered by Michel; one of them, "Au XXIXème siècle: La Journée d'un journaliste américain en 2889" (In the Twenty-ninth Century: The Day of an American Journalist in 2889), was attributable in large part to Michel, and another, "L'Eternel Adam" (Eternal Adam), was mostly by him as well.

L'Etonnante Aventure de la mission Barsac (1919, *The Amazing Adventure of the Barsac Mission*): the supposedly "final" novel of Verne's *Extraordinary Voyages* was written entirely by Michel from his father's notes for a novel to be called *Voyages d'études* (*Study Trip*).

Scholarly reaction to Michel's rewrites of his father's manuscripts has tended to be very polarized. Some have called Michel's intervention in Verne's posthumous works an inexcusable betrayal of trust and a financially motivated scam that severely compromised the integrity of Verne's entire oeuvre. In an attempt to set the record straight, from 1985 through the 1990s, the Société Jules Verne in France arranged for the publication of Verne's original manuscripts of most of these works; English translations of them have been appearing with regularity since 2002. But other scholars strongly disagree with this assessment. They point out that Jules Verne encouraged Michel to publish stories under his father's illustrious name; that during the final decade of his life when his eyesight was rapidly failing, Jules often asked Michel to "collaborate" with him to help bring several of his later novels to publication; and that Michel's sometimes radical modifications of Verne's posthumous works often improved their readability—an enhancement that surely would have received his father's wholehearted approval. The debate continues to this day.

With Michel's death in 1925, the final chapter of Verne's literary legacy was (for better or worse) now complete. Ironically, in April of the following year, a pulp magazine called *Amazing Stories* first appeared on American newsstands. It published tales of a new species of literature dubbed "scientifiction"—defined by its publisher, Hugo Gernsback, as a "Jules Verne, H. G. Wells, and Edgar Allan Poe type of story"—and on its title page appeared a drawing of Verne's tomb, used as the magazine's logo. The popularity of *Amazing Stories* and its many pulp progeny, such as *Science Wonder Stories* and *Astounding Stories*, was both immediate and long lasting. As the term "scientifiction" evolved into "science fiction," the new genre began to flourish as never before. And the legend of Jules Verne as its patron saint, as the putative "Father of Science Fiction," soon became firmly rooted in American cultural folklore.

About the Contributors

ARTHUR B. EVANS is professor of French at DePauw University and managing editor of the scholarly journal *Science Fiction Studies*. He has published numerous books and articles on Verne and French science fiction, including the award-winning *Jules Verne Rediscovered* (Greenwood, 1988). He is general editor of Wesleyan's Early Classics of Science Fiction book series.

FREDERICK PAUL WALTER is a reference librarian, scriptwriter, and former vice president of the North American Jules Verne Society. He lives in Albuquerque, has generated many articles and programs on Verne, and also has translated several of his novels for major academic presses, including the popular omnibus *Amazing Journeys: Five Visionary Classics* (Excelsior, 2010).

The
Wesleyan
Early Classics of
Science Fiction
Series

General Editor Arthur B. Evans

The Centenarian
Honoré de Balzac

We Modern People:
Science Fiction and the
Making of Russian Modernity
Anindita Banerjee

Cosmos Latinos:
An Anthology of Science Fiction
from Latin America and Spain
Andrea L. Bell and
Yolanda Molina-Gavilán, eds.

The Coming Race
Edward Bulwer-Lytton

Imagining Mars:
A Literary History
Robert Crossley

Caesar's Column:
A Story of the Twentieth Century
Ignatius Donnelly

Vintage Visions:
Essays on Early Science Fiction
Arthur B. Evans, ed.

Subterranean Worlds:
A Critical Anthology
Peter Fitting, ed.

Lumen
Camille Flammarion

The Time Ship:
A Chrononautical Journey
Enrique Gaspar

The Last Man
Jean-Baptiste Cousin de Grainville

The Emergence of Latin
American Science Fiction
Rachel Haywood Ferreira

The Battle of the Sexes
in Science Fiction
Justine Larbalestier

The Yellow Wave:
A Romance of the Asiatic
Invasion of Australia
Kenneth Mackay

The Moon Pool
A. Merritt

Colonialism and the
Emergence of Science Fiction
John Rieder

The Twentieth Century
Albert Robida

Three Science Fiction Novellas:
From Prehistory to the
End of Mankind
J.-H. Rosny aîné

The Black Mirror and Other Stories:
An Anthology of Science Fiction
from Germany and Austria
Franz Rottensteiner, ed., and
Mike Mitchell, trans.